Nichole Severn writes explosive romantic suspense with strong heroines, heroes who dare challenge them and a hell of a lot of guns. She resides with her very supportive and patient husband, as well as her demon spawn, in Utah. When she's not writing, she's constantly injuring herself running, rock climbing, practicing yoga and snowboarding. She loves hearing from readers through her website, nicholesevern.com, and on Facebook at nicholesevern.

Juno Rushdan is a veteran US Air Force intelligence officer and award-winning author. Her books are action-packed and fast-paced. Critics from Kirkus Reviews and Library Journal have called her work 'heart-pounding James Bond-ian adventure' that 'will captivate lovers of romantic thrillers.' For a free book, visit her website: junorushdan.com

DEAD AGAIN

NICHOLE SEVERN

WYOMING MOUNTAIN MURDER

JUNO RUSHDAN

MILLS & BOON

First Published in Great Britain 2023
by Mills & Boon, an imprint of HarperCollins*Publishers* Ltd
1 London Bridge Street, London, SE1 9GF

www.harpercollins.co.uk

HarperCollins*Publishers*
Macken House, 39/40 Mayor Street Upper,
Dublin 1, D01 C9W8, Ireland

Dead Again © 2023 Natascha Jaffa
Wyoming Mountain Murder © 2023 Juno Rushdan

ISBN: 978-0-263-30725-2

0523

DEAD AGAIN

NICHOLE SEVERN

For the Mills & Boon Heroes authors:
You inspire me on a daily basis. Keep writing.

Chapter One

Macie Barclay was leaving Battle Mountain.

And she wasn't ever coming back.

It didn't take a tarot reading or a lunar eclipse to tell her things were only going to get worse. Serial killers, bombers, psychopaths out for revenge and now crimes connected to cartels? Nope. She was out of here just as soon as she had everything packed. "Okay. What else?"

She shoved a few more dresses into her already bulging duffel bag and went to the bathroom to see what she'd left behind. She wouldn't be able to take all her things, but she'd done this before. Keep what was important, leave the rest.

It was too bad. She'd really loved this place. The town, too. Her entire house had been built around a one-hundred-year-old tree. Everyone in the police department had joked about her tree house, but this had been the one place she'd actually felt she belonged. Connected. Free to be herself without shame or judgment. Not the woman she'd created all those years ago. Not Macie Barclay. The real her. Her own scoff punctured through the trill of birds outside as she caught her reflection in the mirror over the sink. "You've been lying to yourself for so long, you don't even remember who that girl is anymore."

Macie closed her eyes, taking in the feel of the cool breeze through the window, the smell of the wood that made up these walls. She knew every inch of this house. From the claw-foot tub to the crack in the countertop downstairs in the kitchen. It'd seemed perfect. It'd felt like it was hers.

Macie forced her head back into the moment. Wouldn't do any good to sit around and feel sorry for herself. She'd make the next place perfect, too. No matter where that was.

Finished packing her clothes and toiletries, she headed back to the closet tucked away in the loft she'd used as a bedroom for the past six years. Hangers slid out of her way easily as she reached for the bifold shutters she'd installed at the back.

Anyone who'd come through this place had questioned her taste in decor, especially inside a closet nobody would see, but she'd put them in for a reason. She tugged at the right shutter and swung it wide. The photos and sticky notes she'd taped inside fluttered with the movement. Everything—crime scene photos she'd paid a former cop from Albuquerque PD to get for her, the autopsy report filed by a medical examiner who'd since been charged with corruption, notes of possible witnesses and family members to interview—it all had a place. Even one wrong placement could undo twenty-five years' worth of work.

Good thing she'd looked at this makeshift murder board a thousand times. She'd have no problem reassembling it wherever she ended up but unpocketed her phone and took a photo of the board in case. If anything happened, she could recreate any piece of the puzzle.

She peeled and untacked each piece of evidence she'd gathered since the day she'd left Albuquerque. No one would ever know why she'd joined Battle Mountain's police department as a dispatcher. Or why she'd run from New Mexico. And that was how it'd have to stay. There wouldn't be any goodbyes. No housewarming parties when she got to where she was going or help moving from the local church group. No home-cooked meals from Karie Ford out at the ranch or arguments with the pigheaded second-in-command, Easton Ford. Her heart hurt. A cold case was all she had left. And wasn't that just pathetic?

Macie outlined a photo that hadn't been included in the police's case file with the pad of her thumb. A photo taken of three toothy ten-year-olds standing in front of a bright yellow-and-red hot-air balloon half inflated before the festival. Her fiery hair stood out the most, but Hazel had been beautiful in her own right. That perfect smile—even with one of her eyeteeth missing—had blown away anyone who came in contact with her. Especially Riggs, the other kid in the picture. Right up until Hazel had been murdered. "I gave you my word."

Macie tucked scrawling notes, photos and reports into a file folder and slipped it into her messenger bag. This was it. She scanned the remains of the house. Everything she cared about was in that duffel bag on the bed, but the people she'd gotten to know—the friends she'd made—they all had to stay here. Live their lives. Be happy. Find a way to survive.

She just couldn't do it with them anymore. It was too dangerous. Macie Barclay had been a good name while she'd been here, but that wasn't her anymore. She shouldered her bag and zipped the bag closed. She didn't know where she'd end up tonight. It didn't matter. As long as it wasn't here.

Her keys trilled in her hand as she hauled her belongings off the bed and down the stairs. She'd done all the dishes, wiped down any surface that might hold her fingerprints and cleaned out the refrigerator. She worked with an entire department of cops. She had no doubt every one of them would spend the next few weeks trying to find her, but sooner or later, they'd give up. If they came looking for her, they wouldn't have the slightest idea of where to start, and her heart shuddered at the idea that Chief Ford, Kendric, Isla, Alma, hell, even Easton had never really gotten the chance to know the real her. Never would. That was just how it needed to be.

She gazed up into the exposed rafters and set her hand against the thickest part of the tree climbing up through the roof. "You were exactly what I needed when I needed it." Her throat threatened to close on a sob. "Thank you. For everything."

Macie gripped the handle of her bag. "Time to go."

She swung the front door open. And froze.

A man had raised his fist to knock, and a thread of fear slithered through her. He was handsome, devastatingly so, with piercing blue eyes that widened at the sight of her, but she'd been fooled by good looks before. And somehow, she knew him. Like they'd met before. "Macie Barclay?"

"Sorry. She doesn't live here anymore." Someone had come looking for her. Crap. She'd let herself get emotional about leaving, and it'd cost her. She had to get out of here. "Wish I could help, but I'm running late for my flight. If you'll excuse me." She wasn't flying. Her identity—no matter how many law enforcement databases she'd managed to alter with her access—wouldn't hold up against TSA.

Macie managed to get past him and closed the front door behind her, not bothering to lock it. Instead, she shoved her hand deep into the side pocket of her messenger bag and gripped the taser she'd started carrying out of necessity the past couple of years. She was halfway down the curving stairs before the mystery man tried again.

"Ava?" he asked.

She almost let go of her bag. No one had called her that since she'd been a girl running around with braids in her hair and as much sugar as she could haul in her pockets back in Albuquerque. Macie forced herself to keep moving. To get away. Nobody was supposed to find her here. She'd been careful, hadn't she? Moving every few years, changing her name, not letting the truth slip. What had she done wrong? "Sorry. I don't know anyone by that name. I hope you find what you're looking for."

"It's me. Riggs." He took a step down. Then another. "Riggs Karig. Do you remember me?"

Air crushed from her chest. She looked up at him from the bottom of the staircase. It hadn't been her imagination. The eyes, the shape of his mouth, the note of concern in his voice. For a moment, she saw her childhood best friend in the man he'd become, and her plan faded to the back of her mind. His five-o'clock shadow accentuated the sleepiness under his eyes. He hadn't changed much. Neither had the permanent scowl etched into his expression. It was him. She could feel it. Beard growth matched the dirty blond of his hair. It'd been darker the last time she'd seen him. A button-down shirt, open at the neck, showed off thick tendons and bulky muscle. She'd never missed the opportunity to appreciate a good view.

Riggs. All grown up.

He took another step down. A flash of a badge peeked out from beneath his jacket, and in an instant, the memories were gone. All that was left was regret she hadn't packed faster. The taser felt lighter than it should have hidden in the side pocket of her bag. She switched it on. As much as she hated the idea of pegging someone with fifty thousand volts of electricity, one thing remained clear: if Riggs Karig could find her, so could anyone else. "I told you, you have the wrong woman."

Macie forced herself to keep moving toward her crappy four-door sedan. She tossed her duffel bag into the back seat and climbed behind the steering wheel.

Then suddenly Riggs was there. He was holding her door open, trying to keep her from leaving, but she started the car anyway. "Avalynn, please. I need your help."

He was the only one who could get away with calling her by her full name. Except her mother, and that'd only been when she'd gotten into trouble. So…a lot. Macie gripped the steering wheel, knowing she'd regret not closing the door on his hand and making a break for it. She'd never been able to resist his charm in the past. Why would twenty-five years change anything? She forced herself to take a deep breath. "Help you with what?"

Riggs dug for a piece of paper in his jacket and handed it to her. It was a decoy. In the next second, cold steel latched around her wrist. He secured the other end of the handcuff to the steering wheel and took a step back as Macie tried to close the door on him. "You can start by explaining why my partner was found dead with your name and address in his pocket less than six hours ago."

HE'D FOUND HER. After all these years, he'd finally found her.

Detective Riggs Karig leaned one shoulder into the car, watching Ava squirm. And, damn, was she a sight to behold. Long legs flexing under some kind of billowy floral dress as she struggled, curses that would make a sailor blush falling from full lips and all that fire red hair he'd teased her about as a kid—she hadn't changed. Even her penchant for flashy earrings threatened to bring him right back to his ten-year-old self like no time had passed between them. Avalynn Davis—no, Macie Barclay—was exactly as he remembered.

And everything he wanted to forget.

"So what was the plan here, Detective?" Macie gripped her cuffed wrist and hauled herself back to test the steel, but they both knew she wasn't going anywhere. "Keep an innocent woman handcuffed to her car like some kind of pervert?"

Detective. She was trying to distance herself. Pretend they hadn't gone through the same nightmare back in Albuquerque or that she hadn't known he'd been head over heels for her. He'd searched the entire country for her once he'd gotten hold of the resources after the academy. All this time, she hadn't been more than a state away. Riggs scanned the trees around the property. Not just any property. A tree house. It'd been set in the middle of the San Juan Mountains. Exposed, and ridiculous, and exactly the kind of place he'd imagined she'd go. "You keep doing that, you're going to break your wrist."

"You almost sound like you care about the woman you stalked across an entire state and cuffed to a car." His warning didn't stop her. Instead, it seemed to egg her on. She leveraged a booted foot against the door's frame and tried again. The links between the cuffs actually groaned, but Riggs wasn't letting her get away that easily.

He presented the key. Crystal green eyes that'd put most algae to shame locked on the brass then shifted to him. He could almost read her mind, her thinking of all the ways to pry it from his hand. Thinking of how far she could run before he caught up. She was right. He couldn't leave her like this. Becker's body wasn't even cold yet. Riggs was on the clock to find out who'd put his mentor in a body bag in the first place. That was all that mattered. "I give you this, you answer my questions. Deal?"

The possibility of freedom seemed to take the wind out of her sails, but Riggs had been lied to his entire career. He didn't trust anyone. Especially not a woman who'd stayed on the run all these years. Macie nodded. "All right. I answer one question, you let me go. Make it count. Because you will never see me again."

A flood of questions rushed to the front of his mind. Why had she left him? What had she been running from all these years? Had she been the one to strangle Becker and leave him to die in an abandoned building in the most isolated town he'd stepped foot in? It all came down to the same need for as much information as possible. Personal friendships, childhood memories, old feelings—none of it mattered in a homicide investigation. "Why did my partner have your name and address in his pocket when he died?"

Macie set that penetrating gaze on him and leaned forward slightly. The movement angled her arm against her throat, and Riggs was suddenly reminded of another strangling he'd tried to forget. "I don't know."

"That's it? You don't know." No. There had to be something more here. Becker hadn't come to this blip on the map and tracked her down for nothing.

"I answered your question, Detective." She rattled the cuffs as though to make a point, but Riggs had no intention of letting her rabbit on him again. "I'll be going now."

Something else was going on here. As much as he had to entertain the idea she'd had something to do with Becker's death, Macie Barclay didn't act like a killer. Which meant something had spooked her. "What are you running from, huh? Why are you in such a rush to get out of Dodge?"

A scoff turned her attention out the windshield of her rusted-out car. "You detectives are all the same. All you do is lie. To suspects, to witnesses." She rattled the cuffs again. "To yourselves. It's any wonder you manage to close cases at all."

"Does that make you a witness, Avalynn, or a suspect?" he asked.

"We're through here." Faster than he thought possible, she twisted her hand over the cuffs, and they fell free. Macie handed them off to him as though she hadn't just pulled off the greatest magic trick known to man. "I believe these belong to you."

"How'd you do that?" Riggs had never seen anything like it. She just kept a handcuff key on hand? Why? In case she ever landed under arrest?

"I've got plenty of tricks up these sleeves you haven't even begun to imagine." Her voice dipped into dangerous territory, and a flash of the hell-raiser who'd always gotten herself into all kinds of trouble as a kid surfaced. "I'd say it was nice seeing you, but then I'd be lying. Goodbye, Detective."

She moved to close the driver's side door again, but Riggs couldn't help himself. He couldn't let her leave. "A good man is dead, Ava. A good detective, and for some reason, you were the last thought on his mind before he was strangled. You have to know something."

She didn't even seem to breathe at his plea, as though she were used to people coming to her for help all the time. "This is personal for you. The detective who was killed. Who was he?"

"It was Becker," he said. "You probably don't remember him, but he was the lead detective during—"

"I remember him." Her hand fell away from the key still lodged in the ignition. Already pale skin seemed to drain of the last evidence of color. "What is it you want from me?"

"Did Becker reach out to you? Do you know what he was doing in Battle Mountain?" He just needed something—anything—to make sense of this. Becker had been the best of the best. Yeah, the retired detective had put away dozens of violent criminals, even worked task forces centered around bringing down the cartels moving in on New Mexico, but none of them had made a move like this. None of them had gone after a detective personally. If someone was making a move against the department, Riggs needed to know.

"No. I'm sorry for your loss, but Becker keeping his distance from me was probably for the best." Sincerity laced every word. She kept her hand on the door, ready to close it on him at any second. To walk away all over again and leave him behind. Ava—Macie—handed back the note he'd given her with her contact information sprawled in his own handwriting. It wasn't the original. As long as he was here in Battle Mountain, he didn't have jurisdiction to take the lead on this case, but he'd still handle the evidence as though he did. "Listen, it might not do any good, but you should check in with the interim chief. Battle Mountain PD is pretty good at this stuff."

Riggs's hand released her door. "Oh, yeah? Places consisting of seventeen hundred people see a lot of murder?"

"You obviously haven't been watching the news," she said. "You'd be surprised what a small town like this is willing to do to protect itself. Find Easton Ford. He'll help you."

What was that supposed to mean? Riggs stepped away from the car to give her room to leave. He believed her. Whatever Becker had wanted with Macie Barclay, the detective had taken to his grave, but the thought of letting her slip away again…

Movement caught his attention over the top of her car. From the trees about ten feet away. They were so thick, he couldn't see through to the other side. He hated that. All the greenery and shadows. Back in New Mexico, everything was flat, bare, exposed. Who knew how many threats waited here? His gut said it wasn't an animal, but he wasn't altogether familiar with this place, either. They were out in the middle of the woods. No neighbors for miles. Becker was dead, with Macie Barclay's contact information. He wasn't going to take any chances. "Ava, get out of the car."

"Stop calling me that like you know me, Detective. You

don't, and I've humored you long enough." Macie pressed down on the brake pedal. "I can't stay here."

Riggs ripped open the door, grabbed her arm and dragged her from the car. They hit the dirt as one as a large knife cut through the air. A solid thud registered from overhead.

Ava—damn it, Macie—twisted her face up to the blade embedded deep into her tree house's wood staircase. "Is that a—"

"Stay down!" Riggs shoved to his feet. He took cover behind her vehicle and unholstered his weapon. Adrenaline threatened to tunnel his vision. He was met with nothing but pine trees and a breeze shaking through the wall of green, but the sick awareness of being watched didn't leave. No telling where the attacker had gone. But he wasn't going to stand around and wait for another attack. They needed to get out of here. Now. "Get to my truck. I'll cover you."

"I knew I should've left when I had the chance." Macie reached into the car and dragged a bag from the back seat. She stumbled forward, trying to keep her head down as she raced for his rental about ten yards away. "If I get stabbed in the back, I'm taking it out on you."

The low rumble of an engine broke through the trees and grew faint. Smaller than a full-size engine. ATV, maybe. A hint of diesel filtered through the trees. Riggs kept his weapon aimed as he used the sleeve of his jacket to dislodge the blade. The metal whined upon release. He backed toward his truck, never once letting his sidearm dip. It wasn't just his life on the line. He had a duty to protect the woman who'd left him to rot in New Mexico alone.

He wedged himself into the driver's seat and holstered his weapon. "Hold this." He handed off the knife. After starting the truck, he fishtailed down the dirt road that'd brought him face-to-face with the friend he'd never thought he'd see again. "Someone killed my partner, and I think it's safe to say they just tried to kill you. So start talking, Macie, or whoever the hell you are. Who wants you dead?"

"That's funny." She pressed herself back into the seat. "I was about to ask you the same question, Detective Karig."

Chapter Two

It was happening all over again.

Battle Mountain had just barely started moving on from the last threat, lost its mayor and seen its police chief shot. Guess she didn't have to wonder what would come next. Riggs Karig had found her because someone had killed an Albuquerque homicide detective and now someone had thrown a freaking knife at her. Whether in warning or to actually hurt her, it didn't matter, but she knew what she had to do next.

She glanced toward the chief's office, expecting to find a warm familiar face staring at her through the blinds like Weston Ford so often did. He wasn't there, and her heart shuddered at the thought of not seeing the one person who didn't take her for an eccentric kook again. How long did it take for someone to recover from a bullet wound these days?

Macie checked if her bag was still stuffed under her desk. She'd had to leave her car back at the scene. She could walk out of this station right now—finish what she'd started—but she wouldn't get any farther than the end of Main Street. These particular boots were not made for walking.

It wouldn't be any use anyway. Riggs Karig would find

her again. While she didn't know him personally anymore, collecting information and uncovering answers was in his and every other police officer's nature. And, whether she wanted to admit it or not, she was now part of a mystery he wanted to solve.

Interesting spot to be. She'd spent twenty-five years trying to melt into the background and avoid putting down roots. This place had made her soft.

"Show me your hands and turn around slowly." The definitive human-made click of a gun loading reached her ears.

Her insides lit up at the sound of the voice behind her. She did as she was instructed, raising her hands as high as her shoulders. Macie spun in her chair at the front of the station—slowly, of course—to find enormous blue eyes and the most beautiful wide gap-toothed smile. "You've got me, Officer Dwyer. I stole the cookie from the cookie jar. Would it help if I apologized?"

"Hand it over, scum." Penny Dwyer stretched one hand out, the other busy making the shape of a gun with her index finger and thumb. Her parents wouldn't let her have a toy gun considering what they did for a living. Probably the right choice, but it wouldn't stop the chaotic and vibrant four-year-old from following in their footsteps. "Swowly."

"Scum? That's harsh. Does your mom know you talk like that?" Macie made a big production of following along because honestly, Penny's visits were the only part of her day that didn't remind her of all the evil outside those double doors. Instead, she stood for the innocence of a childhood Macie had never had. "Okay. Okay. I'm just going to reach into my desk."

Macie gripped the item she'd left planted in her desk

for over a week, waiting for this exact moment. "Here you go, Officer."

She made quick work of aiming the water gun at Penny and pulled the trigger. A shriek of glee and surprise filled the police station as Macie pursued the girl down the hall. Water spattered between Penny's shoulder blades and sent her running faster to the break room. "That's what you get, copper. You'll never get your hands on those cookies!"

The chief's door swung open. Riggs set himself dead center in her path. Macie's boots slipped against wet tile, and she flattened into the detective's chest. Hard muscle, coupled with strong hands, flexed against her to keep her upright. Seemed the little boy who'd followed her around as a kid had done some growing up since she'd left Albuquerque. A flash of a yellow shirt and the trail of laughter disappeared around the corner. "Dang it. You let her get away."

"Does this department usually have squirt gun wars in the middle of the day?" Riggs didn't seem too impressed with the way they did things around here, but Macie wasn't too overly concerned with his opinions. He'd dropped into her world. Not the other way around, and he wasn't staying. Then again, neither was she.

"Nerf gun wars, too. If we can manage to fit them into our busy schedule," she said.

Easton Ford stepped free from the chief's office. As interim chief of police, he had every right to sit behind that desk, even if Macie didn't like it. After his brother, Weston—Battle Mountain's true chief—had been shot a few days ago, someone had to step in. She supposed the former Green Beret was the best choice considering what little experience the rest of the officers in this office held.

Easton had at least grown up here, was invested in the town and its people, especially its veterans. He'd even built a recovery center for them out at his family's ranch, Whispering Pines. It was where vets suffering with all manner of mental and physical health issues could go to feel safe and get the help they needed. Including Easton's fiancée, Genevieve. The Alamosa district attorney wasn't a vet, but she was a survivor, and her physical therapy at the ranch would be the only chance she'd get to walk again after she'd been grievously injured and confined to a wheelchair. "Detective Karig here was just filling me in. The body we recovered in one of the fire-damaged buildings this morning now has a name. Kevin Becker. Our coroner is up to her ears working with the military to sort through some bodies that dropped in town during a previous case, but she'll take good care of your friend. I give you my word."

"I appreciate that." Riggs shook Easton's hand. He was proving to have a solid poker face. Macie couldn't read his intentions or what he planned on doing next. Decades of sun exposure had created drought patches on his face, but that penetrating gaze remained clear, keen and probing. Not so quick with a smile. Direct, with a trustworthy face. He also filled out those jeans like he'd been born to them, and she couldn't deny he looked good. No wedding ring, though. Local girls would eat him alive.

"Great. Now you can go back where you came from." Macie set one hand at the small of his back—a very nice shape, if she had to say so herself—and maneuvered him down the hall toward the front of the station. He played along, but Macie had no doubt he could set her on her behind in one quick move. "So nice catching up with you. I'm sure you have better things to do than hang around Battle Mountain. Ford #2 will keep in touch about the investigation and let you know if we find anything. Bye-bye. Safe travels. Get out."

"Ford #2?" Riggs cast a glance back toward Easton.

"He's not going anywhere, Macie." Easton's voice filled the station. Harsher than normal. She turned back to see him hefting her overnight bag from beneath her desk, and her lungs seized. He set it on the second level of her double-height desk but didn't move to open it. Her entire life was in that bag. "And neither are you."

Her hand fell from Riggs's back. Easton didn't have that authority. "What are you saying?"

Her temporary boss rounded her desk, before stopping short in what they'd lovingly called the lobby of the station. "I'm saying the detective told me everything while you were playing cops and robbers."

"Everything?" Her throat dried.

"You were leaving, weren't you?" Easton settled his massive body against the front desk, and irritation stupidly burned through her. It wasn't her desk anymore. She'd given it up to whoever BMPD decided to hire to dispatch next. "For good. Without a word to anyone."

"Do you blame me?" Awareness prickled between her shoulder blades as she became the center of attention. Right where she didn't want to be. "I'm not sure if you've noticed, but it seems every week we've got ourselves a new serial killer or arsonist to contend with. I didn't want to spend the years I have left being told my friends are dying off. Not including you, of course."

Easton's scoff broke the tension in his jaw. "Like you were informed of Hazel McAdams's death?"

The slap of shock took her retort out of her mouth. Rage unlike anything she'd felt before charged through her chest, and she turned on Riggs. "You had no right."

"He needed to know." Riggs didn't even bother to look sorry. "My partner was strangled to death less than a block from here, Macie. Protecting your feelings isn't high on my priority list. So, yeah, I told him. Because I'm not going to keep intel that could help me catch who did it from local police. Besides, aren't you the one who told me to come here? That this department was pretty good at these kinds of things?"

This wasn't happening.

"I talked to the Albuquerque PD captain that oversaw Kevin Becker for most of his career. He didn't have any idea why the detective would've come to Battle Mountain. But he's given Detective Karig permission to aid our investigation, and we're lucky to have him." Easton moved away from her desk, heading back to the office he'd taken over. "Oh, one more thing. Given the victim was found with your address on him, coupled with the attack at your home, Mace, I've asked Detective Karig to keep an eye on you for the duration of the case while we focus on the knife you recovered earlier." Amusement cracked through Easton Ford's controlled expression. "From what I've heard, I'm sure you two will get along swimmingly."

"You've assigned me a babysitter?" Her and Easton's rivalry, their insults and her insubordination—it'd all been one big joke over the years, but this crossed a line. Macie wanted nothing more than to put a curse on him then, but she'd only started learning about ceremonial witchcraft a few weeks ago. "I knew there was a reason I didn't like you."

"And you can keep on not liking me as long as you're alive. I'm looking forward to it." Easton retreated to his office and closed the door. End of discussion.

"Guess it's you and me, Red." Riggs took up space in her peripheral vision.

"Don't get any bright ideas, Detective." It'd take a few hours to get the annoyance out of her system, but apparently, she didn't have any other place to be. "It's just temporary."

Right?

"If you say so." Riggs rubbed his hands together as though he was about to get a grip on a project he'd been looking forward to. "Where to?"

He wanted answers? Fine. She'd close this case for him as fast as possible and get him the hell out of Battle Mountain. She wasn't police, but she'd been around them long enough to pick up some skills. "Back to my house. Assuming your partner's killer threw that knife at us, we should try to retrace his steps."

"That's where I'd start, too," he said.

She buried the wave of pride at his words and headed for her desk to collect her bag.

Penny shot up from behind.

Macie's surprise was cut short as a beam of freezing water splashed into her face.

"I DON'T THINK I've heard anyone scream as loud as you did back there." Riggs couldn't help himself. It wasn't every day he got to see the wind taken out of the sails of a woman hell-bent on making everyone else question their sanity. "Your makeup smeared a bit under your eyes. I think I have a towel in the back seat if you want to try to get it off."

"So glad my misery could make your day a little better." Macie didn't move. Didn't even seem to breathe. It was hard to compare the carefree thrill seeker he'd known as a kid to the woman in the passenger seat. She wasn't anything he'd expected and kind of a pain in the ass but entertaining at the same time. "And I'm fine. Thank you."

The truck bumped and skidded up the same dirt road he'd traveled this morning. He hadn't known what waited at the end, but he sure as hell hadn't planned for Macie. Her self-awareness and moodiness alone outshined any memories of the past, leaving nothing but curiosity. She'd become a police dispatcher, worked with law enforcement and watched every single officer in that department risk their lives for this town. Why? Riggs tightened his grip on the steering wheel to be ready for the tires to slip out from under them. "You don't seem to like the interim chief much. I take it there's some history there."

"What gave it away?" She stared out the passenger window as though convinced just looking at him would give away every secret she'd ever held on to. He was a good detective, but he wasn't that good.

"Calling him Ford #2 was a bit of a hint." It'd taken every ounce of control he had not to laugh at it, either. Other than the straight up insubordination, Macie was proving to be one of a kind. Like this place. He hadn't come across that in a while.

"You were asked to keep me alive, Detective. Not get to know me," she said. "Just because you're my babysitter, doesn't mean we have to be friends."

"Fair enough, but to be clear, none of this was my idea." Jagged cliffs and peaks held on to the remnants of winter around them but still managed to produce entire layers of greenery. If he was being honest with himself, he hated this place. It was nothing like New Mexico. There was a weakness here that came with relying on shade and protective cliffs. Back home, things had to survive. A place like this didn't present a challenge in the least. He couldn't help make the internal comparison. He'd known from the time he'd been ten years old that he wanted to be a detective and help solve crimes, but with Becker out of the picture... He wasn't sure what else was left for him to do. He needed something more. Something to give him that spark that'd died over the past few years. "Seems Ford #2 genuinely cares about what happens to the people in his department. I told him my theory. He came up with the protection gig."

"Yeah, then what's your theory?" she asked.

Riggs's gut clenched. "That Becker's strangling wasn't random. I think he found something. He had your address for a reason. He could've been looking for you because you're connected to the McAdams case, and the killer followed him." Of course, there were a lot of other variables, but his instincts said he'd hit the mark. No one had been arrested in the murder of Hazel McAdams. Someone had been trying to stop Becker from getting to the truth. And they'd succeeded. "But you're right. We don't need to be friends. I was just trying to make the drive less awkward."

Silence pressed in through the truck cabin.

"He's too practical." Macie rubbed her palms against her knees and turned her attention out the windshield. "Easton. It works for him, and a big part of why this town is still on the map is because of him. I know that. He was military. There wasn't a whole lot of room for joking around and fun, and after what he went through to land him his discharge, I can see why he takes everything so seriously. There are lives at risk when he's working a case. He knows the best way to take down a threat and protect the people of this town, but life is about more than getting the job done at the end of the day." She half turned toward him, the sourness etched into her expression draining with every word. It was a sight to behold. "It's about finding meaning along the way."

Meaning. A flash of memory took him by surprise. Hazel and Ava—Macie—jumping over and falling into Las Huertas Creek on a school field trip up the mountain. They'd gotten soaked to the bone, but they'd kept the biggest smiles on their faces. Even when the teacher had chided them. It was that same creek where Becker and a couple police K9 units had found Hazel after her disappearance—an area they'd searched before but found nothing. The killer had returned the body to the scene of her abduction. "Our line of work doesn't allow for much meaning when we have to face the worst humankind has to offer."

"You're right." Macie's voice softened. "But it can't be all bad either, can it? Otherwise, what's the point?"

He didn't have an answer to that. Riggs maneuvered the truck onto another road, giving them a straight shot to her tree house. Which was a bit out of the box itself. What kind of woman lived in an actual tree house? Macie. That was who. Even as a kid, she'd always leaned into the unique. Never stopped learning something new. Like there was a piece of her missing, and she was trying to fill the gap. It was one of the reasons he'd liked her so much. He'd wanted to see what else she'd uncover about the world. He'd wanted to see the brightness in her face as she taught him about it, too.

Riggs pulled the truck into the makeshift driveway he'd parked earlier. A Battle Mountain police cruiser waited across the property, but he didn't see any officers to accompany it.

"That's Alma's and Cree's," she said. "They'll be around here somewhere."

Hesitation had him reaching for Macie before she got out. Soft skin slid beneath his calluses, and if that wasn't the metaphor of the year, he didn't know what was. She hadn't seen the things he had, hadn't been hardened by the realities of the world. No. Instead, Macie Barclay had run from the hard things as soon as she could and never looked back. She got to pretend evil didn't sink into the cracks around them and take over. While he'd been left to deal with the consequences. "Let me take a look first. Just to be safe."

She settled back into her seat. Surprising. He'd expected her to fight tooth and nail and shout about her ability to protect herself if it came right down to it. But it was then he caught sight of the bag she'd been hauling to her car when they'd met this morning, now at her feet. He'd noted the tension in her shoulders when Easton Ford had set it on her desk back at the station. She was protective of it. No doubt. So maybe she was letting him take the lead to get ready to run again.

Riggs hit the dirt, taking his keys with him, and scanned the tree line. He felt more exposed out here than he did in the middle of a flat desert. Unfamiliar territory had always put him off-balance, but he'd trained to handle anything the job threw his way. His personal life was another matter.

Hand poised above his sidearm, he headed for Macie's car. The keys were still inside. With a quick glance back toward his truck, he collected them from the ignition. If her plan had been to accompany him back out here to collect her car and disappear for another twenty-five years, she'd be sorely disappointed.

A breeze shifted through the trees and tightened his nerves. An echo of the engine he'd heard after the attack stalled on the wind. He didn't have that same feeling of being watched that he'd had earlier. Probably just his imagination. Still, he didn't trust his instincts out here. Riggs pocketed her keys, laughing at the hot-pink *coffee, chocolate and me: some things are better rich* key chain. He headed back toward her. Knocking on the window, he then stepped back as she cracked the door. "I want to take a look inside. Make sure nothing is missing, if that's all right with you."

"Did you find anything that would tell you who tried to fillet us?" Macie climbed down from the truck, one long leg peeking out from the split in her dress. Patches of dust had stained the white background of bright flowers and stems, but she'd taken his tackle like a champ. Maybe she wasn't as delicate as he'd initially believed.

"Not yet." He had an idea, but he wasn't ready to make a statement. Considering the use of an ATV and how quickly the killer had escaped down this mountain, whoever killed Becker hadn't followed the detective from Albuquerque. He'd already been here. And he knew the area.

They headed up the grand staircase complete with an extra split in the wood. The door was already unlocked, but he recalled Macie hadn't locked it behind her when he'd confronted her the last time they were here. She'd been set on leaving in a hurry. And from his guess, never intended on coming back. No point in locking a place you're leaving when disappearing for good. She'd done the same thing to her house in New Mexico.

"Oh." Macie pulled up short in the doorway, but even from a few inches behind her, he saw the same thing she did. Absolute destruction. "I don't… I don't understand."

Riggs maneuvered past her, catching a lungful of sensual perfume that seemed to fit her perfectly. But it wasn't enough to diffuse the chaos around them. Broken dishes had been scattered across the wood floor, chairs overturned where the dining set was supposed to be. Chunks of wood splintered away from the tree the house had been built around, as though the killer had been looking for something.

"He must've come back after we drove away." Riggs didn't want to touch anything. Everything in this room could be considered evidence. "Searched for something to connect you to Becker."

Macie didn't follow the same protocols. She carved a path through the mess and headed straight upstairs.

"Macie, wait." He tried to grab her arm, but she was too fast. Determined.

She didn't answer, disappearing beyond the two-story banister separating a loft from downstairs. Shuffling registered from above, and Riggs couldn't help himself.

"Damn it." He waded through the remnants of her personal possessions as carefully as possible. Upstairs hadn't survived any more than the first floor. Pillows spilled their guts, the mattress had been shredded and Macie…just stood there. His heart gripped hard. While she'd intended to leave this house, he understood it'd be hard to come face-to-face with this alienating destruction. Riggs slowed his approach, taking in what looked like hinged window shutters installed at the back of an empty closet. "What was in here?"

She seemed to snap out of whatever thought she'd been stuck in and closed the closet doors. "Nothing."

Chapter Three

She hadn't lied to him.

Macie had emptied that closet a few minutes before he'd gotten to the house, but somehow the killer had known about it.

Or maybe he'd gotten lucky.

She didn't know. Either way, someone had caught on to what she'd been doing all these years. They'd broken into her home, gone through her things. She shouldn't care. She'd planned on leaving it all behind, but she couldn't dislodge the sense of violation. That house had been hers for six years. It'd been home longer than anywhere else. Was that how Detective Becker had found her? Had she made a mistake?

Riggs drove them down Main Street, heading back for the station. Last they checked, Alma Majors and Cree Gregson were still following the ATV tracks through the woods. They'd be out there until the sun went down. Waste of time. Macie already knew what they'd come back with. Nothing. In her experience, the killer would've found a way to disappear. Wasn't that how the past five murder cases in Battle Mountain had worked?

She studied residents enjoying the first real day of spring. Snow still capped the cliffs protecting the town from outsiders, but temperatures were on the rise. "Can we please stop for something to eat? My stomach doesn't feel good."

Heat spread through her as Riggs glanced in her direction. "No problem. Anything good around here?"

"The coffee shop is fine." She pointed out Caffeine and Carbs' new location a few doors down from the station. Normally, she would've gone to Greta's—Battle Mountain's oldest and authentically grimiest diner—but grease wouldn't cure what ailed her. She needed straight up caffeine to settle her nerves.

The detective angled into a parking spot, rounded the hood of the truck and waited. For her. The part of her that wasn't freaked out by a throwing knife and someone going through her house appreciated it, but Macie knew exactly what he was doing. It was what all of the reserve officers in the department had done when lives were at risk: followed orders. He was taking his protection detail seriously. Riggs walked beside her all the way to the door and held it open for her. "After you."

Macie headed straight for the counter, not even bothering to glance at the pastries in the baker's cases on either side. She'd tried not to feed her sweet tooth since she'd made herself sick eating so much candy as a kid. Unlike Isla Vachs, BMPD's newest recruit. Actually, she was surprised the former EMT wasn't already here for her daily hit of sugar and chocolate.

"Hey, Macie." Reagan Allen wiped his hands on a dishcloth from behind the counter. He'd been an institution in Battle Mountain since the day she'd rolled into town. The former competition pastry chef had gotten tired of the rat race and wanted something quiet. Too bad that hadn't really worked out for him considering his bakery had burned down with the help of an arsonist about nine months ago. Not to mention the forest fire on the outskirts of town and all the dead people turning up. No doubt he'd already heard about the one in the next building over. "Get you the usual?"

"No." Her voice shook more than she'd meant it to. Macie leveled her chin parallel to the floor. "Today, I want my unusual please."

Silence descended from the couple a few tables over.

"Hell, woman." Reagan dropped the towel on the counter. "You haven't ordered that since Easton Ford signed up with the department. You sure?"

"I know what I'm about, Reagan Allen. I'm not a child." She could handle the caffeine. No matter what anyone in this town believed.

"All right." The baker held his hands up in surrender. A bandage had been plastered along one side of his left one. Reagan was always trying new things in the bakery. It wasn't uncommon for him to catch a few burns a week. "One blonde roast coffee coming up."

"Am I missing something?" Riggs asked.

"No. I'm just thirsty." She'd forgotten he was there at all. Macie left her money on the counter as Reagan handed her the extra-large coffee. Heat soaked into her hands through the Styrofoam cup, like the contents were trying to be absorbed through her skin. Today she finally understood why people wished they could be hooked up to their coffee intravenously, but she'd do it the old-fashioned way.

Riggs ordered his drink. Something loaded with cream

and sugar, plus a pastry. Whatever he did to keep in shape, it was obviously working.

"You're gonna want to watch her." Reagan tried to keep his voice down as he handed off Riggs's order, but noise carried in a place like this. "Last time she had one of those, police found her out in the middle of the woods in a sleeping bag with a bunch of stuffed animals tucked in tight. She didn't remember any of it."

Every muscle in her body tensed for the laugh, but it never came.

"Good to know." Riggs dropped a few coins into the tip jar. "Thanks for the coffee."

They left together, stepping out into the too bright sun and the slow mingling of townspeople conducting their own business in the middle of the week. But the tension was still there. "You're not going to ask me about what Reagan told you?"

"Why would I?" Riggs took a huge bite of his chocolate glazed donut like he'd never tasted anything so good. Looked like cops really did like their pastries. He followed it up quickly with a big sip of coffee. "Sounds like you weren't hurting anyone or destroying property. What you choose to do with stuffed animals in the middle of the woods is none of my business."

His tone said otherwise. "You're not even a little bit curious?"

"Like I said, it's got nothing to do with me." Heading down the street, he finished off his donut and tossed the wrapper into the garbage can on the way. "Tell me what happened to these buildings."

Macie had yet to take a shot of her overcaffeinated coffee,

but her hands had somehow stopped shaking. She studied the back of Riggs's head, and a flash comparison to the boy she'd known superimposed over reality. He'd always been inquisitive, especially about things he didn't understand. The bizarre and unusual. Like the more knowledge he collected, the farther he could go. Literally and figuratively. But the crest on the badge around his neck said he hadn't gone far. He was Albuquerque born and bred. No amount of education was going to peel him from his hometown.

They stopped in front of one of the first buildings that'd been affected by the bombing at the station. "This was the fly shop. Lake San Cristobal isn't far from here. We get a lot of fishermen and tourists passing through who are looking for a taste of the outdoors. Some regulars. Well, we used to."

"What happened to it?" He surveyed the crumbling concrete structure. The roof had caved in as the resulting fire spread. Remnants of the front sign still clung to the edges, but there was nothing to save.

"There was a bomb." She could still feel the heat of it burning her from head to toe. If it hadn't been for Cree Gregson and his quick instincts, she would've been one of its victims. She was a dispatcher. She wasn't supposed to be caught in the danger. All these years, she'd expected the threat to come out of Battle Mountain. Turned out, this place wasn't the source after all. It'd followed her here. Just like the detective who'd been killed. "Nine months ago. An ATF agent had murdered her sister. She was doing everything she could to stop the department from catching her. Caused the forest fire, too."

"I noticed the burnt trees on the way in," he said. "This place has got a few scars, from the looks of it."

He had no idea.

Riggs walked along a little farther. "What about this one?"

"This was Caffeine and Carbs." This building looked like the others. Maybe a little worse for wear. Macie had no idea why the city hadn't bulldozed these already. Business owners didn't have the money to rebuild after insurance denied their claims, and Battle Mountain didn't have the funds to revitalize any of it. This town had started dying the moment the coal companies pulled out, and it was only getting worse with this new wave of crime. "Reagan's insurance didn't cover a rebuild, so he decided to take over one of the buildings that hadn't been as damaged. Started fresh."

"Becker was here. I don't know why. I don't even know how he found you and what the hell he was doing in this building." His voice dipped, solemn and pained. "It killed him to retire without having an answer to the one case that'd haunted him."

"Hazel's." Macie understood the feeling. It felt as though she'd put her entire life on hold for breadcrumbs when what she really needed was the whole loaf. She could only imagine how hard the detective who'd overseen the investigation had pushed all these years, but the trail had gone cold long before she'd left Albuquerque.

Hazel McAdams had been more of a sister than a best friend. They'd shared the same birthday and were hardly ever apart from kindergarten all the way through fifth grade. She wasn't sure when Riggs had joined their little band of merry hell-raisers, but he'd fit right in as though he'd always been there. Actually, she was pretty sure he'd had a crush on Hazel. Most people did. Hazel had been the city's sweetheart. Perfect in every way with a great big smile and gorgeous blond hair. As an only child, she'd gotten her parents' love with extravagant birthday parties and beautiful dress-ups. Teachers had given her extra gold stars. The girl could've done no wrong, in anyone's eyes.

But Hazel had made a mistake. One that'd cost her life.

Macie tried to keep the memories from encroaching on the moment. The police had spared no expense in the hunt. The entire city had been up in arms with volunteer searches, flyers, pleas in the paper and on the news. The McAdamses had offered a reward, but that'd only thinned the police force out there in the streets and woods by giving them empty leads to chase. Detective Becker had stuck with it, though. He'd been the one to find her three days later. This was her chance to make things right. To move on. "Was there anything he said to you? A lead or someone who came forward with new information?"

"Yeah. There was. I found his notes locked in the trunk of his car. From what I could tell, he'd gone back through the original file. I took a look at the crime scene photos and found a note he'd written on a Post-it. The same shoe tread could be found all over those woods. Like Hazel had run from her abductor. Police figured every child-sized imprint had come from her during a struggle with the killer, but he believed there were two sets of footprints in those woods. Same shoe. Two different sources." Riggs locked that penetrating gaze on her, his index finger extended at her from around his coffee cup. "According to Becker, Hazel wasn't alone the day she was killed."

"WHAT ARE YOU asking me, Detective?" Macie seemed to shut down right then. Those fish bait earrings of hers had a lot to say, though. They caught in her hair as wind cut down the street from the canyon and cliffs southward.

"You were there, weren't you?" He hadn't ever considered the possibility. The evidence had been straightforward. Identical shoe treads all across that mountain. One belonged to the killer—that much had been easily discernible, but the others... "The day Hazel was taken. The day she was killed. That's why Becker wanted to track you down. He must've remembered you two had been inseparable. You dressed alike, sometimes with the same earrings, same shirts. Did your hair the same way. And I remember those shoes, Macie. White-laced sneakers with hot-pink scales. You begged your parents for them for months because Hazel had ones just like them. You were so excited when you finally got them for your birthday."

She tossed her coffee—completely full—into the street bin. "I'm sorry you lost your partner. Really, I am. I don't know why Becker had my contact information in his pocket when he died or why he came here. I don't know who killed him, and I can't help you."

Riggs couldn't let her go. Not yet. He slipped his hand between her arm and rib cage, before pulling her into his chest. Her softness turned hard as she pressed against him. "I think you know more than you're letting on. I think you know exactly who killed my partner and why Becker wanted to find you, but you're either in denial this has anything to do with you, or you're hiding something from me."

Her bottom lip parted, but still, she didn't answer. Like she'd betray some kind of promise if she did.

"That's why you left, isn't it? Why one day I showed up at your house and the entire place had been cleared out."

Riggs released his hold on her. All this time, he'd resented her for leaving him to deal with Hazel's death alone, for disappearing. What if he'd had it wrong? What if Hazel and Macie had been together that day? What if Hazel's killer had taken them both and nobody had known until she'd reported what'd happened to police? "I tried calling for days. I went by your house. Becker was there. I asked him if he knew anything about where you'd gone. He had no idea. One day you were there, and the next day you were gone." The truth set in. It sucker punched him harder than he'd expected. "I thought it was because you couldn't take staying in the same city where you'd lost your best friend, but you and your parents left because you thought Hazel's killer might come back for you. Didn't you?"

A line of tears welled in her eyes, but what little he knew of this new version of her told him Macie wasn't the kind of woman to let them fall. She backed away from him, out of reach. "That's quite a theory, Detective."

"It's not just a theory, is it?" He thought his past cases had emotionally wrung him dry from the inside out, but right then, his heart gripped hard in his chest. Twenty-five years on the run. Terrified. Alone. How had she survived? "You escaped him."

Macie cut her attention to a couple crossing the street. "We went back to that creek. You know, the one where Mrs. Reich took us for a field trip to study algae and insects in moving water that one time. We thought we could win the entire science fair if we were able to grow our own algae, but we figured it was like making sourdough bread. We needed a starter first, a sample. Stupid, I know, but we didn't know any better."

Her laugh died as wind howled down Main Street, rising to the obvious storm churning inside her.

"I don't know where he came from." Green eyes unlike anything he'd seen until he'd met her darkened as clouds blocked out the sun. "One second, we were throwing moss at each other, the next he was standing there."

Tension flooded through his neck and shoulders as though he could intervene on her behalf. "Did he talk to you?"

"He told us he was lost, then asked us if we knew the way back down the mountain. It all happened so fast I never got a good look at his face. He grabbed me from behind. I kicked and screamed, but he was so strong." She hugged her middle. "Hazel grabbed for a dead branch and hit him in the back to get him to let me go. Worked, too." Clarity spread across her expression. "He let me go, but he caught the branch Hazel was swinging and turned on her. I don't remember much after that."

"You must've gotten back down the mountain somehow. You made it home. Your parents are the ones who called the police, but they never mentioned you'd been with Hazel that day." Guilt had obviously been eating away at the sunshine inside of her since she'd left Albuquerque, but children weren't supposed to know how to fight off attackers. They were supposed to know how to jump rope, navigate puberty and do their schoolwork. They were supposed to believe in Santa Claus and fight with their siblings. Not full-grown men. What she'd been through… No ten-year-old should've had to face that, but there was something in her eyes that said she'd held herself responsible ever since. "Where did you go?"

"Canada, at first. It was the farthest my parents could get

me while staying on the continent. We found an isolated plot of land in Newfoundland and acquired it to build a cabin," she said. "They're still there as far as I know."

He didn't understand. "What do you mean? You don't talk to them?"

"I mean I got tired of watching them check the doors and windows multiple times a night. I got tired of the weekly trips to the gun range and stashing our food like the end of the world was coming. I wasn't allowed to go to school. They didn't let themselves get to know anyone. They were suspicious of everyone. As long as I was there, they would've kept giving up their lives for me, and I couldn't take it. I knew sooner or later, they'd resent me for it," she said. "So I didn't give them the chance. When I turned seventeen, I told myself I would never let anyone else put themselves in danger for me, and I left."

He didn't know what to say to that, what to think. "Macie, I'm sure they were just happy you survived. They were doing what I wish all parents would do. Protecting you. What more could you have asked for?"

"I guess I'll never know." The tears were gone. In their place, defiance took control, and Macie was back to being the firecracker waiting to blow up in his face. "You can consider your babysitting duties fulfilled, Riggs. Now you know the truth. Both Hazel and Becker died because of me, and I'm not going to let anyone else make the same mistake. Including you." She swiped a strand of hair out of her face. His name sounded whole and compelling coming from her mouth, like it was some kind of lifeline, and he wanted nothing more than for her to latch on to it. "I hope you find who killed your partner. Becker deserved better. Don't try to find me again. Please."

He reached out again, hating himself for even trying as she flinched. "You can't run from this, Macie. Whoever did this… He's going to find you just like I did."

"I like my chances." They were back at his truck. Macie wrenched open his vehicle door. Lugging her duffel bag over her shoulder, she blocked her face from the incoming rain and headed down the street back toward the police station. Within seconds, the town's drainage system struggled with the amount of water, and he was completely soaked through, from head to toe.

She had a point. Anyone who'd tried to help her had turned up dead or on the run. He'd be stupid to follow after her now that he knew why Becker had come to Battle Mountain. He had another piece of the puzzle in place. By her own words, there wasn't anything else Macie Barclay could give him, but the thought of letting her go without a solid plan for her protection in place gutted him.

"Damn it." Macie was so determined to run, she'd plow straight into a tree if she thought it'd get her out of here faster. Riggs jogged to catch up with her, tossing his coffee on the way. "You're not getting anywhere in this downpour. Your tree house is still a crime scene. You can't go back there. What are you going to do? Sleep in the station? The only beds they have are made of concrete and surrounded by steel bars."

"That's not your problem, Detective." She cut through the storm as though she'd done it a thousand times before. Which was a probability in a place like this. Lightning lit up the sky a split second before thunder shook the very ground he stood on. Hell. Had Battle Mountain opened a hell gate he didn't know about?

"You don't have to do this, Macie." He wasn't sure why he was petitioning for more time other than the simple fact that as long as she was with him, he would keep her alive. He could make up for not being there for Becker when his partner had needed him the most. "Help me. Please."

She turned on him. Water streaked down her high-boned cheeks and framed her chin. "Help you? Do what?"

"End this," he said.

"Did you not hear what I just said, Riggs? Anyone I get close to ends up dead or in some cabin in the middle of Canada. Even if I agreed to stay, I'm not a detective, Riggs." Macie glanced toward the station two doors down. He could see the wheels spinning in her head, see how much she wanted to walk away. But he couldn't do this without her. "I'm a dispatcher. I don't know the first thing about investigating a homicide."

"But you know this killer. You survived him." He held himself back from putting the cuffs on her again, to keep her from leaving a second time. Wouldn't do any good. For all he knew, she'd hidden handcuff keys in the seams of her dress. "Aren't you tired of running, Macie? Don't you want to finally feel safe? If we work together, if we put the bastard who killed our friends behind bars, you can be free. You can see your parents again. You can finally have a life."

Macie gave the station another longing look. "Don't make promises you can't keep."

Chapter Four

She'd lied to him.

About that day in the woods. She'd recalled the memories so many times, there wasn't anything she could do to keep them from haunting her. The secret she'd carried from that day forth wouldn't help find who'd killed his partner, and it wouldn't help catch the man who'd killed Hazel.

Its sole purpose was to punish her.

Riggs closed the door behind them, shutting out the storm. He shucked out of his jacket and ignited a lungful of something along the lines of spicy aftershave and earth in the enclosed space. It pricked at her senses. A perfect distraction from reality. "Make yourself at home."

She scanned the too-small room as she peeled her own jacket free from the dress suctioned to her skin. Single bed, a dresser topped with an old TV. No chairs. A door across the room led into the bathroom. No matter where she looked, brown reigned. In the carpet, the curtains, the wood paneling. Everything looked like it'd taken a flush down a toilet then come back up and spilled over every inch of the place.

Cindy's Motel hadn't been affected by the fires, serial killers, bombers or gunmen. It was the one spot in all of

Battle Mountain that seemed safe, but the pressure in Macie's rib cage refused to relent. She squeezed the handle of her duffel bag tighter as the walls seemed to cave in. "Not sure where I can do that seeing as how the only place to sit is the bed."

He collected a backpack near the door and maneuvered past her on his way to the bathroom. Ridges and valleys of muscle across his back flexed under every move. "Is that you worrying about me sleeping on damp bedding tonight, or your way of talking yourself out of staying?"

Macie caught herself staring at the white T-shirt plastered to him like a second skin. Holy hell. The man had done more than a little growing up. He'd taken very good care of himself, indeed. "Both. I think." She couldn't really remember what he'd asked.

"You're going to want to close your mouth before that spider in the corner finds a new place to stay." He pointed overhead. That crooked smile she'd only gotten a taste of earlier made a full appearance a split second before he disappeared into the bathroom and closed the door. "I might have something you can change into. Get you out of that dress. Unless you're not staying."

Thunder crashed overhead and shook the cheap window at the back of the room as though to make a point. This storm had been waiting in the mountains for three days and was just the beginning of a series that hit every spring. Roads flooded, mudslides blocked entire passages and accidents increased. Unfortunately, she wasn't going anywhere until it passed.

Macie unshouldered her bag and set it on the bed. The canvas had protected most of what was inside. She wouldn't have to borrow any of Riggs's clothes. Sleeping arrangements, on the other hand, would be awkward. Flipping through her files, she ensured Easton Ford hadn't taken anything while he'd manhandled her bag back at the station. Nosy, no-good imposter. She took a cleansing breath, still picking up hints of spice. Everything was there. "You said Becker was your partner. He must've been close to sixty now."

"Sixty-three." Riggs's answer was nearly drowned under the patter of running water. The shower?

"How long were you partners for?" Macie took the opportunity to run through the rest of the room. Nothing in the dresser drawers. Seemed the detective traveled light. Preferred to be ready to go at a moment's notice. She liked that. She understood that. Closing the top dresser drawer, she moved to the nightstands with a glance toward the bathroom door. The motel Bible had seen better days, but it'd been dusted recently. No sign of a phone or laptop. Not even a charger. Riggs would have to keep in touch with his department. He must have taken them into the bathroom with him.

"Three years, but we've been friends longer." The door swung open, and a wall of steam escaped upward. "Can I help you find something?"

Macie slammed the nightstand drawer closed and straightened as fast as her upper body allowed. Not fast enough. He'd caught her snooping. She could see it in the amusement plastered across his gorgeous face. "Floss?"

"Floss." That single word told her everything she needed to know. He was a much better detective than she'd given him credit for. Riggs had lost his shirt, accentuating lean muscle, narrow hips and that little V thing men got when they worked out. He wadded and wrung the fabric stretched between his hands. "And the first place you thought to check for that was my nightstand?"

"I have sensitive teeth." Heat burned up her neck and into her face. He wasn't stupid. He knew exactly what she'd been doing, but he was giving her the benefit of the doubt for some reason. "It's genetic."

"Right. And is snooping through other people's personal belongings genetic, too, or does that come with the Macie Barclay package?" Riggs hung the shirt over his shoulder.

"Fine. You caught me. Okay? I was looking through your room to see what I could find out about you." What was a little spying between friends? "Hard to tell who's actually telling the truth these days. For all I know, you could be the one who killed your partner and were trying to hunt me down."

She regretted the words the moment they'd left her mouth.

The pain registered on his face, but Riggs hid it well. "Kevin Becker was the only person who ever gave a damn about me. My parents pretty much checked out after my brother came into the world. Becker saw what losing you and Hazel did. I was alone. I was scared I was next. He encouraged me to face my fears. When I joined the force, he taught me how to run an investigation, to stick with it and get my own answers. He's the reason I became a detective. Becker was a good investigator, but he was an even better man. I'd never have hurt him. Least of all to find you."

"I'm sorry. I didn't mean…" She wasn't sure what she'd meant, but one thing he'd said had stood out among the rest. Macie took a half step toward him. She didn't know why other than to make herself feel better about her accusation by offering some comfort, but she wasn't good at that, either. "You've been looking into Hazel's case all this time?"

"What else was I supposed to do? Pretend everything was normal. That you'd just show up at my doorstep one day, and you'd go back to being all I had?" He talked as though that'd been exactly as he'd done, and her heart hurt at the thought.

Of course, there'd been times she'd imagined that day playing out differently. That she'd been the one to stay behind and Hazel had made it out alive. That they'd both fought for each other. Maybe even grew up, became pop stars like they'd always imagined. That they'd fall in love and leave Albuquerque to start their own lives. Riggs had been there, too. Doing what he did best by watching out for them.

He tossed his shirt onto the bed's headboard to dry. "Didn't do any good, though. Twenty-five years later, and I'm nowhere other than proving Becker's theory was true. Hazel wasn't the only one there that day."

A thought struck her. Fresh and hard. Macie shifted her weight between both feet. "What if Hazel and I weren't the only ones?"

"You mean another victim? Police ran through missing persons reports at the time. I've even gone back to try to establish a pattern, but Hazel's case was unique." Riggs straightened, and suddenly he seemed so much bigger than he had a moment ago. A force to be reckoned with. Not her childhood friend but the detective. More intense, isolated. Focused. "There didn't seem to be any motive, and neither her parents nor her teacher had noticed anything strange

Dead Again

going on in her life. They both reported she was her normal wild self. Nothing to suggest the killer targeted her specifically, and there weren't any other open investigations in the area."

"But some killers don't stay in one area, right?" As much as she hated the idea of more victims out there, they needed to consider it now. Macie finally took that full step, bringing herself closer to him as excitement built at the prospect of a new lead to follow. "Sometimes they have to adapt and move to keep from getting caught. I'm not saying whoever did this is a serial offender, but from what I've seen in this town, it's never one incident. Bombers practice their art before the big show. Military units run through their battle plans until they've got it ingrained in their heads. What if Hazel wasn't the first? Or the last?"

She should've thought about it before now. She should've—

"You don't think I've looked? Macie, I'm telling you. There's nothing. No forensics to test. No vehicle to track. No suspects to run background checks on. There's no more crime scene. Everything is gone. Every lead has been exhausted." He almost seemed apologetic and took his own step toward her. Strong hands gripped her arms, holding her upright when the world wanted to crash down around her. "The best chance we have of finding Hazel's killer is finding who murdered my partner."

His redirection hit her harder than she'd expected. That wasn't what they'd agreed on. Macie stepped out of his reach. She'd spent the past two decades trying to get answers. For a moment there, she thought they'd been on the same page, that they'd wanted the same thing, but now…

"I don't understand. You told me you wanted me to stay

so we could work together on this. You stopped me from leaving. Twice. What are you saying? You're already giving up?" If she wasn't trying to find Hazel's killer, what was she doing? Who was she? What was she supposed to do with her life? Macie tried to catch her breath, but the temper she'd been warned to keep under control was heating up her chest. "You're just going to forget that she was our best friend and tell me that her case isn't worth continuing? You and Becker have been trying to find her killer all this time, and suddenly you've changed your mind. Why?"

An invisible weight pulled at the sides of his mouth. "Becker and I weren't working Hazel's case together, Macie."

She didn't know what else to say, what to think. Warning triggered in her gut. Telling her to run, to get out of Battle Mountain as fast as possible. Before things got worse.

"A year ago, I put in my papers for a transfer. I got a new partner," Riggs said. "Becker threw his entire life away for a case that went nowhere. I wasn't going to follow after him."

HE'D NEVER SAID the words before.

Hell, he hadn't even had the guts to say them to Becker.

But the old man had known. He'd tried one last time to get Riggs to come around to his way of thinking before he'd walked off the job, but Riggs hadn't taken the bait. Not again. It'd been too many years wasted in hope, in all-nighters, in empty leads and dead ends. Following Hazel's case had cost him promotions, relationships and time he couldn't ever get back, but Becker hadn't seen any of it. At the end of their partnership, Riggs had finally thrown the truth in his partner's face: he hadn't been building a career of his own. He'd followed Becker's path into the same sad dead end.

And some cases just couldn't be solved.

The storm had come inside while still raging outdoors. He could feel it in Macie's icy gaze, the way she tried to get as far from him in the cramped room as possible by sitting on the bed near the door. Word had come down from BMPD. Roads were closed. Neither of them were going anywhere tonight.

The flowy floral dress that'd brought out the color of her eyes had gone somewhat opaque and dim soaked through, to the point he could tell the color of her matching bra and underwear set, but he didn't have the guts to say anything.

What did you say to someone who'd been caught with several stuffed animals in a sleeping bag in the middle of the woods?

"You can stop staring at me. I'm not going to turn into a monster from the black lagoon." Her hair streaked down her back, and it was then he noted the thin raised line of scarring running from the base of her neck beneath her collar. Had that been from the attack or from something else?

It'd hit him a few minutes before that despite the years they'd known each other, he really didn't know her now. Not as Macie Barclay, at least. What she'd been doing all these years, how she'd survived, if she had a husband or lover or kids. The thought shouldn't have taken so much of his mental energy considering a dead body had brought them together, but he couldn't get the idea of her happy, living a full life while Hazel's had been cut short, out of his head.

"There goes my pitch to the paranormal reality show." He could feel her disappointment like a rock in the pit of his stomach. He knew the feeling all too well. That spark of hope going out. He'd felt it more than a few times over the course of his career.

"Why are you here?" Her words barely registered over the pounding of rain at the window. "You and Becker weren't partners anymore. Why are you the one here trying to solve his murder if you don't want anything to do with the case he was investigating?"

He wasn't sure he could explain it to her. He wasn't sure he could even explain it to himself, but she deserved to know what he'd dragged her into. "Because I'm the reason he's dead."

The words had been there since he'd gotten the hit about a body matching Becker's description turning up in one of the most forgetful towns he'd never found on a map. Right there at the edge of his mind. Nagging, digging, destroying him from the inside out. "The last time I saw him, I told him he'd wasted my life. My career. That he'd stolen twenty-five years I couldn't ever get back. He just looked at me. Didn't even deny it. I think he knew I was right. I think he realized he'd wasted his life, too, and it just pushed him harder. It got him killed."

"Do you really think it's a waste trying to help someone else find peace?" Her question settled between them, and Riggs couldn't help but feel she wasn't asking on Becker's behalf.

"Hazel's already at peace." Didn't anyone get that? Closure wasn't for the victims of the cases he investigated. It was for the living. To give them a sense of justice and finality. "Becker wasn't doing it for her. He was riding that case into the ground for himself. And he was taking me and everyone else in his life down with it."

Macie slid off the bed and took a position at the window to peer out. "Yet you became a detective because of her. You worked her case until a year ago, believing you could make a difference."

The accusation cut through him. He hadn't told her as much, but he guessed it wasn't hard to put together, either. Or maybe she saw more of him than he'd meant to show. "You're right. I let myself get sucked into the story. I let myself get so focused on trying to find Hazel's killer that I let friendships go, I stopped climbing the department ladder, my family stopped calling. I lost my wife. I was an addict. Just like Becker. I couldn't stop. I couldn't see what the case was costing me. I convinced myself into believing I could be the hero at the end, but it turns out, the entire thing was just a fairy tale. At least until today."

Now it was more like a nightmare.

"You were married?" Macie asked.

"Ten years." Riggs stared at the invisible impression left behind by his wedding band. It wasn't really there. It'd been two years since the divorce, but he could still feel it. That connection to another person. "She saw what was happening and couldn't sit back and watch me do it to myself. I think the divorce was supposed to shock me out of it, but it just made things worse."

"You thought if you could find who killed Hazel, you could get it all back." Macie crossed the room, bringing an air of fresh rain and perfume in her wake. "Maybe your partner did, too. Becker tracked me down. The only reason he'd want to do that is because he believed I had something to add to Hazel's investigation. Whether we like it or not, these two cases are connected. We solve one, we solve the other. Just like you said. Tell me who Becker liked for a suspect."

"No way in hell, Macie. You had the right idea when I found you." Riggs needed to get out of this room. Away from her and childhood memories that had no right to take up space in his head. He should've let her go when he'd had the chance. "Getting involved in a case in which you were a victim isn't going to help Hazel or Becker. You should leave like you intended. Disappear for another twenty-five years."

"I think Becker proved hiding isn't the answer. Look how he found me. Who knows what his killer got out of him before he died. You said it yourself—the best thing we can do is work together. We're stuck inside until the roads are clear. That's not happening until morning." Macie's thin shoulders rose on a deep inhale. "We might as well make the best use of our time."

"That was before I found out you were there when Hazel was abducted." Damn it. He was getting sucked back in. Exactly where he didn't want to be, but she was right. These cases were connected just as he thought, and there was no avoiding the past. No matter how much he wanted to bury it. Riggs dragged his backpack from against the wall and hauled it onto the bed. Tipping the bag upside down, he dumped it empty. "Everything I'm about to show you doesn't leave this room. Understand?"

"These are Becker's belongings? I don't see a laptop or phone." Macie pushed each file and personal item into its separate space across the bed.

"Becker was old school. Didn't trust technology. He used

to say murders were solved by detectives. Not computers."
The lesson hit Riggs hard when his laptop had crashed with
every single note and crime scene photo of one of his first
investigations before he'd had a chance to add it to the department server. Although, he wasn't entirely convinced
Becker hadn't had something to do with it. Either way, Riggs
had gone for physical files after that. Always keeping a
backup. "I've already gone through it. He had his keys and
his weapon on him. They're with your coroner. I've got a
notebook with a couple pages filled in with Becker's handwriting, a pen, a change of clothes, some toiletries. Nothing
that points to why he was in that building in the first place
or if he was meeting anyone."

Macie flipped through the first few pages of the file,
hesitant and tense. Her voice lost some of its confidence.
"Seems so…empty."

He reached to take the file from her. "You might not want
to look at those."

She dodged his attempt, turning her back to him. "You'd
be surprised what I can handle, Detective."

"Riggs." Riggs shoved a hand through his still-damp hair
as frustration got the better of him. "Hell, we've known each
other for years, woman. You can call me by my first name."

"It's not you," she said. "People I care about end up in
danger if I get too close."

Which meant she hadn't built any new relationships all
this time. No husband. No lover. No kids. No friends. Macie
had isolated herself in the middle of a mountain range to
protect the people around her all this time. And, hell, if
that wasn't admirable. And heartbreaking. As much as he'd
hated the turn his life had taken by following Becker down

this never-ending road, he never would've given up their friendship if he'd known their time had been limited. Not for all the promotions in the world.

He wanted to tell Macie she was safe. That she could trust him, and that nothing bad was going to happen to her, but it'd be a lie. Becker had died with Macie's contact information in his pocket. It stood to reason whoever'd killed Hazel—whoever'd abducted them as kids—knew she was here.

And hunting her.

Riggs took a step forward, still aware of her personal space. "I know you're scared, but I'm not going to let anything happen to you, Macie. I give you my word."

"I made that same promise to Hazel once. That I'd always protect her and have her back. She said the same thing to me. We made a blood oath because we thought we could make it last forever." Macie flipped her right palm upward as a glimmer of tears welled in her eyes. "Look how that turned out."

He dared another step and reached out. Only this time, it wasn't for the case file. Running his thumb down the middle of her palm, he memorized the raised tissue there. So many scars. "I think you're forgetting I'm not a ten-year-old girl."

Her laugh scattered the pressure building in his chest. "No. You're definitely not. You're a lot more hairy, for one thing."

"Is that a bad thing?" He stroked his five-o'clock shadow, and suddenly felt himself wanting to shave it all off. For her. Which was crazy. He hadn't shaved for anyone, and he didn't intend to start now.

"Not when it's in all the right places." Macie's smile held

on longer than he'd expected, but she pulled her hand away. Her focus diverted to the file in her other hand. "This isn't the official case file."

"What do you mean?" Riggs maneuvered over her shoulder to get a better look, getting a lungful of damp hair and soft perfume.

"I've seen the original investigation file for Hazel's case. I know exactly what's inside. This isn't it." She folded the manila file cover to the back, exposing the first page of witness interview statements from twenty-five years ago. "None of these names are familiar."

To him, either. Riggs pried the file from her hand and checked the tab on the side. Something fell from inside and hit the floor. "This doesn't make sense. Becker was extreme when it came to keeping his files clean. Why would there be another file in here?"

"Because Becker wasn't just investigating Hazel's case." Macie collected the photo that'd dropped and handed it off. A crime scene photo, foreign and unrecognizable. "He'd found another victim."

Chapter Five

Sakari Vigil.

Seven years old.

She'd gone missing from her backyard in Dulce, New Mexico, in the blink of an eye. Ten years ago.

One minute she'd been playing in the hose, running through the grass when her mother had gone in to get some more sunscreen and water. The next Sakari had been gone. Three days later, her body had been laid peacefully on the eastern border of the Jicarilla Apache reservation.

Macie's heart hurt as she traced the smile creases around the girl's eyes in the photo. Another victim. The blow had taken the fight right out of her. According to Becker's notes, Dulce police had exhausted every lead within a month. No suspects. No leads within the past few years. The case had gone as cold as Hazel's. "Becker never said anything to you about another victim? About how he'd come to find her?"

"No." Riggs stared out the single window at the back of the room, unmoving and braced against the wall. Quiet. She couldn't read him as well as she used to, but she could feel the same tendril of pain in him. The one that wound tighter with every breath. "Nothing."

"There's a pattern here." Macie hated that fact. That this killer wasn't choosing his victims randomly but looking for a carefully thought-out set of parameters. How many other victims had fallen into the sickening set of rules he'd set? How many more were out there they weren't seeing? "Hazel and Sakari were both only children. He wanted to make sure he could get them alone—that other siblings wouldn't interfere or be able to identify him."

Riggs slid his hand down the cringeworthy wallpaper. "Then why attack Hazel when she was with you?"

She had an answer, but Macie didn't have the guts to tell him the truth. Not yet. "He might not have planned for me to be there that day."

"There's fifteen years between these cases. We can't even be sure both girls were killed by the same person." Riggs shoved away from the wall. "For all we know, Becker was grasping at straws, chasing after another one of his dead ends."

She didn't think so. "Both victims were strangled. The pattern left behind on their throats is similar. Same gender. Same family dynamic. Taken from outdoors. Close in age."

But that raised the question: Why hadn't the Criminal Justice Information System linked the two cases?

"No. They're not." Riggs ripped the photo of Sakari from her hand and turned it to face her, and in that moment, she saw the truth. The agony in his expression. The debilitating guilt contorting his handsome face into something other and dangerous. "Sakari Vigil was seven years old, Macie. Seven. She was waiting for her mom to bring her some water when she got too hot from playing in the backyard.

Not climbing up a mountain without telling anyone where she was going. She was innocent."

Her defenses dumped a dose of adrenaline into her veins. "I'm going to pretend you didn't just blame me or Hazel for what happened that day she went missing, Detective."

"That's not… That's not what I meant." He shook his head as though he could rewind time and try again. "I'm sorry. I just—"

"You want a reason. A motive." Because if they could make one element of this case make sense, the rest would follow. That was how it was supposed to work. But Macie had been at this long enough to know one puzzle piece did not a painting of Lake Como make. "You want someone to blame."

"Yes." That single word pained her more than any other they'd said in the past hour. Riggs practically stumbled back, that photo still in his hand. "Now instead of solving Becker's murder, there are two families out there wondering what happened to their little girls. Who knows how many others?"

The intense detective who hadn't taken no for an answer this morning retreated into the man who'd put so many others ahead of him. Always searching for answers with no hope of achieving a molecule of something significant. The one who'd lost and given up having anyone important in his life for one more chance to do something good. Riggs Karig wasn't like the officers she'd worked with these past few years. Sure, they'd all had their reasons for joining Battle Mountain PD. A job, a trauma or a sense of duty, but Riggs… He took every case personally. It was that kind of commitment that would consume him in the end. "Have you considered homicide investigations might not be the right career choice for you?"

The question seemed to knock him out of whatever downward cycle he was circling. "I was working Becker's path. Not mine."

"But you could've stopped." Macie didn't miss the fact she could have, too. That she could've thrown away the files and photos and reports she'd pinned to the inside of her closet and forgotten about Hazel. That she could've let someone in these past few years, just to take the weight off her shoulders and feel what it was like to trust another person again. That she could've fallen in love or traveled the world or learned to bake all those delicious treats like Reagan. She could've had a whole life had she not chosen to live in the past. "You could've altered your course. Unless there was something you were hoping to find along the way. Something that would've made all this worth it."

Riggs collapsed back against the wall, staring down at the same photo of Sakari Vigil as she had. "There was something. I used to have this friend. She changed my life. Not in any big way, but she made an effort with me. I couldn't say that about anyone else really. Not my parents. Not my brother or my teachers. To them, I was and always would be a screwup. I couldn't do anything right, but to this friend, she treated me like a person. She shared her lunches with me because all I had was a pudding cup that day. She helped me with my homework when math wasn't making sense, and I was on the verge of repeating fifth grade. She made me laugh all the time, except for when she punched me in the nose because I'd pulled her hair."

Macie's insides clenched at the memory. He wasn't just

talking about a friend he'd had over the years. He was talking about her.

"One day, she was just gone, and I was back to being alone." That ache she'd felt solidified in his voice. "I thought maybe if I solved Hazel's case, she'd come back. That we'd pick up right where we left off. Until I realized my entire life had passed me by, and I'd fallen for another fantasy."

Her throat threatened to close in and she collapsed back onto the edge of the bed. Macie tried to swallow around it, but the words weren't there. "I... I had no idea."

"Would it have changed anything if you did?" Sincerity laced every word. They both knew the answer. Her parents had dragged her from Albuquerque in fear for her life. Nothing and no one would've been able to convince them otherwise.

"No," she said.

Riggs closed the distance between them, before setting the photo of Sakari Vigil back onto the file in her lap. "Becker broke protocol. Each case is supposed to have its own separate file, but he combined these two. He was working them as the same case."

"There's another possibility." Macie straightened the file's contents with the side of her finger. "People who hurt others—like the ones I've seen—all have one thing in common. They don't want to get caught. Serial killers, bombers, gunmen—they're all the same. They'll do whatever it takes to keep their freedom, including following media coverage, learning who's involved in the investigation and even taking official pieces out of the game. It's possible Becker knew he was being lured to that building and was compelled to hand over whatever he had. He could've shoved both files in here while handing over an empty folder or one stuffed with random paperwork. The killer most likely knew he liked to keep physical notes. By moving both files to the same folder, Becker could've been protecting the investigation by giving up a decoy."

Riggs stared at her a moment, seemingly in a daze. "You're starting to sound like a detective."

"I might've picked up a few things over the years." Pride and a hint of confidence speared through her. As much as she'd hidden herself from the chief and his officers, none of them had bothered to try to get to know her. She was Macie the Dispatcher—a tool to make their jobs easier. Someone with connections and a tree house to hide out in or a babysitter when they needed to respond to a call. Would any of them have guessed she might know more about Battle Mountain and the people in it than they did? "Hard not to in a town like this."

Riggs moved away from the wall, a little more stable on his feet from the look of it. The storm that'd taken him at his most vulnerable had passed, leaving behind an air of capability and experience. Most of the men who'd tried to insert themselves into her life had kept their masculine armor in place. No emotion. No hint of weakness. It was kind of nice to see one of them break, even just for a couple minutes. "Dulce is about three hours north of Albuquerque along the freeway."

Macie pulled a map up on her phone, and her stomach flipped. He was right. If they were looking for the same killer in both cases, following the freeway from Albuquerque north took him straight through Dulce, and if he kept going north… "Battle Mountain is on that route."

"Where Becker was killed," Riggs said.

Macie didn't want to think about the implications. She didn't want to think of another little girl like Sakari and Hazel being ripped from her family and found three days later. Penny's face materialized at the back of her mind. No. She couldn't think like that. Penny was just four years old. Way too young to be drawn into a case like this, and someone stupid enough to even come near her would suffer the wrath of the entire Battle Mountain police department.

"Let's say Becker was right. Sakari Vigil was killed by the same unsub as Hazel. Whoever we're dealing with, it's not compulsion." Riggs cut another path through the limited space between the foot of the bed and the dresser. So close. "Becker's death was an outlier, a means to an end, but Sakari and Hazel... They're the real data. He's able to hold himself off for years at a time. He's in control, able to make smart decisions. Not being overcome by his needs. If that's the case, why kill Becker after all these years? Why not take him off the board long before now?"

"Could be whoever is doing this was incarcerated. The killer might've been forced to take a break, but without a name to run, that doesn't get us anywhere." There was another reason she could think of. "Maybe it was like you said, you'd never gotten close. No suspects. No new leads or witnesses. Becker must've surprised him. He must've followed the killer here, to Battle Mountain."

Tingling spread down her arms and into her fingers locked around the file. It was only then she realized the rain had stopped. The roads would open soon, and there'd be no reason for her to stay. No reason to keep following this path. Macie studied that smiling face a second time.

Every cell in her body homed in on Riggs. There was no turning back. No running this time. His partner had come to Battle Mountain for a reason, maybe even to stop another little girl from being taken. "He's on the hunt for a new victim."

HE SHOULD'VE KNOWN whoever'd killed Hazel wasn't finished.

He'd just been too stubborn to see what Becker had seen.

Riggs rolled over on the bed. Paper crumpled beneath him. Then he felt nothing but a wall of warmth. Forcing his eyes open, he realized he was face-to-face with Macie. She was still asleep, curled on her side with her mouth slightly parted. Long lashes fanned out across the tops of her cheeks. This close, each lash distinct. Not clumped together with mascara or anything else to hide her natural beauty. A spatter of freckles stood out across her nose that he hadn't noticed until now, and Riggs found himself counting them to block out the world a little longer.

"You're staring again." Her voice cracked on the last word, attesting to how late they'd gone through Becker's file last night. Over and over. No notes as to who his partner had suspected killed the two victims, but he had to have some idea. Why else come to Battle Mountain? Why go to that building?

"Sorry. I had to pinch myself to see if I was dreaming," he said. "Can't remember the last time I woke up to a woman in my bed. At least one that wasn't permanently pissed at me."

Macie pressed herself upright, a yawn peeling back that guarded, sarcastic layer. Look at that. She was real. "Keep pushing your luck. I'm sure you'll get there."

She'd finally given in to changing out of her dress, going for what looked like an oversize men's T-shirt and sweats from her duffel bag. Part of him had wondered whose shirt she'd taken over while the other part lectured him how it was none of his business.

They weren't together. Hell, they weren't even real partners.

They'd been brought together by a dead man.

Riggs peeled the scattered papers of their handwritten notes from beneath his rib cage. "I'd offer you some breakfast, but apparently this isn't one of those fancy places, and I'm pretty sure the owner hates me."

"Cindy? No. She hates everybody." Her laugh tendrilled through his chest and set up residence in his stomach. "Besides, why settle for motel breakfast when Greta's is just up the street."

"Does everyone in this town name their establishments after themselves?" he asked.

Macie scooted off the end of the bed with more grace than he had on a shooting range. Frizz haloed around the crown of her head. Every hair out of place. Quite a change from the hell-raiser he'd met at her front door yesterday. "If they have any chance of surviving around here, yeah. I'm going to get dressed. I won't be long."

"Take your time." He braced himself against her pillow, aggravating a hint of her perfume. The bathroom door clicked closed, and Riggs took the chance to breathe in her light scent. It was calming and invigorating at the same time. Familiar but fresh. It was all Macie, and he'd be lying to himself if he said he didn't like it.

He checked his phone. Two missed calls. One from his

captain, the other from a number he didn't recognize. Dragging himself to the edge of the bed, Riggs popped his neck and shook off the near hangover from lack of sleep and too much talking into the early morning hours. He hit the unfamiliar number and waited.

"Oh, good. Macie hasn't killed you and disposed of your body yet." Easton Ford's voice came with a sudden need to salute and stand up straight. The interim chief had obviously been up for hours, even though the old clock radio on the nightstand read seven in the morning. Military man, through and through. "One less thing on my plate I have to worry about."

"That happen often?" Riggs glanced toward the bathroom door. "Her disposing of bodies?"

"Only to the people she doesn't like," Ford said. "Which is a lot of people, mind you, including me."

"Can't imagine how you've managed to stay alive all this time." Joking aside, he and Easton Ford weren't friends. They were trying to solve the Becker murder and stop a killer from striking again, but humor had long been used as a way to diffuse the tension and violence police faced on a daily basis. It was the only way to survive. "You got something for me?"

"Our coroner is doing the autopsy on your guy today. Thought you might want to be part of the action," Ford said.

"Sounds like a party." He and Macie had gone through everything Becker had kept in his combined file. It made sense his partner had wanted to protect the investigation, but now they had the problem of sorting through notes that could pertain to either case. Only Becker would've been able to tell the difference. Riggs stole another glance at the thin door separating him from the woman on the other side. "Let me ask you something. You ever hear anything about Macie being found in the middle of the woods in a sleeping bag with a bunch of stuffed animals?"

Well, hell, that was a sentence he hadn't ever thought he'd hear himself say. His brain had worked through the night, conjuring different scenarios. Some of them outside the natural law of man. Or woman.

"Please tell me she didn't order a blonde coffee from Caffeine and Carbs." Ford sounded as though he was having a hard time keeping his laugh to himself, and Riggs's curiosity rocketed into overdrive.

What the hell had he gotten himself into here? "I think she tossed it before she got the full effect."

"Let's just say you dodged a bullet. Macie and caffeine don't mix well." Shuffling cut through from the other end of the line. "Penny, not the phone!"

The other side of the line cut short.

Checking the screen, he confirmed the call had ended. Seemed Easton Ford had his hands just as full as Riggs. He made quick work of collecting their notes from last night and organizing everything back into the file as best he could. He changed his clothes faster than he ever had before.

But not fast enough.

The bathroom door swung open. Macie froze, her eyes wide, and he couldn't even blame the smile hitching higher on her mouth. His foot had gotten caught in his pant leg. He'd spent the past few seconds hopping, trying to get it free without falling over. Solely in his boxers. Damn it.

She leaned against the doorframe, crossing her arms. All that fiery hair had been tamed as though she'd come straight out of a salon. Absolutely beautiful in another one of her flowy dresses. This one a deep green with peach flowers that brought out the brightness in her cheeks.

Riggs collapsed against the bed. He finally got his foot free. "Ever heard of a little thing called privacy?"

"Privacy is what you get in a bathroom with a closed door. Not in the middle of the motel room. Besides, I'm not sure why you're being so shy. Compared to most of the guys around here, you, Detective, are a masterpiece. I wouldn't mind adding you to my private collection." Disbelief brought her out of pure amusement into full-on excitement as she closed the distance between them. Wrapping one hand around his arm, Macie forced him to his feet and turned his backside to face her. "Wait. Is that a unicorn, a rainbow and a cat on your ass?"

Unfiltered heat penetrated through his arm and up his neck at her touch. It shot into his gut and exploded into something cleansing and addictive. The reaction triggered him to pull away and get back some control. Riggs ripped his dry T-shirt from off the back of the headboard and shoved his head through the collar. "For your information, I forgot to pack a change of clothes. These were the only pair I could find at the gas station on my way into town."

He managed to get his arms through the correct holes.

"Well, to be fair, I think there's a unicorn inside all of us." That smile was back—the one that couldn't even compare to the way her touch had affected him on a cellular level. "Not sure about cats, though."

"The only thing inside of me is an empty stomach, the urge to solve this case and get back to my life." Riggs shoved his feet into his boots and laced them into place, but his brain just couldn't help sticking on the fact she'd said she wanted to add him to her private collection. Who said exactly what they were thinking like that?

"If I only had a nickel for all the times I've heard those exact words." Macie dragged a small purse from her duffel bag and set it over her shoulder. "Come on, Detective. Let's get you something to eat before that unicorn turns into a bear."

"If I turn into a bear, does that mean I'll end up in your sleeping bag in the middle of the woods after too much coffee?" Riggs couldn't help himself.

"If you're not careful, you'll end up down one of the mineshafts where no one will find your body." Her tone lacked any humor, and a sliver of fear prickled down the back of his neck.

Still, this game they'd created had him wanting more. It reminded him of the stupid jokes and threats they'd thrown at each other growing up in New Mexico. This side of her he knew, and hell, if he was being honest, it was a side that he'd missed.

His phone rang from his back pocket. Same number he'd called back a few minutes ago. Riggs answered, one finger held up at Macie's questioning expression. "Don't tell me the autopsy already started, Ford. It's been two minutes."

"Bring Macie back to the station. Now." The older Ford brother couldn't catch his breath from what it sounded like, and a wave of battle-ready tension flooded through Riggs.

His gaze met Macie's. In an instant, their bizarre humor was shoved aside as he gauged her reaction and what to do next. "Something happened."

"She's gone." Clattering—something like a chair hitting

a wall or the floor—filtered through Easton Ford's heavy breathing. "I can't find her anywhere. The gun is here, but she isn't. She knows not to leave the station while she's here. She knows to check in every few minutes."

Riggs didn't understand. "Slow down, Ford. Who? Who's gone?"

"Penny." Both sides of the phone met with silence for a series of seconds. "She's been taken."

Chapter Six

"I trusted you!" Campbell Dwyer shoved the interim chief against the wall, her hands fisted in his uniform. And Easton Ford let it happen. "You promised me she was safe here, Easton. How did this happen? How could you not check to make sure the doors were locked!"

Macie joined Campbell's husband—Kendric Hudson—in trying to pry Campbell off the chief. A lot of good she could do up against a fully trained investigator more comfortable with a loaded gun in her hand than Penny's favorite toy. Campbell was former Colorado Bureau of Investigation. She worked Internal Affairs while mothering a sociopathic four-year-old and standing up to the man who'd left her as a single parent after an explosion had destroyed his world and half his face. Tears streaked down Campbell's face as she ripped free of Macie's hands and pushed at her husband. Kendric obviously knew better than to try anything else. The woman was a force to be reckoned with outside CBI as much as she had been inside.

"I did, Campbell. I swear it. The back door was locked when I checked in with her twenty minutes ago." Easton straightened, ready to take another attack like the good soldier he was supposed to be. "You know I would never fail to secure this place."

"So what then?" Campbell asked. "Someone just walked through the front door and grabbed her?"

"The back door is unlocked now." Easton's voice turned to glass. "There aren't any fresh scratches on the dead bolt plate, which means they knew what they were doing."

Macie reached out to Campbell, but instantly knocked back into a wall of muscle she'd forgotten had followed her inside. Riggs. He kept her upright, as though ready to shove her back into the ring. "Campbell, we're going to find her. Okay? I know what you must be feeling, but she can't have gotten far."

The grieving mother turned all that rage and uncertainty on Macie. "No. You don't. You don't know, Macie. You're a dispatcher. You're not a cop, and you're not a mother. You have no idea what really goes on outside of this station, and you were supposed to be here. You were supposed to watch her. Where the hell were you?"

Shock slapped her across the face as efficiently as a physical strike. "I…" She wanted to lean into Riggs's strength. She wanted to explain that she hadn't left Penny alone, but that she was trying to find a killer. None of the words would take shape, and a sickening wrenching twisted her insides.

"Campbell, this isn't her fault." Kendric eased his hand around his wife's arm. "Gregson and Majors are out searching Main Street now. Isla and Adan are combing through the neighborhoods, and Karie Ford is keeping an eye out at the ranch. The entire department is on our side. We will find her."

"No. I will find her. Because this wasn't supposed to happen again. Because I promised her this wasn't going to happen again." Something heavy and suffocating drained from Campbell's face, leaving a shadow of the woman Macie knew. It was the same look she'd noted on Hazel's mother's face when the police had finally found the body. Campbell turned into Kendric's chest, but she didn't stop for comfort. She pointed a strong finger into Easton's face—one of the few daring enough to confront the older Ford. That, in and of itself, was enough for Macie to like her, but hurt set up residence where admiration had flourished. Penny had been kidnapped once before. Taken by a madman determined to get away with murder and left for dead in a shed in the middle of winter woods. Campbell and Kendric had fought like hell to get her back, and Campbell was right. Macie had no idea what it felt like to lose something so precious. "You and I both know this never would've happened if Weston was still in charge. You and I aren't finished."

Easton didn't answer, didn't even seem to breathe as Kendric followed Campbell toward the front of the station and out onto the street. Macie had no doubt in her mind Campbell would do whatever it took to find their daughter. But this killer... The one who'd taken Hazel and Sakari... He didn't play by the same rules BMPD followed.

A tremor worked up Macie's arms. Penny was gone. Someone had come into a police station and taken her right under the nose of the most volatile officer in command, and it was her fault. "We have three days to find her."

"You can't know that." Easton had started showing signs of life, but that legendary guard was back in place.

"Actually, we do." Riggs took position at her side. He handed over the case file they'd analyzed more times than

Macie could count last night. "As I said yesterday, Becker was working on a twenty-five-year-old case. It's what brought him to Battle Mountain. Hazel McAdams. We believe he was following a suspect from Albuquerque and found who he was looking for here. Killer must've recognized him. Strangled him before my partner could do anything about it. Both victims Becker identified were missing for three days. It's a pattern. One we're still trying to work out."

"You said both victims." Easton started reading the file. "Hazel McAdams. Found strangled next to a creek in the woods. What makes you think Penny's disappearance is the work of the same attacker?"

"We discovered another case combined with the McAdams case last night, taken from Becker's car." Macie's mouth dried. She didn't even want to think about the sweet girl she'd gotten to know the past couple months found with bruises around her neck. Penny was feisty. She was stubborn, but she wouldn't be able to overcome a full-grown man alone. The only way Macie had been able to escape was with help. And Hazel had died because of it. That urge to lean into Riggs again, to borrow some of his strength, took hold, and Macie let her arm settle against his. His gaze dipped to the point where their skin touched, but he didn't pull away. "A seven-year-old girl strangled outside the reservation in Dulce ten years ago. Missing three days, just like Hazel."

"These notes refer to Avalynn Davis, Hazel's best friend at the time she went missing." Easton Ford set that unreadable gaze on her. "You knew the first victim. That's why Detective Becker came to find you, right?"

He couldn't possibly know that. "How…how do you…"

"I like to know everything I can about the people coming near this department and my family, just in case," Easton said. "When I learned the name Macie Barclay didn't surface until around nineteen years ago, I took a deeper look at you."

"You never said anything." The words barely registered over the kick of the air conditioner. She'd lied to the chief, to Easton, to everyone out of survival, but the sudden possibility of being punished for it—of losing all this—hurt more than she'd expected. "You just gave me dagger eyes every time we were in the same room together."

"People change their names for a lot of reasons. I figured you'd tell us yours when you were ready." Easton handed off the file to her.

"Us." Oh, no. Macie was practically using Riggs to balance now. "So Weston knows, too."

"Weston knows, but he's not keen on sharing that information with the rest of the department. Like I said, I protect my family, Macie. That includes you when the mood strikes." Easton turned on Riggs, leaving her exhausted and shocked and on edge at the same time. "Your name is in that file, too, Detective. Funny how you failed to mention that part when you met with me after Kevin Becker's body was found. Riggs Karig, also best friends with the first victim."

"Yes, sir." Riggs cut his attention to her and held her there for what seemed like a minute straight. "Hazel, Macie and I grew up together. We were the first to be interviewed during the investigation."

He called her Macie. It shouldn't have held so much significance, but it did. Like he was accepting the woman she'd become. That she wasn't the girl he'd known anymore.

But Macie had worked in this department long enough to know what Easton would say next. That they were too close to the case. That personal feelings didn't have any right to be involved in an investigation. That connections to the victim would only lead to mistakes. He was going to forbid them to help with the search or dig deeper into Becker's notes. They'd end up on the bench or worse. Riggs would be sent back to Albuquerque to resume his life, and she'd…keep running.

She studied Riggs out of the corner of her eye. Twenty-four hours. That was all it'd taken for him to get back beneath her skin. All she'd wanted to do was get away from him this time yesterday. Now it felt as though he fit. Here in Battle Mountain.

"Then you two are the ones who have the most to lose if you don't get out there and find Penny." Easton turned back into the office that wasn't his. Only this time, Macie didn't get nausea thinking about him behind that desk. He paused in the doorframe, one hand overlapping the butt on his gun. "Just promise me one thing, Macie. Promise you're not going to try to curse me again. I can't take the acid reflux." Ford closed the door, effectively ending their conversation.

She didn't know where revealing her real identity left them or this department, but Macie was sure of one thing: there was a scared little girl out there because of her.

Riggs maneuvered between her and the chief's door, consuming her attention until the world dissolved around them. "I know what you're thinking, Macie. I don't care what

Penny's mom said. This isn't your fault. You couldn't have possibly known—"

"If I hadn't run, he never would've followed me here. He never would've killed Sakari or targeted Penny in the first place. You and I both know this isn't about them. It's about me. The one who got away." The weight of the knowledge was comforting in a way. They had a motive now. "He'll take her somewhere isolated. Like the woods. Somewhere no one will hear her scream for help. Both victims were found with small amounts of water in their lungs, so I think he'll want to hole up near the lake or a creek. He might even use it to control her."

Riggs nodded agreement. He believed her, like she knew what she was talking about. She couldn't remember a time when anyone else had taken her word for anything. It was just as Campbell had said. She wasn't a cop. When it came right down to police matters, what did she know? "You got a place in mind?"

"Yeah." Macie steeled herself in confidence. "I do."

THE TREES WERE closing in.

Too many shadows. Too much movement. Too much for his senses to process. Damp earth, rustling leaves, the humidity clinging to his skin—all of it worked to break his concentration.

Riggs followed in Macie's footsteps along only one of the rivers weaving out of the south end of Lake San Cristobal. They'd already covered one of the creeks that'd dead-ended and were now making their way north to catch the source of the second. He batted away at something that zinged straight into his face right before something salty and bitter spread across his tongue. "I think I just ate a bug."

"It won't be the last one. After a while, you get used to it. They become protein rather than a nuisance," she said.

He wasn't sure he ever wanted to view insects as a food source, but Riggs was out of his element here. If it came right down to survival, he bet there wasn't much of anything he wouldn't try. Especially if someone he cared about was in danger.

Macie charged ahead, all determination and defiance. That stubborn drive he'd tried to avoid as a kid had ramped up full force in the face of finding a four-year-old girl. She blamed herself. For not being at the station when Penny had been taken, for not being able to comfort the girl's mother, for the fact Penny had gone missing in the first place. He could see it in the way she refused to slow down despite the mosquito bites at the back of her neck and how she clung to the water gun she'd found under one of the chairs at the station. Nothing he said would change her mind or make her see any different.

Then again, maybe that stubbornness was what was going to bring Penny home.

They hadn't found any traces of activity yet. No footprints. Not even a granola bar wrapper or signs of an ATV. It was looking like whoever'd taken Penny hadn't come this way. His muscles ached. He'd sweat as much as he'd had to drink in the past hour, and he was out of breath. How Macie managed to keep going after nearly two hours of searching, he had no idea. "I don't know how you do it. As much as I hate to admit this, I've gotta take a break."

"Okay." She veered toward one of the trees off to her

right, its roots clawing up through the ground like fingers waiting to take her into the dark. Stripping free from the jacket she'd changed into, Macie took a seat at the base and chugged a mouthful of water from her bottle. "We're about a mile from the source of the next river. Should make it there by sunset if we keep up this pace. We'll need the flashlights we brought."

Riggs swiped his mouth with the back of his hand. "My teeth feel like the grille on my SUV."

"Look like it too from here." She set her head back against the bark and closed her eyes. Sweat glistened on her skin, but Macie wasn't the kind of woman to admit she'd lost her fight more than two miles ago. She dumped a good portion of water over her head. "I won't hold it against you."

"We're going to need entire teams of people and K9s to cover this area, Macie. We can't keep going like this all night." They'd come into this area on a hunch, a mere connection between both victims, but what if they were wrong? What if Penny wasn't here like Macie believed? What if they were wasting what precious time the girl had left looking in the wrong place? "For all we know, she's not even out here."

"She is. I can feel it." She pushed herself to her feet. "I'm not giving up."

But feelings didn't solve cases. Evidence did, and so far, they hadn't found any. Time was running out for Penny, and he sure as hell didn't want to be the one to have to tell Macie she was wrong. Riggs straightened. "I'm not telling you to give up. I'm asking you to be realistic."

"You want me to be realistic?" Exhaustion etched into her expression. Her hair was out of place again, her skin sallower around her cheekbones. In a matter of hours, she'd gone from a woman on the run to a woman who had something to stay for, but it'd come at a cost. "Here's reality, Riggs. Penny is scared. She's alone, possibly hurt, and she's already been through this once before. Someone took her from her family to punish them, and now it's happening all over again. An entire department of police officers weren't able to keep her safe. Only this time, he's punishing me. So you can go back to the car or rest as long as you need. You can go back to Albuquerque and your life and keep pretending Hazel's case doesn't affect you anymore, but I'm not leaving until I find that girl."

His heart gripped hard in his chest. Riggs tugged a flashlight from his backpack and compressed the power button. Night would fall fast. There was no way in hell he was going to leave her out here to face it alone. "Okay. One hour."

Macie notched her chin higher, daring him to ask a single thing of her. "What?"

"Going like this half-cocked, desperate, alone and in the dark isn't helping Penny. So I want your word. We turn back in an hour." Riggs hiked the short distance between them. "If we haven't found anything by then, we regroup at the station and come up with another plan. We get ourselves a search team to hit the ground in the morning. We call in whoever the hell we need to call in and start fresh. Give her a real chance of being found."

"One hour?" An internal war played across her face. Push herself to find something—anything—out here that could give them an idea of where Penny was, or do the logical thing and come back to search a much larger area with help. Macie checked her smartwatch. Large numbers ticked down in the limited light still penetrating through the trees. "Fine."

"After you." Riggs set his attention to the ground, keeping Macie's boots in his peripheral vision as he scoured the dirt and plant life for signs of disturbance. The forest fire that'd eaten through a good chunk of the woods hadn't come this far south, but he could still smell the char in the air. Insects trilled within bark and under bushes, out of sight, and set his nerves on high alert. Too many places to hide in here. Not enough knowledge of the area. All he had was Macie. "I'm sorry. About Penny. From the way you two were drenching each other with those water guns, seems like you were—are—close."

Riggs wanted to kick himself for the slip. Penny wasn't dead. Not yet. He had to believe the killer would stick to his MO. That he would give them three days to catch up and bring her home.

"I'm not sure it's possible to be close to a four-year-old." Macie didn't lose a step as she answered, hauling herself over a fallen tree. They were still following the creek they'd already searched, but the water was traveling faster now. They were getting closer to the source threading out of the lake. "All they care about is when they're getting a snack and if you're going to make them take a nap."

His laugh caught him off guard. A branch scraped along the sleeve of his jacket, and he noted the trees had grown thicker in this section of the woods. "Still, she obviously trusts you. I don't know about you, but I don't let just anyone shoot me with freezing cold water."

"She likes to give people hugs when she's soaked. It's their surprise, I think. Their screams make her laugh." Macie's voice dipped an octave. "The first time she did it to Easton, I nearly fell off my chair. You should've seen his face…" She stopped dead in her tracks, every muscle in her body wound tight.

The humor they'd shared had died in a matter of seconds. Riggs set his hand on her shoulder, but she didn't move. "We're going to find her, Mace. We're not giving up."

"Riggs, is that…" She pointed to a clump of fur caught on one of the lower branches.

He stepped around her, before tearing it free. No. Not fur. Hair. Blond with slight waves. Just like Penny's. Son of a bitch. Macie had been right. Riggs scanned the immediate area. Arm stretched out, he maneuvered Macie back from the spot. No footprints. No ATV treads. Nothing to support they were on the right track. "She was here."

A rough exhale escaped Macie's control. "Penny! Penny, can you hear me! It's Macie. I'm here!"

They listened for a series of seconds. No answer. But if their theory was right—that Penny had been taken from the station—had they really expected one?

The same awareness of being watched that he'd experienced back at Macie's tree house dug through him. "Macie, quiet."

"Penny!" She stepped off the trail they'd followed and closer to the trees.

Movement registered from the tree line to his right.

He shoved Macie to the ground, but not fast enough. Pain ignited along his arm as they landed in a tangle of limbs and gasps. He clamped a hand over the wound, but the knife had embedded deep into his shoulder.

"Riggs!" She pulled her legs out from under him, her hands hovering above the wound.

"Macie, go." He hauled himself to his feet. He unholstered his gun and took aim into the darkness. Only he couldn't see a damn thing. His vision wavered, and Riggs stumbled to his left. A growl clawed up his throat, and he dropped to his knees. He tried to get to his feet, but he was losing too much blood. "I'll cover you. Run."

"I'm not leaving you." She tried to hold him steady. Coming around to his front, she shoved him along the trail. "Come on. We can make it."

"No." An outline separated from the trees. "You can't."

Riggs raised his weapon to take aim, but the world went black.

Chapter Seven

A soft vibration reverberated through her wrist.

Music filled her head, but she wasn't sure where it was coming from. Macie tried to open her eyes. All she met was darkness. Cold, cold darkness. Her throat burned from dropping temperatures, like she'd been left exposed to elements. A shiver prickled at her arms. "Riggs?"

Something snapped to her left.

Shoving to sit upright, she leveraged her heels into the ground. The crunch of leaves filled her ears. She was outside. Still in the woods? "Hello?"

Silence pressed in around her. Slices of memory—of blood, of pain, of desertion—filled the gaps. Penny. They'd found a lock of her hair. And Riggs... Her entire body shuddered as she struggled to her feet. He'd been stabbed. So much blood. She could feel it dried in her palms. Someone had attacked them. "Penny?"

"She's not going to answer, Avalynn," an unfamiliar voice said. "In fact, she won't be saying anything at all for a while."

Fear tripled the nausea churning in her stomach, and Macie collapsed into the tree at her back. She searched her immediate surroundings. She couldn't see him, didn't know where his voice had come from. But he could see her. She was sure of it. Her fingertips clawed into the bark as though she could use it as a weapon. She hadn't been strong enough to fight back then, but she could do this for Penny. She could bring her home. "It's you, isn't it?"

"I've been looking for you for twenty-five years," he said. "Canada, New York, California, Montana. I lost you in Colorado. Turns out, all this time you've been in my own backyard."

All the places she'd hidden, never staying put for too long. Because she'd felt like she was being followed. And if what he said was true, she'd been right. Until she'd come to Battle Mountain. This place had provided safety and protection when no other could. Now she knew why. The same terror she'd felt at the edge of that creek when strong arms had locked around her took hold. Macie tried to control the wobble of her bottom lip. She had to focus. "Where is Penny?"

The voice came from her right this time. "Don't worry. I've taken such good care of her."

"She doesn't have anything to do with this." Macie braced herself to leave the protection of the tree. Bending at the knees, she skimmed the ground for something—anything—she could use as a weapon in case her attacker came closer. "She's just a little girl. You have me. You can let her go home to her family."

"But you and I both know the truth about little girls, don't we, Avalynn?" He'd moved again, circling behind her. This was all a game to him. Predator versus prey, but she wasn't going to play. Not fairly, anyway. "They're so much stronger than they look. As long as Penny does exactly as I say, she'll be fine."

"You mean until you get bored of her." Her fingers brushed thin sticks and soggy leaves. Cold settled in the tips of her fingers and toes. She needed something heavy, something that could inflict damage if she had any chance of finding Penny. "The same way you got bored of Hazel and killed her."

"Hazel should've done as I asked." Anger intensified the bite in his words, and dread pooled at the base of Macie's spine. "She knew exactly what she was doing when she tried to escape, and she paid the price for that choice. Just as you'll pay for yours."

The strike came out of nowhere.

It crashed into the side of her face and knocked her off-balance. Macie hit the ground as lightning struck behind her eyes. Rolling onto her side, she tried to crawl back to the tree she'd abandoned, but a second punch took vital air straight from her lungs.

"Do you remember that day I found you in the woods, Avalynn?" The voice was quieter now. Distant and low. Like he'd crouched to watch her struggle. "Do you remember what you did to me?"

Her face pulsed in rhythm to her heartbeat. Macie tried to get onto all fours, but the pain was too much. "Where are they? Where are Penny and Riggs?"

"You elbowed me in the face. Broke my cheekbone if you can believe it." Shuffling filled the night. Purposeful. Trying to pull her focus. "The bone never set right. Now it always looks like I'm smiling. I've replayed that moment in my head so many times."

Stinging pain rippled across her scalp as a strong hand fisted her hair. Her attacker dragged her to her feet. Macie latched on to his hand with both of hers, but every movement pulled another section of hair free. She tried to bury her gasp deep, but she ended up giving him exactly what he wanted. Satisfaction. Blood trickled down her nose and coated her tongue. Her teeth had cut into the side of her mouth. "You deserved much worse."

The whisper of breath tickled one ear as the killer pressed his mouth close. "Such bravery from the girl who left her friend to die."

Macie froze.

"That's right, Avalynn. I know your secret," he said. "I was there, remember? I had you right where I wanted you, but I failed to consider Hazel much of a threat. She hit me with a branch she'd found nearby. I let you go to fight her off, but instead of teaming up on me to protect each other, you did something I was not expecting. You ran. You left her there to fend for herself. What happened next…was your fault. All these years you've been trying to find the person who hurt your friend when all you had to do was look in the mirror."

The scene played across her mind like it had a thousand times before. There hadn't been a single night she hadn't closed her eyes and known what she'd done. Hazel had come to her rescue, just as he'd said, but all she'd wanted at the time was to get away. To be safe. Tears pricked in her eyes. Not from the pain in her head or face. From the truth. She'd been a coward. Plain and simple. "You don't… You don't know what you're talking about."

"Oh, but I do," he said. "Do you want to know what

Hazel's last words were? Do you want to know what she wanted most?"

Her heart threatened to beat straight out of her chest. They'd been children. No match against a fully grown man at the time. Macie had done everything she'd thought was right. She'd run home. She'd told her mother what'd happened. They'd called the police and started the search, but... it'd been too late.

"She wanted you, Avalynn. She wanted you to come back. She wanted you to save her. She begged for you until she lost her voice and couldn't scream anymore. Couldn't cry anymore." His hand lightened its grip in her hair. "Lucky for Hazel, it didn't take long for her to realize nobody was coming to save her."

The tears fell now. She hadn't told anyone. Too afraid to even admit the words to herself, but she couldn't run from them anymore. No amount of changing her name would make her forget what she'd done.

"You and I both know you deserve what's about to happen next." The hand gripped against her scalp released her hair and slid around her neck. Rough calluses scraped against her oversensitive skin. Her attacker pressed her skull back into his chest. "You know this has been a long time coming and that you belong here with me."

"Yes." She'd hidden her secret for so long, she'd almost convinced herself she wasn't that ten-year-old at all. That she was Macie Barclay, Battle Mountain PD's dispatcher. The wild woman who could read your aura, cleanse your house with sage and predict your future with tarot. The one who loved hard and fast and took what she wanted. The one people trusted and relied on. She closed her eyes as Riggs's face materialized at the forefront of her mind. It'd all been a lie. The woman he'd blindly followed into these woods didn't exist. Not really. And she hated that fact. But there was one person who knew her better than anyone. A little girl who gave the best hugs and biggest smiles. The one who didn't care who Macie was in the past, just the one who played with her, gave her unhealthy amounts of junk food and painted her fingernails outlandish colors in the present. Macie wanted to be that person. She wanted to be anything Penny needed. And right now, Penny needed her to fight.

"I deserve everything that's coming to me." Macie slammed her head back as hard as she could. The crunch of bone filled her head, and the hand around her throat released. Her attacker hit the ground, but instead of running, she would fight. She wouldn't fail Penny like she had Hazel. "But Penny doesn't. Tell me where she is, or that broken nose will be the least of your worries."

A low laugh filtered through the brush of wind in the trees. Unease flooded her at that laugh. It was a mixture of humor and victory, despite his position at her feet. "Now, what on earth made you think it would be that easy?"

His leg slammed into her shin and took her down. Macie fell onto her back. Oxygen crushed from her lungs. Before her brain caught up with what was happening, the killer was on top of her. His hands were around her throat. He was squeezing. Air pressurized in her throat, begging for release, but he wouldn't give it. It built and built until she was sure her chest would explode. He expertly used his weight to keep her in place.

Macie tried to bring her knees up, to dislodge his hold, but no amount of bucking and wrenching deterred him. He was going to kill her. Just like he'd intended to kill her that day by the creek.

Only this time, there wouldn't be anyone to save her.

RIGGS GASPED FOR air as though the weight of an invisible hand was strangling the life from him. His skull knocked back into the tree behind him, but he couldn't move.

Vicious pain ignited through his shoulder the harder he pulled at his hands. He tried to hunch forward, to get some semblance of movement, but the thick rope around his neck constricted tighter. Any move he made cut off his oxygen supply. Blood seeped through his jacket and down his chest.

The blade was gone.

The killer must've taken it to keep Riggs from cutting himself loose. Smart. Because that son of a bitch didn't want to know what Riggs had in store for him when he got out of this mess. But the wound wouldn't stop bleeding until he was able to add pressure. Hell. How much time had he already wasted unconscious? "Macie? Talk to me, Red. You hurt?"

Where he'd expected her whiskey-smooth voice, the woods answered. Insects quieted at his added disturbance. He couldn't see much past two feet around him, but his senses were adjusting. No movement. Nothing to suggest she'd been tied to a tree nearby. Which meant the killer had taken her. His brain automatically filled in the blanks of what that meant for the childhood friend he'd lost and for the little girl counting on them to save her. "I'm coming, ladies. I'm coming for you both."

Riggs fought against the ropes crooked in each elbow, his chest splayed wide, and the rope around his neck shifted.

His scream slipped up his throat despite the pressure. Two, maybe three, more moves would silence him for good. How the hell was he going to get out of this without something to cut himself free? He settled back against the tree, and the rope relaxed.

There was only one way out of this.

But the risk of strangling himself before he got free was high.

The past forty-eight hours hadn't come to anything he'd planned. He worked missing persons cases. He investigated homicides. There was an order and a protocol to both. This case had blown everything out of the water. No. Not the case. Macie. She was unpredictable and frustrating in the best of ways. Unique and surprising. Nothing at all like he'd imagined over the years. Definitely not by the book. Her emotional honesty and creativeness outdid him at every turn. It was refreshing and scary yet somehow exactly what he'd needed on this case. And exactly what he needed to shake up his life. For a small town, he'd hated the crowded feeling Battle Mountain elicited with dense trees, claustrophobic cliffs and suffocating niceties, but she'd somehow brought out the mystery and the beauty in a matter of days.

They were here because of her. Because she knew this killer, and they were going to find Penny because of her. Her intensity and commitment to finding that girl would carry them both to the end of this sick game, but he needed to find her first. "You just gotta do it, man. They're relying on you."

Riggs filled his lungs with as much air as they could hold. He squeezed his shoulder blades together, making the rope as tight as possible against the bark. He shuffled back and forth, back and forth. The rope itself wasn't thick, but it was sturdy. He only hoped it'd gone through some wear before he'd been put in the game tonight. And that the tree bark was sharp enough to do the job.

Strands dug into his neck as he shifted and locked oxygen in his trachea. Every move burned more air, but he couldn't stop. Not yet. His shoulder screamed for release the longer he stretched the wound. He wasn't sure if the bark was doing anything, but he had to believe. Warm liquid had soaked his shirt clean through. He was either going to strangle himself or bleed out. Both final endings the killer had most likely bet on, but Riggs hadn't come this far to die in the middle of the damn woods. Becker deserved better.

The rope snapped.

Riggs took his second gasp for breath and crumpled forward. His forehead hit the dirt. He clamped a hand over his shoulder. Blood snaked through his fingers as he pulled himself together. A patter of rain started, blocking out any other signs of life. Dragging himself to his feet, he stepped on something hard. It broke under his weight. Glass? He crouched to get a better look. The shape resembled a gun, but the killer wouldn't have left Riggs with a weapon within reach. "Oh, hell."

Penny's water gun.

Macie must've dropped it after he'd blacked out.

A crack riveted along the bright orange barrel. It'd never work the same again. Riggs dug it out of the damp earth and brushed off as much dirt as he could. Holstering the toy, he stumbled down a slight incline and met up with what he as-sumed was the same creek he and Macie had been searching. It was impossible to tell in pitch-dark, but gurgling water navigated him upstream.

The killer had ambushed them. Which meant they'd gotten too close. Riggs braced against the arc of pain exploding down his shoulder and tipped into a nearby tree to catch his breath. Macie might've helped him see this place in a new light, but it could still kill him. He couldn't see anything out here. One wrong move could send him off the trail. "Get a hold of yourself, Karig."

Shoving off the tree, Riggs closed his eyes. Rain punched through the canopy above and slid down his face. It was colder than the minuscule amount they saw in Albuquerque, keeping him focused and awake. He had to think. He knew this case. He knew this killer. Not as well as Macie, but close. The better part of his life had been devoted to catching this man. He knew the killer's MO and his preferences. It didn't matter he was out of his element here. The same rules applied.

Recover Penny and Macie. Take their attacker into custody.

Riggs opened his eyes and took a step forward. He couldn't rely on any footprints out here. The rain was already destroying the evidence. But he could listen. Insects were still buzzing beneath the patter of rain. He kept the creek on his left, ensuring he didn't venture too close. "All right, you son of a bitch. Where are you?"

He wasn't sure how long he'd walked. Seconds. Minutes. Nothing had changed but the feel of dirt turning to mud beneath his feet. He had to be close to the source of the creek now, closer to the lake. But it was quieter this far up, even with the onslaught of rain. The woods' inhabitants were hiding, avoiding being heard here. Riggs slowed. A hint of smoke tickled the back of his throat. Burning wood. But it wasn't the same odor that seemed to engulf Battle Mountain after the forest fire. This was lighter, fresher. A campfire?

Brushing his hand against his holster, Riggs reminded himself he'd been stripped of his weapons, but that didn't mean he was defenseless. He stepped to his left, losing the scent, and set back on course. The harder the rain fell, the faster the odor died in the air. He was running out of time. And so were Macie and Penny. He picked up the pace. Branches and pine needles scratched at his exposed skin. His legs burned as mud suctioned his boots to the ground. He was close. He could feel it.

A clearing spread out in front of him. Riggs kept to the tree line as the outline of a pop-up tent took shape straight ahead. The camp couldn't have been more than a few hundred yards from the creek. He and Macie had to have walked right by it without noticing. How was that possible? Lightning flashed overhead, highlighting the setup for a fraction of a second. A single tent and a fallen log. No signs of Macie, Penny or the killer. Riggs took a tentative step into the perimeter.

Something caught on his bootlaces, and he froze.

He crouched, reaching out. Thin wire threatened to snap, leading in both directions. "Trip wire."

This wasn't a regular camper on a vacation for the weekend. This was exactly what Riggs had been looking for. A nest. Question was, had it been set to keep intruders out or victims in? Riggs had the feeling the killer had considered both. Straightening, he maneuvered over the line and took his first step into the camp.

The fire he'd smelled was quickly losing strength under the downpour. Embers cast dim orange light in a halo around the pit. One chair, one tent. No vehicle in sight.

The girls weren't here.

"Damn it." Had he been too late? Was this all that would be left behind once the killer moved on? Riggs crossed to the tent and ripped back the front flap. An adult-sized foam pad took up most of the space in the center with a few folded sets of clothing in the corner. A small folding table stood at one side. A backpack consumed his attention a few feet away. He grabbed for it, before hauling the zippers down. An emergency pack. First aid kit, compass, windbreaker— it all looked well used. He shoved the pack back into place. Nothing suggested Penny had been here at all. If the killer was the only one in the tent, where had she been held since this morning?

The answer solidified in his gut. Riggs turned back to the log stretching from one side of the camp to the other. "You've got to be kidding me."

Rounding back into the center of the camp, he then set his hand on the top of the fallen log. It'd been gutted over the years, hollow in the center. Making it easy for the killer to install a chain on either side. Riggs picked up the links glimmering with help from the fire embers. The bastard had kept her here. Out in the open. Chained like an animal. Rage—unlike anything Riggs had felt before—exploded behind his sternum. The killer had chosen this spot. Had prepared to take another victim. Everything here testified of premeditation and intelligence far greater than they'd assumed over the years.

Riggs wound the chain around his forearm and braced

his boot against the log. He ripped the chain free, sending splinters of wood in every direction.

Right before a scream cracked through the night.

Chapter Eight

His scream rang in her head.

She kneed the killer in the groin a second time. His hands released their hold around her neck. She rolled through the mud to put some distance between them. But not fast enough.

The killer grabbed on to her ankle. Macie kicked as hard as she could to get him to let go, but he dragged her back. Fingernails scratched down the backs of her legs, setting her skin on fire. Her elbow knocked into something solid and heavy. She pried it from the mud as rain pummeled into her face. Slamming the rock into the side of his face, she scrambled out from his grip. Her lungs worked overtime as she ran. Every step got her farther away from Penny, but she couldn't do anything for the girl if she was dead.

Macie darted through the trees. Her head pounded in rhythm to her racing heart, but she couldn't stop. A branch cut across her cheek and tangled in her hair. It hurt, but a few strands were nothing compared to the fist against her scalp. She wasn't sure how far she'd run. Not far enough, but flashes of that day she'd run twenty-five years ago infiltrated the present. She'd left her best friend behind to fight a killer alone.

And she was doing the same thing now.

Her energy drained the harder she pushed until she couldn't force herself to take the next step. Rain pitted against her exposed skin as she relied on a large tree to keep her upright. Out of breath, every cell in her body screaming for her to get away, she sobbed through the terror and grief.

She had to go back.

She had to find Penny.

She had to find Riggs.

She was the only one who could bring them home.

Macie swiped the water from her face with the back of her hand and looked down the path she'd run. There was nothing but darkness and pain waiting at the other end, but she'd run long enough. It was time to take a stand. "And cross your fingers you don't die in the process."

She took a full breath and backtracked through the woods. It was dark. It was raining. She had no idea if this was the right direction, but sooner than she expected, she came to the small clearing she'd woken in.

Only it was empty.

He'd already vanished.

Macie spun in circles. Maybe she had the wrong location. Maybe he was still close by. "No. No, no, no, no. Penny!"

"Macie!" That little voice cut through her fear and took up residence around her heart. Air crushed from her lungs. She hadn't expected to ever hear that voice again. Penny was close. "Macie, help me!"

"I'm coming! I'm here!" It was a trap, a way to lure her back into the spider's web, but Macie didn't care. As long as they were together, they could fight. They could go home. She slapped at trees and leaves getting in her way. The thick taste of diesel from somewhere nearby settled on her tongue, and she ran with everything she had.

A pair of small headlights lit up the woods and gave away the ATV's position. It was only then she heard the growl of an engine.

The backs of her thighs burned as she hauled herself over a boulder and through the trees. She didn't gauge the distance. She didn't think twice. Macie launched herself at the ATV and tackled both riders to the ground. The handlebars rammed into her side as Penny's scream pierced her ears. Seconds slipped by as she tried to get her bearings. "Penny, run!"

A fist rocketed into her rib cage.

Unimaginable pain ricocheted through her torso, but all she cared about was protecting Penny. She'd take a thousand punches if it meant the four-year-old could get away. Penny disappeared into the trees. She just had to keep the killer here long enough for her to get away.

He got to his feet, now standing over her. Rain pummeled down onto her face, hiding his. The ATV's headlights darkened his features from behind, but she recognized him for who he was: the monster who'd killed Hazel. "You shouldn't have done that, Avalynn."

She blinked against the downpour. There was no way out. No way she could beat him, but she'd give Penny all the chances in the world to escape. Because she wasn't that scared little girl anymore who only cared about her own survival. She'd become someone else entirely. "That's not my name."

Macie fisted two handfuls of mud and threw them in his face. Thrusting her boot into his shin, she dropped him to one knee and slammed his head against the side of the ATV. She climbed to her feet and ran after Penny. Trees ripped at her jacket and hair, but she wouldn't stop. Not until they were both safe. And Riggs... He was a trained Albuquerque homicide detective. She'd come back for him. She wouldn't give up.

A shadow stepped directly in her path.

But her momentum was too great. She couldn't slow down. Macie collided with Penny's small frame. Wrapping her arms around the girl, she tried to keep her weight off her as they hit the ground and rolled down an incline. Rocks stabbed at her back and legs as Penny's cries drowned out Macie's breathing. She crashed into a boulder twice her size at the bottom and let Penny go.

The four-year-old scrambled out of reach but then knelt to brush her small hand against Macie's face. "I'm sorry, Macie. I didn't mean it. I dropped the water gun you gave me. I'm sorry."

"It's okay. I've got you." Of all the things to be worried about, Penny had chosen the loss of a toy. Macie checked her jacket where she'd sworn she'd stored the bright orange water gun, but found warmth spreading across her side instead. She tested the stinging pain. Not rain. Blood. Her breath shuddered as she considered the chances of them getting out of these woods alive, of not bleeding out, of being able to protect a child that wasn't hers. Macie pressed herself to sit up and wrapped her upper body around Penny's. "You know what, we're going to get out of here. You and me. I'm going to take you back to your mom and dad, and we will get you a new water gun. Okay?"

Penny nodded at the same time a sliver of lightning stretched across the sky. "Okay. Can it be purple this time?"

"I think that's a great idea." She didn't know how bad the wound was or how long she had. Didn't matter. Keeping Penny calm and getting to safety. That had to be her goal. "Are you hurt?"

"My arm hurts." Penny presented her forearm where something had scraped a long line from elbow to wrist. Most likely during their fall. No other significant bruises or cuts as far as Macie could tell. She'd gotten to Penny in time.

"We'll get you fixed up in no time, slugger, but for now, we need to keep moving. That means running and staying quiet. Think you can do that?" She glanced up the hill where the ATV's headlights cast a spread of white light through the woods. She'd bought them some time, but Macie doubted the man who'd taken Penny gave up easily.

"Yes." Penny got to her feet. "If you hold my hand."

Macie clamped a hand over her side. A twig had penetrated through her shirt and embedded deep into muscle. She lowered her voice, all too aware how easy it would be for an experienced woodsman to find them. "Awesome. And when we get you back home, you can eat all the ice cream you want. My treat. Any flavor and toppings you want. You name it."

"Chocolate." Penny looked up at her in excitement. "And strawberry!"

"Shhhh. We gotta be quiet, remember? We don't want the bad man to find us." She pressed her hand against the wound, and the world tilted on its axis for a moment. She

could do this. She would do this. She might not be the chief
of police, a former Green Beret or a bomb technician, but
getting out of tricky situations was a Macie Barclay specialty. She led Penny through another grove of trees. No
telling which direction they were heading or if there was
anything on the other side, but the farther they got from the
killer's last known position, the better. They were going to
make it. She had to believe that. There couldn't be any other
option. Not for Penny.

Thunder rolled overhead, and Macie picked up the pace.

Penny tried to keep up, but her legs just didn't move as
fast as Macie's. At this rate, they'd never make it to help.

A splinter of wood cracked from nearby.

Macie pulled them to a stop, then picked Penny up. Her
wound screamed for relief, but they'd run out of time. "Hang
on tight. You hear me? Don't let go. No matter what, and I
won't let go, either. I promise."

Penny whimpered.

"And here I thought we were becoming friends, Penny,"
a voice said from behind.

Macie spun to face him and backed away one step at a
time.

His outline advanced, countering every move. "I told
you the rules, and you gave me your word you would follow them. It's a shame you're going to have to be punished
for that now."

"You'll never lay another hand on her." Macie's voice
revealed the terror cutting through her. She wouldn't let
go. She'd never let go. Her heel caught on a root clawing
up through the forest floor, but she only held on to Penny
tighter. "Or anyone else."

That same low laugh that'd punctured through her confidence as he'd strangled her filtered through the trees. "You know what I like about you, Avalynn? You never give up. You never stop fighting. That's what's going to make your death so very sweet."

"Stay back." She didn't have a weapon. She wasn't trained to fight, but she did have a little girl to protect, and she'd do whatever it took to get her out of here.

The killer took another step. "Who's going to stop me?"

"I am." A second shadow separated from the trees and swung a hard right hook. The killer dropped to the ground as Riggs looked at her and Penny over his shoulder. "Get her out of here!"

MACIE RAN WITH Penny in her arms.

"I hear you like picking on little girls." Riggs shoved his foot into the killer's gut. He stretched his shoulder back and ignited an indescribable amount of pain. "Wait until you see what a real fight looks like. On your knees, hands behind your back. You're under arrest."

"Your distraction technique won't work, Detective Karig." The man at his feet raised his face to the sky, but it was still too dark to identify anything familiar. "I'll never stop, and you can't protect them both. You'll have to make a choice. The girl or Avalynn."

The swipe of a blade cut through Riggs's jeans and into skin. He jumped back to avoid the next strike as the killer shoved to his feet. The knife whined as it aimed for his midsection. Riggs blocked the attack but was too slow to see it for the diversion it was. A fist slammed into his face and knocked him off-balance. His boots slid in the mud, and another arc of pain slashed down his spine. His scream ricocheted off the trees as he hit the ground and rolled. He didn't have the chance to catch his breath.

The killer launched himself forward, blade angled down to stab Riggs through the gut. He dodged the assault a split second before the knife sank deep into the ground. Riggs turned in time to land another punch to the bastard's face, but it wasn't enough. His attacker blocked the next, twisting Riggs's hand until it threatened to snap.

"And here I thought you were offering a challenge." The killer shoved him beyond the tree line.

Riggs rocketed into a tree but managed to thrust himself away just before the blade struck again. The guy moved faster. Faster than he'd expected. This wasn't a run-of-the-mill killer they'd been hunting. No. This was something so much worse. Something experienced and deadly. "And here I thought you were some kind of formidable villain."

"Well, Detective, you haven't seen anything yet." A knee thrust into his chest and pinned Riggs back against the tree.

Pressure unlike anything he'd felt before consumed the oxygen in his chest. He launched his fist out in a vain attempt to get it to stop and hit nothing but air. His heels dug into the earth, but the son of a bitch who'd taken Penny was all that kept him upright. Complete control.

Was this how Hazel had felt in her last moments? Was this what Sakari had gone through? He'd followed in Becker's footsteps to find Hazel's killer, but he'd found himself at the same end instead. Burnt out with nothing to show for years of work. Somewhere he didn't belong. And alone.

"How does it feel, Detective? Knowing you've spent your entire life chasing me, only to realize you were never enough to help them? That you're not even capable of helping yourself." The pressure on his chest increased until a white blanket encroached on his vision.

His head was pounding. His lungs begged for relief. Riggs wedged one hand against the killer's knee to try to release the pressure and stretched one hand out for something—anything. His fingers grazed a tree branch, and he latched on with everything he had. The last reserves of air were consumed by his holler. The branch detached from the tree, and he swung as hard as he could.

Contact released the weight on his chest. Riggs sucked in as much air as he could take. The killer fell to the side. But not for long. His attacker got back to his feet, but Riggs was faster this time. He secured both hands at the base of the branch and swung up. The end connected with the killer's chin. A guttural groan drowned the pitter of rain as he hit the ground. A pair of headlights coming from above highlighted the man's outline, but it was still too dark to make out much of anything else. Riggs nearly doubled over but held on to the branch. Just in case. "Like I said. You're under arrest for the kidnapping of Penny Dwyer, for the murder of Kevin Becker and for being a straight-up dick."

"All right, Detective. You win." The killer raised both hands as though in surrender.

Instinct warned Riggs it shouldn't have been this easy. Still, he couldn't deny the sense of victory charging through him. It was over. Twenty-five years of interviewing witnesses, crime scene reenactments and searching. It'd all led to this. To Hazel's killer. To Macie's attacker. To Penny's abductor. "On your knees, hands behind your back."

The killer lowered his chin to his chest, doing as he was told. "Whatever you say."

Riggs had no warning.

The blade stabbed deep in his thigh, and he dropped to one knee. His scream stretched far and wide through the trees as disbelief caught him in the moment. Blood seeped into his jeans and trickled down into his boot.

The man in the shadows pulled the knife free, before lowering his mouth to Riggs's ear. "Just as long as you can drag me out of here yourself." A low laugh penetrated through the ringing in Riggs's head. The killer stood, then shoved Riggs onto his back. "Not up for it? I don't blame you."

Rain peppered across his face. Cold and hard. Adrenaline escaped his control as he lay there bleeding out. He had to get up. He had to fight. The bastard at the other end of the knife wouldn't stop gunning for Penny. For Macie. Riggs was the only one standing between a killer and them, and hell, that little girl deserved more than a life on the run and full of fear as Macie had. He could give that to her. He just had to get up.

"The more you fight, the worse it gets for you, Detective." The outline above him limped forward, headlights gleaming off the slick blade in his hand. "That's what I tell my girls. Some listen. Some don't. I hope, for your sake, you don't make the same choice as your partner."

His girls? Those two words penetrated through the pain and the dizziness and scraped him out from the inside. The victims this man had killed weren't his. He didn't get to keep them like trophies. He didn't get to think back on them fondly and congratulate himself for a job well-done.

Riggs summoned everything he had left and launched himself off the ground.

He hiked his wounded shoulder into the bastard's gut and shoved him back into the same tree he'd been pinned against. Riggs went for the throat, but two fists slammed down onto his forearms and broke the hold. He took a gutwrenching hit to the ribs. Once. Twice. Again. Pain exploded from each strike and left him unstable and out of breath. He blocked the oncoming right hook, but he wasn't prepared for the left.

Lightning struck behind his eyes. Blood filled his mouth and gushed down his throat. Shoving back, Riggs battled to catch his breath.

"You know, it's funny. Your partner… What was his name? Becker." The killer sucked in a deep breath from a few feet away. "He warned me about you. Said I'd signed my own death warrant. That I had no idea what I was bringing down on myself. And here you are." The shadow crouched beside him. "I'd have to say, I'm not impressed."

"How about by me?" That voice. *Her* voice. It cleared the haze from his head and gutted him all at the same time. No. She wasn't supposed to be here. "Run."

Macie swung a large branch into the killer's head.

The killer turned to face her. He took the full force of her swing across the face and dropped to the ground, out cold.

"Macie? What…what are you doing?" Riggs scrambled to kick the blade out of the man's hold, before sending it flying into the brush. Pain arced through his thigh. He needed something to tie off the wound before he bled out. "Where's Penny?"

"Just over there." Macie reached for him. Soft skin colliding with his as she gripped him under one arm and hauled him to his feet. "We heard you scream. Couldn't leave you to die alone out here."

"No." This wasn't right. She couldn't be here. She was supposed to take Penny and run. He tried to push her off. "You have to get out of here, Macie. Go. Now."

She refused to budge, her grip tight on his arm. "Riggs, you're hurt. You're bleeding. Let me help you—"

"He's never going to stop." Riggs dragged her into his chest. Didn't she understand? This wasn't over. As long as the man who attacked her all those years ago was alive, this wouldn't end. "He'll never stop coming for you or for her. He used me to bring you back here. He's..." He looked back to keep the killer in his sights. And froze. "Where is he?"

"What?" Macie's grip lightened on his arm. "He was... He was right there. He couldn't have gotten up without either of us noticing."

That was exactly what the son of a bitch had done.

Riggs's heart rate rocketed into his throat. Hell. He scanned the trees.

A scream pierced through the night.

"Penny." Macie dropped her hold and ran into the tree line.

The killer couldn't get far on foot. Riggs headed for the incline as a shadow crossed in front of the ATV's headlights. He clawed through slick mud and despondent root systems. The wound in his leg protested every step. The growl of an engine filled the trees. Then the odor of diesel. Just like he'd smelled at Macie's home. He was going to lose them.

"Penny!" The girl's name tore up the back of his throat. He'd lost the feeling in his fingers and toes. He'd lost too much blood. He'd lost the only shot he'd had of ending this. He couldn't take another loss. Riggs found a foothold and pulled himself onto solid ground.

The ATV fishtailed through mud and deeper into the woods, brake lights lighting up the trees. Too fast.

Macie broke through the trees to his left and ran after the trail left behind. "No!"

He grabbed Macie around the waist to keep her from following. It wouldn't do any good. Not anymore. They were beaten. They just hadn't accepted the truth yet.

Penny's voice trailed back to them and settled in the pit of Riggs's stomach. "Macie!"

Chapter Nine

She should've gone after the ATV.

Macie winced as the nurse swiped an antiseptic pad across the cut along her side. The wound wasn't deep. They'd been able to get the twig out in one piece. No splinters. The lights were too bright here. Everything was so sterile. Like a morgue instead of an emergency room. Her head hurt, and she was pretty sure she'd cracked a tooth, but none of that compared to the emptiness inside.

Penny was gone. Again.

They'd been so close to bringing her home, but Macie had failed. She'd let her out of her sight mere seconds too long. Just enough for the killer to steal her right out from under her care. Tears burned in her eyes.

"Does something hurt?" The nurse took a step back, studying every inch of Macie's exposed skin not covered by the flimsy gown.

Her entire body hurt, but it was her insides that couldn't take the damage of what'd happened. What was she going to tell Campbell? What would she say to Kendric? After all the years of not knowing his daughter, the former ATF instructor had only been allowed a mere few months with her. That wasn't long enough. Macie shook her head. "No. I'm...fine."

The small clinic in the center of town was equipped to handle minor injuries, concussions and broken bones. Not so much teeth. She'd have to see Dr. Corsey for that. As for Riggs, she wasn't sure where he'd been taken. He'd collapsed after they'd lost sight of the killer's ATV. The stab wounds in his thigh and shoulder had caused him to lose too much blood too fast. She'd done what she could to stop the bleeding, but her destructive nature insisted it hadn't been enough. That she'd never see that lopsided smile or get to reminisce about some stupid thing they'd done as kids. The downward spiral of grief and anger and hurt she tried to ignore intensified. He'd been innocent in all this, but he'd gotten too close. She tried to warn him. She certainly hadn't been enough to save Hazel or Penny. How on earth did she convince herself she could've saved him, too?

"All done." The nurse discarded her gloves in the trash bin and reached for the clipboard on the small table beside the bed. "Looks like you got lucky. Just some minor scrapes and bruises. You'll want to keep ice on that jaw up to twenty minutes. Then I'll come back with your discharge papers and a set of scrubs you can wear since the police took your clothing."

Macie wasn't entirely sure she'd heard everything. Her mind was someplace else. On someone else. "Have you... Have you heard anything about the man I came in with? Riggs Karig? He's a detective. He was stabbed during the struggle."

"I'm sorry. Unless you're family, I can't give you any information. I'll be back in twenty minutes." The nurse closed the curtain around her bed. If only it were that easy to shut out the world.

Macie held the ice pack to her face. Family. That single word had been blurred over the years. Of course, it'd started with her parents, but even then, Hazel and Riggs had become something more than friends. And here, in the middle of nowhere, the men and women she'd sent into the night after killers and bombers and gunmen, on searches and evidence collection and into interrogation, had crossed the line she'd drawn between them.

She'd tried. She'd tried to distance herself and keep them safe in case the man who haunted her nightmares returned, but deep down, she didn't want to be alone. She was tired of moving town to town, of changing her name and settling for people believing what they wanted about her. She couldn't think of a single person in all these years who knew her for who she really was. But in Battle Mountain, she'd made mistake after mistake, letting them in.

Letting Penny in.

Then Riggs.

Two days really wasn't enough time to get to know someone, but they hadn't just met, had they? He'd known her since before she was ten years old. The real her. The self-conscious, misunderstood and moody woman she'd always been. And, still, he hadn't walked away.

She might've gotten him killed, though.

The curtain parted, and the face she couldn't seem to get out of her head came into focus. Riggs. He was here. He was alive. On crutches but alive. Hallelujah. "You look like you got in a fight with a bear."

Macie dropped the ice pack from her face and buried the

urge to smooth her hair as she shot out of bed. One step. That was all there was between them, and she closed it as fast as possible. Encircling her arms around his neck, she accidentally rammed him off-balance. One of his crutches hit the floor and claimed the attention of nearly every nurse and physician in the vicinity. She pressed herself to him, hoping to provide him a bit of support, but mostly to convince herself this wasn't a hallucination. "You're alive."

"Not if you keep strangling me like that." Riggs didn't move to pry her free. As though he might've needed the contact, too. Just for a little while.

His warmth penetrated through the thin gown and chased back the effects of the ice pack. She didn't know how long they'd been at the clinic. Hours based on the sun peeking through the window, but he looked more put together than she did. And showered. Macie loosened her hold and lowered onto the soles of her feet. Rubbing at her face, she studied him up and down. "Could you have at least tried to put your face in front of his fist or something? Looking at you makes me feel like a dirty punching bag."

"You look beautiful." That lopsided smile was back, and Macie felt the need to sink into his arms. "Your backside waving in the wind and all."

Embarrassment checked her fast as she jerked to collect both sides of her gown in the back. Only to realize the stainless-steel instrument cart on the other side of her closed-in area had given him a full view of her rear end. "Forgot about that part."

"It's not every day women are that happy to see me." Riggs couldn't seem to keep from smiling, and the tight knot in her chest gave her a bit more room to breathe. "You've set the bar quite high."

"Glad to add a bit of flair to your life." Her attention was back on that smile. On the split in his lip. Without thinking, Macie trailed her thumb over the laceration. "How bad is it?"

He set his hand over hers, that intense gaze softening on her. "The blade went through a good chunk of flesh. Lucky for me, it didn't hit anything major. Not having time for leg day the past few months has paid off. Few stitches, and these bad boys have got me covered." He tapped the remaining crutch. "My shoulder is another matter. Good thing I'm a righty."

"I'm sorry." She didn't deserve to have a few moments of laughter after what she'd done. To him and to Penny. Macie pulled her hand back, instantly cold again. "For all of this."

"Don't do that." Riggs framed one side of her face with his free hand. "You and I both know there was nothing we could do for her in our condition. We fought for her, Macie. We bled for her. She knows that, and she knows we will not stop looking for her. We're not done."

"He said Hazel begged for me to save her before she died. That she died thinking someone was coming for her." Memories of last night—of the terror and desperation in Penny's voice—fed into the growing hollowness in her chest. Like a piece of her had been stolen. "That's all I can think about. Penny out there, cold, restrained, crying for someone to help her. I had her, Riggs. I had her, and I let her slip through my fingers. I knew what would happen if I left her alone again, but I… I couldn't let you face him alone. What kind of person does that make me? Leaving a four-year-old to fend for herself."

"Hey." Riggs wrapped her in his free arm while keeping balanced on the crutch. "You had an impossible choice to make, and because of you, I'm standing here. You saved my life, Mace."

Mace. She liked that. The way he seemed to accept not just her name, but the person she'd been hiding deep down. The one who'd run the moment she'd gotten a chance twenty-five years ago. The one who'd spent that time trying to make things right and who'd inadvertently brought Penny into danger. "I don't know what he'll do to her now. The other two victims had three days each, but Penny tried to escape him. She almost made it. He's going to punish her. Because of me."

He'd spent the same twenty-five years trying to fix what was broken with Hazel's case, but Riggs couldn't fix this. No matter how much she wanted him to.

"He won't go back to his campsite. It's been compromised. Your interim chief has already dispatched the entire department into those woods. They're tearing apart his camp inch by inch." Riggs rested his chin at the crown of her head, fitting her against him. Perfectly. Like a puzzle that'd been waiting for its partner. "They'll find something to tell us where he might've taken her. Until then, we have the knife he threw at us at your house. Ford didn't recover any fingerprints, but it's custom. Someone will recognize it."

Confidence never came easy to her, and she sure could've used some of his right then. Battle Mountain PD had been built from the ground up with a collection of determined, insanely capable and caring individuals from all areas of law enforcement. Coroners, former military, ATF, state investigators, district attorneys—people who had made their mark on the world long before they'd helped this town. But Macie… She wasn't any of those things. Actually, she didn't know what she was, but Riggs looked at her as though she were important. Like she could do something to bring Penny home. "What now?"

"Now we get you dressed and the hell out of this place." He gave her one last glimpse of that smile before tugging the curtain closed behind him.

She clamped her hand back to the opening in her gown. Right. Because she was still naked as a jaybird under this damn piece of fabric. "And then what?"

"Then we find out where the son of a bitch who took Penny is going," Riggs said. "And you and I bring her home."

THIS PLACE WAS worse than the motel.

He wasn't sure who the hell had thought it was a good idea to buy a run-down cabin in the middle of the desert, but it hadn't been a good one.

The floorboards protested with every step. Dust had congregated on every surface, and Riggs was pretty sure those were bullet holes in the wall.

"It's not much, Karig, but it'll do. This place isn't on any map. Isla's husband made sure of it." Adan Sergeant took up more space in the dilapidated postapocalyptic kitchen than anyone else. At well over six-foot-six, the former sniper was not easy to hide. "We planned on fixing it up and moving out here, but Mazi insists on being part of every design decision, and so far, those decisions include a whole lot of pink, purple and glitter. No one will look for you here."

The man was right. It wasn't much, but all he needed was a place for him and Macie to keep a low profile for a couple days. Just long enough to get their bearings after nearly dying in the middle of the woods. Riggs pressed his thumb into a hole almost the size of this thumb. A sniper bullet. Something had happened here. Recently. "You're married to Isla Vachs, one of Ford's officers?"

"That's the dream, man." Adan slapped Riggs on the back, and he nearly coughed up a lung. "I'm sure you know what it's like. The incessant waiting for the right time, the planning. Hell, I don't even know if Mazi wants me as a dad."

He caught sight of Macie crossing the hallway at the back of the cabin, and his entire system lit up in awareness. That was all he'd felt since they'd left the clinic. A connection as though his body knew exactly where she was at all times. He hadn't ever felt that with his wife. Back when they'd gotten together, getting married had just felt like something they were supposed to do after dating for five years and some months. Both of their families had expected it, and neither of them had been getting any younger. Turned out, that wasn't the best way to ensure a healthy marriage. It'd all started falling apart when he'd spent more time with his nose in Hazel's case file than with his wife. Riggs had just…made her disappear. Long before the divorce. "Yeah. I know how that feels."

"I've stashed some weapons under these floorboards and in the cabinets. Just in case." Adan motioned to a few key locations. "Isla had me put in an alarm system, too. Anyone or anything comes onto this property you aren't expecting, you'll be prepared."

"You expecting trouble?" He'd trusted BMPD's newest recruit and his—whatever Isla Vachs was—with Macie's life at her insistence, but how well did he really know these people? Protocol dictated local PD take jurisdiction on any crimes in the town boundaries. That didn't mean they were on the up-and-up, and it didn't mean they had any clue as to what they were doing. Not like big-city police.

"Always." Adan Sergeant straightened to his full height, and one thought settled at the front of Riggs's mind. Anyone stupid enough to take on a former sniper protecting his family, his property and his town deserved whatever came for them. "We take care of our own out here, Riggs. We don't have anyone else."

With that, the military man nodded goodbye and closed the front door behind him.

"Did Adan give you the 'we take care of our own' speech yet?" Footsteps registered from down the hallway, and Riggs turned in time to catch Macie wipe a bit of dust from her high-waisted slacks.

It was part of an ensemble she'd pulled from that duffel bag she insisted on retrieving from his hotel room. This whole place was covered in dust, but it looked damn good on her. Although the mint green color of her pants was bound to give them away if they had to make a run for it out here in the desert. Still, they accentuated the shape of her hips, the clench of her waist. The dresses had complemented her personality, but the slacks and tank top combination put everything on a whole other level. All he could think about right then was running his hands along several inches of creamy smooth skin.

Her voice graveled to mimic Adan's as she flexed both

arms. "'We don't have anyone else, Macie.' I swear all the man thinks about is where the next bullet is coming from. He's pretty, though."

Riggs forced himself back into the moment. "Makes sense. Seeing as to what him and his partner went through. Especially with an eight-year-old in the mix."

"Yeah." Macie swiped ChapStick across her mouth. The movement hollowed one side of her face and exaggerated the head wound. A small butterfly bandage pulled two sections of skin together at her temple. The killer had done that, had hurt her the way he'd always intended, and now he had someone else to take all that anger out on. "No way to live, though, is it? Looking over your shoulder all the time. It gets exhausting."

She would know. Riggs memorized the notches where Adan had marked each cabinet and floorboard. One for each weapon the soldier had hidden. Smart. Riggs imagined that hadn't just been for himself but for Isla, too. The way Adan had talked about fixing the place up, how their eight-year-old wanted to be involved in all the design decisions—Adan Sergeant wasn't miserable with his choice. "He seems happy. As exhausting as constantly worrying about what threat comes next can be, I'm sure it makes you appreciate what you have. Pushes you to live in the moment."

Macie slowly capped her ChapStick and slid it into her pocket. "Yeah. It does. Makes you realize what you don't have, either."

His instincts said they weren't talking about Adan Sergeant anymore, and Riggs hobbled to close the distance between them. Damn crutch was bruising the underside of his arm, but the other option was crawling on his hands and knees. And he wasn't even sure he could do that. He lowered his voice, catching a quick shrill of wind through one of the windows. "What is it you think he's missing out on?" Riggs tried to hold her attention. "He's got a partner, a girl who has him wrapped around her little finger, a job protecting the people of this town. What more could he want?"

Her voice sounded small as she crossed her arms. A protective gesture, one meant as armor against this line of questioning, and it was then he had his answer. This wasn't about Adan. This was about her. "A job—relationships—is well and fine, but without purpose, what good is it? What good is any of it if you don't know who you're actually meant to be?"

Meant to be? Riggs studied her a moment longer, and understanding hit. He took the risk of stepping another inch closer. All these years, he worried about following in Becker's footsteps rather than leaving some of his own. Of leaving a legacy behind after he was dead and gone. He'd at least had a guide. Someone to show him the ropes and give him the choice of what kind of man he wanted to become. But Macie... She'd never had that chance. "You've spent twenty-five years on the run out of survival. A man attacked you and intended to kill you, just like he killed your best friend. You didn't have the time or the mental capacity to figure out purpose or who you are."

"I felt safe here. For the first time in years, I felt safe," she said. "That's why I stayed so long. I've been in Battle Mountain for six years, Riggs. During that time, I've watched the officers in the department risk their lives for each other and this town. I've seen them fall in love and start families and live entire lives from behind my desk. They're out there doing the hard things to ensure every single person in this town has the same opportunity, and what am I doing? I'm on the sidelines. I'm answering phones and tracking down Greta Coburn's husband's urn for the thousandth time because teenagers ran off with it after she locked it outside on the porch. Or I'm making a run to Caffeine and Carbs for the chief like I'm some damn personal assistant or babysitting one of these hellions locking themselves in the drunk tank." She was out of breath, her shoulders rising and falling in erratic rhythms. "This…this isn't a life, Riggs. This isn't me."

Riggs dragged her against his chest with his free hand, inhaling that hypnotic scent he'd associated solely with her these past few days. Delicate and sensual. One hundred percent Macie. Her hands spread across his lower back, her head resting against his heart but careful of his shoulder. Right where he needed her. Where she belonged. Because despite the pain of her leaving all those years ago, she was the one holding them together. "Then tell me what it is you want, Red."

"It doesn't matter." She pulled away. "Penny is out there. We're no closer to finding where the killer took her than we were yesterday, and Campbell and Kendric need my help more than ever."

Riggs didn't let her get far, his hand trailing down the back of her arm.

"It matters to me." And it did. Somehow over the course of this investigation, Macie had become something more than his childhood friend. More than a potential witness. More than a victim. Just…more. What she felt, what she had to say, it mattered. Dozens of cases had taken their toll on him, had hardened him in ways he'd never imagined. But in less than a week—out of his comfort zone and faced with the failings of his past—she'd left her mark. Something permanent and irrevocable. Even if he went back to Albuquerque tonight, a piece of her would stay with him.

She didn't answer right away, to the point he wasn't sure if she would. "I want to be happy. Is that too much to ask? To just have one moment of unfettered joy without worrying where the next threat was coming from." Macie set her hand over his chest. "To feel something real and honest and exciting. I know it can't last forever. I know it's stupid when I'm stuck in the middle of a case, but I want—"

Riggs captured her mouth with his.

The momentum maneuvered her back into the wall ridden with bullet holes. Her hands fisted in his collar, pulling him closer, and his heart rate rocketed to keep up with the desire pulsing through his veins. Heat speared down his spine and into his gut so fast he had to catch his breath. Staring down at her, he tried to gauge her reaction. "Is that exciting enough for you?"

"I'm not sure." A smile tugged at one corner of her mouth. "Let's try it again."

Chapter Ten

That...hadn't been part of the plan.

At all.

Her body ached in all the places she'd forgotten could pleasurably ache. Battle Mountain was a small town. There were only so many rides she could take on the merry-go-round of eligible men and come back for seconds, but none of them had compared to the detective who'd blown her pity party out of the water last night.

Macie brushed a thin layer of dust off her face as she opened her eyes. Ugh. It was everywhere. Her hair, her teeth, up her nose. It'd take days to get it all out. This place was dreadful. And exactly what she and Riggs had needed.

"Good morning." Riggs lay across from her, wide awake, as though he'd been waiting for hours. Probably had in order to look like he'd stepped fresh from the shower. Did the man ever show signs of mortality?

Macie sniffed his damp hair and pressed a hard finger into his muscled chest. A chest she'd gotten to know very well over the past few hours. Because, she had to be honest, when was she ever going to get the opportunity again? "You showered, didn't you? You used all the hot water so you could wake up next to me looking like that. How dare you."

"Well, I mean, you compared me to a masterpiece a couple days ago." He motioned down the length of his body, the lower half hidden beneath the same sheets she clutched to her chest. The movement cost his shoulder, though. "I had to hold up my reputation. Who knows how long this is all going to stay in one place?"

Wind whistled through the cracks in the window seal and forced a veil of glittery sand into the sunlight. It could almost be romantic. If they hadn't been relegated into shacking up in a literal shack. Grittiness exfoliated her arms as she tugged the sheets higher. "And to think, I was going to let you have your way with me again. Now I'm thinking you're going solo."

Her confidence waned as she got a full memory of what'd happened between them last night.

"Well, where's the fun in that when you have the real thing right in front of you?" Riggs maneuvered closer, that intense gaze locked on her. At the time he'd cuffed her to her own steering wheel, she'd been uncomfortable with that perceptive focus. Now she couldn't seem to look away. He tilted her head back with his thumb braced under her chin, his hand cupping her neck. Her skin started itching where he touched her. The bruising around her throat was still sensitive, but he was careful. Planting a kiss there, he lit up every cell in her body until she was practically shaking. "What if I apologized?"

She gasped as he nicked her throat with his teeth and nearly collapsed back against her pillow in surrender. Who was she kidding? He'd given her the greatest gift her soul craved: peace. And there was no way she was giving it up so soon. Not after years of living on the edge of survival. "I'd say too bad. You should've saved me some hot water."

"Mmm." The vibration of his voice reverberated all the way through her. Riggs angled his uninjured leg between her knees. "I'm sure I could keep you warm in there. Or maybe we could share once the tank heats back up."

An echo of Penny's scream pierced through her mind. Macie stilled, any semblance of desire lost. Riggs had done exactly as he'd promised. He'd made her forget the horror that'd followed her all these years and given her a reprieve, but he couldn't make it go away entirely. That was impossible.

Riggs pulled back. Humor evaporated, replaced with concern. That same hand that'd exposed her throat to his mouth angled her face down so he could look at her. "Hey, tell me what you're thinking."

"I…" She didn't know what to say at the possibility of losing the only semblance of quiet she'd felt in years. She'd had an entire lifetime of misery and fear. Couldn't it leave her alone for this?

"You can still hear her, can't you?" His gaze dipped to her mouth, then back up. "Penny."

That invisible guard she liked to keep close pulsed in defense. Impossible. Last time she'd checked, he hadn't been able to read her mind. "How did you know that?"

"Because I can hear her, too," he said.

A new wave of appreciation flooded through her and pushed tears into her eyes. Macie secured her arms around his neck, their bodies fitting one against the other. Days of uncertainty, terror and pain fled in an instant. Until all that was left was the man in her arms. She'd convinced herself no one would ever understand her. That no one had gone through what she had, but if there was one person in this world who even had an inkling, it was him. Riggs knew her past and gave her permission to be herself. Not the alias she'd constructed. She wasn't alone. She never had been. She just hadn't realized what it would take to find her way back to him.

Or who would've had to die.

Macie buried her nose in his neck, trying to steal a bit of his warmth for herself. "We need to find her, Riggs. Before it's too late."

"I keep my promises." He rested the side of his head against her chest, right over her heart, and she swore the battered thing tried to reach him with how hard it pounded. "I intend to see this through. No matter what it takes."

She skimmed the back of her bruised and scraped knuckles along his jaw. Bristled hair—softer than she'd expected—tickled her oversensitive skin. It was amazing to think of what'd changed since he'd shown up on her doorstep. She'd wanted nothing more than to get out of Battle Mountain and away from him as fast as possible. He'd been a boulder in her way and a reminder of a past she wanted to forget. Now, after everything they'd lived through, she realized Riggs might be the only one who could get Penny through this. The only one who could get her through this. Because it wasn't over. "Thank you. For everything."

"I'm just glad I cuffed you to your steering wheel. Otherwise, who knows where we'd be." His fingers grazed the scar running down her back, like he was trying to memorize the shape. His rumbling laugh shook through her and loosened all the tension and kinks from falling asleep beside someone who took up more than half the bed.

"Right. About that… I'd say it's time for some payback." Macie shoved him off of her as hard as she could.

He disappeared over the side of the bed and hit the floor with a loud thud. "Hey!"

"Oops." She kept the sheets for herself. Daring a peek over the edge of the mattress, she checked to make sure he hadn't torn any stitches and got a full view of the magnificent specimen that'd chosen her to cavort with last night. Still a masterpiece, even with a couple stab wounds. "Forgot you can't catch yourself. Sorry."

Riggs climbed to his feet with the help of the nightstand. "Just for that, I'm eating whatever Adan stocked in the pantry. All of it."

"Be my guest. I can already tell you what you're going to find. Mazi's favorite food is Pop-Tarts, and that man has no problem giving in to her every whim." She pressed her back against the headboard as he rounded the end of the bed, the sheets still clutched around her. He limped, rubbing at his shoulder. "Looking good, Detective. How about a spin?"

"How about I take these with me?" He ripped the sheets from her grip, leaving her exposed in every sense of the word. Tying them around his waist, Riggs disappeared through the bedroom door. "Pop-Tarts, here I come."

"This isn't over!" Macie scrambled to cover herself with the pillows he'd left behind. Her laugh escaped her control but died just as quickly. Oh, hell. Pressing the pillows against her, she sat up in bed. It wasn't about how far he'd go to find Penny or what'd happened between them last night. It wasn't about his attempt to learn as much as he could in order to be ready for threats, his intensity when he looked at her or that he could read her better than anyone else. The banter, the jokes and teasing, and connection they shared...

It was all of it. And she wanted more.

For the first time she could remember, she wanted to get close to someone. She wanted Riggs to know her, inside and out. She wanted to wake up like this every morning with someone keeping her warm and happy to see her. She wanted to know him. His likes, favorite foods, if he watched sports, the women he'd been with. Every scar, mistake and regret. She wanted it all. More importantly, she didn't want to run anymore. Not from him.

Living at one extreme end of the emotional spectrum had made her highly sensitive to changes in her mood, especially given she hadn't allowed anyone to influence her or get close. But these past three days... They'd blindsided her until she wasn't sure which way was up.

Macie tossed the pillows and gathered her change of clothes from the floor. Muscles she didn't even know existed cramped, and she fell into the side of the mattress with a *humph*. Her side stung a bit, but it was nothing compared to what she'd put Riggs through last night. "Now, this is just ridiculous. Pull yourself together, woman."

It wasn't like she'd never been interested in a man before. She'd gone through dozens, but this one hit differently. Did something funny to her insides, which didn't make sense. She and Riggs were friends. It wasn't like he was going to stick around Battle Mountain after they closed this case because he'd gotten laid. It wasn't like they had a chance together. He'd go back to Albuquerque and solve more homicides, and she...

Didn't know what she was going to do.

Macie lowered herself onto the edge of the bed, Riggs's question loud in her head. What did she want? It'd been easy to answer him last night because a moment—or a couple hours—of bliss had been exactly what she'd needed to break from the past. But life didn't come with never-ending orgasms and men willing to provide them on a whim.

The nightmare that'd followed her for most of her life was finally coming to an end. She could feel it—the killer closing in.

She just hoped she was strong enough to face him the next time.

RIGGS TOOK ANOTHER bite of stale pastry.

Macie had been right about the inventory in the pantry. Who the hell lived off of Jolly Rancher-flavored breakfast pastries? He dropped the rest onto the paper plate he'd found and shoved it away. What he wouldn't give for one of the donuts from Caffeine and Carbs to wash out the aftertaste.

His attention slid to the hallway where movement registered from the bedroom at the back. Or someone to help get rid of the taste. Phantom sensations prickled in both hands. Silky hair fisted between his fingers, curves of creamy skin at his command, a sharp exhale against his fingers—it all worked to make him forget the past three days. Last night, wrapped up in Macie, feeling her become part of him, had given him a focus he hadn't experienced since the start of his career. When he'd had a purpose. Every case he'd worked had always come with a question at the back of his mind. It didn't matter if it was a homicide, a missing persons investigation or a burglary. That single question had remained the same in each instance.

What would Becker do next?

The man had guided him into the department and through the ranks from the time Riggs had been ten years old. Help with homework in high school, advice on college essays and which courses would fast-track him into the department, pop quizzes and bloody dioramas built from homicide cases Becker had worked in the past. All in an effort to turn Riggs into the detective Hazel McAdams deserved on her case. A hint of PTSD flared at the thought of all those mornings Becker had broken into his apartment with a bullhorn to start Riggs's day off with a five-mile run. "You don't get to run my life anymore, old man."

But if there was ever a moment he needed Becker, it was now.

This case… It was important. He couldn't afford to screw this one up. He'd convinced himself finding who'd killed Hazel had been solely for her family. To give them peace of mind and a way to move forward. Now he realized they hadn't been the only ones hurting all this time.

He needed to do this for Macie. And for Becker.

Riggs pulled Becker's case file in front of him. His mentor had combined the McAdams and Vigil cases into one file. He'd broken protocol, but the late detective wouldn't have done it without good reason. *First rule of homicide investigation, kid—keep your file clean. You can't solve a murder if you can't find your damn notes.* Becker was a better detective than that, so there had to be a reason these two cases ended up together. Then again, for all Riggs knew,

Becker was having his own brand of petty revenge by making a mess for Riggs to sort through.

The wound in his thigh pinged as he shifted closer to the table. Riggs had sifted through every note, every report, and separated them into two separate piles. He'd studied Hazel's case backward and forward for years. He recognized the investigative plan and crime scene photos and made quick work of dividing those pages into their rightful place. As for Sakari Vigil's case file, it was all fresh. Anything that didn't match up with Hazel's murder went into the other pile. He'd gone through the entire folder in a matter of minutes. As he and Macie had already concluded, there were no notes conveying why Becker had come to Battle Mountain, how he'd known the killer had come here or why his body had been found in an abandoned building. It was as though an entire section of the file had been taken, leaving them at a dead end. Riggs leaned back in the chair.

This was what living in his partner's shadow for so long had gotten him. Dead ends, no new leads and three unsolvable cases. He'd never had a chance. All those cases he and Becker had worked, the old man had taken the lead, had come up with the plan and had narrowed down a suspect. And Riggs… He'd just been along for the ride. A tourist. He wasn't a detective. He was a fraud, incapable of solving a single case on his own. He was going to end up just like Becker. A has-been, a joke to the department, forced into early retirement. And Penny Dwyer would be the one to pay for his mistakes. "Hope you're proud, Becker."

His phone vibrated with an incoming email. He scrubbed both hands down his face and flipped the screen upright. Becker's preliminary autopsy report. He'd missed the exam,

but considering he'd been trying to stop a killer from strangling two victims at the time, Riggs couldn't feel anything
more than mild regret. He skimmed the first couple of pages.
"Multiple bruises around the neck, defensive wounds on the
hands and forearms."

The scene played out in his head in full color. Becker
hadn't gone willingly. He'd fought. For his life, for the victims'. In the end, his partner had believed he was the only
one who still cared about Hazel's case. He'd known the risk
of pursuing the investigation, and it hadn't stopped him.
You have no idea what you're bringing down on yourself.
Wasn't that what the killer recalled Becker had said in his
final moments? Even at the edge of death, his partner had
believed in him. Had believed Riggs would do the right
thing and take this thing to the end.

"You had to have known what you were getting yourself
into." He discarded his phone on the table and went back
into the case files. "Come on."

He scanned through each handwritten note, over and over
again. Names of neighbors from the canvass at both scenes,
interview notes, theories written down, then scratched
through. He and Macie had been through all of it at least a
dozen times in the motel. And none of it was getting them
anywhere. His attention drifted back to his phone. To the
autopsy report of the one man he could credit for getting
him out of the hellhole where he'd been raised. Becker had
had his faults, but he'd been everything Riggs had needed
in the end. The old man wouldn't leave him hanging now.

Riggs dragged his phone closer, reviewing the photos
taken of the body. Becker had let his beard get out of hand,
more gray than the dark brown Riggs recognized. Few more

wrinkles, too. Hell, his partner had aged a matter of years without anyone noticing. Least of all him. Didn't change anything it seemed. Becker was still wearing sweaters under suit jackets. Riggs battled the urge to look away, but his partner had trained him to take in every detail.

Even the ones that didn't seem relevant…

Like a rash Riggs had never seen before. He pinched the screen to make the photo bigger. There. Just under Becker's left cuff at his wrist. Red splotches stood stark against the paleness of his partner's skin. He closed the window and went back to the report. A rash would be documented in the autopsy report. His heart beat faster as he searched through any marks discovered on the body at the time of the exam. He needed a better view of the reaction.

"Please tell me there's coffee." Macie swept into the room and headed straight for the pantry to start the search. She'd be sorely disappointed unless her favorite food matched that of an eight-year-old. His gut clenched as he caught sight of her in high-waisted slacks that showed off her figure. Having her this close alone was enough to shove reality back a few seconds, but then Riggs noticed the red marks along the side of her neck. Not bruising. Something else.

"What's that?" He shoved to his feet, making sure to take the sheets he'd stolen from her with him. Angry welts pimpled in a cluster near her throat. They weren't like the mosquito bites he'd suffered from the woods. These were like blisters. "You've got some kind of rash."

"Oh." Macie covered the area with her hand. "I've been scratching."

His mind instantly tried to connect the two instances. Becker came into contact with the killer, as did Macie.

In fact, the rash seemed to follow the same pattern as the bruises darkening around her throat. "Does it hurt?"

"It itches. Happens sometimes. It's just an allergy I've always had. It's nothing. They'll go away in a couple hours as long as I leave them alone. Kind of like hives but smaller and more annoying." She continued pulling the mountain of stacked boxes of lime green breakfast pastries from the shelves. "Okay. I promise I was joking about the pastries. Is there seriously nothing else to eat?"

Riggs pushed her hair back behind her shoulder to get a better view, exposing the affected area. "I didn't notice them last night. What are you allergic to?"

"Peanuts." She tossed one of the boxes back into the pantry. "Riggs, I promise, I'm fine. This is the worst it gets. I've had in-office allergy tests every year to keep on top of it. I'm not going to go into anaphylactic shock, and I don't need an EpiPen. Stop worrying."

"Does this kind of reaction happen a lot?" he asked.

Her eyebrows crinkled in the middle. "No. I'm pretty good about staying clear from anything with peanuts. You'd be surprised how much food contains nuts. They're everywhere. Even these things." She tossed a box of pastries back in the cupboard and closed the pantry.

"Becker was allergic to peanuts." He wasn't sure of the relevance to the case or how it would lead them to recovering Penny, but it was a lead. Something to tie the man they'd fought in the woods to both attacks. "His body was found in a burned-down bakery. No amount of peanut residue could've survived that fire, which means the killer had to have had it on his hands when he killed Becker and attacked you."

Macie rubbed at her neck as if suddenly conscious of the fact she'd been strangled a little more than twenty-four hours ago. A shiver chased across her shoulders. "Makes sense. Direct contact with allergens can produce the rash."

"He's not going to hurt you again, Macie." Riggs stepped in close enough for a hint of soap and clean woman to tickle the back of his throat. "It doesn't seem like much, but this is something new we can focus on."

"You want to hunt a man who has peanut residue on his hands. That's not exactly a telltale marker of a killer, Riggs. Plenty of people handle peanuts in their jobs or to just snack on," she said. "What are you going to do? Have an allergist test everyone in town?"

She was right. It was an impossible task to follow. "Then we're back at square one."

"Maybe. But if there's one thing I know about you, it's that you don't give up. Even when the chips are down and you're bleeding out." She ripped the sheets from his hand and crumpled them in her arms, leaving him completely and utterly exposed to the elements. "Now, if you'll excuse me, Detective. I need to wash these."

Macie sauntered back down the hallway.

Chapter Eleven

She couldn't stop scratching her neck.

Macie shoved her hair out of the way to get a better view in the small bathroom mirror. The rash was getting worse. Damn it. She hadn't lied when she'd told Riggs it usually went away within a couple hours. What was this? Super peanut? Didn't matter. A rash wasn't going to help them find the killer, and it sure as hell wasn't going to help them find Penny.

Their best shot was going back through Becker's files, but they'd already done that. Ad nauseam. Penny was smart. Her parents taught her to beware of strangers and all the other rules of interacting with a scary world. She wouldn't have gone with a killer willingly just like Macie hadn't gone with him all those years ago. She would've screamed, fought, bit, punched—anything and everything she had to do to get free. She would've let Easton know she was in danger.

Unless…she hadn't been able to. Unless she'd been knocked unconscious or drugged or restrained. The killer had twenty-five years to get his skills up to par. Because of her. Hazel, Sakari, Penny—they'd all been taken. But she could still help one of them.

Macie stared at Campbell Dwyer's name in her phone contacts, her thumb hovering above the entry. She feared for what waited on the other line, but they'd already wasted so much time Penny didn't have. She'd taken refuge in the bedroom as Riggs reviewed his partner's files from the beginning. She couldn't just stand there. She had to do something. She pressed the screen and raised the phone to her ear. The call connected almost instantly.

"Do you have something?" Campbell's voice shook, tearing through Macie with every quaver. The pain was real and suffocating and uncomfortable, but ignoring it wouldn't make it go away. Shoving it deep down only made things worse.

"No. I just…" She wasn't sure exactly why she'd called. The seconds stretched between them, like she and Campbell had somehow become strangers overnight. Macie rubbed a clammy hand down her slacks. Didn't help her nerves in the least. "I wanted to see how you were doing?"

"How I'm doing, Macie? Really?" A humorless laugh staticked from the other side of the line and sucker punched Macie in the gut. "My daughter has been abducted for a second time, you're hiding instead of out here with us to look for her, and you want to know how I'm doing?"

The attacks just kept coming. Macie closed her eyes. Hiding. The word took up so much space, it was hard to breathe. She had been hiding. Not just since the attack in the woods. But practically her whole life. She'd looked at Hazel from the sidelines, all the while protecting her own skin. Because she was afraid. For her life, for what she'd find, for the people she cared about. She forced herself to take a deep breath and keep the emotion lodged in her chest from breaking free. "Someone has to. Have you eaten or gotten any sleep the past couple of days?"

Campbell didn't answer right away, didn't even seem to breathe, but she hadn't hung up. It wasn't much, but it was progress. "There will be plenty of time to sleep when I find her."

Her pulse thudded hard in her throat. Thoughts that'd been circling her brain for years rushed into focus. She'd lived this exact moment every time she'd opened the closet where she'd hidden the pieces of Hazel's investigation she'd collected. She knew everything going through Campbell's mind. Every fear, every hope, every justification—it'd all been leading to this moment. To someone else taking up the mantle, and her being able to walk them through it. To keep others from having to do it alone as she had. Tears burned in her eyes. "It wasn't my fault, Campbell."

"I…" A deep inhale registered. "I know that, and I'm sorry. I'm sorry I blamed you. I just feel so…"

"Helpless." Campbell and Riggs were similar in that respect. Macie glanced toward the door, not hearing anything from the kitchen table anymore. He must've given up on the files. Or fallen asleep. Neither of them had gotten much rest over the past few days. "I know it feels that way, but I promise you are a good mother. I see you with Penny. I see how she looks at you and how far you were willing to go to get her back that first time. You almost died bringing her home, Campbell. How many other mothers would've gone up against a psychotic killer to protect their child? I know for a fact you're in the middle of the woods right now, searching for her, trying to kill yourself all over again."

A crunch of leaves confirmed her theory. "I can't stop,

Macie. I can't go home. No matter how many times Kendric tells me I need to take care of myself or that I need to eat or get some sleep, I can't do it. Because I know the second I do is when she'll need me the most."

The duffel bag she'd carted from her tree house consumed her attention from the corner where she'd dropped it the night before. The files inside were still there. She'd double-checked. Hazel had been her best friend, and still, all these years later, that need to keep going, to find the next lead, to do something worth doing, gripped her hard. "They're going to tell you that you can't do anything for her unless you take care of yourself. They're going to have the best intentions. They're going to try to make you see reason. Screw reason, Campbell. Don't listen to them. Eat a granola bar, take a power nap in your car, then get back out there. If it's permission you're looking for, you have it from me. Penny needs you, so suck it up, buttercup, and focus on her. Let us take care of everything else."

The silence was back. Just for a moment. "I'm glad I didn't have to kill you."

A smile notched her mouth higher. "Me, too. Good luck out there. I'll check in with you as soon as we have news."

The line disconnected, and she stared down at the phone. The timer she'd set to run in the background was still ticking down. Forty-eight hours had somehow diminished in the blink of an eye. Now they had less than twenty-four to find Penny.

Movement registered from the doorway. Riggs.

"It's not polite to eavesdrop, you know." Macie tried to force a smile as the weight on her chest increased, but she was tired of carrying around all the facades she'd relied on over the years. For once, she just wanted to be. No expectations from others. No internal compulsion to stay bright and cheery and reliable.

He moved into the room, all predatory-like and smooth, carrying a grace she'd never had. Taking a seat beside her on the bed, Riggs let his arm settle against hers. "You told Campbell exactly what she needed to hear. You're good at that. Reading people."

"I've always wanted a superpower." His warmth added to the sensation overload closing in but soothed the raw edges of the past few days at the same time. "Maybe next I can start reading minds."

"You were one of the kids in chemistry who ignored the safety rules to see if you'd turn into a superhero, weren't you?" he asked. "Mixing up things the teacher told you not to, just to see what would happen."

"You know me so well." Her laugh took her by surprise. It was so easy to forget the world existed outside of these four walls with him here next to her. As though twenty-five years had been a blip of time, and they'd picked up right where they'd left off. "Did you find anything new?"

"I've gone through Becker's autopsy report and called in to your interim chief. Easton and the rest of the department are all hands on deck, but nothing at the campsite we uncovered gave them anything. Every printable surface had been wiped down. Same with the knife we recovered. I'm beginning to think the killer made it himself. It was like the bastard had known we were coming." Riggs shook his head. "Did you happen to catch the model or license plate of the ATV while you were out there?"

"No. It was too dark." She tried. She'd gone over those

terrifying minutes again and again, but nothing new had come to mind. They were still dead in the water, and Penny was drifting farther out to sea. "I couldn't even pick out a color, to be honest, and trying to track one of those will be like trying to find a needle in a haystack. Everyone who owns property around this town has them to help work the land."

"Last I heard, Ford was calling in some favors to the surrounding departments, trying to get as many boots on the ground as possible," he said. "Your guy Reagan from the coffee shop has even volunteered to keep everyone hopped up on caffeine and pastries. Whole town's involved now. The killer can't last out there forever."

"And what if he's not out there?" Ice slid through her veins. "What if he's already done with her? What if what we did out in those woods pushed his timing? He'll just move on to the next town and do this to someone else. We can't sit around and wait for news, Riggs. We need to do something."

"You were strangled twenty-four hours ago, and I lost two pints of blood the last time we went up against this guy." Riggs set one hand against his thigh. "If you've got a plan that ends with who we're after in cuffs, Penny on her way home and us still alive, I'm all for it."

That was a tall order but one they couldn't walk away from. All that mattered was bringing Penny home safely. Whatever it took.

"Come with me." Macie shoved off the bed and rounded back into the living space. The kitchen table was still covered with files, now separated into two distinct cases. Hazel McAdams and Sakari Vigil. "Look at the photos of the victims." She pointed to the first photograph, unable to bring herself to study them again. It wasn't Hazel and Sakari she saw anymore. It was Penny. "The only marks found on their bodies during the autopsy were the strangulation bruises."

"Okay." Riggs didn't sound convinced of anything yet.

"He's preserving them while holding them captive." It was a long shot, but they had nothing else to go off of. "He's being careful with them, making sure not to damage them in any way until the finale. I don't have proof, but I know for a fact Penny wouldn't have gone with a stranger willingly. She knows what her parents do for a living, and they taught her everything she needed to know to fight back, but he wouldn't have wanted to knock her out or sedate her because that would leave a mark."

Riggs picked up that first photo and took another look, clarity and determination spreading across his face. "If that's the case, he would've had to convince her to leave with him. How?"

Macie hated the theory that'd taken hold, but it was the only one that made sense. "I think Penny knew her abductor. I think she went with him willingly."

Willingly. That was a big leap.

But if Macie was right… If Penny knew her abductor…

Hazel could've known hers. Sakari could've looked into the face of a man she trusted while slowly suffocating, all the while believing he would loosen his grip. That left Macie. She'd been the killer's original target all those years ago, hadn't she? He'd gone after her first. Would she recognize the man determined to keep to the shadows?

The primal need he'd tried to ignore when it came to this case had returned with a vengeance. He couldn't pretend anymore. He couldn't turn his back. He had to see it through to the end. He had to know who'd done this. Too many people had died from his refusal to acknowledge the truth. Innocent lives. That was on him. Which meant both Penny's and Macie's lives were on him.

"You're chasing a damn ghost, Karig." Riggs scrubbed a hand down his face. A rise of frustration powered through him, and he shoved the stack of cases off the table. The papers scattered into a mess of blurred words and stark images. Every other homicide he'd worked had left a trail of clues for him to follow, even on the tailcoats of Becker's career. There'd been evidence, motive—something—he could use to find the right answer, but this case… It wasn't like the others. This killer wasn't like the others.

A washed-out photo of Becker on the slab had landed on top of the rest from BMPD's investigation file, separated from the preliminary autopsy report. The final wouldn't come through until the case was closed. *Second rule of homicide investigation, kiddo—don't make it personal.* A scoff escaped his control. Too late for that. This was personal. Every inch of it. He'd known the first victim and the last. They'd both played an integral part in shaping him into the man sitting here with nothing but a handful of crime scene photos and a witness getting under his skin. He collected the photo from the scattered pile. "You knew I'd come running, didn't you? You knew I'd do whatever it took to see this through. Because that was how you trained me."

The hole he'd tried to fill with case after case collapsed in his chest, leaving nothing but hollowness and grief. His eyes burned. Why hadn't Becker retired like he was supposed to? Why couldn't the man have found a hobby or traveled the world in an RV like everyone else his age?

The answer solidified as the seconds ticked by.

Macie.

Becker had wanted to find her. To help her. To protect her as he hadn't been able to protect the others. And when he couldn't—when he'd died trying—his partner had trusted him to take up the cause. He'd come to Battle Mountain in a last-ditch effort to save lives, and instead, had lost his own. Doing what he loved.

Riggs tried to rewrite their last conversation in his head, but there was no getting around it. He'd accused the old man of controlling his career from the get-go, but in reality, Becker had led him here. To Macie. "You always were trying to set me up on dates."

"You know there are doctors who can help with the voices in your head." Macie settled against the wall beside the hallway—the same spot where he'd kissed her. Damp hair waved down her shoulders, curling in the front and waving in the back. Hints of citrus and something compelling and rich. He'd smelled it on his pillow a few hours ago when he'd woken beside her, and instantly imagined falling asleep with that same scent on him tonight. "Personally, I think mine are more interesting than the people around me."

Riggs memorized everything he could about her. He could still taste her, feel that perfect mouth beneath his, and there wasn't a single cell in his body that wanted to stop him from doing it again. He could get used to this. Despite the case that'd brought them together, Macie had blown his organized and routine world apart, and he didn't miss a single moment of it. In as little as three days, she'd given him a renewed energy he hadn't felt since graduating from the academy. A fresh outlook. She gave off a light when his entire life had become dark and lonely. It wasn't just about saving lives anymore. It was about living his own. Doing as she had done in choosing her own path, looking out for the people she cared about and staying curious. "The only voice I have in my head these days is yours."

"You say that like it's a bad thing," she said.

He shifted his weight into his good leg and stood, closing in on her. His uninjured hand found her hip as though it'd been carved just for his touch. Full, soft and enticing. "Took some getting used to, but now, I can't imagine it any other way."

"I've heard I have that effect on people." Macie wound her arms around his neck, lighter over the patch of gauze and tape on his shoulder. "None as handsome as you, though."

Hell, she was beautiful. Vibrant. Confident in all the right ways. His total opposite. Maybe everything he'd been missing in his life. Somehow, even in the middle of all the violence and terror and uncertainty, she'd become a lighthouse directing him through the dark and doubt. He needed her. Today, tomorrow and the day after that. Longer if they could manage it. There wasn't anything or anyone waiting for him back home he wasn't willing to give up right this second. For her. He fit her against him. Absolutely perfect. "How do you do it, Red? How do you manage to make things look so effortless and easy when the world wants nothing but chaos and challenge?"

"Practice makes perfect." Macie seemed to test the words for a few seconds. "But nothing is as easy as it seems."

Her answer lacked that sarcastic and lighthearted flair

he'd come to associate with her. Riggs loosened his hold to get a better read of her expression. "What do you mean?"

"I wasn't always like this, Riggs. These past few years, on the run… I used to know who I was. I didn't have to lose myself in things like astrology or fifteenth-century plants, and read any book I could get my hands on, hoping something would light a spark," she said. "I think that's one of the reasons Easton Ford doesn't know how to talk to me. No one in this town knows how to talk to me. To them, I'm the airheaded dispatcher preaching her voodoo and giving herself manicures at her desk. But the truth is, I don't know what I'm meant to do on this planet and that scares me. So, yeah, I guess that I might make this look easy, but that's because I have no idea what I'm doing. I'm lost."

Lost. The word snaked through his mind and settled at the forefront. It was an uncomfortable feeling. All this time he'd relied on Macie to get them through this investigation—to lead him in the right direction—and it turned out, that confidence he'd acquainted with her didn't exist. But the longer he looked at her, the longer he had her in his hold, Riggs knew one thing for certain.

"I know who you are." He pushed a strand of damp hair back behind her ear. "I'll admit, I was confused there for a while. The stubborn girl I knew twenty-five years ago was still stuck in my head. Avalynn was powerful, confrontational and never liked anyone telling her what to do. She only cared about one thing. Being in control. Everything was a test of wills, especially when it came to her best friends. But it's never been clearer to me than right this second, Macie Barclay. You're not her."

She moved to argue with him.

"You're sensitive to everyone else's needs but your own. You're willing to put yourself in harm's way for the sake of a four-year-old girl and a burned-out detective who'd rather be in the desert than the woods." Riggs smoothed his thumb along the seam of her blouse at her side. "You're the most self-aware and honest person I've ever met and able to take the lowliest situations and make light of them. The world needs that. I needed that." He took another step into her, her chest pressed against his. "You're creative, and intelligent, and feisty in the best of ways, and I can't imagine going back to Albuquerque without that light you bring in my life."

Her mouth parted on a sharp inhale. "What…what are you saying?"

"I'm saying when this case is closed—when Penny is home safe and the man who took her is behind bars—I want you to come back with me. It's taken me this long to figure out all these years, I haven't just been looking for Hazel's killer, even Becker's killer. It's you, Macie. I've wanted you back in my life since the moment I realized you'd left." Pain registered from his leg, but he pushed it to the back of his mind. He'd stand here on a bum leg for a hundred more hours as long as Macie waited at the finish line. "I came to Battle Mountain to make up for a mistake, but Becker's death is more than one of a hundred homicide investigations I've worked. It's a chance to start over. For both of us."

"Wow. I don't know what to say." Her tongue darted across her bottom lip. "I've been thinking about that question you asked me. About what I want. I built a life here. I have friends here. For the first time in years, I think I've made a home, and I don't want to lose that feeling." His gut checked him hard as hesitation contorted her features.

Those wide green eyes locked on him. "But I've also never felt closer to another person than I have with you, and I've missed that connection."

"I'm not going to try to convince you one way or another." That would be a losing battle, with him as the sore loser. "It's your choice. Not mine, but know I'll accept whatever decision you make."

"I've already made my choice." Her full-blown smile nearly knocked him on his rear end. Macie launched onto her tiptoes and fused her mouth to his. Before he had a chance to fully enjoy the taste of her again, she dropped onto her feet. "But if I'm going to come back to Albuquerque with you, if we're really going to give this a chance, there's something you need to know first."

"What is it?" he asked.

"That day with Hazel in the woods." Her voice dipped into a whisper. "Everything I told you was true, but I didn't tell you the whole story."

Confusion cut off his air supply for a second. "What else is there to tell?"

"Hazel came to my rescue when the killer grabbed me, like I told you, but I lied when I said I didn't remember much after that," she said. "I remember everything."

Chapter Twelve

The admission should've lifted the weight off her chest, but Riggs hadn't responded yet. Her heart rate notched higher the longer silence reigned. "Say something."

His hand faltered on her hip as he took a step back. That unreadable guard was back in place, and the warmth charging through her veins at his proximity cooled significantly. She didn't know what was going through his mind, but it wasn't every day a witness came forward to recant their story.

"Okay. You'd said he asked you for directions, right before he attacked you. You didn't get a good look at his face because he surprised you from behind. You remember Hazel hitting her killer with a branch to get you free." Riggs released her entirely. No longer comforting or supportive. He was back in detective mode. Unreachable. "What happened after that?"

"I ran. Down the mountain." She could still feel the wet spots on her shirt where Hazel had hit her with clumps of moss. They'd crusted the longer she'd run. Macie clenched her hand into a fist to keep from testing her blouse for the same stains now. "I don't know for how long. I looked back to make sure Hazel had followed after me, but she wasn't there. Once I saw his face, I just ran faster."

And the truth was out. Her shame and her guilt right along with it.

"Wait. Now you're saying you saw his face? And you... didn't tell anyone?" Horror widened his gaze, and everything went cold. "You said you couldn't identify her killer. That you didn't remember anything distinct about him."

"I lied." Those same words had played through her head thousands of times. They'd kept her up at night, followed her into every friendship she'd tried to build when she took the risk and driven her to take a meaningless job for the smallest police department in the country. But coming from him... They cut deeper than she'd ever imagined. "You have to understand. My parents were convinced I was next, that he would come for me, and that fear became a part of me. I lived with it for days. I couldn't sleep. I couldn't eat. I refused to leave the house or be alone. I didn't know what else to do."

"It sounds like you did, Macie. It sounds like you could've given police a chance to catch Hazel's killer, but you chose to save your own skin instead." A hardness she'd hoped never to witness again solidified across his features. "What if your account could've helped Becker solve the case? What if Hazel's family could finally have the answers they deserve, and you were the only person keeping them from moving on? Hell, Sakari Vigil and Becker might still be alive if you'd told the truth." Riggs shook his head as he backed away. "All this time, you could've done something, and you chose to stay silent. That's not the kind of woman I want a relationship with."

Dread pooled at the base of her spine. Macie locked her jaw to keep the tears from burning in her eyes, but it was no use. She'd known this day would come—the one where someone saw her for what she truly was. A coward. She just hadn't expected it to hurt this much. "I made a mistake. Okay? I should've told you, but I lied because I wanted you to see the real me. The one you said you wanted to come back with you—"

"I was wrong." His voice lost any semblance of emotion. He'd detached faster than she'd expected, leaving nothing but a shell of the man she'd fallen for. Dark eyes assessed her every move, seemingly seeing right through her. "You haven't changed, have you, Avalynn? You're still that girl who only gives a damn about herself."

Avalynn. He'd stopped using that name over the past few days. He'd accepted her as who she was now, not who she'd been. At least, that was what she'd told herself. Hearing it now severed the connection they'd shared and left her empty and wanting. Macie rolled her lips between her teeth and bit down. It was the only way to keep the grief and heartbreak from tearing her apart. She leveled her chin parallel to the floor, trying to hold her ground. "I'm not that person anymore."

"Could've fooled me. Then again, you're good at pretending to be someone you're not." Riggs stared at her as though wishing he could take it all back. The night they'd spent together, the support and promises he'd let slip through that intensity he carried—it'd meant nothing to him right then. Now facing toward the door, he walked over the mess of files and grabbed his keys off the counter.

The killer was still out there. He knew Riggs now. He

couldn't just leave. Macie moved to stop him. "You can't go. It's not safe."

Riggs pivoted on her, and she pulled up short. His anger centered on her and destroyed the remnants of feeling in her veins. "Lucky for me, I can take care of myself. Unlike Penny. Someone has to have her best interest at heart."

"Didn't I try to do that the other night? Didn't I try to save you, too? You don't know anything about me, Detective, or how far I'll go to bring that girl home." If he was going to try to erase their time together, she would, too.

"You're right. I don't. Whose fault is that?" He wrenched open the door, his limp more prominent then. "I'll let your department know where you are. Until then, do what you do best, Macie Barclay. Look out for yourself."

The door slammed closed behind him.

After a few seconds, Macie flinched as dirt kicked up against the windows during his escape, leaving her alone. Without a vehicle. Without support. Another layer of dust cascaded down from the exposed rafters like a wall of glitter. It got under her collar and made her itch. She grabbed at her neck, aggravating the rash along one side. "What the hell is happening?"

She hadn't eaten peanuts, and even if she had, the reaction should've calmed down by now. Unless…

Unless this wasn't a food allergy as she'd assumed.

Macie tore her gaze from the SUV speeding across the desert landscape. Riggs had said something about Detective Becker being allergic to peanuts, too. She dug through the papers strewn across the floor until she found the photo focused entirely on the rash at the man's wrist. It looked the same as hers. That was impossible. Everyone reacted to allergies differently. What were the chances the rash would show the same pattern? "He had it on his hands."

Not peanuts. Something else.

She discarded the photo, pouring herself into the case and not the ache growing bigger in her chest. Riggs was gone. He wasn't coming back here. Not for her. The only way she could help Penny now was on her own. "Think."

Food, medications, insect bites, latex—there were dozens of sources of allergic reactions, but none of them seemed to fit the bill now. But chemicals might. In fact, now that she thought about it, she'd heard about this kind of reaction when she'd first started as a dispatcher for BMPD, and there was only one place in Battle Mountain this specific rash could've come from. If Penny was there, they had more to worry about than bringing her home.

Macie pulled the file together and ran to the back of the cabin. Adan and Isla were survivors, and they did everything they could to protect their eight-year-old from danger. Not from diabetes, but they'd want to keep a fueled vehicle ready to go. She raced through the back door and kept on going to the newly built shed positioned between the cabin and the cliffs less than a mile away. Hauling the garage door overhead, she then rounded the fender of the monster truck parked inside. It'd been built by and belonged to Isla's late husband. Fully decked out and stocked for emergencies. "Bingo."

It took two tries to get herself behind the wheel. She shoved the key in the ignition, and she could've sworn the engine growl was about to shake her fillings loose. She shoved it into Drive, leaving the cabin she'd learned to love in the rearview mirror.

There was nothing to look back for. Only forward. If there was one thing she'd learned the past few days with Riggs, it was this place—these people—they were worth risking her life for. All of them. She was done running. "I'm coming, Penny."

Macie stepped on the accelerator and tore across the desert back toward town. Meeting up with the dirt road that would take her up the mountain took less than twenty minutes. The truck's shocks threatened to give out as she forced the vehicle along rocky terrain. With her luck, she'd pitch the oversize beast backward, but before any real fears set in about becoming a crash test dummy, the mouth of Desolation Mine materialized through the trees.

"This is it." She'd never come up here, but the teenagers set on making her and Weston Ford's lives miserable a couple times a year had told her everything she needed to know. The mine had been abandoned once the coal companies pulled out. Workers had started getting sick. They didn't know from what, but it hadn't been worth the investment when so few could keep digging. Macie slid from the truck, the ground unsteady. Or maybe that was just her. Mud suctioned at her shoes from the storms from the past few days. She pulled a flashlight from one of the emergency containers in the back seat and compressed the power button. The beam lit up the dirt ahead of her but disappeared into the mouth of the mine. "Here goes nothing."

Goose pimples budded along her arms as she trekked the few yards to the mine's mouth. Only darkness waited. An emptiness that felt like it could swallow her whole if she wasn't careful, but if Penny was in there, she didn't have a choice. A rock rolled under her flimsy shoe, the sound of which echoed deep into the cavern. Something shifted inside. "Please be here."

Macie let the darkness consume her. She took a step, then another. The temperature dropped the deeper she treaded. It was more humid in here than she thought it'd be. The flashlight didn't help much, but it was a reassurance to hang on to at least. Her pulse thudded hard at the base of her skull. She felt as though there were a thousand eyes watching her every move, but she couldn't see any of them. "Penny?"

She wasn't sure how far she'd gotten, but it was enough to make doubt start clawing in her head. There were plenty of spots in a place like this that weren't safe. Not just from asbestos as she feared had caused the reaction on her neck, but open shafts, collapsed areas miners didn't dare venture, gas pockets. The list went on. But she couldn't go back. Not without Penny. Glancing the way she'd come, she misstepped. Her foot hit something solid and out of place.

The thin piece of wood broke under her feet.

And she was consumed by the earth.

HE SHOULD'VE KNOWN BETTER.

He should've known not to let himself get wrapped up in this investigation. In Macie. Becker had tried to warn him about letting things get personal, but he hadn't listened. There was a reason detectives needed to keep their distance. Because the moment emotion played into a case, mistakes were made. And he'd made the biggest one of them all.

Riggs shoved the SUV into Park and hit the pavement. Battle Mountain's police station looked the same, but his entire world had turned upside down. Nothing he'd done the past few days made sense anymore. He wasn't this person.

The kind that fell for a woman in three days. Who believed every word of a traumatized witness on the run, then managed to climb into bed with said witness. Macie had gotten in his head and put his conscience in a blender. Hell. She'd lied straight to his face, and here he'd been thinking about a future. With her.

Wasn't going to happen.

He shoved through the back door of the station and maneuvered down the hall to the left. The chief's office was empty, but Easton Ford wouldn't have just up and abandoned the place. Someone had to be here to answer emergency calls—

"Detective Karig." Kendric Hudson got to his feet from his position behind the dispatcher's desk. Macie's desk. Gruff facial hair shadowed a strong jaw and a path of scar tissue that immediately put Riggs on edge. This was a man who didn't appreciate small talk or beating around the bush. No time or patience for anything but the truth, and didn't put much stock in anything but. Riggs had met plenty of investigators like this one over the years, but there was something unique. Something capable and quick and tested. "We haven't been formally introduced, and you seem to be missing our dispatcher."

"Officer Hudson. Good to see you again." Riggs extended his hand, his shift in weight aggravating the stab wound in his thigh. "And no, Macie's not with me."

A knowing smile hiked one corner of the man's mouth higher, but clear frustration bled into his grip as the former ATF instructor shook his hand. "So what was your plan, Detective? Because the way I see it, a killer took my daughter and is using her to get his hands on Macie. If Macie's not here, he's got no reason to keep Penny alive. You were the one who was supposed to make sure she didn't leave town. That we actually had a fighting chance." Hudson advanced on him, every inch the federal agent and father Riggs had expected that first day. "You don't know me, Karig. You don't know my wife. You weren't here that first time Penny was taken from us, but I promise you, if anything happens to my daughter or Macie because you refused to follow orders, I will not protect you from what's coming."

Plan? If he was being honest with himself, Riggs hadn't had a plan. He'd gotten so caught up in his anger—in his disappointment—with Macie's lie, that he hadn't seen anything straight until he'd walked through the station door. She'd left Hazel to defend herself against a full-grown attacker, without looking back, without trying to help. He'd meant what he'd said. She wasn't the person he believed he'd known, and there was no changing that. "Macie didn't leave town. She's safe. As long as she stays put and you let me do my job, Penny still has a chance."

Kendric Hudson sank back against the edge of the desk, pain clear in his expression. Grief did that. Caught you off guard, made you weak. The man was in no position to contribute to this investigation or protect this town right now, but Riggs would be an idiot to think Kendric would let anything keep him down. "If you don't mind my asking, Detective, given what I know about you and Macie's past friendship, what on earth makes you believe she'll stay where you left her?"

Cold infused his veins. "She doesn't have any transportation out there in that dust bowl. Where is she going to go?"

"I haven't known Macie as long as the others around here,

but she's one of the reasons I get to hug Penny and Campbell every morning and kiss them good-night after every shift. She keeps me and the people I love safe. She's unique, I'll give you that, and frustrating beyond belief at times, but she loves harder than any other person that's come through these doors. I don't care what's going on between you two or why you abandoned her to fend for herself out there in the middle of nowhere. You'd be surprised how resourceful she can be when she feels the need to help, and you'd be stupid to cut her loose." Hudson studied him as though seeing straight through into his head. "You've spent three days with her, Detective. Surely, you've seen by now she can read anybody in a matter of seconds and tell you everything you need to know about their habits, their relationships and how far they're willing to go to protect what they love."

His mind clawed to put Hudson's riddle together for himself. "Adan Sergeant was former military."

"He was. Now, from what I've heard, you're a damn good detective. You've solved more homicides in the Albuquerque PD than anyone else, including the man who mentored you." Hudson dragged himself to stand, no evidence of struggle. "Do you honestly believe a trained sniper who lost everything would leave his fiancée and eight-year-old without a way to escape that cabin in an emergency?"

Oh, hell. Gravity took what energy he had left right out of him. What had he done?

"Majors and Gregson will meet you out there." Hudson headed for the chief's office. "And might I suggest you stop wasting what little time you have to make things right. You never know when you'll run out. Take it from me."

Riggs rushed for the back door and was behind the wheel

of his rental faster than he should have been with two fresh wounds. Rubber screamed in his ears as he fishtailed out of the parking lot to catch the main road. Panic strangled him at the throat. For as angry and betrayed he'd felt at learning Macie had lied to him all this time, he wasn't the type of man to let her get herself killed. They didn't have a future together, but she deserved to live the rest of her life free.

Hudson was right. Macie had never taken a command to heart that didn't suit her own parameters. That determination and stubbornness had been one of the things he'd loved about her the most, but he'd been stupid to think she'd do anything for her own good.

Loved. No. He didn't love her. Because he couldn't love someone who hid part of herself from him, who insisted on staying stuck in the past. But he'd keep his promise. He'd make sure she walked away from this alive. Just like he should've done for Becker.

Asphalt turned to dirt as Riggs skidded down the single road that would take him out past the town limits. Greenery thinned on either side of the SUV, raw dust and barren landscape stretching ahead. This was his element, where he thrived. Where he'd learned to survive. No shadows. No places to lash out from the dark.

He skidded to a stop in front of the cabin and shoved the SUV into Park. Dirt gritted between his teeth as he ran for the front door. Another car pulled up behind him, but Riggs didn't have the attention to focus on anything but Macie. Of making sure she was alive. Safe. He charged through the front door. "Macie!"

Pushing himself through the cabin, he searched every room. There was no sign of her. Their shared breakfast still waited on the table with the files he'd scattered under his feet. But something was different. The photo on top of the pile... That wasn't the one he'd been looking at last.

Heavy footprints registered from the porch. Two sets. "You Karig?" a male voice asked.

Riggs knelt on his good leg and collected the photo of Becker's wrist, inflamed and blistered. He could just make out the shape of the killer's fingers wrapping around the skin. Macie's neck had developed the same rash. The autopsy report hadn't come to anything conclusive about the source, but both Macie and Becker were allergic to peanuts. Was that why she'd dug through the photos for this? "She's not here."

He tossed the photo back into the pile and turned to face the officers at the door.

Cree Gregson took up more space in the run-down cabin than Riggs had gauged from their limited contact at Macie's tree house. Not with his sheer size but with a heaviness that seemed to fill every inch of the place. Like he'd taken on the weight of the world and hadn't let go. The former ATF agent kept close to his partner. Protective. Devoted. Riggs knew the feeling, but the woman on his mind would never feel the same. She couldn't. "Isla keeps her truck in the back garage. The rig was installed with a GPS system by her husband before he died."

"If Macie took it, it won't be hard to track her down." Alma Majors tugged her radio from her belt. He recognized the name from a huge wave of media coverage a few years ago, but why the foremost researcher of Mexican archeology had disappeared to a town no one had ever heard of escaped Riggs. Didn't matter. All he needed was her help. "I'll hail Isla now. See if we can get a location."

There had to be a reason Macie had left the safety of the cabin. She was impulsive, but she didn't have a death wish. Even for Penny. He treaded down the hallway, ignoring the imprints of two heads in the pillows on the bed and rumpled sheets. He didn't have time to think about the rush of hours spent wrapped up in a woman who'd given him so much. The second Gregson and Majors searched this place, they'd know what happened between him and Macie. They'd know he'd broken protocol and gotten mixed up with a witness, but he'd keep the rest to himself. As much as he hated the idea of what Macie had done, those had been the best hours of his life. For once, he'd gotten a glimpse of life outside of what Becker had created for him. He'd forgotten about the job, his divorce, the pain in his body, and he'd been able to just...be.

Because of her. He owed her that.

Her duffel bag consumed his attention from the corner. She hadn't gone anywhere without it the past few days. Why leave it behind now? Unless it wasn't useful anymore. Dragging it toward him at the edge of the bed, he then unzipped the bag. No spell books or weapons or stuffed animals from an escapade in the woods. He pulled a manila file folder from the depths.

A picture had been paperclipped to the front cover. One of three idiot kids with a hot-air balloon behind them. He remembered the day it was taken. He and Ava—Macie—had gotten into a big fight, but the balloon festival was too grand and fantastic for either of them to remember what about. He'd slung his arm around her and smiled as Hazel's

mother took the photo. It would've been one of the last before their friend's body had been found.

Riggs set it aside, not daring to lose himself in that feeling all over again, and cracked the file open.

This was something far more dangerous. Familiar photos spread in a sort of timeline across the file, handwritten
notes written on scraps of paper, official reports with ink
smudges. It was all here. Every shred of evidence. Every
witness statement. Plus her own memories. Some of these
had to have been years old. Decades.

Riggs couldn't believe it. Each report looked as though
it'd been tacked with a pushpin. Maybe to a corkboard or…
"The closet. That's what you were hiding."

Hell. The killer had gone looking for this file during the
search of her tree house because he knew. He knew Macie
had been investigating Hazel's case from the beginning.

Chapter Thirteen

The flashlight beamed straight into her eyes.

Macie blinked to clear the confusion and haze, but the only thing that followed was pain. So much pain. She'd landed on her right arm. A groan echoed off the enclosed walls and reminded her where she was. It stretched the bandage on her side. Forcing her gaze straight up, she tried to make out the top of the shaft she'd fallen down. There wasn't a particle of light from above. Thankfully the shaft had run diagonal, or she'd be dead. "Hello!"

Her head protested her voice ricocheting back at her. Pushing up on her uninjured arm, she hissed at the ache in her hips and feet. No telling how far she'd fallen. Only that she wasn't getting back to the surface.

Bracing one hand against the closest wall, she climbed to her feet. Her skull struck a jutting rock before she had a chance to straighten fully. Lightning speared across her vision, and she pressed her palm against the sore spot. "Can anyone hear me? Hello!"

She'd gone down a mineshaft. No one could hear her.

The weight of that reality squeezed the air out of her chest. Her hand shook as she felt for the next stretch of wall.

From what she'd studied about the mines in these mountains, shafts like this were used to get spoils to the surface, for ventilation or to access raw treasure troves. Macie collected the flashlight from the mine floor and shone it straight overhead. Considering the size of the hole she came through, she bet ventilation. Which meant it would've been man-made, right? There'd have to be an end somewhere. She just had to find it.

Then again, what did she know? She'd put her whole heart into a man who'd left her the minute she'd trusted him with the truth. She hadn't expected that, but it went to show she was right all along. No one would understand her. No one could understand what she'd gone through that day or what she'd been through the past few years. Least of all a detective who'd given up trying. Macie pressed her injured arm into her rib cage, but it was nothing compared to the hurt inside.

Riggs had chiseled past her guard with promises and support and pleasure and taken up space somewhere he had no right to occupy. Then he'd taken that privilege and used it for his own benefit. To give himself permission to push her away. Just so he could go back to his comfort zone, to being alone. Macie stumbled into the side wall, rocks scraping along her skin. "Come on, woman. Survival first. Love life later."

She felt her way along a passage that was getting more confined with every step. The walls were closing in on her. Literally. And she had nowhere else to go. She couldn't climb back up the shaft with a possibly broken arm, let alone reach the opening she'd come through. There had to be another way. "Please! Can anyone hear me?"

"I hear you," a voice said from the dark.

Goose pimples budded along the back of her neck. Not just any voice. His voice. She'd been right about the rash on Becker's wrist, about the one on her neck. They hadn't come from a peanut allergy, but asbestos. The killer had been in this mine. Just like all the men and women who'd walked away sick. She backed into the wall, trying to make herself as small as possible. Clicking off the flashlight, she cast herself into darkness in hopes he couldn't see her, but the sensation of being watched refused to let up. "You."

"Yes, Avalynn. Me." The voice that'd lodged into her mind all those years ago surrounded her, bumping off the walls and attacking her from every angle. It elicited a guttural reaction that shoved acid into her throat. "I was hoping to see you again, but I have to admit, this is the last place I expected to find you."

She licked at her dry, dust-caked lips. Her voice cracked. "Penny... Where is she?"

"Ah. And here I thought you'd come to pay me a visit." The direction of his voice changed. How? Where was he hiding? He was playing games with her—she knew that—but the effect triggered a kaleidoscope of insignificance and doubt. "After all, we're old friends, aren't we?"

Shuffling registered from her right, and she moved farther along the wall, away from it. A kick of dirt seemed to hitch right in front of her. Macie crouched, clutching the flashlight with everything she had. She was ready. To end this. To leave the past behind. To have a life outside of trauma and fear and loneliness. "Friends? Is that what you'd call this? You tried to kill me. You killed Hazel and Sakari.

Now you have Penny. I'm sorry to be the one to tell you, but this friendship is really one-sided."

"Oh, that's not the way I see it, Macie," he said.

Her instincts picked up on the use of her current name. Something he hadn't done until now. It was…almost familiar. Friendly. Terrifying.

"I mean, you talked to me every day, never knowing I was the one who found you in those woods with little Hazel all those years ago." He was moving again, trying to confuse her. "You smiled at me. Laughed with me. You trusted me with your deepest frustrations at work and recommended the books you'd read. Puppetry, how humankind relates to and reacts to plants—all kinds of subjects I never would've considered without your interest. That's what I love about you. Your curiosity. I like to think that makes us similar in that respect. You see, I'm very creative as well. Not in the same way as you, but Hazel and Sakari certainly appreciated my art."

An outline solidified a few feet away, then moved away, and realization struck. He didn't know where she was. He was trying to keep her talking to get her location. Just as she was doing to him. "There I go again. Talking on and on about myself, and you listening so intently. If that's not friendship, what is?"

Horror churned in her gut. No. It wasn't possible. She would've known. She would've known the second he'd spoken to her that first time. She would've recognized him for what he truly was. Wouldn't she? Macie ran through the massive catalog of people she interacted with on a daily basis. There were just too many faces. She'd recommended thousands of books over the past six years and had complained to most people in this town about her job as a dispatcher. It was how she'd gotten so many of them to stay on the line until help arrived.

The man in the dark could be anyone.

"I feel you need a moment," he said. "And I agree, it's a lot to take in. I'm sure it's not every day you realize you brought this—all of this—on yourself."

A flashlight lit up in the too small space and blinded her. Macie brought her uninjured hand up to block the light, but it was too late. He'd found her. She launched off the ground and ran for the way she'd come.

Pain spiraled across her back as a collision of muscle tackled her. The wall rushed to meet her face, and she was suddenly pinned between her attacker and the mineshaft that'd nearly killed her. Strong hands flipped her around to face him, but still, the beam of the flashlight blocked his features.

He swept his thumb above her upper lip, coming away with blood seeping into dry, cracked fingers between them. "Well, now, look what you made me do." Real disappointment dipped his voice into dangerous territory. "I'll have to adjust my plans accordingly. No bother. I like the challenge."

"I don't know what you're so upset about." Macie tried to ignore the deep ache exploding across her face. It was a small price to pay to turn her into a victim. Because that was the only way he wouldn't consider her a threat. He couldn't divide his attention between her and Penny. If she wasn't a threat, he might take her to wherever Penny was being held. It was a solid plan. Riggs might've been proud. If he was here. "I'm the one who's bleeding."

"Bleeding or not, I'm going to enjoy this." He dragged her away from the wall, and Macie released her flashlight.

As much as she wanted to use it as a weapon, she needed to get to Penny. These tunnels went on for miles and in every which direction. The deeper she searched, the faster she'd get herself lost or killed. But he'd have a map. Either mentally or physically, he could work his way back to his captive. She let him shove her ahead of him, his beam only lighting up a couple steps ahead. "Glad one of us is."

"You're awfully chipper for someone about to die." Another hint of familiarity brushed against her mind.

Macie almost wanted to laugh. She wasn't going to die. At least not until she got Penny out of this literal hellhole. By then, maybe Riggs would realize she hadn't stayed put at the cabin. Her heart thudded harder at the mere thought of his name. And with that one thought came an array of memories, starting from when she'd first set eyes on him more than twenty-five years ago to him showing up on her doorstep and beyond. Staring down at her with the sheets tucked over their heads, their hands interlaced together after they survived the attack in the woods, to his cringe when he took a bite of Jolly Rancher breakfast pastries at the kitchen table.

He'd turned his back on her, thought of her as nothing more than a coward, but she wanted him. Warts and all. His constant alertness, his difficulty in trusting people, the isolation he insisted on carrying with him everywhere he went—all of it had molded him into the man she'd started falling in love with as a ten-year-old. The one she'd probably always loved. "Whether I die or not isn't going to change anything. You'll keep looking to scratch that itch that compels you to terrorize and kill little girls, and the rest of the world will keep turning. But in the end, I'll know I did everything in my power to stop you. Just like Detective Becker did."

A hard shove thrust her forward, and Macie hit the dirt. Her arm bellowed for relief. She rolled onto her back, ready for the next strike, but it never came.

"Well, you saw how that worked out for him." The killer moved into the light, exposing an all-too-familiar face. He was right. She had considered him a friend. All these years, she'd been blind, coming to him for advice and shared jokes. How hadn't she seen it? "Let's see how that works out for you."

"Isla's not able to get an exact location." Alma Majors brought up a local map on her phone and set it between the three of them on the dusty kitchen table. "Wherever Macie is, it's too remote. The best she can do is give us the truck's last position it pinged."

Riggs didn't know the area. He had no idea where to look for Macie, but a last position was better than nothing. He pointed to the small blue dot superimposed over the map with pale brown background. "This looks like mountain terrain. Where exactly is this?"

"It's a one-way road heading up the mountain. Only problem is that single road meets up with Cinnamon Pass." Majors expanded the view on her phone. "From there, she could be anywhere west of the range. Ouray, Ironton, Ridgway— those are just a few of the towns on the other side. She didn't say anything about where she was headed?"

"No. We… I left her here. Alone." And it'd been the biggest mistake of his life. Right up there with turning his back

on Becker last year. He'd given her his word he would protect her, yet he'd done to her just as she'd done to Hazel all
those years ago. That didn't make him any better. Hell, it
made this whole thing worse. The photo he'd discarded at
his feet pulled his attention from the phone. Seconds were
ticking by—too fast. Penny's countdown had reached under
twelve hours. Whatever they were going to do, they needed
to do it now. "This photo was on the top of the pile on the
floor when we got here, but I know for a fact it was closer
to the bottom when I left. Macie dragged it out. She saw
something. Something that convinced her leaving was the
best option."

"That looks like an allergic reaction." It was Majors's
turn with the last photo taken of his partner. This was all
he'd have when this case was closed. Just photos. He only
hoped the next autopsies weren't of Macie and Penny. The
thought sickened him.

"You think the killer had something on his hands that
transferred to them?" Gregson studied the pattern across
Becker's wrist. "Macie's allergic to peanuts. She threat-
ens to curse me every time I bring trail mix into the break
room. What are the chances your partner had the same allergy and the killer happened to have traces days apart still
on his hands?"

"You're right. It doesn't make sense. Even if he hadn't
washed his hands, he was in those woods, he handled Penny
and fought me. It would've wiped off." Riggs was studying the photo upside down now. In a different perspective,
he could make out the angry edges of each blister. Like a
burn. He took the photo from Majors and flipped it around.
"I don't think this is a food allergy."

"Chemical." Majors glanced at her partner, her features softening. "Chief Ford pulled a body out of a refrigerator over a year ago, before any of us got here. One that'd been buried underground. A young woman the killer had to get rid of before she informed Dr. Miles she was in danger."

He straightened. Macie hadn't told him any of that. How many homicides had this town seen lately?

Gregson maneuvered around the table to close the distance between him and his partner, almost like he didn't even know he was doing it.

Majors collected her phone from the table and tapped the screen. Once. Twice. "I've seen the case file and the autopsy photos. The victim suffocated inside that refrigerator. There were signs of a struggle all over her body, but she also had burns like this on her hands and the side of her face. Like she'd laid down in something." She handed the phone over, leaning back into Gregson's support. "Dr. Miles wasn't able to match the reaction to anything at the time. Her operation is pretty small at the funeral home, and everything has to go through the state crime lab, but it's been long enough. She might have the results."

He skimmed through the case file. Everything Majors had said lined up with the report. Female victim, died of suffocation due to lack of oxygen in the refrigerator. Bruising, lacerations and a rash-like reaction had all been noted in the report. All bodily fluids, bone, organ, muscle and skin samples had been sent to Unified Crime Lab in Denver. Nothing to notate of any updates or what had caused the reaction. "Call Dr. Miles. I want to know if she's received the results back from the crime lab on the samples she sent."

"You got it, boss." Gregson slid his hand over his partner's stomach and whispered something in her ear before he headed for the door, phone in hand.

Riggs didn't have the courage to take in the full interaction. Not without his heart squeezing so tight he couldn't breathe. Less than twenty-four hours ago, he'd had that. That connection with another person. That one-of-a-kind, hurl yourself off a cliff determination to throw your life away and forget everything you believed in optimism. Because of Macie. He couldn't deny that he'd thought about what might've happened between them if he hadn't left her here on her own. He certainly wouldn't be searching for her now—that was for damn sure. Riggs swept the rest of the files off the floor and stacked them in random order. He'd have to go through them all over again to straighten them out. "You're pregnant."

Majors hitched her thumbs in her service belt. "You're good. No one else has said anything. Or maybe they're too scared to say anything to me. Not sure which."

"You know what you're having?" Riggs was suddenly invested in the answer. As though it mattered. Any of it. Macie was out there. Possibly fighting for her life, for Penny's, and he wanted to know about the intricacies of two officers—partners—starting a family and their lives together.

"Too soon to tell." She shook her head. "Cree doesn't let me out of his sight. He tried to convince the chief to take me off duty, but I shut that down the second I found out. I've wasted too much time being scared. I gave up an entire career because of it. Moved to a town I didn't know where I was isolated and alone before getting my head on straight. I let it rule over every decision I made. I'm done with that.

I want to live every moment of the life I have left. On my terms and with the people I love."

Love. The word battered through Riggs's brain until it was all he could think about. He'd been in love before. He'd married, had plans for the future, and when that future hadn't played out, he'd committed himself to the work to try to make up for it. And when the job hadn't fulfilled him, he'd taken a hard look at where his life had derailed, blaming it all on Becker. But with Macie... That word felt different. Real. He'd spent years trying to come to terms with losing Macie and Hazel all in the same week. He'd hitched his life to Becker's, joined the academy, worked his way up the ladder into detective and homicide—none of it had made him feel the way she had in three short days.

"The cases we work, the victims we seek justice for," Majors said. "It takes a toll, doesn't it? Sometimes we forget what's important and who we are. We become the work to the point it's consumed our lives, but take it from me, Riggs, it will never be enough."

She was right. He needed Macie back. Needed to make things right. Because he loved her. The good, the questionable, the obsessive—all of her. A piece of him had been missing the day she'd extracted herself from his life, and he'd only had a taste of what that wholeness had felt like when he'd come to Battle Mountain. He couldn't give it up again. "How did you stop?"

Majors glanced toward the door her partner had exited, that permanent hitch to her mouth deepening. "I realized I didn't have to save the world alone. I could make more of a difference with a partner who had my back in a small town who needs my help more than ever."

Riggs didn't have an answer for that.

Gregson shoved through the front door, fighting back a rush of dirt and wind. "Dr. Miles is sending over the lab results. We should have them in a couple minutes." The former ATF agent took his expected position at his partner's side. "You good?"

"Never better." Majors smiled, and Gregson's face dissolved from duty to outright adoration. His feelings for the woman showed in perfect balance. Not all or nothing, and Riggs couldn't look away from the easiness of it all. These officers trusted one another, would put themselves in harm's way for each other—all the while starting their own lives away from the department.

Gregson's phone pinged with an incoming email. "That should be the lab results." The reserve officer swiped his index finger across the screen, his hard gaze narrowing. "That doesn't make sense."

"What is it?" Riggs rounded the table, trying to get a better look at the screen.

"This says the rash found on the victim's face and hands from the refrigerator was caused by a direct contact reaction to asbestos," Gregson said. "But she was found in a mine."

"A mine?" Hell, there had to be dozens of them in Battle Mountain. The town had been built from the profits and economy of big mining. They weren't any closer to an answer than when they'd started, and the killer wasn't just going to wait for them to catch up. They had to do something now.

"The road Isla's truck's GPS pinged." Majors set her phone back on the table and widened the map view on the screen. "It meets up with Cinnamon Pass, but there's a branch that passes the last mine to be shut down. It's the same one where the chief found that first victim."

"Which one?" He was ready. Not just to fight for Penny and Macie but for their future. And nothing was going to get in his way this time. Especially not himself.

"It's not safe, Riggs." Majors shook her head. "The government shut it down for a reason. None of us know the conditions or if we'll even be able to breathe in there."

He didn't care. He'd already lost everything. Now was his time to step up and take it back. "Which mine, Majors?"

She glanced at her partner, who nodded, then back to Riggs. "Desolation."

Chapter Fourteen

The dark was playing tricks on her mind. She was hallu-cinating the face of the man who'd hidden in the shadows. Or maybe it was her brain mixing up signals. Right? That was the only explanation.

"You…" Macie shoved her heels into the ground, hoping to gain some distance between her and her captor, but she couldn't leave. She couldn't abandon Penny the way she'd abandoned Hazel all those years ago. "How?"

"Uncomfortable, isn't it?" Reagan Allen stood over her, offering his hand to help her up. The lines in his face had deepened since she'd seen him three days ago, his nose a bit more crooked. The strike she'd delivered during their altercation in the woods must have broken it, turning him almost unrecognizable. Such a small difference, but one that changed everything. "Seeing someone for who they really are."

It was all coming back to her now. The flashes of memory she'd tried to bury. His hair was the same color, if speck-led with a few silver strands at the temples. He had a beard now, too. Better to hide his face. All this time, she'd con-vinced herself she would see him coming, that she would know his voice, but the preparation, the fear, the drive she held on to get her through—it'd all been for nothing. He'd been right in front of her this entire time. "You've been hiding in Battle Mountain all these years. You pretended you were a pastry chef and a coffee shop owner and joked with everyone who came into Caffeine and Carbs. Why?"

"I wasn't pretending. I'm a very good pastry chef. I didn't lie about that, and I didn't lie about my background. The pastry world got the best of me. The pressure to compete and become the best after years of study and burns and thousands of hours of pushing myself to the top... I'll be honest. I snapped." Reagan retracted his bandaged hand when she refused to take it. "I found myself in the middle of the woods, walking aimlessly, until I heard two little girls laughing. They were throwing chunks of moss at each other, like nothing in the world could take away their joy. I wanted that. What they had. So I took it."

She couldn't breathe, couldn't think. All of this—the lives stolen, the years living in fear alone and as someone else—had all started because a pastry chef couldn't handle the pressures of his career? She had to suppress the desire to laugh. No, something in him snapped long before that. He'd just needed an excuse to go over the edge entirely.

Reagan latched his hand around her arm and hauled Macie to her feet like she was nothing more than a rag doll. "But to answer your question, killing people requires income, Avalynn. Strategy. Equipment. I had to hold a day job and make myself part of the community. Here, in this pathetic, going nowhere town, I could still do what I did best. Bake. But when that pressure starts getting to me again..."

"You kidnap and murder innocent girls." That was why

she and Riggs hadn't been able to discern a pattern between Hazel's, Sakari's and Penny's abductions. This wasn't compulsion. This was pleasure. A reward for a job well-done.

"You of all people should understand. When the pressure gets to be too much for your job with the department, where do you come?" He didn't wait for an answer, maneuvering her along the tunnel, deeper into the mountain. "My misuse of violence is the same as your misuse of caffeine, Avalynn. They might be different mediums, but we both get what we want in the end. Release."

She tried to memorize every step, to make sure she and Penny took the right way out, but there were too many turns. Too many ways to get lost. "Strangling people and drinking too much coffee aren't the same. I don't hurt anyone."

"True, but to each our own." Reagan led her into a larger cavern. The walls gleamed with metallic flecks that would turn any miner's head. Braces held up the ceiling, angling out to take the weight of the earth above, but she'd read enough stories to know one shift in the rock, one more pound of pressure, could bring it all crumbling down on top of them.

A whimper echoed off the cavern.

Macie ripped her arm out of Reagan's grip. Her heart shot into her throat. She took two more steps inside, searching every corner and shadow. "Penny, is that you?"

"Macie?" The little girl moved into the flashlight beam. The sound of chains rubbing against each other stopped as the fetters pulled tight when Penny tried to run for her.

Macie took another step to meet her but was wrenched back against the killer's chest.

"Ah, ah, ah. I believe that's far enough." He set his mouth

against her ear, triggering a rush of disgust and shivers. "I've seen what the two of you can do when you work together. If you don't mind my caution, I'd prefer you to sit over here." He hauled her to the opposite side of the cavern and forced Macie to sit. "Mind the patch of asbestos." He waved his bandaged hand in front of her. "It's a real buzzkill."

Rock bit into the backs of her thighs and aggravated the soreness from her fall. She stared up into the face of a man she'd trusted with pieces of herself. All this time, he'd just been using them against her. But she'd found Penny. The four-year-old chained a few feet away was the one and only goal. In the end, Macie recalled the turns they'd taken from that original tunnel she'd fallen into. She might not be able to make it back up the shaft to the surface, but Penny could. She just had to get her there.

"Now, don't you worry, Avalynn. There's plenty of time for you and I to get reacquainted with each other. After all, you're going to be here awhile." He turned his back to her, closing in on his younger victim. "Penny, on the other hand—her time is up."

Not as long as Macie could help it. She felt along the wall he'd set her against. It wasn't uncommon for miners to leave tools behind after their shifts, but she couldn't find anything. The killer had ensured nothing could be used as a weapon against him. Except the very earth holding them captive. She ran her hand behind her. Penny's soft cry grew louder now. Macie clutched a section of the wall jutting out, filling her palm with its size. It broke away in her hand, and she clutched it with everything she had left. "Not yet."

Macie shoved to her feet, swinging the rock as hard as she could. The makeshift weapon connected with Reagan's skull. He dropped to his knees, then face-first onto the ground. She didn't have time for victory. She needed every second he was unconscious to get Penny out of the chains and back into the tunnels. After tossing the rock, she collected the killer's flashlight, then darted for the girl. The shackle had been bolted into what looked like a long stretch of railroad steel. There was no way Penny could move in these tunnels with a ton of metal dragging behind her. Macie tested the strength of the anklet. It was bolted shut. No key. No tools in sight, but there had to be something Reagan had used to secure her. "It's okay. I'm here."

"Don't leave me, Macie." Penny latched on to Macie's injured arm, digging her fingernails deep into sensitive skin. "I want to go home. I want Mommy."

"I won't leave you. I promise." Macie ran dirty fingers through the girl's hair. "We have to hurry. Did you see where he put the tool to tighten this?"

Penny pointed past Macie's shoulder. "It's in his pocket."

She turned back. Reagan's outline hadn't moved. He was still unconscious from the look of it, but that could change at any moment. Shifting his weight might even trigger his brain to reboot, but she had to risk it. There wasn't anything else in this cavern that would get Penny free from the cuff. "Stay back."

Macie got to her feet, before approaching Reagan as quietly as an echoing chamber of emptiness allowed. Her stomach rumbled, and she closed her eyes, wishing it to stay quiet. Only her breathing registered. She stilled near his head, then slowly worked her way around to his midsection. He was wearing a coat. Any one of the pockets could hold the tool she needed, but her instincts said he'd used one of his pants pockets so it'd always stay with him. Her exhale sounded too loud in her ears, and she waited to see if it brought Reagan around.

Nothing.

She could do this. For Penny. For all the other little girls who would be caught in the bastard's web if she didn't. Macie bent down, pressing one hand into Reagan's shoulder, and shook him gently. No response. With a last glance toward Penny, she felt her way through his back pockets, then the ones in his jacket that hadn't been pinned between him and raw earth. The tool wasn't there. She took a deep breath.

Then rolled Reagan onto his back.

His head flopped to one side, away from her in the shadow. Macie felt along his front pockets. There. The length of a wrench peeked out from the right side. She slid it free as quickly as she dared. Her heart threatened to beat straight out of her chest. Too hard. Too fast. Steel warmed in her hand as she backed away. She couldn't believe Reagan was still unconscious.

Macie fit the end of the wrench against the bolt keeping Penny hostage and twisted until it started unscrewing. "Almost there."

The bolt hit the ground. Penny was free. She grabbed the flashlight and hauled the girl into her arms. Her injured arm screamed with every movement, but she had to push through. They rushed for the entrance Reagan had brought Macie through. She'd taken a left in. She went right this time. The number of steps had gotten lost sometime in the mix of pain and surprise, but this section of the tunnel looked familiar.

Penny's arms tightened around her neck, keeping her

grounded and in the moment. It'd be easy to panic, to suc-
cumb to the fear they'd never make it out of this maze alive,
but Macie had lived afraid long enough. It was time to start
taking action. No more false identities. No more lies or
distance from the people she so desperately wanted in her
life—people like Penny and Weston and Campbell, even
Easton. No more running. Battle Mountain was her home,
and she was sure as hell going to fight for a life here.

The tunnel came to an abrupt end. Macie pulled up short,
one hand secured at the back of Penny's head. She dropped
the flashlight, giving them just enough light. "We're here,
but you're going to have to climb up this shaft. See?" Macie
pointed straight up, to the hole in the ceiling. "This will take
you right to the surface. I want you to run as fast as you can
to the entrance of the mine and down the road. Understand?"

"You can't climb that. Your arm hurts." The four-year-
old had more awareness than anyone gave her credit for.

"You're right. I can't. I have to find another way out."
Tears burned in Macie's eyes. The chances of finding another way out, without running into Reagan to finish the
job, were slim. But that was the cost of loving someone,
wasn't it? Risking it all. "But you can bet your little behind
I'm going to get out of here. Okay?"

"Promise?" Penny asked.

"Promise." Macie offered her little finger and made it
official. "Okay. Up you go, squirt." It took three tries to
maneuver Penny onto her shoulder to lift her toward the
shaft, but from the stories Kendric and Campbell told, the
troublemaker had gotten herself into far more precarious
situations than this. "Use your feet and grab on to anything
you can. You can do it."

Penny tested the climb out for herself, managing to make it a couple feet.

"Great work. Keep going." The tears were streaking into her hairline now. It didn't look like it, but this was goodbye. "I'll be seeing you soon. Okay?"

"Okay." Penny leveraged her feet against the rock wall and moved up another couple of feet. Faster than Macie expected, she was gone.

Pain exploded across her face as a fist connected with her cheek. She hit the ground. White spots flittered across her vision, blocking out the threat.

Reagan's voice surrounded her a split second before a hand latched around her neck. "I'm so very disappointed in you, Avalynn, and I'm tired of this game."

RIGGS STUDIED THE footprints cast into the dirt leading straight into the mouth of darkness. Too many to get any idea of who'd come and gone. For an abandoned mine, Desolation seemed like the place to be.

Wind rustled through thick pines on either side of the short incline leading up to the entrance. A low whistle reached his ears from inside, almost like a warning. "Light it up."

Both Majors and Gregson powered their flashlights and took a position at his rear. They were headed into an unknowable situation, with an unknowable killer and an unknowable amount of danger. Mines weren't closed or abandoned on a whim. The three of them crossed the threshold into pitch-blackness as one.

Riggs watched his every step. Thick supports braced up along either wall and crossed the ceiling above him in expertly measured intervals. The familiar scent of gravel and humidity dived into his lungs as he searched along the tunnel. His footsteps echoed off the walls the deeper he walked into the mountain. The beam from his flashlight landed on a mound of dirt up ahead. Like someone had dug a hole. In reality, someone had. Weston Ford and Dr. Chloe Miles had dragged a body out of a refrigerator in that hole less than two years ago.

Seemed where this town's history with violence had started, Riggs had the privilege and duty to see it through to the end. "Keep an ear out. Anything out of the ordinary, you send out the warning."

"What's out of the ordinary for a mine that hasn't been operational for six years?" Gregson grunted after a hard thud. His partner had sucker punched him. "Hey, I think it's a valid question."

A pattering reached his ears, and Riggs pulled up short. His instincts homed in on the sound, trying to differentiate it from familiar noises. "Hear that?"

The same rhythm thumped hard from the inky darkness.

And it was growing louder.

"Footsteps," Majors said. "One set. Coming fast."

Riggs unholstered his weapon. Whoever it was, they wouldn't be expecting three armed officers. Since the first time he'd joined this investigation, he and his backup held the advantage here.

"Police!" Gregson's voice rang too loud in Riggs's ears. "Slow down and approach with your hands behind your head."

The footsteps didn't falter.

Tension tightened the tendons along Riggs's neck and

shoulders. Those footsteps. They weren't normal. Weren't heavy. Understanding hit. "Put down your weapons." Riggs broke his position and rushed forward, causing both Gregson and Majors to lower their aim. "Penny?"

A quiet sob joined the rush of footsteps as the girl broke through the shadows. Riggs dropped to his knees, arms out to catch her. She collided with his chest, nearly knocking him off-balance. "It's okay. You're safe, Penny. You're safe." He tried to pry her small face from his shoulder. "Where is Macie?"

"She couldn't climb up with me. Her arm was hurt. She said to run as fast as I could." Penny wiped grimy fingers across her face. "I did what she said. Can I go home now? Can I please go home?"

Couldn't climb? His brain worked to translate a four-year-old's perspective. Climbing could mean a shaft. If Macie had fallen, she could be hurt. Not to mention she was still being hunted by a killer. "Penny, where did you climb from?"

"Back there in the tunnel." The girl pointed behind her. Into the unknown. "She pushed me up inside, and I climbed all the way up. Just like she told me. Before the bad man got us."

"The bad man's here?" He felt more than saw her nod. That was all the information he needed. Riggs handed Penny over to Majors, who instantly secured her arms around the girl. He had no doubt the duo who'd had his back would do whatever it took to keep Penny safe. "Radio her parents. Tell them where we are, and make sure you get her home to them."

Gregson stepped forward. "You can't go in there alone, man. This place is a maze. You'll never make it out."

"Albuquerque caves aren't too different from Battle Mountain mines, and I've investigated plenty of them." Riggs removed his jacket and rolled up his sleeves. The less he had to carry, the better. Never knew when the walls would start closing in. "Just make sure she gets home."

"At least take one of our radios and an extra flashlight. We'll send another unit your way as soon as we can." Gregson stretched out his hand. "Good luck."

Riggs shook, feeling that spark of partnership and community for the first time in years. He'd had that once. With Becker. Hell, he wasn't sure he'd ever feel it again. He accepted the extra equipment. "Thanks."

He didn't wait to watch them take Penny back to the patrol car. Every second Macie was down here was another second she might not make it out alive, and he just couldn't live with that outcome. Not after everything it'd taken for him to get her back in his life. He was here for her, and he wasn't going anywhere until she was back in his arms.

The mine seemed to breathe around him, fluctuations in smells and some kind of breeze changing with every step. Places like this had to have airflow to avoid gasses getting trapped in certain rooms where miners had been working, but the possibility of death at every turn kept his nerves at a high point. It was worth it. Every risk, every potential for a life-ending step. For Macie.

The ground sloped downward, taking him deeper into the belly of the beast. He wasn't sure how far he'd gone or if he was even walking in a straight line anymore. The walls were more narrow here, funneling him into unfamiliar territory. Rocks reached out and grabbed for his gun, his extra flashlight, his shirt. They were everywhere, but none of it detracted from that feeling of being watched. The same feeling he'd experienced in the woods before losing Penny a second time.

"I'll give you until the count of three to release her and come out with your hands behind your back." His words echoed back to him.

"Detective Karig, I knew we'd meet again." It was the same voice. The one that'd haunted Riggs's nightmares for the past two days. "Unfortunately, Macie is unavailable at the moment. Perhaps I can take a message. Let her know you'd stopped by when she's conscious. You see, she took somewhat of a nasty fall. She's going to need to save her energy. You understand."

Riggs halted his approach. As much as he wanted to believe his senses, he couldn't trust them in a place like this. He'd learned that the hard way when he'd gotten stabbed in the thigh. Clutching his flashlight, he hit the power button and cast himself into darkness. Relying only on what he could see would waste time. Time Macie didn't have. "You're trapped in here, you son of a bitch. BMPD has the place surrounded. Every exit. There's no way out for you, and the more time you stall, the worse it's going to be. Why not save yourself the trouble?"

"Where's the fun in that?" the killer asked.

The air shifted, and Riggs took a step back a split second before a blade slashed across his face. He grabbed for where he believed the killer's upper body to be and clenched both hands into the bastard's shoulders. Riggs thrust his head forward and connected with flesh and bone. His shoulder screamed at the impact, but he only pushed himself harder.

The killer cried out.

Riggs threw a right hook and landed a hard blow. The blade whined again. He caught the killer's wrist and tucked his shoulder beneath the man's rib cage. Hauling him overhead, Riggs slammed Penny's abductor to the ground. He fought to take a whole breath. "You are under arrest for the abduction of Penny Dwyer, for the abduction of Macie Barclay, wanted in the questioning of Sakari Vigil's murder, wanted for questioning of Hazel McAdams's murder, for killing my partner, Kevin Becker, and whatever the hell else I can pin on you."

He unholstered his cuffs and dragged the killer into the flashlight beam. Disbelief crushed air from his lungs, and his grip faltered. The baker from the coffee shop? All this time, he'd been watching Macie, getting her to trust him. Riggs ratcheted the cuffs into place. "The building Becker was found strangled. It was your building, the one that burned. You lured him there, didn't you? Right before you killed him. Why?"

"You know, I couldn't believe it when he walked right into my bakery asking if I knew of anyone named Macie Barclay. He told me everything," Reagan said. "How he believed she was part of a murder investigation from twenty-five years ago in Albuquerque. That he needed to find her to ask her about the day her best friend had been abducted and murdered. You see, Avalynn made a mistake. She's been investigating Hazel's case all this time, relying on others to get her the information she needed. Seemed one of them spilled the beans to Becker, and he came running. But I wasn't going to let him take her from me."

Riggs tightened the cuffs more than needed. "She's not yours, you son of a bitch."

"She's not yours either, Detective. Did you really think after staying under the radar for twenty-five years, this would be easy? You arrest me, Avalynn dies." Reagan Allen heaved to catch his breath. Blood leaked from a gash on his head, bruising darkening his nose and cheekbones. Nothing like the man who'd given him a donut a few days ago. "You're going to have to make a choice. Take me into the station or keep Avalynn from dying a horrible, painful death. You couldn't save your partner. Are you going to save the woman you love?"

Riggs shoved the bastard against the opposite wall. "Where is she?"

"I'll give you a clue as soon as you get me out of these cuffs," he said.

Variables raced through his mind. Arrest Reagan and save dozens—if not hundreds—of more girls just like Penny and Hazel, or save the one woman he couldn't see himself live without.

"I'll take it from here." Another flashlight brightened in Riggs's peripheral vision, blocking out the man behind the beam. A ten-gallon hat took shape in the shadows as he sauntered closer with all the time in the world. "Seems Mr. Allen and I sure have a lot to talk about anyway."

Riggs raised one hand to protect his retinas. "Who the hell are you?"

"I'm the chief of this town, Detective." A man, similar in stature and features as Easton Ford, stepped into the light. Maybe a few years younger. A day's worth of beard growth intensified the sharp angles of his oval face and brought out the seriousness in his eyes. The rightful chief lowered his flashlight with one hand and aimed his sidearm at Reagan

Allen with the other. "You've done good. Now, I'm going to need you to bring my dispatcher home. My entire department is falling apart without her. Take the radio. I've got this covered."

"Yes, sir." A renewed energy lit him up from the inside, but without Reagan's clue as to where he'd set up Macie, he was looking for a needle in a five-mile deep mine haystack. Horrible, painful death. That was what Reagan had said. The killer's MO had stuck with strangulation thus far. All past victims had suffocated. He wanted the control, to make them suffer and lead them through a slow death.

Riggs didn't believe the bastard would change at the end. He'd have her somewhere that was possible. In a mine, that could mean a small room with low oxygen or a contraption that applied pressure. His instincts said the former was the easiest to set up quickly. He just had to find her in time. "Macie!"

Chapter Fifteen

Her name spliced through the comforting warmth she'd buried herself inside. *Macie!*

Heavy. Everywhere. Her fingers had gone numb. She couldn't feel her feet. Something was strapped over her nose and mouth. The forced air froze her nostrils and throat. But the pain in her arm had settled to a dull ache. How was that possible?

"You got your wish, Detective," a female voice said. "She's coming around. I'll give you two a minute."

Macie willed her eyes to open. Dim lighting infiltrated her cracked lids. There were no lights in the mine, but she'd had a flashlight. A dark outline blocked the assault, and every muscle she owned tightened with battle-ready tension. Reagan. She gripped something cold and solid, ready to fight back with everything she had left. No matter how weak she felt.

"Macie, it's me," he said.

She knew that voice, but this had to be some kind of dream. Her brain synapses were probably firing all kinds of information in the last minutes of her life. Riggs wasn't here. Reagan had won. He'd finally claimed her in the end.

A calloused hand smoothed over hers. So real. "You were down in the mine. You fought back, and we arrested Reagan Allen. You're in the hospital now. You did it, Macie. You brought him down. You found Hazel's killer."

Was this...real? She wouldn't make that up, would she? The feel of his hand in hers felt solid. If this wasn't real, she sucked at coming up with ideas of heaven, that was for sure. This place was worse than the cabin in the desert. Macie tested her hold on him, and a sob broke free. "Am I dead?"

"No, Red. You're very much not dead," he said.

"It's over?" She'd spent years trying to find the man who'd killed her best friend, but there was only one small soul she cared about right then. Her throat convulsed around the dryness. The memories were there. No sense in burying them this time. It wouldn't make the pain go away. Just as trying to forget what she'd done to Hazel hadn't destroyed her grief. Macie tried to bring her hand to her face. Her fingers collided with a rubbery mask. An oxygen mask. "Penny. Where's—"

"She's home." Riggs's face cleared with every inhale. So stupidly handsome. This was real. He was here. He threaded his hand in her hair, and her skin goose bumped at his touch. "She's got a couple scrapes and bruises, but she's been checked out. She had very little exposure to the asbestos, it turns out, and she should live a long and happy life. Because of you."

Penny was safe. The weightlessness of that truth took the oxygen straight out of her lungs. She closed her eyes as the past slipped from her grip and a bright future took hold. It was over. She was free. Reagan Allen would pay for what he'd done to those girls, and she could finally choose a life on her terms. "What happened?"

"Reagan trapped you in one of the small ventless caverns. The gasses from the mine were pretty strong. Doctors weren't sure you'd ever wake up with oxygen levels as low as yours." Anguish shook his voice, and Riggs tightened his hold in her hair. "I don't know how long you were in there, but you were close to dead when I found you. It's a miracle you're still here. I don't know what I would've done if I hadn't gotten to you in time. You've been out of it for about three days. I thought I might have to go beat the living daylights out of Reagan if you didn't wake up."

"What do you mean?" Her heart rate picked up the pace. She didn't dare hope. Not yet. Because hope led to disappointment and hurt, and she didn't want to go through that again. He'd accused her of only looking out for herself. Said that she hadn't changed from that selfish ten-year-old he'd known.

"I mean I was wrong." He tested a cut across her temple, so gentle and warm. Riggs wasn't looking at her, not directly. "About everything. About this case, about you. I found the files, Macie. In your duffel bag. You never said anything. You've been looking for Reagan Allen all this time."

What was there to say? Of course, she had. "It was my fault Hazel died. I was just trying to—"

"To make it right." That unreadable gaze was on her then, and the world threatened to tip on its axis. He had that power—the one that changed her perception and made her forget anything else existed. He could turn her world upside down in the blink of an eye, and she wouldn't even mind.

Because she trusted he would put it right back where it belonged. Riggs interlaced his fingers with hers and traced her busted knuckles with his thumb. "You risked your life all these years trying to identify the man in the woods, knowing what would happen if you did so. You left your family, ended friendships, went on the run. You sacrificed an entire life to bring him down. You knew any steps you took could alert Reagan to what you were doing, and you did it anyway."

She didn't know what to say to that.

"And I was wrong, Macie." He kissed the back of her hand, triggering a whirlwind of butterflies in her stomach. "You're not the same girl I knew back then. Not even a little bit. You're so much more. You're brave, and selfless, and loving. You're everything I want in my life and everything I've been pushing away, and I love you, damn it. I always have. And I'm sorry I wasted what little time we've had trying to prove I don't need you. Because I do. All of you."

She wanted to believe him. She wanted every word out of his mouth to be true. Macie swallowed around the ache in her throat. The mask was making it hard to breathe, despite the steady flow of oxygen, and she moved to pull it down. "You broke my heart, Riggs. You told me you didn't want me in your life—just as you told Becker you didn't want him in yours anymore—and then you left me in that cabin to protect myself after everything we'd been through. What's going to stop you from cutting ties the next time? What's going to happen when you realize this isn't what you signed up for?"

He focused on their hands intertwined. "I will have to live with those decisions for the rest of my life, Macie, and believe me, it won't be easy. You know the toll it can take. Your mistakes. You've been living with that, too." Riggs retracted his hand from her hair. "I was so convinced I'd been following Becker's career instead of my own path, I rebelled against everything he ever taught me. I'd relied on him for so long, I didn't know if I could catch his killer. Then I found you."

He brought his attention back to her, and an epic shift stripped him of that invisible armor he'd carried since they'd met. "You showed me the worst parts of myself and the best. You showed me what trust feels like and that it can change your entire life. Without you as my partner, Reagan would still be out there, Penny might be dead and I'd spend the rest of my life agonizing over the one case I couldn't ever solve. I'd die just like Becker. Alone, worked to death and without hope. You gave me purpose. You showed me experiencing life comes with letting people in and believing there is good in them. I came to Battle Mountain broken, Macie. You made me strong enough to fix myself. How on earth am I supposed to walk away from all that? From you?"

Her lungs shuddered on a shaky inhale. The tears were back, but they were different than they'd been over the past few days. He loved her. She was the woman he wanted to be with, and for the first time since she'd left Hazel in those woods, she felt whole. No pieces of her missing. She had everything she needed right here. "You know, if you'd just started with that, you could already be kissing me, Detective."

"You got it, Red." Riggs leaned forward off his chair, pressing his mouth to hers. Heat speared through her as he tested her lips, then penetrated the seam of her mouth.

Fisting his shirt in both hands, she dragged him fully into the bed and laid one on him. "I love you, too."

"That's what I like to hear." His laugh diluted the remaining ache in her chest and limbs. "Careful of the shoulder. I'm still recovering from a stab wound."

"We've worked around it once before, and you're still alive." Her arm hadn't been placed in a sling, but she could still feel the muscle soreness from when she'd hit the mine floor after she'd fallen down the shaft. Whatever the case, they could tend to each other's wounds. Physical, mental, emotional. They had all the time in the world.

"I guess now is as good a time as any to ask." Riggs framed her jaw with one hand. "What were you doing with those teddy bears in your sleeping bag in the woods after you downed all that coffee?"

Macie considered her next words very carefully. As much as she loved Riggs, some stories were best left to be doled out in portions. Not an avalanche. Although it would be fun to see his reaction. "You know that secret you promised me and Hazel to never tell? The one where—"

"We made a blood oath, Macie." Shock contorted his handsome face. Riggs straightened, setting one finger over her heart. Right where he'd taken up space. "I still have the scar in my palm to prove it. We promised never to speak of it again."

She raised her hand in the Scout's honor. "And I haven't. I swear, but…" Macie bit her lip, dragging this out as long as possible. It was fun seeing him like this. A combination of the kid he'd been and the man he'd become. It was the start of something new, and she couldn't wait to see what happened next. "The caffeine may have convinced me you and Hazel were the bears."

"You threw a tea party in the middle of the woods with a bunch of stuffed bears." Not a question. But he wasn't running from the room, either.

"It's one of my favorite memories, even if I'm not allowed to talk about it, and I was hopped up on caffeine." She actually didn't remember a whole lot of that night, but she remembered one thing: she'd been happy imagining him and Hazel there. "Do you blame me?"

"I'm never going to be able to unsee that in my head." Riggs locked that molten gaze on her and maneuvered closer. "What did my bear look like?"

"Oh, he was definitely the most handsome. Had the softest hair." She skimmed her fingers through his short hair. "The darkest eyes. And you know what else? He didn't complain about the tea I made."

"Now I know you're making this all up." He leaned back into her, taking her mouth with his, and a flood of laughter caught her by surprise. "But the oath still applies. We're never talking about that tea party again."

HIS TRANSFER WAS OFFICIAL.

The papers had taken a week, and Macie didn't know anything about it yet, but Riggs had no intention of returning to Albuquerque. Not when his life was here in Battle Mountain. From now until she said otherwise, he worked for BMPD.

He hiked the long dirt driveway leading up to Whispering Pines Ranch, his hand in Macie's. She'd hit every milestone her doctor had set for her in the hospital, blowing everyone's expectations out of the water and granting herself an early discharge. She did that. Surprised him at every turn, and he couldn't wait to see where she led them next. He caught a hint of a wheeze as they neared the large main cabin up ahead, and Riggs intentionally stopped to check his bootlaces.

"I know what you're doing," she said.

He couldn't stall anymore. She'd caught him in the act. Riggs straightened, taking her hand in his again. They were late, but he didn't care. The more time he got her to himself before they each went back to work, the better. "I don't know what you're talking about."

"Sure, you don't." She bumped her shoulder into his as they continued up the too long driveway. "I'm fine. You were there when the doctor said there's going to be some adjustment off the oxygen. The wheezing is normal."

"I could go without the snoring, though." Riggs chanced a glance at her, trying not to smile.

She shoved him away. Shock widened those brilliant green eyes. "I do not snore!"

This was what he loved about them. The easiness, the fluidity between subjects, as if they were reading each other's minds. In truth, he didn't mind the snoring. Just meant she was still in bed with him and not getting wise enough to ditch him for some other guy. Reagan Allen had been arrested and charged for the deaths of Hazel McAdams, Kevin Becker and Sakari Vigil, and it looked like his lawyer was going to get him to plead guilty to avoid the death penalty. The district attorney—Easton Ford's fiancée—would make sure there would be no leniency. The bandage on Reagan's hand had revealed an allergic reaction to asbestos, which sealed the deal of his involvement. Riggs's partner's remains had been released, and without any family to claim Becker, Riggs had taken the old man's burial upon himself. What better place than a small town no one had heard of and where Becker had done one last good deed? "I promise not to tell anyone."

"Thank you." Macie dragged him back to her side and hooked her arm in his. "After all, I have a reputation to uphold."

Jagged peaks fought to pierce the bright blue sky. A gaggle of geese called over rocky canyons and high valley floors. He'd noted a crystalline river flowing alongside the dirt road they'd taken up here, promising adventure and spurred endless exploration, before it widened into an impossibly green-blue lake nestled in a small valley. No matter where he looked, the possibility captivated him all over again. Yeah. He could get used to this.

Riggs led her up to the main cabin adorned with a bright green roof and trim. Smaller satellite cabins had been positioned no more than a few hundred yards in every direction. From what Macie had told him, Whispering Pines Ranch had started as the Ford homestead but had since become more bed-and-breakfast since the death of their old man last year. Since then, Easton Ford had built a rehabilitation center on the other side of the property. Riggs could just make out the roof through the trees. This place… It definitely wasn't a tree house.

"Aunt Macie!" Penny Dwyer practically lunged down the cabin's steps and raced for Macie's arms.

"Oh, my gosh. Did you somehow get bigger since the last time I saw you?" Macie hugged the girl tight, and Riggs's gut clenched as he envisioned what lay ahead for them. He'd never really thought about a family given his circumstances and background, but seeing Macie's incredible smile on a bunch of kids would be worth thinking about. "You nearly knocked me over."

"No, I didn't!" Penny laughed.

"You made it." Campbell followed behind her daughter, Kendric positioned at the top of the stairs, watching over his girls. "I was starting to think you'd changed your mind."

"And miss one of Karie's legendary breakfasts? You're out of your mind." Macie let the four-year-old lead her back into the cabin ahead of Riggs, but he was stopped at the top of the stairs.

Kendric Hudson stretched out his hand. "Detective, I just wanted to say thank you. For everything you did to find Penny. I can't imagine where we would be if you and Macie hadn't fought for our daughter. I'm honored to start working with you."

"Same here." Riggs shook, this time without worrying if he was about to die, and nodded to Campbell on the way inside.

Heat closed in on him the moment he stepped over the threshold. A massive stone fireplace climbed two stories up the open main living space. Builder grade wood, lighter than the exterior of the cabin, absorbed the sunlight penetrating through floor-to-ceiling windows on one end of the house. A frayed multicolored crocheted rug took up a majority of the hardwood floor. A small carved bear holding a bowl of fruit demanded attention from the table that stretched the length of the back of the dark leather sofa, with similar carvings strategically positioned around the open kitchen and against the grand staircase leading to the second level. Handcrafted lamps, varying shades of animal fur and muted nature paintings finished the space in old-style hunter decor. This wasn't just a place for people to live. It was a home. Something he'd never had.

Macie smiled at him from her position at the kitchen counter. There were a lot more guests here than he thought there would be. Easton Ford toasted a cup of coffee his way with one hand, his other interlaced with a dark-haired woman in a wheelchair at the head of the massive wood table. From what he could tell, the older Ford and Genevieve would have some news of their own to announce soon given the size of her lower abdomen. A blonde—the coroner—laughed at something Weston Ford said in her ear while an older woman came to collect the baby from her arms.

Everyone was smiling, joking, at ease with each other. Macie seemed right at home, sneaking fresh fruit from the arrangement on the counter. And he…didn't know how to do this. The closest thing he'd had to family was Becker, and he'd screwed that up to hell and back.

"Don't make direct eye contact. They'll sense your fear." Isla Vachs clenched a cup of coffee, positioning it in front of her mouth as she spoke beside him. The former EMT turned reserve officer tried not to smile at him. And failed. "It's a little overwhelming, isn't it? How invested in each other they all are. You'll get used to it, but if you show any hesitation, they'll throw you in the deep end, make you tell them your whole life story and take personal responsibility to fix it."

"You sound as though you're speaking from experience." Riggs scanned the massive living room. "You're missing the giant you usually have following you around."

"Adan's trying to get a handful of glitter out of his hair for the third time today." Her smile finally gave into a full-blown flash of brilliance. "Mazi believes the world can always use more glitter. In our food, in our bed. Her new idea was in Adan's duffel bag. The whole thing exploded in his face when he opened it."

"Looks like you got hit, too." He pointed at her neck where Isla seemed to sparkle past human capabilities. He had the distinct impression that hadn't been from a duffel bag, though. More like transfer. "I never got to thank you for hiding us out in that dust bowl of yours in the middle of the desert."

"Anything for Macie. Actually, anything for these guys." Isla hugged her coffee into her chest. "That experience you're talking about. We all have it in spades. There isn't a single one of these people who wouldn't have mine or Adan's or Mazi's backs if we asked, and I wouldn't be here if it weren't for them. I was an outsider. I came out here after I lost everything, and this department welcomed me and Mazi with open arms. They took us in. Made us part of the family."

Riggs didn't understand that. Albuquerque PD had housed nearly nine hundred officers, detectives, administration and specialized department members. Sure, he'd gone out for beers and darts a few times with his fellow teammates, and when the situation called for it, he could trust his brothers and sisters in blue to be at his side. They didn't have brunch together. They didn't hand off their kids to be held by someone else or throw a piece of fruit at another officer's face. He hadn't even done any of that with Becker. Their relationship had been about the work. About saving lives. This… What BMPD had here was more than a department. This was a community. One he wanted to be part of. "That doesn't sound so bad."

"It's not. It's…kind of nice." Isla peeled off to meet Adan coming down the hall, and Riggs worked through the small crowd to join back up with Macie.

"Coffee, Riggs?" Alma Majors lifted a fresh pot and took a mug from the cabinet, Gregson not far from her side.

"Yes, ma'am, but there's something I gotta do first." Riggs dropped down onto one knee in front of Macie, memorizing every change in her expression. "Macie Barclay, Avalynn Davis, whatever the hell you want to be called, I've wasted enough time trying to go through life on my own." He produced the small gold band with diamonds set in intervals all the way around. "I'm ready to have a partner again. Forever."

The room went quiet, all eyes on them.

Macie's face lit up, and Riggs couldn't get enough of the sight. "You're talking about Adan, aren't you?"

"He's not really my type." Riggs slid one hand beneath hers and pushed the engagement band into place on her finger. "But I'm sure we could work something out, isn't that right, Adan?"

"I told you. We're seeing other people, Karig," Adan said. "It's over."

Laughter filled the room.

"Does this mean I'm going to have to give Cree his vial of blood back?" Macie asked.

He should've been surprised at her question, but it was only one of the things that made Macie so unique and impossible to resist. "Only if you agree to marry me."

"In that case." She dipped her hand into her slacks pocket and pulled a necklace with what looked like an actual vial of blood hanging from the middle. "I'm not going to need this anymore." She tossed the vial at Gregson and launched herself down into Riggs's arms.

The momentum knocked his bum leg off-balance, and they toppled to the floor. Hoots and hollers exploded throughout the living room, followed by a handful of clapping as Macie pressed her mouth to his.

This was it. Everything he'd wanted since he'd been ten years old and in love with a girl way out of his league.

And it'd only taken about twenty-five years and a serial killer to get to her.

* * * * *

WYOMING MOUNTAIN MURDER

JUNO RUSHDAN

To the gung ho Rushdan tribe. You are my everything.

Chapter One

"He's going to kill me."

Charlie Sharp recognized the panicked voice on the other end of the burner phone. It was a VIP client. A woman who not only took classes with her but also was in the process of using some of Charlie's *off-the-books* services.

"Slow down." Cradling her cell phone between her ear and shoulder, she turned the key in the dead bolt and finished locking up for the night. "Did he find out you're planning to leave him?" She adjusted the strap of her gym bag on her shoulder. "Tell me what happened."

Haley groaned, as if in agonizing pain.

A fist of tension gathered in Charlie's chest. She understood all too well the type of brutality her client—*her friend*—endured at the hands of her monstrous husband. Charlie tried not to get too close to any of the customers who came to Underground Self-Defense—USD—the school she'd built all on her own. There were hazards in getting emotionally attached, but she had a soft spot for survivors of domestic violence and invariably got sucked into their lives.

"Haley, talk to me."

"There's no time. He hurt me pretty bad." Haley sobbed

over the line. "You have to help me." The terror in her voice was palpable, chilling Charlie's blood. "Oh, God, he's coming back."

The call disconnected.

For a moment, Charlie stared at the screen, thinking. Should she call Haley back? If her husband heard the phone ringing, would it only make him angrier?

The same applied for a text message.

Charlie hopped in her Dodge Hellcat, tossing her bag in the passenger's seat, and cranked the engine. Tearing out of the parking lot behind her USD school, she hit the side street, Garfield, and then at the stop sign made a right onto Third, the main road through town.

Once she cleared downtown, taking Highway 230, the Snowy Range Road, she gunned the accelerator, pushing the seven hundred horsepower supercharged V-8 of her leather-lined beast to the max.

Logic told her to call the police. That was what a reasonable person would do in a potentially life-threatening scenario.

But Charlie couldn't, for the same reason Haley had called her instead of the cops.

Haley's husband was a detective in the Laramie Police Department. His brothers in blue had protected him countless times. Looking the other way. Not filing reports. Her husband's threats had always coerced Haley not to press charges against him no matter how badly he'd beaten her. The cycle of abuse simply continued.

Drawing in a deep breath, Charlie struggled to suppress her own childhood memories. Of her mother's screams. The sight of her bruises. The endless excuses she had made to justify her husband's violent nature.

The first six years of her life, Charlie had grown up in a constant state of fear.

Fear of what would set off her father the next time. The television tuned to the wrong show. Dinner not ready on time. Meat loaf served when he had a craving for fried chicken. Back talk from her mother. Charlie playing with her dolls too loudly. Sometimes it was just the weather. Too hot. Too muggy. Too much snow.

Sometimes there wasn't any reason at all, except that her dad was a cruel man, who didn't need one.

On and on it went until the summer she turned seven.

That was when her life changed forever.

She cut left, taking the turn for the dirt road that led out to the Olsen ranch. The twenty acres had been divided between the two brothers. Seth had Ranch B, eight acres with a lake large enough for fishing. The other brother, Abel, who had Down syndrome, had gotten Ranch A, with more acreage and the pig farm.

The road forked. She took the right path, headed for Seth's place. Slowing down, she didn't want to give the impression that she had been driving like a bat out of hell or skid as she navigated the ruts of the gravel road. The dread that had been gnawing at her since Haley's desperate phone call took another bite.

Beyond the wrought-iron arches that had Olsen scrolled along the top, the modest house appeared in the moonlight. Charlie stared with apprehension at the small wooden cabin. It was so plain and simple. And *dark*. Haley's car, a white sedan, was parked in front of the attached garage. From the windows, nothing stirred inside the house.

Charlie brought her Dodge to a stop on the path before reaching the garage, far away from the house, and stuffed her cell phone in the pocket of her leggings.

Hopping out of the car, she hustled around to the trunk and popped it open. She fished around in the crate that she kept back there and found a flashlight. The big metal one, long and thick with hefty weight. In a pinch, she could use it as a weapon.

Closing the trunk, she scanned the area. There was nothing nearby. No other houses. No odd sounds. Only the trees swaying in the quiet, the croaking frogs and crickets, and the lake behind the house. She couldn't even make out Ranch A in the distance.

The night air smelled of dying lake grass and still water, and held the heat of the day.

A breeze stirred the birch limbs overhanging the house. As she approached the sagging wooden porch, there were no sounds coming from inside the cabin. No yelling. No crying.

Nothing but an eerie stillness. Goose bumps prickled her arms. She rubbed them away as she marched across the overgrown lawn.

Was Haley okay? Was Seth still there?

His car wasn't parked outside.

But why was the house so dark?

Something about this was off, wrong. So wrong. She crept up the rickety porch steps, each groan from the wood warning her to tread carefully. Floorboards creaked as she drew closer to the front door.

There was no bell on the jamb. She pulled open the screen

door; hinges in need of WD-40 squeaked. With two knuckles, she rapped on the door, and it yawned open like someone hadn't closed it all the way for the latch to catch.

"Hello?" she called out.

No answer.

Haley could be unconscious, bleeding to death. Or worse. Seth was pond scum. Well, actually, he was lower than pond scum. He was the type who would leave his wife injured, alone, in desperate need of medical attention, and in the dark for sheer spite.

The type of man Charlie wouldn't spit on if he was on fire.

She nursed her anger to keep at bay the worry flitting around her belly like fireflies.

"Hello? Haley?" Every muscle tightened as she listened intently, straining to pick up the slightest whimper.

Still not a peep.

Forget about trespassing if it meant she could save a life. She stepped over the threshold, letting the screen door slam shut, and edged into the house.

With a sense of foreboding ballooning inside her, she slowly eased deeper, into the living room. She pressed the button on her flashlight, the sound of the click reassuring, but it didn't turn on. Shaking it, she hoped the problem was just a short and that the flashlight might at least flicker.

No luck. The batteries were dead. She usually changed them once a year. But there should be a new twelve pack of D cell alkaline batteries in the trunk.

She debated going back outside to change the ones that weren't working. But it was better to find Haley first. Every second counted in a life-or-death situation. It had taken

Charlie twenty minutes to get there. No telling how much damage Seth had done to Haley in that amount of time. Broken bones? Swollen eyes? Internal bleeding? Concussion?

All good incentives to hurry.

The curtains were drawn back, letting in plenty of moonlight for her to see. She wanted to avoid touching light switches or much of anything if this turned out to be a worst-case scenario—a crime scene.

In the living room, a tired leather sofa faced a fireplace and flat-screen TV. Magazines covered the coffee table: everything from gossip rags, recipes, to *National Geographic*. An ashtray filled with cigarette butts sat on top of a *TV Guide*.

She stepped into a bedroom. Looked like the primary. A king-size bed with a blue-and-white quilt dominated the space, only leaving room for a couple of nightstands. On one of the bedside tables was a glass of water. Moving on, Charlie peeked her head into a cramped bathroom next door. The shower curtain was pulled back, revealing an empty tub. But something on the sink caught her eye.

Dark spots on the porcelain gleamed in the moonlight. She stepped inside and leaned over the sink for a closer look.

Blood.

Not much. Only a few drops. Maybe from a nosebleed. But it was enough to spur her on quickly throughout the rest of the house.

The dense, muggy air was thick as soup indoors thanks to the lack of air-conditioning.

She came to a second bedroom, similar to the first and also empty. From the hall, she entered the kitchen, coming up to the peninsula on the right side. The space was small and jam-packed, even with just the basics and a slim top freezer fridge.

But the back door was wide open.

She walked around the peninsula and halted.

A bright spill of moonlight, cutting through the kitchen, spotlighted a swath of something dark smeared on the floor all the way out through the back door. She stared at the grimy strip. It wasn't mud.

Glancing around the kitchen, she saw more. Splattered on the cabinets and wall.

Was it blood?

Panic welled up inside her. She edged closer to the trail on the floor, careful not to step in it. Squatting, she held up her phone, activated the light and illuminated the smear.

Oh, God. Definitely blood. Black. Sticky. And a lot of it. *Everywhere.*

Dizziness swept over her, like the wind had been knocked right out of her.

Regaining her equilibrium, she could only gape as the full import of what she saw registered. Then she was struck by a wave of horror. Outrage. Utter disbelief.

She swallowed with difficulty, tasting bile, struggling to regain control of her emotions.

"No," she whispered to herself. But her gaze swept across the kitchen, skated over the back porch, out to the grass.

It was true.

That was the kind of appalling trail left behind after dragging a bloody body.

Charlie wasn't sure if the blood led to the lake, where a corpse could've been weighted down in the water, or to the garage, where it could've been loaded into the trunk of a car and disposed of elsewhere.

She stood, and skirting the edge of the blood, went out onto the porch and headed toward the lake, to see if she could spot anything in the water. Not wanting to step in the evidence, she stayed clear of the possible path of blood.

Sweat dripped down her spine. Her stomach churned.

She dialed Haley's number and desperately hoped. Hoped that it hadn't been her body dragged out of the house. Hoped that the woman had finally gotten the upper hand on her abuser and killed him before he got to her first.

Charlie knew how to handle a situation like that. How to help Haley get through it.

The call went straight to voice mail.

The sliver of hope withered inside her, leaving a bitter taste in her mouth. Guilt clogged her throat.

What was she going to do?

Calling the police was a necessity. But it was also something she would not, could *not* do.

The boys in blue would use the good ole boy system and do whatever was possible to protect one of their own. Somehow the line of questioning would implicate Charlie instead of Seth. She was the one at the crime scene. Hell, she'd just contaminated it.

Then Charlie's off-the-books services would inevitably be discovered.

No. Calling the cops was out of the question.

So, she did the next best thing and dialed the one person in the world she trusted.

"Hello," Rocco Sharp answered.

Technically, he was her cousin, but they were as close as siblings and she loved him like a brother.

"I need help. I've got a problem."

"Make it quick. I'm working. Can't stay on the phone long."

As a Bureau of Alcohol, Tobacco, Firearms and Explosives agent assigned to a special joint task force in town, there was no telling what work entailed for him this evening because he couldn't discuss it.

"Haley Olsen called me. He was beating her again. I'm out at their place. I think Seth did something to her. Killed her."

"Sure you're not overreacting?" Rocco asked. "Look, I get that Haley, her situation, is a trigger for you."

Seeing any abused woman sparked Charlie's anger, and she wasn't unwilling to accept that she might be more sensitive to Haley's circumstances since it reminded her of her mother. Woman married to a violent cop who was protected by the force. Charlie had already lived through the nightmare once and knew how that story was going to end.

Maybe it already had.

"I'm not overreacting. It's dark inside the house," Charlie said. "And I found blood. Lots of blood. Like there was a body that was moved. No sign of Haley or Seth, but her car is still here. Her phone goes straight to voice mail."

Rocco swore. "You broke into the house?"

"The door was open."

More curses from him stung her ear. "This is bad."

Squeezing her eyes shut, she nodded to herself. "I know."

"You're always up to your neck in trouble," he said, and

she didn't bother trying to deny it since it was true. "You've got to call 911."

"No way." She shook her head, a reflex even though he couldn't see her. "If you were here, I *might* consider it. Otherwise—"

"I can't come. I'm sort of stuck in a situation outside of Laramie." Rocco sighed. "But I can send someone else."

There was no one else she trusted. No one who would give her the benefit of the doubt. No one who would take her at her word. Not like Rocco. And he was out of town. "Who could you possibly send?"

"Someone who'd be on your side. That's what you need."

She groaned at the lack of a name. "I need to know."

"Bradshaw," he gritted out.

"What? Is this a sick joke?" Brian Bradshaw was one of them. "He's a cop." Which made him the last person she wanted getting involved. Better for her to hightail it out of there right now.

"He's a friend. With a badge. He can look out for you. Act as a buffer between you and the rest of the Laramie PD."

Technically, his friend was on loan from the police department, currently assigned to the same joint task force as her cousin. During the time they had worked together, she was painfully aware that the two guys had grown close. Hung out. Had dinner. Watched football games. She often teased Rocco about their bromance, but that did not mean she trusted their mutual acquaintance to protect her back.

Clutching the phone tighter, she hated the idea for more reasons than she was able to count. She would do anything to avoid that man.

Brian Bradshaw had an insidious way of staying so warm

and upbeat, regardless of how icy and rude she was to him on purpose. His unflappable congeniality rankled her senseless. No one was that nice. All the time. He was hiding something behind his saccharine facade and annoyingly handsome face. One she admittedly enjoyed looking at too much. Even though no man would ever make her go weak in the knees or soft in the head, no matter how attractive he was. But Brian was simply too much…of everything. Too talkative. Too ingratiating. Too persistent.

Not that any of it mattered because everything boiled down to one insurmountable fact.

He was a cop.

Just like her father.

It was bad enough her cousin was an ATF agent. Although she had grown up with Rocco, trusted him with her life, she even kept him at a distance. Never letting him get too close. She made sure that he didn't know anything about her illicit activities. He was smart enough not to ask her questions he didn't want answers to. The secrets she harbored remained off his radar. She planned on keeping it that way.

For her sake as well as his.

On the breeze, she caught a smell in the air. Her stomach flip-flopped as she put a name to the distinct scent.

Smoke.

Charlie spun around. Flames were visible through the windows of the house. Flickering. Spreading. Very, very, fast.

"The house…" She swallowed, staring in disbelief. "The house is on fire," she muttered, half to herself.

"What? I don't understand," he said, and neither did she. "Didn't you say the place was empty?"

Charlie started walking toward the cabin, mind scrambling to make sense of it, every nerve ending alight and crackling like a fuse.

This was the epitome of bad.

Another thought occurred to her. Somewhere in the darkness of the property was whoever set the fire.

A chill crawled under her skin. "I'm getting out of here. Got to go." She ended the call without another word and ran, heading for her car.

Charlie bolted across the lawn, and as she came around the side of the cabin, she caught sight of the three-hundred-gallon propane tank used to heat and power the place. Her mouth went dry as dust. She veered away from the combustible tank, sprinting faster, heart pumping double-time as adrenaline surged through her veins. But by then, it was too late.

The house exploded. The blast concussion hurled her off her feet. Heat seared the air. Singed her hair.

Her back slammed against the ground, her head hitting something even harder. Pain spiked through her.

And the world went dark.

Chapter Two

"Will you help Charlie get to the bottom of things while keeping her out of trouble with your guys?" Rocco asked, referring to the police department.

"Are you sure you really want me on this, bearing in mind what I just told you?" Brian would understand if Rocco reconsidered, but it was important for him to know. "You can get someone else. Maybe Nash."

Nash Garner was the FBI lead and supervisory special agent of their task force. The guy could be a bit brusque and taciturn, but he was fair. Too bad Becca, the other agent on their team, was on vacation.

"I'm sure. It needs to be you." There was no hesitation in Rocco's voice, which was encouraging. "I think you're the only one who can get it done, even if it means a delicate balancing act on your part. Just don't tell Charlie what you told me. She'll panic if you do. Take care of her for me, won't you?"

"Yeah, all right," Brian said, realizing he had just made a promise that was going to be nearly impossible to keep.

The second he hung up the phone, he wondered what he was about to get himself involved in.

A sliver of unease wormed in his gut.

Helping out a buddy and coworker didn't require a second thought. Much less asking too many questions. He was tight with Rocco, but this situation was tricky. Especially when it came to Charlie.

The woman was an enigma wrapped in ice. He longed to chip away at her permafrost. No matter how long it took. He estimated it was going to take a while because Charlie was cold, cold, cold. Completely unattainable. On every level unavailable.

Not that it deterred him from wanting to make Charlie his one day.

What could he say?

He enjoyed a *challenge*. That single word summed her up perfectly.

Last year, Rocco had been added to the special joint task force and had moved to Laramie. That was how Brian had met Charlie. Funny, she'd been living there for years, and before then their paths had never crossed. Almost as though she hadn't existed. But once he had seen her, been introduced, it was like he kept getting sucked into her orbit. Running into her everywhere. His thoughts always veering back to her.

Charlie on the other hand wanted nothing to do with him. You would've thought he had the bubonic plague the way she steered clear of him. Every one of his attempts to get to know her she had stymied, despite his best efforts. His offer to teach self-defense classes at her school for free, to take care of a plumbing issue at her house—once again, no strings attached, to fix her flat tire when he'd once seen her broken down on the road, to buy her a cup of coffee, had all been met with stone-cold rejection.

When they'd bumped into each other at a charity gala for a women's shelter in Cheyenne—both without dates—he'd sworn it had been fate. That things between them might change that night. For a couple of perfect hours, it had. The evening felt like the beginning of something.

Then she'd gone back to barely speaking to him while he couldn't stop thinking about her.

It was maddening.

Doing this favor for Rocco might be the key to getting closer to her.

Or it could be the biggest mistake that he ended up regretting.

Either way, this was going to be problematic. He'd already explained the potential complications to Rocco. Nonetheless, his friend trusted his judgment and had given him the green light to assist since Rocco was busy out of town, doing some undercover work.

Brian set down his first beer that he'd been nursing outside on his porch while enjoying the balmy summer air, stargazing. Wyoming in general, but specifically, out here in the countryside, boasted some of the darkest skies. An ideal spot for spying constellations. Even the Milky Way.

Great for clearing his head, restoring his soul.

Fortunately, he wasn't too far from the Olsen place. Or Charlie's. About ten minutes to each, but in different directions. Seemed as though folks who lived out on the outskirts of town, close to the mountains, liked their space. Made sense to swing by the Olsen ranch first, take a look. Then he'd check on Charlie and have a chat.

Pushing his concerns aside, he grabbed his badge, his gun, clipping the holster to his belt, hopped in his truck and drove off. He took out his cell and dialed dispatch over at the Laramie PD.

"Hey, this Detective Brian Bradshaw. I received a report about a fire at Detective Seth Olsen's place over on—"

"Already got it, Bradshaw. Seth's brother phoned in something about hearing a huge boom. Then he saw a fire."

His gut tightened. "There was an explosion?"

"Apparently."

Things had gone from horrible to worse faster than he had expected.

"Station twenty-four is there now putting out the fire," the dispatch said.

Brian did a quick calculation in his head, factoring in the location of the fire station from the ranch. "How did they get there so fast?"

"They were already in the area responding to another incident. The one over at the Olsen ranch took priority, with the explosion and fire."

Brian peered through the windshield in the direction of the ranch. Smoke billowed in the night sky. The scent was carried on a breeze through his rolled down window.

Charlie. "Were any bodies found on-site? Anyone injured?"

"No casualties yet," the dispatch said, and *yet* echoed in Brian's head. "They've requested canines to go through the place and look for remains once the fire is out."

"Any idea what caused the fire or the explosion?"

"Haven't heard. The new fire marshal is out there, too.

I'm sure he'll report back soon as he's had a chance to properly investigate."

Brian had heard a new guy had taken over the position. "What's the name?"

"Powell. Sawyer Powell."

He wondered if he was related to Holden Powell, the chief deputy of the sheriff's department. "Okay. Thanks." He disconnected.

Change of plans. Slowing down, Brian made a U-turn and headed toward Charlie's house instead. No one was found at the scene out at Seth's. Investigators had the situation in hand. There was nothing for him to do at the ranch now besides get in the way. Not to mention that his presence would only have others questioning why he was there.

Finding Charlie and getting details firsthand was the best way for him to start.

She was only a couple of miles away. He'd had no idea that she lived so close to him until the day he'd spotted her on this road with a flat tire. Meaner than a rattlesnake, she had made it crystal clear that she didn't need his or anyone else's help. End of discussion.

Hopefully there had been a tectonic shift in her perspective in that respect since then.

It only took Brian a few minutes until he pulled into her driveway alongside her Hellcat. Nothing sexier than a strong, beautiful woman behind the wheel of a sleek muscle car. Even the color suited her. Frostbite blue.

She didn't have much land. About an acre and a half, maybe two. Neighbors had plenty of breathing room, not on top of another. The house was set close to the road, which he didn't care for, with most of the land behind it.

Grabbing his cowboy hat, he climbed out of his truck. He smoothed his hair back before putting on his Stetson. As he passed her car, a twinge of jealousy zipped through him over all that speed and torque. But nothing offered a better view of the road or more rugged protection than his F150.

He strode up to her porch, wondering what kind of reception he'd receive. Cold or lukewarm?

Brian hoped for the latter. For once.

The curtain in the front window closest to the door was yanked aside. Charlie appeared. She glared at him, shook her head as if exasperated, and stormed away.

The welcome was going to be icy.

As usual. *No big surprise there.*

Footsteps pounded inside, drawing closer. The door flew open. Charlie put a fist on her lean hip, cocked her head, and up went those eyebrows. He met her striking green eyes, a volatile color he could never forget no matter how hard he tried. As he drank in the sight of her, it was as if the world dropped out from under him.

The woman took his breath away every time he saw her.

Although she and Rocco were cousins, they were remarkably different. Rocco was big and imposing, with dark hair and brown skin thanks to his native Hawaiian heritage on his father's side. While Charlie had a creamy porcelain complexion, white-blond hair, and a slender yet athletic figure, though she still managed to be equally intimidating. Her personality was a force of nature.

But tonight, she looked as though she'd been the one put through the wringer. His gaze slid over her disheveled hair, which had grass and splinters of wood in it, down her mud-spattered T-shirt and dirty leggings, but then whipped back up to the fresh scrapes on her arms and chin.

"You're bleeding." He reached out to touch her face.

Charlie slapped his hand away and stroked the spot he was referring to. She glanced at the drops of blood on her fingertips. "It's nothing." Straightening, she looked back up at him. Even though she was five-nine, he still had a good four inches on her. "I told Rocco that *you* were the last person on earth I wanted him to call."

Brian let the sharp-tongued remark roll off his back. Something he was good at. Most survivors were.

He gripped the brim of his Stetson and tipped his hat at her. "Nice to see you, too." Undeterred by her thick veneer of cool disdain, he mustered a smile, determined to kill her with kindness. "May I come in? It would be better to discuss things inside, ma'am."

Her scowl faltered as she rocked back on her heels. "Don't ma'am me. I'm not a gazillion years old. I've told you before it rubs me the wrong way."

"I assure you that is not my intent. But if you want to tell me how to rub you the right way, I'm all ears." Her eyes narrowed to slits at that, and he thought it best to fill in the awkward silence before she slammed the door in his face. "My use of *ma'am* and *sir* is an old military habit that's hard to break. My apologies."

"You're prior service, huh." Her face softened, a little. "What branch? What did you do?"

"Army. Intelligence Support Activity. A Special Operations unit."

"Were you Special Ops or did you support them?"

"Both." It was hard to explain to civilians, but from the

skeptical grimace on her face, he needed to try. "My old unit and our counterparts, SEAL Team Six, Delta Force are all considered Tier 1. You don't hear about ISA in the news, and they don't make movies about *The Activity*," he said, as they were often called, "but if not for us, Delta and DEVGRU—the SEALs—would have a tough time being successful." That was pretty much it in a simplified nutshell.

"Why did you quit Spec Ops to become a cop?" she asked, making *cop* sound like a dirty word.

He thought he was the one who was supposed to be asking the questions. Was she screening him to see if he was fit to assist? "This really isn't relevant."

"It is to me." She folded her arms across her chest. "You don't step foot across the threshold until I get an answer that satisfies me."

Brian tamped down the sigh rising in his chest. "My dad got sick. My mom couldn't handle the ranch on her own and couldn't afford to hire someone. So, I chose to stop doing something that I loved." He was no quitter. "To help the ones that I love. Joining the force was the closest fit for my skill set. But two years after I came back here, my father suffered a massive stroke. I had to put him into the Silver Springs Senior Living center. My mother couldn't bear to be away from him and moved in there also."

He'd given up his career for nothing. His specialized skills were going to waste. In the end, he had to sell the horses to pay for the exorbitant fees at the special care facility for both his parents.

Now, he was stuck. Back home. In Wyoming. As a cop. Living alone on land that he had no idea what to do with. Only thing stopping him from selling that, too, was his promise to his parents that he would hang on to the Brad-shaw legacy.

The one good thing to come out of it was getting assigned to the joint task force.

"Satisfied?" he asked. This time when he smiled, he didn't try to hide the sadness behind it. Not just for himself, but also for his father's tragic decline.

At least his parents were together. To this day, they made him believe in true love. Not in finding a soulmate, which he doubted was real, but in connecting with someone who understood you, whose faults you could tolerate if not appreciate, who brought light into the other's darkness, and vice versa.

"Not entirely, but enough," Charlie said, after a long moment. She stepped aside, letting him in. "How long have you been a *cop*?" Once again, contempt laced the word.

"Four years." The short period of time made him sound green, which he wasn't. She wouldn't be dealing with a patrol officer. "But I was fast-tracked to detective two years ago because of my military background."

She frowned when he'd thought she would find that reassuring. Obviously, he was missing something important.

"Let's get one thing straight," she said, shutting the door. "Just because Rocco trusts you doesn't mean that I do. Got it?"

Man, she was tough.

One more reason to like her.

"Fair enough." He removed his hat. "But you need to remember that I come in peace. To help you. In any way that I can."

"We'll see about that."

Stepping deeper into her home, he looked around. Minimalist, utilitarian furniture. Plain white walls. A few abstract pieces of art that provided hints of color. No knick-knacks. No personal photos. A flat-screen TV sat on an empty bookcase opposite a taupe sofa. The coffee table was nothing more than a scratched metal storage trunk. Unopened cardboard boxes lined the far wall.

Since she'd gotten a flat tire on the road nearby almost nine months ago, he knew she hadn't just moved in. "How long have you lived here?"

"Two and half years."

It was as if the place was merely functional. A place to eat and sleep. Not a sanctuary. She hadn't even fully unpacked.

"You don't spend much time here, do you?" he asked.

"No. The USD is open seven days a week, fifteen hours a day to give anyone interested in taking a class a chance to fit one into their schedule." Glancing around, she stiffened. "Why do you ask?"

Not one to lie and not willing to get sidetracked by offending her, he said, "How about we get your face and arms cleaned up."

Charlie shook her head. "It's only a few cuts and some singed hair," she said, fingering a bunch of strands. "It can wait. Have a seat." She gestured to the living room.

She dropped into a chair across from the sofa. Beside her was an end table. On top of it was a lamp and a glass with amber liquid. He noted a hole in her leggings that exposed pale skin on her calf and blood.

Tending to her wounds, no matter how minor, should be the priority, but he also sensed this needed to be on her terms. "It's going to be hard for me to focus with you injured and bleeding. Let's compromise. We get you bandaged up while you explain why I'm here. You do know how to compromise, don't you?" He was half joking. The other part of him wondered just how stubborn she really was.

A groan, fraught with impatience, rolled from Charlie. "I do." Her jaw clenched. "I simply don't do it often. There's generally no need."

Since he was making headway, he figured he'd push a bit further. "Where's your first-aid kit?"

Gripping the arms of the chair, she started to rise.

"Allow me to get it for you." He dared put a hand on her shoulder, urging her stay seated.

She flinched from his touch like his palm had scalded her. "I'm not an invalid."

"Clearly, but Rocco made me promise to take care of you."

"I don't think he meant like this."

No, he hadn't. "Still, he'd be happy if I did, and it'll earn me some brownie points with my mom." Hopefully with Charlie as well.

"I can't believe you care about brownie points with your mother." She looked him over, from head to toe and back up to his face. "Then again, I take it back. I can."

Why did that not sound like a compliment?

"Were you a Boy Scout, too?" she asked.

"As a matter of fact, I was. Cub Scout first." He left out the part about the Cubs being the equivalent of the Brownies where the term brownie point originated.

Charlie rolled her eyes. "Oh, give me a break."

How was that a bad thing?

She was a hard case. Only intensified the itch he would one day scratch.

He was an eternal optimist if nothing else. "Where's your first-aid stuff?"

"Lower kitchen cabinet, next to the pantry. Don't expect to find some fancy, tricked out med bag like you probably have."

With a curt nod, he went to grab it. In the cabinet, there were basic supplies that paled in comparison to what he had in his truck, much less in his house. At home, he had a complete suture kit. She didn't even have hydrogen peroxide or alcohol.

Not that it was necessary. The saline solution and antibiotic ointment would suffice. He also grabbed gauze along with bandages and paper towels.

He returned to the living room and knelt in front of her.

"No comment?" she asked, eyeing the supplies in his hands.

"You've got the essentials." Brian shrugged. "What's there to say?" He imagined her pantry and freezer to be the same. Basics only.

He tugged up her pant leg past her knee.

She grimaced. "Ouch."

Peering closer, he spotted what caused the pain. He yanked out a rather large fragment of wood embedded in her calf. Blood spurted from the wound. He pressed a paper towel to it first. With the saline solution, he flushed the cut, eliciting a hiss of pain from her.

Wincing, she clutched his shoulder.

He poured a bit more solution on the deep gash.

Her grip on him tightened, and she swore. "Sorry. I'm not usually such a big baby."

"No problem." He dabbed at the wound with gauze, pleased the bleeding slowed. "Feel free to grab on to me anytime."

She glanced down at her hand on his shoulder. Her eyes flared wide as though she hadn't realized she was touching him. Pulling away, she grabbed the glass on the end table and took a healthy sip.

"What's your poison?" he asked, applying antibiotic ointment.

"Scotch. Twenty-one-year-old Glenfiddich."

Two things she splurged on, her car and her Scotch. It certainly wasn't her home decor.

He put a bandage on the cut. "At that price point, I bet it's pretty smooth. I'm more of a beer drinker myself."

"Of course, you are," she said with a slight sneer.

"What's that supposed to mean?" While he waited for a response, he cleaned the cut on her wrist above her smartwatch.

"It's the quintessential alcoholic beverage of the USA."

"And?"

Lowering her gaze, she shook her head as though she wasn't going to say anything else. But she did. "It's very on brand for you." She looked at him. "Fits with your whole Captain America vibe."

That was nicest thing anyone had ever said to him. At the same time—she had hurled the words at him, sharp, little stones not intended to flatter—it was also the meanest.

Good thing he didn't have a big ego, but it was better

she thought of him as a capable superhero than a dimwitted Dudley Do-Right.

If he searched hard enough, there was always a silver lining.

Rocco had once admitted that although he was the closest person to Charlie, they weren't exactly close. By her choice.

In that moment, Brian understood why she was alone. Why she had no pictures of family or friends hanging on the walls. It was because she had a knack for pushing people away. The sort of talent that was bred from pain. Or fear.

Perhaps both.

"You'll come to learn that my brand is more along the lines of Timex," he said, dabbing gauze saturated in saline solution on the cut on her chin. "I take a licking and keep on ticking." He winked.

Give it your best shot, Charlie.

She stared at him with an inscrutable expression on her face. Up close, she was even prettier. Mesmerizing eyes. The sultriest mouth. He tried hard not to think how her chin-length hair would feel tickling his bare chest. Then he tried even harder not to think about her lips doing the same thing.

With a gentle fingertip, he applied some ointment on her chin. She let out a shaky breath, her lips parting at contact. His pulse raced. His blood pumped hard through his veins as he took her in. The scent of her making its way deep into his lungs. Feminine musk, grass and smoke. Something passed between them, hot and intangible.

All too soon, she leaned back, pulling her face from his fingers.

Needing to get it together around her, he got up from the floor and sat in the chair on the other side of the end table.

"Tell me the reason you called Rocco, and why you were at the Olsen ranch."

"First, you have to agree not to haul me in as a witness."

"Depends on what you tell me."

"Either you agree that this stays between us for now, off the record, or I have nothing else to say."

Brian had made a promise to Rocco, and going into this, he knew Charlie wouldn't make things easy. "I'm capable of coloring outside the lines, but I won't aid and abet."

Resting an elbow on her thigh, she pressed the heel of her palm to her forehead and stared down at her muddy sneakers. "I guess this is harder, repeating everything to you than it was telling my cousin."

Totally understandable. Normal even. "But I need to hear it from you."

"To see if I'm lying?" Those green eyes flashed up at him.

"When you play a game of whisper down the lane or telephone, details in the message tend to get lost." As a former human intelligence officer, getting information from people was his specialty. Firsthand was always best.

To weed out the lies.

To dig deeper to the truth.

To read between the lines of what they didn't want you to know.

"I was locking up USD when Haley called me." Tension was evident in the stiffness of her neck and bone-white knuckles of her clasped hands. "She told me that Seth was going to kill her. He was beating her again."

Frowning, Brian scooted to the edge of his seat. This was precisely what he wanted to avoid. A game of whispers. "What were her exact words?"

"He's going to kill me. He hurt me. It's bad." She made a noncommittal gesture as if she wasn't completely certain. "Then she asked me to come help her."

"She said *he*, not Seth?"

"Yeah, so what?"

There were rumors that Haley was unfaithful. The same applied to Seth. If true, they were both cheaters. "It's possible she was referring to a third party. Maybe a lover."

"At her house? Beating her?" Charlie yanked down her pant leg and jumped to her feet. "She never mentioned having a lover to me."

Most cheaters didn't go around bragging. "Doesn't mean it isn't possible." He wouldn't sugarcoat this. "What I don't understand," he said, standing and striding closer to her, "is why Haley would call you instead of the police."

"Calling the cops was useless. The lot of you stick together." She waved an accusatory hand in his direction. "The one time she dialed 911, he had coerced her to say that she fell to explain her injuries. After those boys in blue left, he made her regret it. Most of the abuse was psychological, but not always. Many times, he left bruises and scars that I saw myself."

Brian's mind reeled. He had always considered Seth to be a good guy. Not an abusive jerk. Hell, Seth was not only a fellow cop, but they played tackle football together with some other guys on the force. Hung out from time to time afterward, having a few beers. Occasionally dinner. They weren't quite friends, like he was with Rocco, but they were certainly chummy.

All things he had shared with Rocco in full disclosure. Things his buddy thought best not to tell Charlie.

"That still doesn't explain why you," he stated. "Surely she has family or friends. Why did Haley Olsen call you?"

No way they were BFFs. Charlie wasn't the type to have a best friend. She was a lone wolf. Tortured and forbidding. All he wanted to do was get her to stop running. To show her that she didn't have do it all on her own. To chase the shadows from her gaze.

Could he?

She picked up her drink, took a swig and gave a one-shouldered shrug. "I don't know."

He stepped toward her. "I think you do."

A beat. A second's hesitation. She blinked before looking away and setting her glass down with a *clink*. "I don't. She shared a lot with me during training sessions at USD. It's good to vent while you're sweating. Maybe she felt that she could trust me to help her."

"What would instill that degree of trust? To ask you to intervene with her husband?"

She nipped her bottom lip. A subtle gesture, but a telling one. At best, she was hiding something. At worst, she was lying.

Damn it.

He shook his head. She had no idea who she was dealing with. His gaze dropped back to her mouth. Those rosy-pink lips pursed in a way that made him imagine she was holding back an avalanche of secrets. Made him want to kiss those secrets right out of her. Slowly. One by one.

A technique he had never employed before. His specialty as a human intelligence officer had been uncovering the truths others sought to bury. He'd been extremely proficient at his job, doing whatever was necessary. Some skills were never lost. He might be rusty, but it was like riding a bike.

He'd find out what she didn't want him to know. Once he was on to something, he was like a bloodhound that didn't stop. "If something has happened to Haley," he said, still not entirely certain that something had, "the police will come to question you once they check her phone records."

"The cell phone is a burner I gave her so she could communicate without Seth knowing. The number I gave her to contact me is to my own burner. The cops won't be able to trace it back to me."

A vehicle tore up to the house. The dull sound of tires spitting through the lawn drew their gazes to the front window.

"Are you expecting someone?" he asked.

She shook her head. "No."

Years of ingrained training had him grasping the hilt of his weapon. He inched over a step and looked through the window. High beams were focused on the house, like a spotlight, blinding him.

Next thing he knew, there were gunshots.

Chapter Three

Charlie reached for Brian, to get him away from the window. Out of the line of fire.

But he was already in motion, lunging for her with startling speed. He grabbed hold of her, taking her down to the floor, his body covering hers.

Pop, pop, pop, pop. Four more rounds blew out her bay window. Shattered glass rained down. A lamp exploded. Bullets bit into the walls.

An engine revved, tires spun outside and peeled away.

Heart pounding violently, she lay there, frozen for a minute. Even if she had wanted to move, it would have been impossible. His solid, heavy body had her pinned to the floor.

Slowly, he uncurled the strong arm he had wrapped around her head. He stared down at her, his warm chocolate-brown gaze caressing her face as lean, masculine muscle brushed against her. An electric jolt ripped through her that had nothing to do with their close call with death and everything to do with him.

You're just confusing the rush of adrenaline with something else.

That's what she tried to tell herself anyway. "They're

gone." Her voice was a whisper she didn't recognize. "You can get off me now."

When he didn't immediately move, she pressed her palms to his chest to shove him away and instantly regretted it. Hard, taut muscle shifted beneath her fingers. The ridges and valleys teasing her, tempting her. His warmth penetrated through clothes and skin, deep into her bones. The weight of his body was so comforting that she couldn't bring herself to push him off.

"I just wanted to make sure they didn't swing back around for another try," he said, his soft breath grazing her cheek.

"Oh." She hadn't considered that possibility.

He cradled her face with a tenderness that had her throat growing tight and her heart drumming harder.

Part of her couldn't wait for him to move. The other part wanted to cling to him a little longer, holding him close, soaking up his heat. Even the scent of him was sunshine and happiness and sexy sweat. He smelled better than anyone she'd ever met.

She struggled to catalog the terror tangling with the thrill that stung the insides of her veins as she found herself slipping into a strange passivity trapped beneath him.

God, she hated the effect he had on her.

"Think it's safe now?" she asked in a hushed voice.

"Yeah, I think so." He gave a little nod, his mouth a hairbreadth from hers. "But stay down and let me check to be sure." Rolling off her, he pushed to a crouch with his sidearm in his hand.

The chill that swept over Charlie in the absence of his body heat made her shiver. She glanced at the shattered glass, holes in the wall and the mess left behind from the bullets meant for her.

Brain crept to the window, pressed his back against the wall and craned his neck around the sill. A moment later, he said, "All clear. It's safe to get up." He strode back over to her and offered his hand.

But she couldn't take it, actually more afraid of what might happen, of how she might feel if she touched him again, than of the shooter coming back.

She got up on her own. "Thanks. You're quick on your feet."

"Any idea who was shooting at you? Or why?"

"No." The only thing she could think was that it was somehow related to whatever had happened to Haley. "Maybe it was Seth."

A frown tugged between his dark brows. "Why would a cop drive by your house and shoot at you?" he asked, sounding as though it was outside the realm of possibility.

"Cops commit crimes, too. Premeditated. Out of passion. Desperation. Don't look at me as if I'm delusional."

Jaw hardening, he rubbed the back of his neck. "You're right. Some cops are bad. But not most. I would know."

"Maybe you don't see too clearly with the rose-colored glasses you wear."

"I've been through the carnage of war, endured physical nightmares that would traumatize most and seen how ugly humanity can be. Trust and believe, I see clearly." He took a deep breath. The corners of his mouth lifted in a soft smile. He raised his palms, like a white flag, suggesting peace. "Let's not get sidetracked. I get you've made being mean your hobby, but it's not going to get you answers or help Haley. How about a truce since we're on the same side. What do you say?"

She took a step back. Something inside her deflated, all the anger and annoyance fizzling away at that one little benign act. Perhaps what made it so powerful was that it seemed sincere.

This man kept throwing her off-kilter, softening her despite her efforts to maintain her hardened edge. Part of her regretted giving him a hard time. The other part remembered he was a cop.

Snap out of it. He was probably just trying to get her to lower her guard. No one was ever that nice. At least not to her.

Being mean wasn't a hobby. It was a defense mechanism. The best one she had, but she couldn't ignore that working together was the only way to get answers. "Okay, truce."

"What motive would Seth have for coming here? Why would he shoot at you?"

"Because I know what he did. I saw the blood in the house. Then someone set a fire and the whole place went up. Someone set it on fire deliberately. He'd shoot at me because I'm a witness."

"You fled a crime scene?"

"Don't say it like that, as if I'm the one who committed the crime. I'm not. I was only trying to help a friend. Then I panicked."

"First, I'm going to call in this shooting," he said, and she opened her mouth to protest. "A report has to be filed about this. It's nonnegotiable. Then you're going to walk me through exactly what happened after you spoke to Haley tonight."

Gritting her teeth, she relented with a nod. "But I don't want the report filed with the Laramie PD. If you've got to call this in, do it with the sheriff's office. Deal?"

One LPD officer in her home and another possibly shooting at her was more than enough. She didn't want to involve any more.

"I can live with that."

CHARLIE RELIVED THE details of the evening for Brian, enduring his relentless barrage of questions as he tried to pick apart her story.

"Then the cabin exploded. I was knocked out for a minute or two from the blast. When I came to, I left." There had been fiery debris everywhere. Strewn across the yard. Covering Haley's car. She was lucky to be alive.

"You didn't actually witness anything other than arson," he finally said, standing beside her in the kitchen.

"What about all of the blood in the house?" She took another sip of scotch from her freshly poured glass. This was her *only drink in case of emergency or celebration* bottle of Glenfiddich. The night called for two more fingers worth. "I'm telling you it's from a dead body. Haley's."

"But you didn't see a body, did you?" he asked.

"No, but Haley's missing. She's not answering her phone and her car was at the house. It was blown up in the explosion."

"Maybe she got the drop on her husband. Did something to him. Used his car to transport the body. Then set the fire."

"Seth Olsen is no featherweight. Haley is a hundred and twenty soaking wet. Seth's got to weigh at least as much as you." She estimated two hundred pounds of muscle easy.

"She couldn't have disposed of a body on her own. Why would she even try, knowing that I was on the way?"

Straightening, he narrowed his eyes, studying her suddenly with a measured glance.

She had tipped her hand, said the wrong thing. But what?

"You're the *friend* someone calls when they need to get rid of a body. That's why she dialed your number and no one else." It was a statement. Not a question.

No, no. He was not going to turn this around on her, making her a suspect.

She swore under her breath, wanting to curse her cousin for sending Brian. "Haley hadn't been plotting to kill her husband. She'd been planning to leave him. I think Seth might've found out and that was the reason he beat her tonight. I honestly don't know why she called me. Other than she must've known I'd come regardless of the risks to myself. For the record, I've never helped anyone get rid of a body." But there was always a first time for everything.

Brian seemed to mull that over while assessing her. "Let's stop speculating. The police will be looking for Haley and Seth. One or both will turn up. No casualties were reported at the house. I'll know for certain once the canines go through the debris. The cadaver dogs will pick up whatever is left of any blood."

"Someone started the fire," she insisted. "Deliberately. To cover up what I saw in there." That same person was also probably the one who had shot at her. Well, they had messed with the wrong woman. Because now she wasn't just scared and appalled. She was angry.

"I'm not doubting it."

"You only doubt that Seth was responsible."

"I didn't say that." Brian sighed. "Look, jumping to conclusions is counterproductive. It'll get us nowhere. I prefer to investigate and let the evidence speak for itself."

A car pulled up outside with red and blue flashing lights. No siren wailing.

"I'm not going to say anything about Haley's phone call," she said, "or about going to the ranch."

His brow furrowed. "You have to."

"No. I don't. I only agreed to let you report the shooting."

"You were at a crime scene. You need to give an official statement."

"I will. After we find evidence. Discreetly." There was a knock at the door. "Let's see if I can trust you." She doubted it. "Play this my way. Got it?"

"This isn't a game."

"I know." It was a gamble.

She answered the door.

"I'm Chief Deputy Holden Powell. I take it your lack of a front window is from the shots fired?"

"Yes. Please, come in." She opened the door wider for him.

The deputy stepped inside.

"Holden." Brian strode over and extended his hand.

The two men shook. "I was surprised to hear from you tonight, Brian."

"Unfortunate circumstances made it necessary."

"How many shots were fired?" the deputy asked.

Charlie closed the door. "Five."

"Did either of you see who it was?" Holden looked between them.

They both shook their heads.

"No. The shooter sped off," Brian added. "I thought it

best not to pursue. I wanted to make sure Charlie was all right. Also, in case there was more than one, perhaps a second shooter on foot meant to finish the job."

Another terrifying notion that hadn't occurred to her. Then again, she hadn't expected anyone to shoot at her in her home. With her side business, she sometimes encountered people who wanted to do her harm. It was usually up close and personal. But she could handle herself in a physical altercation. This attempt to hurt her by taking cowardly potshots was something else.

"Did you happen to see the make or the model or color of the vehicle?"

Another shake of the head from Brian and her.

"Any idea who might want to kill you?" the deputy asked. "Or why?"

Brian fixed her with a stare. One that pleaded with her to do what he thought was the right thing. She tensed under the intensity of his gaze, but she wasn't changing her mind.

She needed his cooperation. Not his judgment. "I've made a few enemies in town, but I can't say with certainty who might've done this or why." She glanced at Brian.

Could she count on him to keep his mouth shut?

Or would he disappoint her as so many others in her life had?

Folding his arms, he stayed silent, laser-focused on her, with disapproval he couldn't quite hide beneath his careful lack of expression.

To her amazement, there was no breach of trust.

The deputy walked through her living room, looking around. He put on gloves, pulled out an evidence bag and tweezers. "The good news is," he said, pulling out a shell casing embedded in the wall, "I didn't spot anyone watching the house like they planned to try again tonight." He dropped it in the evidence bag and plucked another from a different hole. "Still, it would best to keep your guard up."

She nodded in full agreement. "I plan to."

"You shouldn't stay the night here," Brian said.

The deputy clucked his tongue. "I have to agree. Best to sleep somewhere safer until we can figure out what's going on. Who's targeting you and why."

"First of all, there's no way I'm letting anyone run me out of my house. Besides, I've got nowhere else to go." She was ashamed to admit it, but it was the truth.

"Crash at Rocco's," Brian said. "He won't be back for a couple of days, and I've got a spare key to his place if you don't."

She was his cousin and didn't have a key. But his buddy did. How embarrassing. Not that she had given Rocco one to her house.

Still, it irked her.

"Or you could stay with me," Brian added. "I've got a comfy guest room."

The offer was generous. Even sweet. Suspiciously so, considering he assumed she had a hobby of being mean. Nobody was that nice to someone who was acting downright awful. The man was too good to be true. There was something wrong with him. Other than the fact that he was a cop. She just couldn't put her finger on it yet, but whatever *it* was would come back to bite her if she wasn't careful.

"I'll be fine here." She glanced over the hot mess of her living room. "Once I put some boards up on the window and clean up."

"I can help you with that," Brian said.

"No need. I'll take care of it."

Brian turned to the deputy. "Can you have forensics come out to take prints of the tire tracks out in the yard?"

"Sure, no problem." Holden nodded. "Won't do you much good until you have a suspect."

Brian slid her a knowing glance. "Yeah. Hopefully, we'll get one."

"Well, I'll leave you to it." The deputy headed for the door.

"One more thing," Brian said. "Is Sawyer Powell, the new fire marshal, any relation to you?"

"He's my brother. Why?"

"I heard there was a fire and subsequent explosion over at the Olsen ranch and that he's the one investigating. I plan to speak with him tomorrow."

"There's nobody better to have on the job than Sawyer."

"Glad to hear it." Brian shook his hand one more time. "Thanks again."

"No problem. I'll show myself out."

Once the chief deputy was gone, Charlie trudged back to the kitchen. Staring at the wide opening in her home, left by the shattered window, she took another gulp of scotch. Too bad she didn't have any spare wood boards to put up. But she wasn't handy and didn't tackle home projects often.

"I've got some extra plywood at home that I don't need," Brian said, as though reading her mind, coming up alongside her.

She set her glass down with a sad chuckle. "Of course, you do."

"Next, you're going to tell me you don't need it."

Mind reader indeed. "Of course, I am."

"Why?"

The question was so simple. A single word. Yet so hard to answer. She tipped her head back and met his curious gaze. "Force of habit." She shrugged. "It's safer to rely only on myself."

That way she wouldn't be disappointed when someone let her down. She never tested things with Rocco or his parents. They were the only family she had left. She didn't want to risk losing them, too, if they'd failed her in some way. Instead, she accepted the love and kindness they'd given and never asked for anything else.

"Not asking for help isn't strength, Charlie."

There was something sexy about the way her name rolled off his tongue. She realized she was staring and had to pull her gaze from his mouth.

"It's time to form new habits," he continued. "As you pointed out earlier, you're not old. You're capable of learning some new tricks."

At thirty, she was a far cry from old. More than capable of change, if she wanted to. She wasn't weak either. She had called Rocco for help, hadn't she?

But she didn't bother to highlight that since she also saw Brian's point.

The fact was he didn't know her, or understand what she had witnessed as a child, what she had survived.

The walls she put up around herself did keep others from getting in, but sometimes they were the only thing holding her together. It was about self-preservation. Not isolation.

"Your brand is Captain America," she said. "Not Dr. Phil *come sit on my sofa.*"

He grinned, and her pulse stuttered. "I'd love to get you on my sofa sometime," he said, his voice smooth and deep, making that flutter inside her dip lower. Dropping his gaze, he cleared his throat. "For now, I'm going to run home, grab the plywood and patch up your window while you get started cleaning. And for the sake of clarity, I'm not doing it for you. It's only out of a sense of obligation to Rocco. Captain America keeps his promises." He winked again.

It was so damn sexy, she struggled to come up with a witty retort, some snide remark that usually came to her as naturally as breathing.

"Do you have a gun?" he asked.

"Locked up in my safe." There were times when she needed one but preferred not to always carry it.

"Good. Get it. Keep it with you while I'm gone. I won't be long."

Brian grabbed his cowboy hat, and then he was gone.

By the time she had swept up the debris and finished tidying the living room, he was back. He really did live quite close.

Without any fuss, he rested the plywood on the nook in front of the window and hammered in nails until the boards were secured in place.

"Thank you," she said, fatigue beginning to override adrenaline. "I know it's late and you probably have better things to do. Like sleep."

"No need to thank me. I'm not doing it for you. Remember? It's all for Rocco."

She didn't hide the smile that surfaced. "Sorry I don't have a beer to offer you."

"I'll have what you're having, if you're in a sharing mood."

How could she say no?

She noticed he was very good at that, finding ways to turn a "no" into a "yes." Must be one of his superpowers.

Taking out a heavy glass tumbler from the cabinet, she wished she had asked him if he wanted something sooner. It was one thing to give someone a cold shoulder. Quite another to be flat-out rude. Her aunt Cecilia, Rocco's mom, would be ashamed of her lack of manners.

She poured him a nightcap and held out the glass.

As he took the tumbler from her, holding her gaze, his fingers stroked hers a tad longer than necessary. A snap of sexual awareness rocked her to the bone.

She pulled her hand from his. Took a sip of scotch as he did likewise. Tried not to stare at him. Which was impossible.

There was something magnetic about those chocolate-brown eyes staring back at her with the same intensity. Something about him overall that tugged at her.

He was tall, broad-shouldered. Had a tumble of mahogany hair that was so thick and luxurious she ached to run her fingers through it. Down the sculpted muscle of his shoulders and arms. Not only was he good-looking, but he was also shrewd.

Still, there was more to him. But she had to figure out what it was.

"Smoother than I imagined," Brian said, his voice, like whiskey and velvet rolled into one, would have made a weaker woman shiver. He stepped closer, erasing the space between them, sucking the oxygen from her lungs. "Sweeter, too."

As he looked at her, that delicious mouth curved up in

one of those smiles that tempted her to believe his good-natured friendly style was genuine.

Her brain screamed at her to get away from him, cross the room, but her feet wouldn't budge, her body betraying her by leaning in. She had never experienced the allure of another person that strongly, pulling her toward him, like gravity.

The sensation was unnerving.

He dipped his head, bringing his face closer to hers.

She thought he might lower his mouth to her lips for a kiss. Her heart thundered in her chest at the prospect. But was it because she she wanted him to kiss her, or not?

His gaze fell to her mouth, his eyes darkening. He bent closer still until the whisper of his breath brushed her skin.

A quiver shot to the pit of her stomach and knotted down to her toes.

"You better get some sleep," he said. "You've got an early day tomorrow."

Her mind stuttered. "Huh?" Disappointment flared under her skin at the lack of contact she craved. Which shouldn't have been such a surprise considering it had been a long time since she'd felt the tension and heat of a man's body. An even longer time since she'd wanted to.

The real shocker was the appetite, the interest, *this* man sparked.

"USD opens at six. Doesn't it?" he asked.

"Um, yeah." Charlie nodded. She had forgotten about everything besides Brian Bradshaw, standing in her kitchen, close enough to kiss her. "I'm usually up by five fifteen."

"It'll be a busy day for me as well. I'll make some inquires, quietly investigate."

"You believe me?" Was he going to help?

"I believe something bad happened at the Olsen ranch tonight. I believe whatever is going on has now put you in danger. There'll be an investigation, but I'm the only one who can connect the dots between the two since you've decided not to make a full statement. I also believe you're not telling me everything I need to know." His voice was gentle, even understanding, instead of accusatory, not raising her hackles. "Let's meet tomorrow night. My place."

"Why are we meeting? And why at your place?"

"I'll share whatever I find out over dinner. You've got to eat. Kill two birds with one stone." His mouth hitched in a smile, and there went another zing of scintillating energy. "I'll text you my address." He slugged back the rest of his scotch, put his glass down on the counter next to her .45 SIG Sauer, grabbed his hat and strode out the door.

Without waiting for an answer.

But he hadn't asked a question. He'd simply declared they were having dinner as though it were a foregone conclusion.

The tingle still flowing through her body was a warning sign. Brian was dangerous.

Not the first time she'd sensed it. Whenever they were within arm's reach, something inside her lit up. Made her want to know more about him. Get closer to him. Something she could not afford to do.

Not with a cop.

Chapter Four

A loud horn blared. Brian jackknifed upright. His ears rang as his gaze flew around. He was still in his truck. Parked out front of Charlie's place. Early morning sunlight poured through the rolled-down windows. Charlie stared at him, standing on the running board of his truck with her hand bearing down on his horn.

His blood surged at the sight of her. Right along with his blood pressure. "Stop it," he snapped.

Charlie removed her hand from the horn. "Morning." She handed him a disposable cup of piping hot coffee, black. "Imagine my surprise when I leave for run and find you here."

"What time is it?" He wiped the sleep from his eyes.

She glanced at her smartwatch. "Five forty-five. A better question is, what are you doing camped outside of my house? Since you're in the same clothes, I presume you were here all night."

He sipped the coffee. Scalded his tongue. A string of curses flew from him.

"Oh, my." Charlie batted her lashes. "I thought your brand of superhero was PG. No foul language permitted."

Every time he looked at her his thoughts nosedived straight into the gutter. Definitely X-rated. He'd been in the company of beautiful women before, dated a few, too, but there was something about Charlie that kept him spellbound. "Goes to show how little you know about my brand."

He blew on the coffee and tried again. The hit of caffeine was just what he needed.

"You didn't answer my question." She raised an eyebrow. "Do I need to lay on the horn again to clear your head?"

"You wouldn't dare."

She reached for the steering wheel. "Want to test me?"

No. He did not.

The sun broke through the clouds, framing Charlie in an ethereal light. Made her look like an angel. A fallen one sent to corrupt him.

Brian had always had a thing for feisty blondes, but he wasn't sure why out of all the ones in the great state of Wyoming, or even in the world, he was so fiercely attracted to her.

But without a doubt, he was.

"It wasn't safe for you to spend the night in your house," he said. "Someone tried to kill you. Same shooter could've easily returned. I noticed your alarm system, but now you're missing a window. I wouldn't have been able to sleep worrying about you. Trying to get you to see reason seemed like it'd be a waste of time. You can be obstinate."

She folded her arms across her chest. "I prefer to be called headstrong."

Semantics. Same outcome. She wouldn't have listened to him.

A yawn scratched up his throat.

She propped her forearm on the door. "How many nights do you plan on sleeping out here?"

"Until you get your window fixed." He took another glorious sip of coffee. "Or you take pity on me by staying somewhere else." Stretching, he groaned. "This isn't the best sleeping arrangement for my back."

She pushed her pink lips out into a pout. "I'm not big on pity." She patted his unshaven cheek. "For myself anyway. I'll see what I can muster for you," she said, flashing a smile.

He couldn't help but return it. The grin spreading wider on her face, the feel of her palm on his skin, that electric thing always between them crackling with a new kind of energy.

"How kind of you," he quipped.

"Blasphemy. I don't have a kind bone in my body," she said with a wink. "I'm all fire and ice."

With either one, when it came to Charlie, he got the feeling he was going to get burned. "To be forewarned is to be forearmed. I'll be sure to handle you with care." He turned the key in the ignition, starting his engine. "See you tonight. Let's say seven thirty."

"No can do." She stepped down from the foot rail. "I don't close USD until nine. Call me with an update. No need for me to stop by for dinner."

Under normal circumstances, if this was a date, Brian would have offered to bring dinner to her at the self-defense school.

Tonight, dinner was about work. He needed her face-to-face, on his territory, where he could control the environment, get her to lower her guard. It was the easiest way to find out what she was hiding.

"You can. And you will. If you want to know what I discover." He knew how to dangle a carrot.

Charlie laughed at that. Still, she seemed to be considering it. "Who knew Captain America could play hardball?"

"I keep telling you, but you're not listening." He put his truck in drive. "You've got the brand wrong, sweetheart." He winked back.

Brian espoused virtues such as honor, integrity and courage. But he wasn't as noble as a fictitious character, who followed duty despite all costs. Not anymore. Not after the things he had done in the military. The things he'd seen.

How long would it take Charlie Sharp to figure out who he was, to see the real him?

The one thing she'd gotten right so far was that he did have a superpower. Getting people to spill their secrets.

She smirked. "I'll figure something out at USD. I wouldn't want to miss an opportunity to compare notes."

That suggested she intended to have some new information to compare.

"Go sticking your nose in the wrong place and someone is liable to chop it off," he said. "Please tell me you learned something from last night."

"I did. Don't stand in front of the window with the curtains drawn."

Not the lesson he was thinking of, but still a worthwhile one. "Seven thirty. Don't be late." With a wave, he drove off.

Punctuality was not only a sign of respect, but also a measure of trustworthiness.

Charlie could trust him, even if she didn't believe it. He needed to know if it was a two-way street. Right now, he had serious doubts.

About her.

THIS WAS THE third window installation service Charlie had contacted. Everyone's response was the same. "Are you sure you can't replace it any sooner?" she asked, not wanting frustration to overwhelm her.

"Four weeks is the best we can do," the manager said. "A bay window with the dimensions you gave me has to be ordered. Even with putting a rush on shipping, you're looking at a month. But once we receive it, we can install it the next day."

She swallowed a groan. "Okay. I understand."

"Do you want me to order it?"

"I need the window." Even if it would take four weeks. "Go ahead."

"All right. I'll call you once it's in."

"Thank you." She hung up.

There was no way she could have Brian sleeping in his truck in front of her house one more night, much less for a month. The busted window was also a legitimate security concern that he had brought to her attention. She'd have to figure something out later.

Right now, she needed to start doing some investigating of her own. Brian might follow-through, but she couldn't rely on him. She wasn't going to take any chances of Seth Olsen getting away with this.

Charlie pushed out from behind her desk, left her office and found Dustin Lee, one of her instructors, putting away equipment from one their most popular lunchtime classes.

"Any luck on getting your window replaced sooner rather than later?" he asked.

If only. "Unfortunately, not."

"I still can't believe someone shot at you."

Neither could she. "I know. It's crazy."

The front door opened. In walked Mercy McCoy.

"Hello," the young woman said. Charlie guessed she was in her early to midtwenties. "Is Rocco here yet?" She was dressed the same as always when she came in. T-shirt and leggings, all in white.

Come to think of it, Charlie had never seen her wear anything but white. She lived on the Shining Light compound, where her father was the leader of a cult. Charlie had heard that they had a color system, where each hue held a different meaning.

She'd always wanted to ask Mercy but didn't want to make her or anyone in USD uncomfortable. This was a safe space for everyone.

"Afraid not," Charlie said. "He's not coming in today." Sometimes her cousin popped in for afternoon sessions. But she could usually rely on him to cover a couple of evening classes one night a week.

Mercy frowned, the disappointment in her eyes evident. "We were supposed to have a one-on-one training session."

It hadn't been on the schedule. Mercy had started out taking group classes, but once Rocco offered individual training, Charlie hadn't seen much of her.

"Sorry about that," Charlie said. "He's caught up with work today." She had no idea how long Rocco had been out of town. "I posted on the website that training sessions with him would be canceled until further notice."

"Internet access is limited on the compound." Mercy glanced around as if lost or as though she wasn't quite sure what to do with herself.

"If you want, Dustin can fill in and train you before the next group class."

"Oh, no." Shaking her head, Mercy eased back toward the door. "I don't want to inconvenience anyone."

"I was about to take my break, but it's no trouble," Dustin said. "Just give me ten minutes."

"That's okay. I should've checked the website for changes."

If Charlie had known about the appointment, she would've called Mercy to inform her.

"It's no problem," Dustin said. "Honest."

"I'm used to Rocco's style of teaching. I'll just wait until he gets back."

Charlie suspected that the young woman didn't want to get used to a different trainer. Whenever Rocco and Mercy were in the same room together, she stared at him like she was captivated.

Charlie would have to be blind not to see the effect her cousin had on women, but this time she thought it might be mutual. Rocco seemed equally taken by her. Mercy had a glow to her, radiating light. She was one of those natural beauties, who looked fragile on the outside, but if she was anything like her father, Marshall McCoy—Empyrean, as his acolytes called him—she was far from weak.

Underestimating Mercy would be a mistake.

"Are you sure?" Charlie asked. "You're already here."

"I'm sure."

"Sorry about the confusion," Charlie said.

"Please let him know that I stopped by." With a wave, Mercy left.

Charlie turned to Dustin. "I need a favor," she said.

"Anything. Just ask."

"Make that two favors. Can you cover things here on your own?" It was a lot to ask. Her other trainer, Teddy Williams, had failed to show up yet again. Sometimes he came in late. Or left early. Called in sick. Regardless of the warnings she'd given him, Teddy was growing more unreliable. She understood that working at USD was only a part-time gig for him, but if this continued, she was going to have to let him go.

"Sure." Dustin didn't look enthused. "What's going on?"

"I need to take care of some things. That brings me to favor number two."

"Which is?"

"How do you feel about swapping cars?" She held up the keys to her Hellcat.

With a new gleam in his eyes, Dustin smiled. "I've been trying to get behind the wheel of that beauty since I started working here."

"Now's your chance."

"Say no more." He fished in his pocket, pulled out the keys to his SUV and handed them to her.

"I'll be back in time to close."

Once she grabbed her things, she headed to his SUV. The Jeep was ideal for surveillance. It had black-tinted windows, plenty of room to spread out and it blended in. Best of all, in case Seth noticed the vehicle, it wasn't registered to Charlie.

She tucked her hair into a baseball cap and took off. Next on her to-do list was finding Detective Olsen. Today, that might be a crapshoot.

Three weeks ago she had surveilled him, taking pictures and meticulous notes. The purpose hadn't been to ascertain if he was up to something nefarious, like now. Then it had been to see if he had a routine in order to pick the best day and time for Haley to leave him. To help a person make a smooth transition into a new life took months of preparation. Time to arrange fake credentials and build an online history. The documents that Haley would have needed weren't even ready. The plan was for Haley to disappear in twelve days once everything was in order.

While following Seth, Charlie had quickly learned two things. It was easier to do undetected if she had a tracker on his truck. The second being that the most predictable part of his schedule was in the early morning. Later in the day things got hectic, but he always hit the gym at the crack of dawn, no matter what. Beyond that, he ate at Delgado's bar and grill about three times a week. The only other places he frequented with any regularity was the local strip club out on Raven Drive—sometimes in the middle of the day or late at night since they were open from noon to 2:00 a.m.—and the station.

Charlie cruised past the police station. Brian's truck was parked out front. She took it as a hopeful sign that he was there investigating. Normally, he was at a different facility where the task force worked.

Turning the corner, she drove by the adjacent parking lot in the rear of the building and spotted Seth's gray Chevy pickup. Charlie made a U-turn farther down the block and pulled over, where she had sight of the station as well as the lot. While she waited for him to leave, she took out her camera, which had an attached telephoto lens. She wanted proof of whatever he was up to.

Her timing couldn't have been any better. Seth shoved through the back door and strode into the lot, wearing jeans and a T-shirt. Clean-shaven. Slicked-back hair.

She wasn't sure what she had expected. Perhaps for him to appear disheveled, at the very least distressed. Certainly not groomed and undaunted with a smug smile on his face. He lit up a cigarette as he crossed the lot. She zoomed in closer on him, making sure she got a shot of the carefree grin on his face, right before he hopped into his truck.

If she was a betting a woman, she'd wager a kidney that Seth Olsen had just given the performance of his life inside the station. Playing the part of the grieving, confused husband.

What a fake and a liar. The man was no good.

It didn't take long until he drove out of the parking lot, headed in the opposite direction. Charlie put the SUV in drive and followed him, keeping as much distance as possible without losing him. Even though she was in an inconspicuous car, she didn't dare get too close. She had hoped to catch sight of another vehicle tailing him, a detective conducting a thorough investigation. But she was the only one on him.

Not surprising.

They were headed toward the outskirts of town, where it was going to be difficult to follow someone surreptitiously. With long, wide stretches of plains and winding mountain roads, there would be few, if any, cars to hide behind, but she was too stubborn to give up.

As soon as she had an opportunity, she'd put a GPS tracker back on his truck. That would enable her to keep a good mile between them without the threat of being discovered. In the meantime, she pulled into the lot of a feed store. It was the last retail shop, or much of anything, before leaving town. If Seth came back to Laramie, he'd have to take this road.

To bide some time, she used the facilities inside the store, bought some water and hunkered down in the SUV. The store had open Wi-Fi. She piggybacked off it, using the laptop that she'd brought along, and kept an eye on passing traffic while she got some work done.

Two hours later, she spotted a gray Chevy pickup. It was Seth's.

She set her laptop to the side and started the engine. Once he passed, she gave him a few seconds, then drove out. Back through town they went. Until he headed east.

The moment he turned onto Raven Drive, she knew where he was going. The audacity of it had her gritting her teeth.

Across the street from the Bare Back Gentlemen's Club, she found a place to park that offered a prime view. Rather than staying visible from the front seat, she climbed into the back of the Jeep and managed to get a few pictures of him entering the club.

Now all she could do was wait. She glanced at the time on her cell phone. If only there was some way for her to get out of dinner with Brian. Tailing Seth was a higher priority. In her gut, she knew it would lead to something, eventually. But Brian had made it clear that he wasn't going to share whatever he learned over the phone.

She needed all the pieces to put together the puzzle.

So as much as she wanted to get out of it, later tonight she had to have dinner with Bradshaw.

As BRIAN LIFTED the strainer basket from the large pot on the stove, the doorbell rang.

He looked at the time on the oven. Seven thirty on the dot. He dumped the seafood boil into an aluminum pan and shook the mound of fresh shrimp, lobster tails, crab legs, sweet corn and halved red potatoes before setting it on the outside dining table that he'd lined with newspaper. Then he wiped his hands and answered the door.

"Smells good." Charlie removed a ball cap from her head and finger-combed her hair as she stepped inside.

"Hope you're not allergic to shellfish."

"Lucky for you that I'm not."

"I should've asked." The safer choice would've been steak. "But I like to gamble from time to time." He led the way through the main living space of his house and out the back door.

Entering the patio, she glanced at the table, where beside the food he had a bucket of ice with beers and a nice chardonnay to complement the dinner.

"Wow. Look at this spread," she said. "You made enough food for at least four."

"I like to cook large meals, so I have plenty of leftovers. Saves time in the kitchen."

She picked up the bottle of twenty-year-old Glenfiddich he'd also bought. "You even shelled out the big bucks for my favorite scotch."

It had set him back two hundred dollars, but if it got her talking, then it was worth it.

"For future reference," she said, "I only drink the stuff on rare occasions. Horrendous day. Best day ever. That sort of thing."

He was stuck on the prospect of future dinners. With her. He hoped like hell he'd get to explore the possibility. "Good to know. Have a seat."

"Mind if I clean up first?" she asked.

"No, go right ahead. Second door on the left." He indicated the hallway.

While she used the bathroom, he went back to the kitchen for the melted butter, seafood sauce and warm crusty bread. By the time he had it on the table, she reemerged. As she sat across from him, she grabbed a beer.

"I didn't think that would be your beverage of choice," he said.

"I'll have a cold brewski from time to time. But tonight, I just want to taste what you enjoy."

He smiled, unable to help it. "What's with laying on the charm?"

"I've been accused of being many things. Obstinate. Impulsive. Too smart for my own good. But charming? Never."

Tonight, they were both playing games. Did she think she had to butter him up for him to share information? Or was there more to it?

She popped the cap off her beer and took a long swig.

"Verdict?" He took a bottle of beer also and opened it.

"I like it. The pale ale will go well with the seafood. Do you eat out here often?"

"Weather permitting, every chance I get. My father made this table himself. And a few years back, I built the pizza oven."

She glanced at the outdoor kitchen that also included a grill and smoker. "Nice setup."

"Yeah." He wanted it to be nice for his parents. "I've had plenty of family meals here." Brian loved the fresh air, the land, the green landscape, surrounded by mountains. If only he had been able to do more to keep his parents living in the house longer. "Dig in."

They both helped themselves to the food, loading their plates, and began eating. He had set the table with all the utensils and tools they'd need, including wooden mallets.

She cracked crab legs, plucking out succulent meat and licking her fingers as she devoured the meal. "Did you learn anything?"

He had, but he wasn't going to rush this. "First, there's something I've been meaning to ask you."

"Oh, yeah." She tore off a piece of bread. "What's that?"

"When I offered to teach classes for free at USD, why did you turn me down without giving me a chance?"

She grunted and chewed bread. "Honestly?"

"Please." He was dying to know.

"Because you're a cop."

That stung. "So, what. Rocco is ATF. You let him help out at your school."

Munching on shrimp, she shook her head. "Not the same thing."

"Both law enforcement."

She shrugged. "Still different."

"What have you got against cops?"

She clearly had some grudge. A big one, too, if she had declined his offer to work for free based solely on that.

"I see right through this little plan of yours," she said.

"What plan is that?"

"Serving sumptuous seafood to get me talking."

She was right, but he wasn't letting on easily. "How so?"

"There's a surprising intimacy to it. The informality that comes when you eat with your hands."

It was hard to be aloof with someone while sucking tasty bits of crab from your fingers. That was the reason he'd chosen the meal instead of steaks.

Brian gave a knowing smile. "Guilty as charged." She was changing the subject. Trying to lead him down a different path. "Spill it." He kept his features soft, his tone inquisitive not defensive. "Why do you hate cops?"

"If I open that can of worms, things will get heavy, fast, and not in the way that you want."

She had no idea what he wanted. If she did, it would probably scare her off.

"I want to know you," he said. "Want you to know me." All true. "This is an important subject, considering I'm the thing you hate."

"All right. Remember you asked for this." Dropping crab legs into her bowl, she looked up at him. "My dad was a cop. He used to beat my mother. She never dared call 911 because he told her that he would make her disappear if she ever did. But the neighbors called the police a couple of times. When they showed up, they would take my dad outside, talk to him on the front lawn. Neighbors watched from their yards or from their windows. Then they'd let him go. They claimed it was because my mom wouldn't make a statement or press charges. Bottom line, calling them was pointless. I learned the hard way that blue wall of silence is real."

The same thing that had supposedly happened with Haley. At least according to Charlie.

But in this day and age, once a victim or someone else called the police to report domestic violence, the matter was usually out of the victim's hands. If a law enforcement officer believed a crime was committed, they were obligated to arrest the alleged offender, regardless of whether the victim wanted to press charges.

Who was to say how strictly that had been enforced when Charlie was a kid?

Today, with the legislation that had been passed to protect victims of domestic violence, the law was upheld.

Of course, he wasn't so naive as to think that there weren't any cases that slipped through the cracks.

This was a small town. Seth did have a lot of friends on the force. Some who might have been inclined to look the other way. Not that Brian ever would have.

"I remember, vividly, the last time my father beat her. It was summertime. I was seven. There was a heat wave. A scorcher of a day. The cicadas were so loud, it was kind of frightening. Meat loaf for dinner set him off. Because he'd wanted fried chicken. He beat her so badly, I thought he might kill her. So, I called the cops. When they came, I finally mustered the courage to speak up. Even though my father looked at me like he wanted to strangle me, hollered at me to shut up. I kept talking, told them everything that happened. The two officers had an argument outside. One finally came back. Arrested my father. Five hours later. Five," she said, holding up her hand, "he stormed back into the house. My father snatched me out of bed by my hair. Grabbed his gun. Dragged me to their bedroom.

Mom begged him not to hurt me. He looked at me with these glassy eyes, had the strangest expression. Told me that this was my fault. Then he shot my mother. Next himself. And left me alive."

To live with the memory of that horror. Surely with survivor's guilt as well. Losing both her parents in such an awful, ugly way, to be traumatized at such a young age. What a terrible thing.

"I'm so sorry you had to go through that," he said.

"That's the summer I went to live with my aunt and uncle, Rocco's parents."

It explained a lot about Charlie. Even why Rocco was the closest person to her without the two of them actually being close.

"Something like that changes you forever. Leaves an indelible mark. I've never experienced anything of that magnitude. After I lost two teammates during a dangerous mission, I almost turned into a cynical, bitter wretch." If he'd gone through what Charlie had endured, at seven, who knows what it would've done to him. As a grown man, there had been times where the darkness tugging at him had threatened to drag him under. But every day he woke up grateful, to be alive, for a chance to make a difference in the world. "Somehow, I force myself to still see the glass as half full. But it's not always easy."

He knew the situation for Charlie was far more complex.

"Enough of this pity party," she said lightly, as though they'd been making small talk. "This isn't why I'm here. Are you going to tell me what you learned? Unless you came up with nothing."

He was fascinated by more than her beauty. It was the whole package. Her mind. Her heart. Her secrets.

Her scars.

"Earlier this morning, I spoke with the fire marshal." Sawyer Powell had been helpful. "It was arson out at the Olsen house, which you already suspected. An accelerant was used. Smokeless gunpowder."

"The type of accelerant a cop would use."

She wasn't wrong there. Someone knowledgeable about firearms would've chosen it. "That's not evidence Seth was responsible for the fire. No evidence was found in Haley's car. The canines went through the debris of the house. They didn't find a body, but they did pick up some DNA. Traces of blood."

Charlie stiffened, and he could feel the tension radiating off her. "Only traces? But I saw a lot. There was so much blood."

Staring in her eyes, he believed her. "The fire destroyed quite a bit of evidence."

"What about Detective Olsen? Has he been charged?"

Brian shook his head. "No. Haley is considered a missing person. Seth has an alibi for the time in question and has been put on administrative leave."

Her brow furrowed. "What alibi?"

"Another detective who works with him." Whether they were on duty at the time was unclear, but Brian would find out for certain.

"Are you kidding me?" The tone of her voice pulled at him. "One detective protecting another. Next, you're going to say that neither of them would lie and that Seth isn't capable of murder."

People were capable of horrible things with proper motivation, under the right circumstances. Seth had worked Vice first and now Narcotics, but any smart cop would know how to get rid of a body, as well as evidence, and craft an alibi. Also, it didn't give Brian a warm and fuzzy that Seth was pals with another detective who turned out to be his alibi. But he didn't want to feed into Charlie's mistrust. "There's an experienced detective investigating. A good guy."

Although he knew the cop assigned—and there were more pros than cons with Kramer on the case—the detective had some shortcomings that made Brian wonder if it might impact the investigation. While Brian had been at the station, he hadn't been able to get the guy alone, but he needed to soon.

"Are you telling me that if Olsen is responsible, if he did something to Haley and blew up his own house to cover it up, that it's impossible for him to get away with it?"

Brian had asked himself the same question while he'd nosed around the station earlier. There were potential cracks in the system. A lot of the cops on the force had been embedded for many years and had forged deep loyalties. At times even Brian was treated as an outsider and had to struggle to break in.

"Not impossible, but improbable." He hoped.

"Are you going to wash your hands of this?" She fixed those green eyes on him. "Or are you going to look into it deeper? Will you help me?" she pleaded.

"I can't investigate a possible homicide without someone in the department catching wind of it."

"Thanks for dinner." Tossing her napkin on the table, she stood.

He got to his feet and cupped her shoulder, stopping her. "You told me that we'd compare. What did you learn?"

Charlie frowned. "When Olsen left the police station, he paid a visit to the strip club on Raven. Stayed two hours."

That wasn't a crime. "Maybe he needed to blow off steam. Disconnect for a while." Different strokes for different folks.

At the station, Seth had seemed bereft and bewildered. All the guys offered to donate clothes since he'd lost everything in the explosion, except for the things he kept in his locker at work.

"Then he went to a house on Mulberry." She gave him the exact address. "He had a key and let himself in. Can you find out who owns the place?"

"Yeah, I can, but do you have any idea how dangerous it was to follow him?"

"Somebody has to. Apparently, nobody in the LPD cares enough to bother. I feel responsible for Haley. I was the one who convinced her to leave him and was helping her prepare. She was scared enough to be willing to upend her life and move halfway across the country. If he got wind of it and did this, then it's on me. I feel like I failed her." Charlie's gaze clung to his as everything about her softened.

The heavy weight of this, her concern for Haley along with her guilt, this striking moment of vulnerability in the impervious Charlie Sharp, shone clear in her eyes. Still, he couldn't shake the sense that there was more to this story, to her involvement, that she wasn't telling him. If only she could trust him enough to be completely honest.

A big ask that would take time. Good thing he was a patient man.

"Can you understand?" she asked in a low voice that trembled.

He sighed, knowing he was going to regret what he was about to say next. "I do and I care. I'll investigate further if you agree to back off." Her getting involved any deeper wasn't going to help resolve the case or keep Charlie safe.

"Sure," she said after a moment of hesitation. "I'll take a step back while you handle it."

Brian wanted to believe that she'd let it go. He really did, but he sensed her stubbornness was only surpassed by her determination. "Let me put the food away, grab my keys and I'll follow you home."

Another frown. "To camp out again?"

He nodded even as his back protested.

"No need," she said. "Give me the keys to Rocco's. I'll crash there until he gets back."

Brian was confident that her cousin wouldn't mind, but he'd texted his buddy earlier to be sure and got a thumbs-up. "Can I trust you to follow through? To sit on the sidelines of this and stay at Rocco's?"

Charlie gave a sad, slow smile that brought every one of his senses to red alert. "I guess you'll just have to wait and see."

Chapter Five

Guilt churned through Charlie as she maneuvered Dustin's SUV through the parking lot of Seth's gym.

It hadn't been her intention to lie to Brian when she'd agreed to keep her nose out of this. The deal had been made in good faith, albeit reluctantly. Later at Rocco's last night, she'd tossed and turned on the sofa, unable to stop thinking about Haley. Worrying about what had happened to her. Wondering whether Seth would slither free from any blame. Wishing she had the power to do something about it.

Then she realized that she did have power.

To do something no one on the police force was willing to undertake.

In the early morning lights, she spotted the gray pickup at the back of the lot.

Looked as though the creature of habit's routine hadn't changed since Charlie ran surveillance on him earlier in the year. If he did as she expected, he would spend another ten minutes pumping weights. Then wrap up with a three-mile run on the treadmill before hitting the showers. Since he was on administrative leave, she had no idea where he'd go after that.

She parked with an empty space between their vehicles, tucked a baseball cap on her head, slipped the hood from her black zip-up jacket over it and got out. Glancing around to make sure the coast was clear, she edged closer to the Chevy.

Once she was sure no one would see her, she shot around to the passenger's side and dropped to the ground near the back wheel. Planting a tracker inside a vehicle was ideal, but it took longer and circumventing an alarm system wasn't simple with a modern car. Placing it outside did run the risk of the device breaking or getting lost, but she'd had good luck in the past. She took the GPS tracker from her pocket and reached up past the wheel and mounted the magnetic box, the size of a deck of playing cards, on a flat surface on the frame. Unless he had to change the tire, he'd never see it.

Unfortunately, it wasn't a motion-activated unit that would only turn on whenever the vehicle started moving, which preserved the life of the battery. But she hoped there wouldn't be a need to follow him for months.

She got up and hopped into the SUV.

None too soon either. Seth pushed through the doors of the gym in deep conversation with another man who wore glasses. The guy had a slight build and was jumpy. Kept looking around with a nervous expression.

Charlie grabbed her camera and got a few quick shots of the two speaking.

Olsen started walking through the parking lot. He put his hand on the man's shoulder. Glasses stiffened, then nodded as he listened.

A couple more photos. Time to get out of there before he noticed her.

Now she'd be able to follow his every move. Document whatever he was up to.

The way Haley talked about her husband, Charlie had discovered one important thing about him. His hubris was his weakness. Seth Olsen thought he could do anything and get away with it. Maybe even murder.

Well, not anymore.

IT HAD BEEN over a year since Brian had been in the police station two days in a row. Every time he stepped inside the building claustrophobia set in. He'd grown accustomed to being on loan to the task force, far removed from the others on the force. Having a sense of purpose that better suited his skill set. Getting to work with the FBI and ATF had broadened his horizons and had gotten him thinking about what was next in his career beyond the LPD.

Detective Kent Kramer wasn't at his desk, but Brian found him in the breakroom filling up his travel mug with coffee.

"Hey, Kent." Brian strode up to him.

"Well, look at who it is. Decided to grace us with your presence again."

The detective met his gaze. Heavy bags under his bloodshot eyes bolstered Brian's concerns. After the death of his wife in a car accident, Kent hadn't been the same. It was no secret he drowned his sorrows every night at a bar. Before Brian's assignment to the joint task force, he'd never caught the smell of alcohol on Kent's breath, but there had been times when he'd wondered if the detective had become a functioning alcoholic. Kent still could get the job done, but his drinking was also a potential liability that Brian couldn't ignore.

"I was hoping to run in to you. Alone."

"Oh, yeah," Kent said, with an easy smile. "Something little ole me can do to help you on your *special* task force?"

Kent had taken a shine to him from the beginning and had been the one to encourage Brian to go for detective early. Not quite a mentor, Kent had been more of cheer-leader. Rooting him on. The first to tell him "atta boy." The only one to congratulate him on being picked as the police liaison for the task force.

"No," Brian said. "Actually, I was wondering if I might be of any assistance to you?"

Kent's brow furrowed as the smile faded. "How so?"

"I was driving by Seth's place last night," Brian said, "and saw the smoke from the fire."

"Really?" Kent smoothed a hand down over his wrinkled suit jacket. "According to dispatch, you got a report about the fire. No mention of you seeing it firsthand."

"Both, really." Brian poured himself a cup of coffee. "I was wondering why you're the only one investigating." For a case this big, involving one of their own, there should be two detectives working on it.

Kent glanced around, causing Brian to do likewise. They were alone in the room. No one was in the hallway. "I asked the lieutenant the same thing," he said, lowering his voice. "Apparently, it's complicated. This doesn't look good for Seth, you know, considering his first wife, Linda, died under suspicious circumstances."

Brian wasn't aware that he'd been married before. "What happened to her?"

"Too much wine. Slipped down the stairs. Broke her neck. Coroner ruled it an accident."

"But Seth lived in a one-story ranch."

Kent shook his head. "They used to live in Linda's house. Massive place. Three levels."

"Do you remember her blood alcohol content?"

"Looked it up once I got this case. She had a .30 BAC."

Brian whistled. That was high enough to severely impair walking, even speech. At .08 a person was considered intoxicated.

"After she died, he sold the house," Kent said. "Used the proceeds to stop his family ranch from going into foreclosure. Seth said that it was the only good thing that came out of her death. That she was his angel taking care of him from the beyond."

"That doesn't explain why you're the only detective on this." If anything, that gave even more reasons as to why this was a two-person investigation.

Kent's gaze swept the hallway. He waited until an officer passed by. "Rumor has it there are dirty cops in the LPD."

Brian had heard rumblings of the same and presumed the new police chief, Wilhelmina Nelson, had been brought in to clean up the problem before it was verified as credible and made headlines. One more reason Brian had been grateful to be assigned elsewhere. But the chief was in for an uphill battle.

If there were dirty cops, Vice and Narcotics would be a good place to start looking for them. The odds were there would be others at different levels, working in various areas. A tight-knit group.

Kent took a gulp of his coffee. "Chief Nelson told the lieutenant that she doesn't want anyone close to Seth working on the case. You're looking at the one detective who isn't, besides yourself. He's bosom buddies with all the others."

Laramie was a small town. The size of the entire police force was tiny compared to a single precinct in a large city like New York or Chicago.

"Internal Affairs is going to get involved," Kent said. "They're sending someone down from Cheyenne next week. Until then, it's just me."

"Have you made any headway? Got any leads?"

Kent added cream and sugar to his coffee. "One dead end after another so far. No pun intended. Seth claims if anything happened to his current wife that her boyfriend is behind it. I talked to the guy. He clammed up as soon as I mentioned the name Olsen. Refused to say anything else. But he denied being Haley's lover, and he's got a solid alibi that checks out." Kent took another furtive glance toward the corridor. "Which is more than I can say for Seth."

More surprising news. "I thought Colvin was his alibi."

Sipping his coffee, Kent nodded. "Yeah. Supposedly. But they weren't on duty at the time. I can't verify that they were even together or what they were doing. I've only got Colvin's and Seth's word to go on."

Wonderful. "What's the alleged boyfriend's name?" Brian asked.

Tipping his head to the side, Kent gave him a wry look. "Why?"

"Maybe I can take another pass at him for you. It can't hurt."

"Listen, you're the only other detective I'd even consider talking to about this. It's a big mess. Nothing adds up. My gut tells me this one is not going to end well. As much as I could use someone else on this case with me, it's got to be official. If you want more information or intend to question suspects, you have to get the lieutenant's blessing. Then I'll be happy to share everything I've got, and you'll be free to take a crack at the alleged boyfriend. But you should know that Olsen has some serious connections in town. You won't be doing yourself any favors hitching a ride on this circus."

Brian gave him a two-finger salute. If Kent was already seeing red flags, the need for a second detective investigating was essential. And urgent. IA's involvement was a good sign, but a lot could happen between now and their arrival. Evidence had already been destroyed in the fire. Who was to say what else could happen.

Carrying his cup of coffee, Brian made his way to the lieutenant's office. He rapped his knuckles on the door.

Lieutenant Malcolm Jameson looked up from the computer. "Bradshaw." He beckoned for him to enter. "Surprised to see you. What can I do for you?"

Brian closed the door behind him. "Can I speak frankly?"

"I wouldn't have it any other way." The lieutenant gestured for him to take a chair. "Are you having a problem on the task force? Supervisory Agent Nash Garner speaks very highly of the work you're doing over there."

"That's nice to know and no, I'm not having any problems. I heard about the investigation regarding Detective Olsen and the disappearance of his wife. I understand the situation is complicated, but Kramer would welcome a partner on this."

Lieutenant Jameson pressed his lips into a thin, hard line. "He's the only one Chief Nelson would sign off on. We need to make sure there isn't a conflict of interest in the investigation. Kramer is seasoned and capable. Besides, he only has to manage a few more days. IA will be here soon enough."

"Do you think the chief would sign off on me?"

"Don't you already have an assignment? A fairly high-profile one at that."

Since Brian had joined the force, he kept his nose to the grindstone, never taking vacation days or calling in sick. Only handling family affairs in his spare time. Nash had been pushing him to take some time off. So when Brian had finally asked this morning, his last-minute request had been approved.

"As luck would have it, I can be spared for a few days. I've got the free time. Rather than slack off, why not put me on the case?"

The lieutenant leaned back in his chair and folded his hands on the desk. "I have to admit I'm surprised you've taken such a keen interest in this."

"If my wife went missing and my house blew up, I'd want it to be all hands on deck. This is a two-person case, yet only one detective is working on it."

Jameson narrowed his eyes. "I still haven't figured you out yet. What drives you to push so hard. Ambition? Accolades? Some other angle? I know you don't do it for the paycheck."

Smiling, Brian lowered his head. He could offer the truth. That the driving force in him was simple—a call to serve. To protect. To see justice served. Never to miss the opportunity to fulfill his purpose.

Instead, he said, "I owe Kent. If not for him, I wouldn't

be a detective. He's still going through a rough patch and needs a partner until IA gets here. I'd like to do it."

The lieutenant nodded. "I can respect that. It's good that you've had distance with the department for a while. You've got a reputation for getting along with everyone, and yet, not really being pals with anyone." Then he frowned. "Don't you play football with Seth and a few of the others? Yeah," he said, as if remembering now. "You scored the winning touchdown in the annual game against the fire department."

"The season is about to start back up. This week in fact. I can make excuses not to participate. I only played for fun and the extra exercise. Sometimes we grabbed a drink afterward. I assure you there's no conflict of interest."

After a moment of consideration, he said, "Okay." He picked up the phone. "If Chief Nelson says yes, which I think she will, you're Kent's partner. Temporary basis. Avoid coming to the station. No one will know you're on this. It's best to keep it that way. And when football starts up again, you should play like you normally would. You never know what you might learn."

"Sure, I can do that."

CLICK. CLICK.

Charlie snapped photos of Seth leaving Delgado's. He'd finished having dinner with a man she recognized. The guy had a couple of well-placed ads touting him as the sharpest real estate agent in the Cowboy State.

Pretty big claim if you asked her.

After Seth climbed into his truck, she threw the SUV into drive and followed her target. Luck had been on her side this morning when she'd found Seth at the gym. From there, tailing him all day had been simple, even if it had turned up absolutely nothing so far. Nonetheless, she'd keep at it, tracking him, photographing whatever she could.

When the time was right, she'd come clean to Brian and admit to him that sitting on the sidelines wasn't her style. There had to be different terms they could agree on where he'd still help look into this.

Sighing, Charlie turned down Raven.

Good grief, again?

Part of her considered not even bothering to follow him to the strip club, but she'd devised the plan to see what eventually turned up. That required her to stick to it, no matter how dull or repetitive the task.

After she parked in the same spot she'd found yesterday, she took a few pictures of him entering the club. Then she settled into the back seat of the SUV with no idea how long the wait could be.

This was dull work, but her fingers were crossed that it would pay off in the end.

An hour later and one power bar eaten, the front door of the club swung open. A redhead with voluminous, curly hair strutted out, wearing a robe that was tied closed and sky-high heels. Charlie slumped down in the back seat, ready to dismiss her until she realized the woman was making a beeline straight over to the SUV.

What in the world?

Setting the camera to the side, Charlie considered hopping in the front behind the wheel and taking off, but she'd already been made. Better to find out what the woman wanted.

The redhead marched up to the vehicle and knocked on the driver's side rear window. "Get out of the car."

"Excuse me?"

"You heard me. Get out. Right now."

Questions tumbled through Charlie's mind. The woman posed no physical threat, yet Charlie had a bad feeling about this. It wasn't often that she followed people and staked out a place, but this was the first time something like this had ever happened.

Bang, bang, bang.

The jarring sound came from the roof of the vehicle, snatching Charlie's attention to the passenger's side.

A tall, beefy man stood at the other window. Wearing a black T-shirt that exposed sculpted biceps and black pants, he was clearly a bouncer. He must have left the club out a different door and crept around.

They'd gotten the drop on her.

"You heard the woman," he said in a deep baritone voice. "Out of the car."

Her options seemed limited but doing as they ordered wasn't at the top of her list of preferences. "I'll leave, okay," Charlie said, climbing into the front seat.

As she fumbled for the keys, the redhead drew something from one of the robe's pockets that glinted in the fading light of day. It was a switchblade. "I bet I can flatten two tires before you pull off," the woman said, holding up the knife. "What's it going to be? You get out and we chat, or you get flat tires?"

That narrowed her choices down to two. Both undesirable. What did they want from her?

Had Seth spotted her and sent them to check her out?

Charlie glanced over at her purse where her gun was stashed. Drawing it might dial up the tension unnecessarily. If need be, she could disarm the woman and take on the bouncer. Violence was always a last resort for her. She unlocked the door and did as they demanded. "Is there a problem?" she asked, raising her palms in a conciliatory gesture.

"That's what I'm here to find out." The redhead pointed the tip of the blade at Charlie and propped her other hand on her hip. "This is the second day I've seen you scoping the place out. The last time someone cased the club, me and two other girls were robbed after our shifts."

The aggressive approach now made sense and was even warranted.

"This is a misunderstanding." One that could hopefully be cleared up easily and quickly. "I'm not casing the club or planning to rob anyone."

"Then why are you out here?"

"I'm following a husband." Charlie gestured over her shoulder to the back seat of the car, where the camera was visible.

The redhead looked inside. "All right. I believe you. Now, that'll be fifty bucks for each of us."

Charlie lowered her hands. "What exactly am I paying for?"

"Our silence." The redhead smiled. "Otherwise, Hammer," she said, pointing to the bouncer, "is going to tell every dude inside to be on the lookout for you, along with your description, the make, model, color and license number of your car."

This was a shakedown. How many private investigators had they put through the same process?

With a groan, Charlie got her purse and fished out what

little cash she had. "It's all I have. Eighty bucks will have to suffice."

"This will do." They divided the cash between them. The bouncer headed back to the club while the woman stayed. "The husband inside yours?"

"No."

"What's his name?"

Charlie folded her arms. "I'd rather not say."

"And I'd rather that you did. Believe it or not, I'm all about women helping women."

A harsh chuckle flew out of Charlie's mouth. "Forgive me for not believing you, considering you just extorted me for money."

"We all got to make a living, sweetheart. Even you're getting paid by the hour to sit out here with your camera."

"This is pro bono for me. A friend of mine is missing, and I'm trying to figure out if her husband is responsible."

Something passed over the woman's face, perhaps a flicker of curiosity or concern. "Most of the men in there treat us like meat. Disposable. Not like working women, trying to pay their bills, who deserve respect. I don't owe any of them anything. What's his name?"

There were a hundred reasons not to trust her and if any of them were valid, then forty dollars was going to buy her silence anyway. "Seth Olsen," Charlie said, figuring she had more to gain than to lose.

The redhead reeled back. "Haley is missing?"

"You know her?"

"Yeah." She nodded. "We're friends."

Friends? Charlie hadn't seen that one coming.

"We can't talk out here," the woman continued, glancing back across the street. "Drive around to the back of the club and park behind the dumpster. Wait about thirty minutes. Give me a chance to do my performance and I'll come out afterward."

"Okay." Charlie opened the car door as a thought struck her. "Hey, I didn't get your name?"

"Aubrey. Who are you?"

"I'm Charlie."

Once she had parked in the rear of the building, where Aubrey had told her, it was the longest thirty minutes of her life as she waited. Hard to believe that Haley was friends with Aubrey, stripper and extortionist. Haley was always Miss Prim-and-Proper. As a housewife, she had plenty of time to volunteer at the hospital and for social clubs like the Kiwanis, the cache of crocheters, and running the weekly bingo game down at the VFW—Veterans of Foreign Wars.

This didn't fit her image. Then again, when Aubrey was fully clothed and not wielding a knife, maybe she enjoyed crocheting, too.

Charlie's pulse spiked when the redhead pushed through the back door, once again wearing a robe.

The staccato *click-clack* of Aubrey's heels echoed in the alleyway as she approached the vehicle. She hopped in the passenger's seat and shut the door.

One question kept repeating in Charlie's head. "How did you and Haley meet?" she asked, hoping it didn't come across as offensive.

"At the club," Aubrey said. "Haley used to work here. That's how she met Seth. She caught his eye and made sure to keep his attention. At first, he was adoring, even sweet. She reeled him in, and he swept her off her feet. After they got married, he made her quit. Haley didn't mind. She thought he just didn't want her taking her clothes off for other men, but soon enough she learned that he wouldn't let her get a job anywhere. Insisted that she stay at home."

He wanted her isolated, alone and completely dependent on him for money. "That's the classic behavior of an abuser."

"You know?" Aubrey turned toward her and leaned against the door. "That he beats her?"

Charlie nodded.

"Once they got engaged, he became controlling." Aubrey wrung her hands. "I told her he wasn't going to stop after they exchanged vows. Something like that always gets worse. But she wouldn't listen. She thought he was her Prince Charming."

No such thing. A perfect example of why Charlie hated fairy tales. Rather than be a damsel in distress, she believed in rescuing herself.

"What happened to Haley?" Aubrey asked.

"I don't know. I'm trying to piece it together."

"He used to tell her that if she didn't do as she was told that he'd make her disappear. I guess he finally made good on that promise. Not the first time, either. You know his first wife died? The newspaper said it was a tragic accident. Stated Seth had been cleared of any suspicion."

The coincidence of two women Seth had been married to snatched out of his life—one an accident, the other disappeared—was too strong, too far a stretch to be happenstance. Or to be ignored.

"Did you ever hear him threaten Haley?" Charlie asked. "Witness the abuse firsthand?"

Aubrey shook her head. "No. Only what Haley told me."

Then the cops would dismiss it, calling it hearsay. "When was the last time you spoke to her?"

"It's been months. Not since Seth started coming to the club almost daily. I noticed he started paying less attention to the girls while he's here. He's always meeting with somebody. This is like his second office. I told Haley about it. She asked me to spy on him. But it was too dangerous. I told her no. Then she stopped talking to me. I ran into Rafe a few weeks ago. Asked him how she was doing. But he hadn't seen her in ages, either."

"Who's Rafe?"

"Rafael Martinez. Her *friend*," Aubrey said, using air quotes on the last word.

Maybe Brian was right about a third party. "Was Rafe her lover?"

Aubrey shrugged. "I don't know for sure, but I kind of got that feeling. Like she was relying on him to help her break free of Seth. Haley had this way with men, of luring them in, making them feel special. As though they were the center of the universe. When she wanted to be, she was mesmerizing."

"Any idea where I can find Rafe?"

"He works at the floral shop on Grand Avenue."

"Thanks for talking to me." Charlie was sure that this conversation could put Aubrey at risk.

"If you really want to thank me, don't come back here again. Not unless it's to tell me that you found Haley. Or Seth has been arrested."

Chapter Six

Charlie pulled into a spot a couple of doors down from The Prickly Poppy floral shop. She took off her baseball cap and ran her fingers through her hair before she climbed out and headed for the door.

"Please tell me this is a happy coincidence," a familiar male voice said from behind her just as she reached the shop, "and not something that's going to stick in my craw."

Swallowing a sigh, she turned on her heel and faced Brian. "Let's call it a coincidence and leave it at that." Although surprisingly, she was happy to see him.

"Are you here to buy flowers?" he asked, drawing close enough that she had to tip her head back to meet his eyes.

A quiver ran through her belly, but she steeled herself against it.

Her first instinct was to lie. It would've been simpler, avoiding the discussion that they needed to have, but Brian had been a stand-up guy with her to this point. As far as she knew, he hadn't betrayed her trust. Not only did she owe him honesty, but he also had an easy way about him that made opening up more comforting than cringeworthy. Which was a first for her.

"No, I'm not here for flowers," she admitted.

"Is the reason going to—"

"Stick in your craw?" she said, finishing his question. "Yeah, I think it will."

Brian stiffened. "We had an agreement. I've kept my end of the bargain. I'm now assigned to the case. Free to investigate. While you're lying to me, running around, still endangering yourself."

"I thought I could do it. Sit back, do nothing besides wait. Turns out, I'm not built that way. I'm sorry. I didn't mean to lie to you last night."

He gazed down at her. "I'm only trying to keep you safe."

Even though it was obvious he was perturbed, it was the worry in his eyes that made her look down at her feet and swallow around the sudden lump in her throat. It didn't help that he was genuinely nice. And downright sexy.

She'd never been much for cowboys, usually going for the bad boys instead. But a Stetson and jeans looked really hot on him. He was so clean-cut with the kind of wholesome qualities that made her want to get him dirty.

The dangerous combination was beginning to wear her down.

"Whose car are you driving?" he asked, glancing at the SUV.

"It belongs to Dustin, one of my trainers."

"What happened to your Hellcat?"

"Nothing." Shoving her hands in the pockets of her jeans, she straightened. "Now, please stop asking questions that you won't want to hear the answer to." At least Rocco knew better. "I'm not used to this." She waved a hand between them. "Sharing. Cooperating. Making deals and sticking to them."

"It's called working on a team."

He'd hit the nail on the head.

"Yeah," she said. "Not really my forte. I usually go it alone."

"I get it, but you're going to have to figure out how to meet me halfway. I'm putting my neck on the line here, and I don't feel like it's a two-way street."

Tension knotted in her shoulders. "What do you mean?"

"You're not willing to go out on a limb with me. Instead, you're still keeping things from me. I need to know what you're hiding that might help me put it all together."

Her gut clenched. She didn't like that he could see through her, but he had no idea what he was asking of her.

"Charlie." Brian took her by the arm, his grip soft, almost soothing, like his voice. "I don't expect you to spill all your secrets to me on the sidewalk. But telling me the truth is the first part of what I need from you."

The first? "What's the second?"

"You're going to keep digging into this, aren't you?"

She nodded. "I have to do everything that I can."

"I realize that now. So, I'm going to need you stay at my place while you do," he said, and Charlie pulled her arm free. "Before you give me a hard time over the idea, you need to understand that if you insist on putting yourself in danger, then this is the only way I can keep you safe."

"I can protect myself." She'd packed her gun along with other essentials when she'd gone to Rocco's. If ever there was a time to carry it with her, it was now.

He sighed. "Someone already shot at you. You keep poking around, they might try again. If you're with me, you won't be an easy target like you would be alone at Rocco's." His gentle tone made her chest hurt. "Those are the new terms. Nonnegotiable. Or I stop sharing information."

Charlie's mouth dropped open.

How could he box her in like this with an ultimatum? She stepped back, away from him, anger building against her rib cage despite his calm, caring approach. All she could do was glare.

"I'll give you time to think about it while I question Rafe Martinez."

"I'm coming with you," she said.

"I can't have you tagging along with me. This is official. You're staying out here. And while you sit back, try to gain some perspective. Working with me is your best option, but I require full disclosure."

"As well as me sleeping in your bed."

He quirked an eyebrow. "Was that a Freudian slip? I never said anything about *my* bed. I was thinking you'd sleep in the guest room, but whatever you prefer. You're welcome between my sheets anytime." An irritating grin tugged at his mouth as he leaned toward her. Closer and closer. So close that she smelled his aftershave—sandalwood and cedar. "You don't need to fear it or fight it." His breath was warm against her ear.

"What's that?" she asked, his proximity fuzzing up her thoughts.

He met her eyes and brushed her cheek with the back of his hand. "Chemistry."

That one word rang true as a bell, echoing inside of her, dredging up all the loneliness she often tamped down out of habit. A visceral attraction and curiosity and that stupid tingle suppressing her rational mind drew her to him.

She was loath to admit it, but this thing between them was combustible.

Their *chemistry*, and everything about Brian Bradshaw, scared her senseless.

"Other options besides fight or flight," he said softly, his lips an inch from hers, his breath a caress on her face. "More pleasurable ones, too." He cupped a hand around her neck and pulled her mouth to his.

All the reasons not to get close to Brian, that this was a mistake, melted away. The kiss was a slow, hot, all-encompassing thing that was more persuasive than possessive. Everything about it, his warm mouth, his tongue sliding against hers, his rough hand holding her still, was right. As if every interaction prior had been leading up to this moment—stacked dominoes waiting to fall.

But when he broke the kiss, gently easing his body from hers, doubt flowed in like the tide. Waves of it telling her this was wrong.

She only stood there, the breath backing up in her lungs, her pulse throbbing hard and thick. No one had ever kissed her like that, with so much… What was the word for a perfect mix of fire and sweetness? It was like the world had turned upside down, the aftershock leaving her a quivering mess. Her insides turned to jelly.

Brian didn't move. Didn't say anything. Not that he needed to because his hot, penetrating stare spoke volumes.

She glanced away. Cleared her throat. "I'll wait here." Turning, she licked her lips, tasting him again, and went back to the SUV. She leaned against the vehicle and folded her arms across her chest so he wouldn't see that her hands were trembling.

As Brian opened the door to the shop, there was a little chime, and he stepped inside.

The memory of the kiss tingled across her lips. One little kiss and she was struggling to steady herself. What would happen if she slept with him?

He had left her with her brain a little scrambled and two big demands to consider. Both had been issued out of his sense of decency, his nobility—which she was finding harder to question and even harder to resist. Her mind worked overtime to clear it of thoughts of him.

One thing stood out in the haze. The way Aubrey spoke about Haley, as a mesmerizing stripper capable of making a man feel like the center of the universe.

The meek, mousy woman who had skulked into the Underground Self-Defense school all of two months ago, desperate to claim some power over her life sounded like a different woman. Was it possible that Seth had beaten the light out of her, turning her into a husk of the person she used to be?

Or had Haley been acting, playing a sick game?

The florist shop door opened with a chime and Brian strode out. From his grim expression, the conversation hadn't gone well.

"That was fast," she said.

"Because he wouldn't talk to me. He already spoke to another detective and didn't have anything to add to his statement."

"Now what?" she asked. "Any ideas for a next step?"

He rested a shoulder against the car, facing her and hooked his thumbs in his belt. "Did you make a decision?"

She had decided. "For future reference, I hate ultimatums," she said, and his mouth curved a little bit. "But we'll do it your way." Getting shot at wasn't a pleasant experience. If staying with Brian reduced the likelihood of it happening again, then she'd go along with his plan. As for telling him about her illicit activities, maybe that was for the best. Better to scare him off now. Nip this thing between them in the bud once and for all.

She only prayed she didn't end up in jail as a result.

"Then the next step is for you to give it a try with Rafe," he said.

"I thought he wouldn't talk."

"Not to a cop." Brian brushed strands of hair from her face, those chocolate-brown eyes of his direct. "I think you two can build a rapport on common ground," he said in that husky scrape of a voice that sent a tingle down her spine.

Her gaze dropped to his mouth. Just for a second until she remembered Rafe. "I'll give it a go."

"We'll meet back up at my place," he said, heading to his truck.

"Where are you off to?"

"You wanted me on the case. Now that I am, I've got to investigate. I looked up the address you gave me to the house on Mulberry. It's owned by an offshore LLC. The more I dig, the murkier it gets. It's not as easy to hide your identity as it once was, but the owner has done an impressive job. I'm going to speak to an attorney. See what I can find out."

She nodded. "Okay, and so you know, I won't make it to your house until late. I've got to lock up USD tonight."

Teddy was a no-show again and Dustin had a life. Unlike her. She couldn't expect him to work her grueling hours, especially with little advance notice. With the way things were going, following Seth whenever she could, she was going to have to close USD. Perhaps for a few hours every day. Maybe even for a whole day.

"Good luck in there," Brian said, tipping his hat to her.

She entered the shop. The chime sounded. Fragrant, cool air perfumed by flowers curled around her. She met the gaze of the man who was looking at her from behind the counter.

"Hello," he said, snipping a stem of a rose. "Welcome to The Prickly Poppy. Is there something I can help you with today?"

She went up to counter. His name tag read *Rafe*. "I hope so. I'm Charlie Sharp."

"I know who you are." His smile faltered. "You own Underground Self-Defense."

"Haley attended classes there. We're friends. She went missing two days ago."

His features tightened into a wary expression. He set down the shears. "The cops told me. Was that your buddy who was just in here, the one with the badge?"

"I don't like cops. Don't trust them. It worries me that Haley's husband is one and now, she's disappeared."

He gave a slight nod. "What does that have to do with me?"

"I heard you two were friends. Anything you can tell me about Haley might help."

"We used to be friends, but I haven't talked to her in a while."

"It was my understanding that you two were close," she said. "What happened?"

"If Seth finds out that I told anyone—"

"He won't. I promise." She hoped he believed her. "Why did you stop being friends?"

"Last February, that maniac caught me outside, in the back of the shop as I was locking up one night. He was wearing a ski mask," Rafe said. "He beat me up and told me to stay away from his wife. If I went near her again, he'd kill me."

Now she understood why he was being tight-lipped with the police. "That never should've happened to you." Charlie put her hand on his. "Did he say her name? Are you sure it was him?"

"He didn't need to say her name," Rafe scoffed. "I knew who he meant. Recognized his voice. Have nightmares about it."

"I hate to pry, but were you and Haley having an affair?"

Lowering his gaze, Rafe shook his head.

"You can tell me if you were. Her husband is a monster." A wife beater and possibly a murderer. "He treated her like garbage."

"We weren't. Haley needed someone to lean on, to listen to her problems. We clicked. You know?" Rafe said. "There was this one moment when we were having drinks, she did kiss me. It caught me by surprise. I wasn't expecting it. I'm gay, and thought she knew. After I told her, we laughed it off. No big deal. I grew to love Haley. It was hard not to once you got to know her. But it was platonic. I tried to explain to her husband, but he didn't give me a chance."

"Do you know if she was involved with anyone else?" Charlie asked.

"Not while we were friends. I think she would've confided in me if she had been."

"Did Haley mention anything about leaving Seth?"

"Only that she wanted to, but she was scared. I was the one who suggested she take classes at the USD. Then Haley got it into her head to get her friend Aubrey to spy on Seth at the strip club. Something shady was going on. Haley figured that if Aubrey could find some dirt on him that it would give her leverage."

"Don't you mean Haley asked her, but Aubrey refused?"

"No." Rafe shook his head. "They would meet up once a week. Aubrey would tell her everything she found out."

"Are you certain?"

"Positive. Sometimes they spoke in the back here. Or at the pastry shop, Divine Treats. Even the library. Haley was excited about it. Not just the clandestine nature, but it seemed like she might actually get something on Seth."

But why would Aubrey lie?

It was getting harder to figure out who was lying and who was telling the truth.

"How many times did they meet?" Charlie asked.

Rafe shrugged. "I have no idea. After her husband's violent warning, I cut ties with Haley. I know she needed me, and I feel bad about doing it, abandoning her, but I felt like I had no other choice."

The look in his eye was familiar.

Charlie was doing everything in her power to push beyond the crushing sense of failure, but it was rooted deep. The only thing that would ease the mounting pressure was getting answers to her questions.

Chapter Seven

Holding a bag of pastries from Divine Treats, Brian knocked on the office door of assistant district attorney, Melanie Merritt.

She looked up from a stack of papers on her desk, her gaze bouncing from his face to the white paper bag. She groaned. "I told you to stop bribing me for favors. My waistline can't afford it."

With a chuckle, he strode in and removed his hat.

Melanie was savvy, smart, sophisticated and easy on the eyes. The kind of workaholic who only took a break to eat, sleep and exercise.

"Who are you trying to kid?" He placed the bag in the center of her desk. "You're more fit than I am. Besides, you probably didn't even have lunch." *Busy* was the woman's middle name.

A twinge of guilt coursed through him for imposing on her.

Mel frowned. "Got me there. I haven't had anything to eat since breakfast. Unless you count my steady stream of coffee."

"I do not. Can't subsist off caffeine."

"Says who?" Opening the bag, she peered inside and melted at the sight and smell. "My favorite."

A chicken, spinach and artichoke puff pastry tart. The last time she had spent countless hours helping the task force on a case, he noticed how much she enjoyed them.

"I even had them heat it up for you," he said.

"You're going to make some lucky woman very happy one day."

He was working on it. "Can you spare a few minutes?"

"You've come bearing gifts. How can I say no?" She gestured for him to sit.

"I'm working a missing person case, trying to piece things together. A possible suspect was seen at a house." He gave her the address and she made a note. "Tried to find out who owns the place. Got the name of an offshore limited liability company. NHB, LLC. I thought it would be simple to see who was behind it." The Corporate Transparency Act was designed to prevent true anonymity. The CTA maintained a registry of actual owners that was only available to law enforcement, not to the public. "When I looked them up in the database, an offshore holding company was listed."

"Well, the CTA only requires all US registered corporations, LLCs and similar entities to report beneficial ownership."

"So, it's foreign owned?"

"Maybe. Maybe not." She leaned back in her chair. "There are loopholes for both. A beneficial owner is one who owns at least a twenty-five percent equity stake. Say there were five individuals, if each owned twenty percent, they could get around the requirement. Another way is to bury their identities in layers. One offshore LLC behind another and then a holding company after that. Either way, it took someone with legal expertise, who was extremely well-versed in navigating the cracks in the system to do it."

"How do I find out who owns it?"

"Without a subpoena?" she asked.

He nodded. "For now. It's possible a dirty cop is involved. I need this to stay quiet."

"That's going to be tricky. It'll also take time. But I can look into for you."

"When? Are you going to do it instead of sleeping?" He was only half-joking.

She smiled. "I've got to pay you back for this tart some way, don't I?"

Not enough pastries in the entire Cowboy State to earn her assistance. "Thanks. I appreciate it." He stood and headed for the door.

"Brian," she said, stopping him. "You should be careful. It's not often that I've seen insulated layers like this."

He put on his hat. "But you have seen it before?"

She nodded. "The only time I've seen double or triple layering like this is when the cartel has been involved. Throw a dirty cop into the mix and this could blow up in your face. Literally. Watch your back out there."

CHARLIE LOCKED THE front door of USD for the night and checked the GPS tracker on her phone again. This evening Seth had spent time in Centennial and Woods Landing-Jelm. Both towns were a thirty-minute drive from Laramie. She recalled Seth had trekked out there three weeks ago when she'd followed him while prepping for Haley. At the time, she hadn't been concerned with what he was doing, only *where* and *when*. Now she wished she knew what he was doing out there, but she'd had to relieve Dustin earlier.

The exact addresses were logged in the GPS history. Maybe she could ask Brian to research them.

Now, it appeared that Seth was at the house on Mulberry again.

She had enough sense not to go skulking around the place in the darkness by herself. But that didn't mean she couldn't stake it out from down street for a bit. She locked the back door of USD and strode into the parking lot.

As she started up the SUV, which Dustin had agreed to let her hang on to for a couple more days, her stomach grumbled. She hadn't eaten since noon. On the way to Mulberry, she swung through a drive-through. Ordered a double cheeseburger and fries, but she denied herself the milkshake she was craving in lieu of water.

The warm, hearty smell that permeated the car was divine. She dug french fries from the bag and noshed while she made her way to the house.

The lights were on inside. Out front were two cars behind Seth's truck that hadn't been there the last time. Shadows moved behind the drawn curtains. Three, possibly four individuals were inside from what she could see.

There weren't many cars on the street. Most were parked in driveways.

Charlie chose a spot across the street and two houses down behind a sedan. She set her camera on top of her duffel bag, ready to take pictures if an opportunity presented itself. Biting into the burger, she stayed focused on the house, silently nibbling on her food until there was nothing left.

As she wiped her mouth, the front door opened. Three men strode out, including Olsen.

Chucking the napkin in the paper bag with the rest of her trash, she grabbed her camera and zoomed in on the men. She took pictures of them talking while they walked down the front steps. At the sidewalk, they spoke for a few minutes. The one with close-cropped dark blond hair pointed back to the house. Another glanced at his watch, the one who was balding and had a bit of a belly.

Seth nodded at them and waved goodbye. He started toward his truck.

She got pictures of the license plates of the other men's vehicles.

Olsen crossed in front of his Chevy into the street. As he grabbed his door handle, he looked down the block. Right at her.

Charlie's pulse spiked. She lowered the camera.

Had the lens reflected the light from a streetlamp and caught his attention?

His gaze was locked on her, eyes narrowing. Letting go of the door handle, he stalked down the street. Headed straight for her.

She tugged on the bill of her cap to hide her face. Cranking the key in the ignition, she fired up the Jeep. Seth took off in a jog. She threw the SUV in reverse and raced backward, swerving around the corner. On the perpendicular block, she whipped the steering wheel, doing a one-eighty, put the gear in drive and sped off. She glanced in the rearview mirror.

Olsen rounded the bend.

Flooring the accelerator, she made a hard right, running a stop sign, tires screeching.

Her heart pounded wildly, adrenaline flaring hot in her system. That was a close call. Too close. She only hoped that Seth hadn't gotten the license plate number.

Charlie made a few more sharp turns and checked to be sure she wasn't followed before slowing down. She stuck to the speed limit, adhering to every traffic rule all the way to Brian's driveway.

Relief poured through Charlie. Not only to have gotten away from Olsen, but to be at Brian's. The knowledge she wouldn't be alone tonight was a comfort.

There was safety in numbers, but more than that, Brian's concern for her was genuine. Exceeded some loyalty to her cousin. He truly was nice.

All the time.

And their chemistry…

The thought of his bed and him in it sounded tempting.

Charlie stuffed the camera in her duffel, uncertain if she'd mention to Brian what had just happened. He'd only berate her and worry. She could do without a lecture.

Drawing a deep breath, she shut her eyes for a moment. All she saw was Seth. The way Olsen had stared at her, seething. Like he wanted to tear through the glass and metal of the car to get to her.

Charlie's heart was still pounding.

Shake it off. Don't let Brian see it.

She hid the camera in her bag and got out. At the door there was a sticky note telling her it was open.

Strange not to ring the bell or knock first without having a key, but Charlie went in and locked the door behind her. Down the hall, the back door to the patio was open. Although the porch light was off, she glimpsed one of the rocking chairs in motion. He must really love it out there.

She set her duffel on one of the stools at the island in the kitchen. On the countertop was a plate of food, steak and veggies, covered with plastic wrap along with another note that read, "In case you're hungry."

His thoughtfulness knew no bounds. Had she known he was going to go out of his way to fix dinner, she would have chosen the home-cooked meal over greasy fast food. She put the plate in the fridge and grabbed the bottle of wine. Turning, she opened a cabinet. Dishes. She tried another one. Glasses. She pulled one down and poured a hefty amount of chardonnay.

She strode down the hall and out onto the covered deck.

He tilted his head to the side, catching her gaze. "Join me," he said, indicating the rocker next to him.

She sat, sipped the cool, crisp wine. Tipping her head back, she stared at the evening sky. An unfamiliar yearning flooded her chest like starlight. For this peacefulness never to end.

For him to kiss her again.

"I was worried," he said, his voice low, soft. "You didn't call to let me know you'd be late. You closed USD more than hour ago."

She stiffened, not accustomed to answering to someone, much less checking in. "Brian, I—"

He took her hand in his, linking their fingers. "I know. Just saying I was concerned. Next time, call, so I don't have to go looking for you. Okay?" His tone was calm, understanding—impossible to balk at.

Lowering her head, she pulled her hand free into her lap. "I don't let people close for a reason. It's not just to protect myself," she said, "but also the few people I have in my life. I keep Rocco at a distance because I don't want my world to taint his. You asked me for full disclosure. I'm willing to give it, but you should know beforehand that it'll compromise you. As a police officer."

Fixing her with a stare, he stopped rocking. "Compromise how?"

She shook her head, exasperated. She wanted his help, not to ruin his career. Dragging him into this was a mistake. One she didn't want him to regret.

He put a hand on her shoulder and squeezed. "Let's start with you telling me what you learned from Rafe Martinez. We'll work our way up to the full disclosure part. Baby steps. Yeah?"

Charlie's stomach flip-flopped. She'd warned him his job could be jeopardized and he was more concerned about her taking baby steps than about protecting himself.

Her style was to rip off the Band-Aid and get it over and done with, but if he wanted to delay the inevitable ugly part, then she'd do it his way.

She sucked in a deep breath. "Rafe told me that he and Haley were only friends. Never anything sexual between them."

"Do you believe him?"

Another sip of wine. "He's gay."

"Oh." Brian nodded. "But he's definitely hiding something."

"Rafe claimed that Seth believed he was having an affair with Haley. Jumped him one night as he was closing the shop. Wore a ski mask and beat him up."

Brian leaned forward, resting his forearms on his thighs. "Why didn't he report it?"

"Too afraid. Seth threatened to kill him if he talked."

"Allegedly," Brian said.

"You still don't think that a cop, one you know, is capable of something like beating up his wife, or her best friend, or murder?"

"That's not what I think."

She waited for him to tell her what was going through his head, but only stared back, cool and collected. "You can't put the assault in an official report. Rafe is worried about it getting back to him."

Brian looked insulted. "Give me some credit," he said. "Listen, Internal Affairs is going to investigate Seth. They're impartial, coming in from Cheyenne. Talk to Rafe again. Let him know. See if he'll speak to them."

"I can try." But she doubted he would be receptive to the idea. She wouldn't be if she was in his position.

"When was the last time he has seen Haley?"

"Not for months. Not since the assault." Poor guy. His story tracked with Seth's history of abuse and violence according to what she'd learned from Haley.

She tipped the glass up to her lips, letting the wine slide down her throat.

"Dead end on who owns the house on Mulberry," he said. When Charlie frowned, he added, "More like a closed door. My friend, Melanie Merritt, is going to help me pry it open."

"The assistant district attorney?" she asked, choking on

her wine, and he nodded. "Must be nice to have friends in high places."

A look crossed his face like he wanted to say more but was hesitant.

"I've got two more addresses for you to look into. One in Centennial and the other in Woods Landing-Jelm."

"Please tell me this doesn't mean that you're still following Seth."

"Then I won't. I'll text you the addresses."

"It's dangerous following him. You need to stop. If he's not on to you now, it's only a matter of time. Then you'll have more to worry about than what happened to Haley," he said, and she shifted her gaze to the sky. "Are you listening to me?"

Sighing, she was annoyed by the parental tone, and the fact he was right. Olsen was on to her because she'd gotten sloppy, ventured too close to the house on Mulberry. Confessing it to Brian, after his little lecture, would only upset him. And worry him.

To her surprise, it was nice having someone concerned about her welfare. "I hear you."

"I checked out Seth. The story of domestic violence."

She perked up in the rocking chair. "And what did you find?"

"Nothing official documented about abuse. Not a single 911 call from Haley. No complaints. No medical history at the hospital to support it either."

"You don't believe me." Charlie's breath caught. "After what I told you, about seeing the bruises myself."

"Haley Olsen never reported any kind of domestic violence. Not at the hospital. Not in a 911 call. Detective Kent

Kramer spoke to her family. Not a word to them about it, either. Nothing. While Seth's record is clean. Not a blemish on it."

She couldn't believe what she was hearing.

"Did you know Haley used to be a stripper at the Bare Back?" he asked.

Not until today, but she nodded.

"Rumor is, Haley was cheating on Seth. If not with Rafe, then maybe with someone else. The only report, the only evidence I could find, was about Haley. Taking a baseball bat to Seth's truck."

"What? When?"

"Six months ago. On Valentine's Day no less. Want to guess where?"

No, she didn't.

"In the parking lot of Delgado's. Other cops were there and saw it. The only reason she wasn't arrested is because Seth said it was a personal matter and that he didn't want her charged."

Six months? Valentine's. "I bet she did it because of Rafe. The assault. It happened last February." Maybe that was the final straw. What drove her to USD a few short months later.

"It doesn't matter why. What does matter is that there's evidence, with eyewitnesses on record, of Haley, an alleged abused wife, terrified of her husband, being violent. Being the aggressor. In public. While her demon of a husband defended her. Protected her. Kept her out of jail. The dots don't connect. It's not adding up."

She heaved a breath.

This didn't sit well with her. For one thing, the night Charlie had talked to Haley about the possibility of fake credentials, starting a new life somewhere else, Haley had been a quivering, frightened victim who'd gone through a box of tissues. The entire time she'd blamed herself for the beatings, worried about what might happen to her if Seth discovered her plan to leave and questioned whether it might be better to stay.

Was it possible that there was another side to Haley, a side Charlie knew nothing about?

She got up, strode to the railing of the deck, leaned on it. "Did you find anything to give you a grain of doubt about him?"

"I did." Brian stood and joined her. "His alibi, being with Detective Colvin, can't be verified. They weren't on duty. No one else saw them together. They weren't caught on traffic cameras, either."

"Then he's not free and clear," she said. "His record might be clean, but maybe it's because he hasn't been caught yet. It doesn't mean his hands aren't dirty."

"You're right. It's not cut-and-dried. There's more to it all, and I'm going to get to the bottom of it."

"You do care about this," she said. "About what happened to Haley."

"Of course, I care. A woman has disappeared. Her husband, a cop, might be responsible. And if not for that, then possibly other illegal things. This matters to me, but you matter more."

She drew in a deep breath, held it, exhaled relief that Brian wasn't giving up. The part about mattering to him, she was quite sure what to do with it.

Easing in front of her, he closed the gap between them and pinned her with a long, steady look that made her stomach flutter. "I need to know what you're keeping from me. What are you afraid for me to find out?"

"I'm not exactly a model citizen."

"Are we talking dead bodies buried somewhere?" he asked, easy-breezy.

It wasn't as bad as that, still, she grunted her frustration. This was serious. Life-changing. Career-ending. She wished he'd act like it. "What if I told you I had killed someone? What would you do?"

His dark brows knit together. "I'd ask you why you did it."

His reasonable response, the best she could really hope for, didn't make her feel any better.

He gazed down at her calmly. "Stop testing me. Tell me what it is."

She gulped the rest of her wine. Why did he have to push this?

"Hey," he said. "I want you to think of this deck as a safe space. A confessional. You share with me, and I'll never violate your trust."

She frowned at the monumental promise he couldn't possibly keep.

"Give me a chance, Charlie."

"For what, to let me down?"

He cupped her face in his hand and stroked her cheek with his thumb. "Have I disappointed you yet?"

No. He hadn't.

"You're no coward," he said. "This isn't the time to start acting like one."

Now he was testing her. Pushing her. Right out of her cagey comfort zone.

BRIAN WAITED FOR Charlie to respond, bracing himself for… Well, for anything. It was a given that her confession involved an illicit act. But he knew that Charlie wasn't a murderer, despite her earlier question.

He stared into her eyes, willing her to trust him.

Something in her was broken. Leftover from her childhood, haunting her. To ever heal from it, she was going to have to put her faith in someone. He wanted that person to be him.

"I didn't just convince Haley to leave her husband," she said. "I was in the process of helping her do it."

"Helping in what way?"

"New location. New name. New everything. Get her off his radar. Make it so that he could never find her."

She was talking about illegal, fake credentials. "Is this the first time you've done this?"

"What?"

"Make a person vanish by giving them a new life."

"I've been doing it for three years. A handful of clients. Only women and children who were in a violent situation. Never for criminals."

He lowered his hand from her face, his gut tightening. "Do you make the fake IDs?"

It was tough to get credentials that passed scrutiny. Required specialized skills, and while Charlie was talented, he didn't see *forger* fitting into her wheelhouse.

Then again, she was full of surprises.

"I act as a liaison. The middleman so to speak. My client buys it from one of my contacts. But I make nothing from the deal."

Relief trickled through him that Charlie wasn't a forger

or personally selling fake credentials. Not that it was good that she was acting as a go-between, but she should have told him this sooner.

"Maybe Haley decided to leave town early," he said. "Staged the scene at her house to implicate Seth as a going away present."

"Why are you so cynical about this?"

He shrugged. Came with the territory of being a detective and working a case.

"In my heart, I think Haley is dead. There was so much blood. Too much." She shook her head. "If she left, where would she go? She doesn't have a new identity yet. None of her credentials are ready. The clients never have any interaction with my contact. Only I do. And that still doesn't explain who shot at me."

Foul play was certainly possible. The blood found at the house matched Haley's DNA. Forensics also detected latent bloodstains and stated that close to two liters of it had been in the house, though, they'd only been able to analyze traces.

But the fact that a body hadn't turned up was nagging him.

"This is a dangerous business you're in," he said. "Not only for you, but more so for your clients. They have no idea what they might be buying with a fake ID. They could be getting a host of issues from credit problems to a criminal history." There was no telling.

"The identities are solid. There's never been a problem."

"How can you put the lives, the futures of these women and their children, into the hands of some shady scumbag hacker that you don't really know?"

Charlie rested her head back against a wood post and lowered her gaze. "But I do know him."

"How well?"

She took a deep breath, released it. "Intimately. Once upon a time."

A cold lance of jealousy stabbed him. "How long ago?" The words came out harsher than he intended.

She looked up at him, surprise flashing in her eyes.

Yeah, he'd finally lost his cool. Over a former lover of hers, who was also a criminal and still embedded in her life.

"We called it quits four years ago," she said.

He swallowed some of his irritation. "Did you love him?"

She shook her head. No hesitation.

It relieved him to know she hadn't given him her heart only for the guy to break it. "Why did you two end things?" Dating a criminal was the polar opposite of a cop. Should've been exactly what she was looking for, the ultimate bad boy.

"You think I have trust issues?" Charlie arched an eyebrow. "Orson kept hacking into my phone and computer. It was a lot to have my boyfriend constantly spying on me."

"Other than that, he was Mr. Right?"

"Hardly." She gave a chuckle devoid of humor. "Orson likes variety. I'm not big on sharing. We weren't together long. But he was willing to help me even after the breakup. For a price. There aren't many women's shelters in the state, much less this area. I only do this for women who believe their lives are in danger and need to relocate permanently."

"What's Orson's last name?" He was going to dig into this guy, unearth every dirty thing he could about him.

She narrowed her eyes. "Asking me to trust you is one thing. Asking me to violate someone else's is another."

He sighed. "You shouldn't use your ex's services any-more. There are better ways to help someone disappear. Legal ways. Get them off the grid. Plant misleading tracks online. Tell them to only take jobs that pay in cash. That kind of life is significantly harder, but safer."

"If you need to arrest me, to protect your job, I under-stand. All I ask is that you don't stop investigating what happened to Haley."

Arresting her hadn't been a consideration, especially after she had warned him. It became a *don't ask, don't tell* situa-tion. And he'd made the choice to keep asking. "You shared in the Bradshaw confessional. Your secret stays here."

He respected what she tried to do for Haley. How she saved and protected those who needed her. Even if he didn't agree with her methods, which were legally in the gray, he respected *her*.

"Really?" she asked. The disbelief in her voice chafed him.

A little.

He nodded. "You're safe with me." Maybe now she'd start to believe it.

"I doubted it was possible for us to share the same per-spective about this." Putting a palm on his chest, she relaxed her body against his. "I guess I did have your brand wrong."

"I think you might be pleasantly surprised at what we share." He ran his hands down her arms, to her waist, and gripped her hips. She was all lean muscle and soft, subtle curves. "At what we will share." He ached to kiss her.

The same thing must've been on her mind because she slid her hands up into his hair and brought his head down for precisely that. It was hungry and demanding as he wrapped his arms around her. Earlier, she'd been hesitant, caught by surprise.

Now she kissed him back like she was as impatient and needy and eager as he was.

She tugged his shirt out of his pants, slipped her hand under and across his skin. One of her lean, toned thighs eased between his.

The kiss deepened, turning heady, and she gave a little moan.

He wanted her in the worst way. Had for a long time. Ever since their chance run-in at the charity gala in Cheyenne. They'd lowered their guards, had drinks, dinner, real conversation. Deeper than casual chitchat. Laughed together. Brian had taken her hand. They'd ventured into the murmuring crowd where the band played something soft and romantic. On the dance floor, he'd pulled Charlie close, slid his hand down the bare expanse of her back, felt her shiver at his touch. Heard her breath catch in her throat. They moved in sync, two pieces of a puzzle that fit. Others dressed in sequins and tuxes eddied and swirled around them. Overhead, hundreds of tiny lights twinkled like stars. He gazed down at Charlie's upturned face. Captivated by her beauty, by her smile, he'd kissed her without thinking, tasting the champagne on her lips. As she opened her mouth, sliding her tongue over his, wrapping her arms around his neck, pressing even closer, he'd thought he could tell where the night might lead.

Then she backed away and bolted. Fled home to Laramie and returned to giving him the cold shoulder.

For them to have a future, they couldn't sleep together

like this. Where she'd take him for a test drive and in the morning, dismiss it as a mistake.

He pulled back and met her gaze. "Not tonight." He wasn't going to blow it by being impulsive. "I made up the guest room for you."

"Why?" she purred. "I thought I was welcome between your sheets."

"You are welcome. In my home. And in my bed. But you're not ready for the latter."

She reached down, cupped his groin and massaged the unmistakable hardness of his desire. "It feels like we're both ready to act on all that *chemistry*. How about some sweaty, no-strings attached fun," she said, low and breathy, her fingers stroking him.

He groaned, yearning to have the feel of her touch all over his body, but he eased her hand away. Kissed her knuckles. "That's just it. I want strings and attachment. What I *don't* want is for us to make love, only to have you run afterward, like some skittish wild horse that's been spooked."

Charlie stilled as if stunned, but she didn't wilt. She was silent. Simply stared at him.

The uneasy quiet stretched between them.

"I want more than sex with you," he said, making sure he got through to her. "I want a relationship."

A sad warmth filled her eyes, along with tears. "I have had walls up for more than twenty years, Brian. I'm not sure I'm capable of tearing them down."

"They're not walls. Merely high fences. I'm rather good at jumping over those." He smiled at her. "You just have to let me." He dug in his pocket and pulled out a key. "It's to the front door. You can come and go without needing me to be here."

She took the key from him. Their fingers grazed and she clung to his hand. "What if you're wrong about me? What if I'm…" Her voice trailed off. A tear rolled down her cheek, and she quickly whisked it away.

"I'm not wrong." He caressed her cheek. "And there's no rush. I can wait." No matter how long it took, even though he knew there were no guarantees. "I'm not asking you to give me forever." Not yet anyway. "Only a chance."

Chapter Eight

Tiptoeing down the hall in her running shoes, Charlie did her best not to make a sound. She didn't want to disturb Brian. Truth be told, she was anxious about seeing him this morning. Their conversation last night had been nerve-racking. She hadn't a clue how he'd take the news about her helping victims of domestic violence procure fake credentials.

But he'd taken it in stride, as usual. Brian had seemed more bothered by her continued association with her ex, Orson, than with her illicit activities. She'd never figured him for the jealous type. Or that he'd tolerate her operating in the gray. Or that he'd reject her offer of sex. Something easy. Casual.

She tried to shrug it off. *No big deal.*

But it had been. A huge deal in fact.

Orson never would've turned her down. Not even after they'd broken up. Sometimes he still tried to have an occasional hookup. Her attraction to him hadn't gone away, but she didn't want to be a part of his revolving door of women. Anything physical or romantic with Orson was dead and buried. Never to be resurrected.

But what kind of guy turned down a no-strings attached good time between the sheets?

She crept around the corner into the kitchen and stopped.

Brian sat at the island, wearing his shorts, a T-shirt and running shoes, drinking a glass of water. He must have been silent as a ninja as he'd gotten ready. She would've sworn he was still asleep.

He snapped his gaze up to hers, direct and penetrating. Heat flooded her cheeks.

Turning to face her fully, he leaned against the counter. He flicked a look over her from head to toe, like he was striking a match against her body.

Something flared under her skin, the warmth in her cheeks spreading lower.

He was the kind of guy who knew exactly what he wanted and wouldn't settle for less. No denying it was a turn-on.

But she hadn't been any more prepared for his blunt declaration than she was for this face-to-face ambush while she was trying to sneak out. She had always been worried about others disappointing her if she got too close. With Brian, for the first time, she was afraid of being the disappointment.

"Figured I'd join you on your jog." He stood, scraping the stool back against the hardwood floor. "If you don't mind the company."

Of course, she minded, and surely he realized it. Hence the reason for this surprise attack. "Suit yourself." She made a beeline for the door.

"How far are we going?"

She heard the scuff of his sneakers on the floor behind her. "Only three-point-nine miles," she answered, leading the way to the road.

"That's fairly precise."

"Mapped it out on my smartwatch. We're only going to the rifle range and back. I didn't realize you lived quite so close to me."

His arm brushed hers, sparking a tingle in her belly. "Feels good to be close to you."

He wasn't only talking about the proximity of their houses, but if she focused on that, he'd see her blush.

"Let's go." She took off, setting a brisk pace down Rogue Canyon Road.

He maneuvered to the other side of her, putting himself on the outside where any cars would pass. His protective instinct never quit.

Casting a sidelong glance at him, she admired his excellent posture and the fit of his T-shirt stretched taut over his muscles. With his powerful stride and those big hands, he seemed like he knew his way around a woman's body.

He looked at her.

Busted. Caught her ogling.

"Rocco told me that you left your aunt and uncle's house at seventeen. Right after you graduated high school."

"Yeah."

"He said you bounced around a lot. About every two years."

Rocco talked too much. "That's right."

"I had to move a lot, too, with the military. Not by choice. Why so often for you?"

She shrugged. "Thought I wanted the hustle and bustle. Action. Kept trying different places. New York. Los Angeles. Miami. Chicago. Denver." During her time in Colorado, she'd met Orson.

"Is that why you haven't unpacked everything at your house? Too used to leaving?"

"I guess I like mobility." She hadn't really thought about it before. "But the big cities drained me." Inevitably, it felt as if her soul was being sucked dry. "I feel grounded here. Something to the great outdoors. The simplicity." She never thought the wild west, the landscape and cowboys, would be for her. Glancing at Brian with mountains as the backdrop, she was glad to be wrong.

"You've been in Laramie a while. Almost three years."

She nodded. "Uh-huh." Long time for her.

"Think you'll stay?"

What was this, twenty questions? "USD is the closest thing to putting down roots." That was the best, most honest answer she could give.

She picked up speed, determined to nix the conversation.

With their ridiculously fast pace, they made it to the range and back to his house in almost no time.

Once they reached his driveway, she bent over and clutched her knees, catching her breath. Somewhat recovered, she stood upright. The sun cast sharp shadows over the hillside and mountains. A cool breeze stirred the trees around them.

Charlie closed her eyes, tipping her head back and inhaling a deep breath; the scent of sweet wildflowers hung in the air. "I love this smell. Different in the morning than at night."

When she opened her eyes, she looked at Brian. His back was to her. A sheen of sweat covered his skin, but he wasn't winded, breathing hard like she was.

He spun on his heel, strode up to her and threw his arms around her in a tight hug.

She went rigid, startled by the intimate contact. Then she found herself melting against him, curling her fingers in his damp T-shirt, soaking in his masculine, sweaty scent.

It felt good to be close to him, too. Scary, but good. She could stay like this a while, wrapped in his arms.

He pressed his mouth to her ear, his breath warm on her neck. "We're being watched. When I let you go, look to your two o'clock. Behind the peachleaf willows. There's a car. Black compact SUV."

She swallowed hard, a knot twisting in her gut.

"It wasn't there when I got home last night," he said. "But it's been there since we left."

He let her go and bent down, pretending to adjust his shoelaces.

Charlie couldn't tell a peachleaf willow from a weeping one, but he'd told her enough to properly orientate her.

Sure enough, behind a cluster of trees was a black car. Through the branches the sun glinted off the windshield.

"Act natural," Brian said. "I'll climb up to the roof. See if I can get a license plate number. Then we'll get ready and leave in separate vehicles. I want you to go someplace well-populated. Maybe Delgado's."

It was close to USD. Busy from the time they opened until closing. Good spot.

"Then we'll see," he said, "which one of us is being followed."

THE EARLY EVENING heat was sweltering even though the sun was low in the sky. Perspiration rolled down Brian's temples, his mind roiling with worry for Charlie. No one had followed him to the sheriff's department, which meant that Charlie was the target.

At the sheriff's, he'd gone to ask the chief deputy if there were any leads on who shot at her. Also, he had them run the license plate number he was able to get while on the roof.

Came up with the oddest result.

"It's showing as blocked," a deputy had said. "Maybe it's a government vehicle. Or possibly an undercover police vehicle. Wouldn't you be able to find out at the LPD?"

So, he'd passed the plate number on to Kent.

Lowering his binoculars, Brian didn't like the looks of the large house sitting at the address in Woods Landing-Jelm that Charlie had given him. It was on the back side of Jelm Mountain. About three acres bordering what might be state land. No neighbors nearby.

The place had all the telltale signs of being a meth house. Blackened windows. An unusual ventilation system that pumped wisps of smoke through small pipes on the roof. The smell of rotten eggs carried on the breeze. A couple of armed guys out front smoked cigarettes, presumably security. Dead vegetation around the property. Burn pits in the grass.

The house at the other address in Centennial hadn't been quite the same. Protected by armed guards as well, but it had a different feel to it. Maybe it was used for distribution or storage. He hadn't been able to get too close to that location, either. With it being isolated, security could see someone coming from miles away.

Nothing odd about a narcotics detective checking out

such a place. In fact, it could be a sign Seth was only doing his job.

But the thought of Charlie being out here, sneaking around this house, made Brian's blood pressure rise. Meth labs, their cooks and users were extremely dangerous and unpredictable.

He hoped like hell that she listened to him and stayed away from Seth. Was she trying to incite him by following him?

She was certainly underestimating him. He wasn't stupid. And if he was guilty of being dirty and harming his wife, then there was no limit as to what he would do to Charlie.

Last night, he felt as though they'd had a breakthrough. She'd opened up, daring to share a dicey truth in spite of the risks. Showed real trust that he thought they could build upon.

This morning, he wasn't so sure. She hadn't been icy. Only quiet. Like she wasn't certain of the way forward. He had a niggling fear in the back of his mind. About Charlie. That she was going to make excuses to him, even to herself, why they couldn't be together. They might not have slept together, but it didn't mean she wouldn't be inclined to run. She'd been doing it for so many years that it was second nature to her.

As long as she understood that following a detective, who might be dirty and might have killed his wife was too dangerous to continue, then the rest was doable. He'd find a way to scale her fences.

Thinking about Seth, he glanced at his watch. Six twenty. He needed to get going. The first football practice of the season was starting in forty minutes.

Brian slid down the hill he was perched on. Dusted himself off and climbed back into his truck. He pulled off onto the road, heading back to Laramie.

In town, he ignored the fast-food signs calling his name. Charlie had *made* breakfast, which consisted of smoothies. Apparently, she wasn't much of a cook. He'd skipped lunch and could have used a burger something fierce. It would be hours before he'd get a chance to grab dinner.

His cell phone vibrated in his pocket. He took it out. Glanced at the screen. It was Kent. He put the call through Bluetooth. "Did you find something?" He'd expect the guy to wait until Monday to check it out.

"Nada. Sorry. I got the same result as the sheriff's department. It's weird. If it's one of ours, I should be able to see it. Unless someone deliberately wanted it hidden. Or it could be some other explanation. Listen, I'm still in the office looking at something. Got a minute?"

He'd been there for hours.

"It's a Saturday," Brian said. "Your day off."

"I've got no life. Sue me." Kent gave a dry chuckle that Brian suspected was hiding a deep layer of grief. "Anyway, I want to run something by you."

"Yeah, sure," Brian said. "What is it?"

"A woman came into the station yesterday, Donna Williams, to file a missing person's report on her son, Theodore. He goes by Teddy."

"Okay. So, what?" Brian turned onto Grand Avenue, going straight to the field where they played. He'd change in the cab of the truck since he'd packed his gear this morning. "I'm not tracking why you're asking me about it."

"Well, Mrs. Williams says the last time she saw her son

was on Monday. He checks in with her every couple of days. When she hadn't heard from him, she swung by his place. The mail in his box has been piling up since Tuesday. She thinks that's when he went missing. Haley disappeared on Wednesday."

"You think the two cases are related somehow?"

"It's been bugging me. That's why I stayed at the office. To look at some stats. Guess how many missing persons we have in the state so far this year?"

"I don't know. A hundred?"

"Forty-five. And I'm talking about folks who didn't turn up after a day or two. In the county, eight. In Laramie, three. Two in the last week."

"You've got my attention. You're thinking it's not a co-incidence." Sure didn't sound like one.

"Yep. I went back through Haley's file, searching for a connection. Her family mentioned that she's been taking classes at the Underground Self-Defense school on Third Street for a little less than a year," Kent said, and Brian's gut tightened. "Guess where Teddy Williams worked?"

Brian stifled a groan. "As an instructor at USD."

"Bingo. But that was only his part-time job. Want to know where he worked full-time?"

"You've got me hanging in suspense. Where?" Brian asked.

"At Nelson's gun shop," Kent said. "They sell premium muzzle-loading gunpowder. How much you want to bet it's the same brand that was used as the propellant at the Olsens'?"

"I'd venture to guess that'll be a winning bet. But how many other gun shops carry the stuff?"

"I'll find out. I'm going over to Nelson's now to ask some questions. Then I'll hit up USD."

"Don't worry about USD," Brian said. "I'll handle it. I know the owner."

DITCHING HER TAIL hadn't been easy. The one good thing was now she knew what vehicle to be on the lookout for. A Subaru Forester. But she wasn't able to get the license plate.

How long had she been followed?

It burned her to the bone that she hadn't known, and Brian had to be the one to spot the tail.

She lifted the camera and zoomed out for a wide shot of all the men on the field that Seth was stretching alongside. Ten of them. She got close-ups of each and every one.

Two were familiar. The balding guy and the one with dirty blond hair. She'd have to show their pictures to Brian. He might be able to help figure out who they were.

Another truck pulled to the parking lot beside the field. Looked familiar. The door opened and a man jumped out.

Speak of the devil.

Charlie gripped the steering wheel, leaning forward, and stared at Brian.

Smiling, he ran onto the field. Gave a few high-fives, including one to Seth, and started stretching.

What the hell?

For an hour, she sat spellbound and steaming, watching Brian play football with his buddies. With Seth Olsen.

Bitterness welled inside her. She snapped photos of them, having fun together, huddling, tackling one another, extending a hand and helping each other up from the field. What was next? Having a drink together? Dinner?

The scene nauseated her.

Brian had gone on and on, warning her about following Seth. Was this the reason why? So she wouldn't discover that they were friends?

Why wouldn't he tell her about this...unless he had something to hide? Was he even seriously investigating Seth? Or merely placating her by letting her think that he was?

No wonder he didn't think Seth was guilty.

Brian Bradshaw—too good to be true.

She banged her skull back against the head rest. She had believed all the things he'd said, wanted to believe *in him*.

Whenever they spoke, he really looked at her. Listened to her. As though he could see into her soul. Like he appreciated what made her unique. What a fool she'd been getting sucked in by his niceness, his consideration, his patience, his empathy. His hotness.

His whole brand.

Was any of it real?

The only thing she should have put her faith in was the power of the blue wall. Cops stuck together. The proof was right in front of her, wrapping up their football game.

Brian slung an arm around Seth, clasping his shoulder, like they were close chums. All the guys headed to the parking lot.

A little knife twisted in her chest. He had been holding out on her. Not telling her every little detail was understandable. This was major. Tantamount to lying.

In an hour or two, Seth would probably be at the. The idea of Brian being there with him, and the rest of the fellas, made her stomach turn.

Then it struck her. That's why he had given her a key.

So he didn't have to wait at his house for her and was free to hang out with Seth. His good pal. She wanted to spit the disgust from her mouth.

Well, she'd be there, too. It was time she found out what was going on inside that club and why Aubrey had lied to her.

No more lies. She was going to get to the truth.

She backed out of the lot across the street from the field and drove to a salon she'd been to a couple of times. Hair Dreams and Beyond. They specialized in makeovers and wigs.

At the reception counter, she put down her credit card. "I don't have an appointment. But I need someone to make me look totally different. Like a new person. Right now. Whatever the cost, I'll pay double."

The receptionist spun in her chair. "Carey! I've got a client for you. She wants the Lover's Quarrel special, and she's in a rush."

"Let me grab a pop! Send her back."

The receptionist whirled back around. "Go on. Last chair on the right."

Charlie marched back and plopped down in the chair. She dumped her purse on the floor and drummed her fingers on the arm of the chair. And waited.

She remembered she'd told Dustin she would close tonight. Now her plans had changed. Groaning, she dug her phone out of her handbag and called him. "Hey, do we have anyone scheduled for any training sessions tonight?"

"We did. But they called to cancel, and I just finished the last group class of the day."

"And no word from Teddy?"

"Nope."

She shook her head in frustration. "He's been dodging my calls, not picking up." She didn't want to fire the guy in a voice mail, but it was looking like that was what she'd have to do. "Get out of there. Post a note on the website and on the front door. Say that we'll be closing early for the next week." She'd have to call any clients scheduled and apologize for the inconvenience. "Then lock up and skedaddle."

"Okay. Sounds good. Don't forget that I have to leave by four tomorrow. You'll have to close."

"Sure. No problem. I appreciate how flexible you've been."

"Enough to give me a raise?" Dustin asked in a hesitant voice.

Well, she was down a trainer. Why not reward the dependable one. "We'll talk about how much, but yes. You've earned one. Thanks, again." She clicked off.

Finally, someone strutted through the hanging string beaded curtain, holding a can of Coke. "Bonsoir, cherie. My pronouns are they, them and theirs," Carey said, wearing a low cut, formfitting top, slim pants and chunky platform boots. "What can I do for you? Do you want me to transform you into someone else or are you looking to slay, become so drop-dead gorgeous that we call it revenge?"

Deep down, slaying sounded like it'd be satisfying. She was angry enough to spit nails. "I need to look like a different person for a few hours. Nothing permanent. Feel free to wave your wand and add in the gorgeous, too. But I need you do it fast."

"All possible, sugar. Although looking at you, I'm picking

up way more spice than sweetness. How do you feel about going to the dark side?"

"Been there and never really left."

Carey chuckled. "I hear that. By the time I'm done, you'll be unrecognizable."

Chapter Nine

After an hour of tackle football, Brian was starving. He'd set a pot of water to boil while he showered. Only bothering to throw on boxer briefs and a pair of jeans, he finished making spaghetti and meatballs.

His preference would have been to wait for Charlie, but she was going to be at USD a while longer and he was hungry enough to eat cardboard.

He scarfed down the food and was wiping up the last of the sauce from his plate with a piece of garlic bread when his front door opened. If he'd known she'd be back early, they could've eaten together.

Swiveling on the stool to face her, he was about to apologize, but a fit of helpless choking stopped him. A stunning raven-haired woman, wearing a tad too much makeup, stalked past him, without a glance in his direction or saying a word.

"Charlie?" It was her...but didn't look anything like her. He was off the stool and hurrying down the hall after her. "What is going on?"

"You don't get to ask me questions anymore." She stormed into the guest room, and he was on her heels.

"Clearly, you're upset about something," he said, keeping his tone calm. "Please tell me what it is."

She grabbed her large travel backpack that could hold a week's worth of clothes and fished around inside.

Up close, he got a better look at her. Thick black eyeliner drawn at an angle gave her sexy cat's eyes. Crimson red lipstick popped against her creamy, porcelain skin. But it was the shoulder-length jet-black hair with cascading waves that he couldn't stop staring at.

Why was she wearing a wig?

Brian caught her arm to stop her from whatever she was doing. "Hey. Talk to me."

Finally, she glanced at him. Her gaze dipped to his bare chest. She faltered a second and then met his eyes. "I don't blame you. It's my own fault. I should've known better than to ever let a cop in my house, much less my life. I don't know what I was thinking." She jerked her arm free of his grasp. "That's the problem. I wasn't thinking. I was an idiot. Lost my head."

Gritting his teeth, he wished they were speaking the same language. He was so confused.

"I know you're afraid of this, Charlie," he said, taking a wild stab in the dark at what the issue could be. "Of having a relationship. But you can't run forever. One day you're going to look around at your life and realize something huge is missing. By then, it might be too late."

She yanked a black lace bra and something else from the bag. "A relationship?" she scoffed. "You think I'm running from you? That I'm afraid of what? Falling in love? Oh, please." She pulled her T-shirt off over her head, revealing a sports bra and smooth, taut abs.

Lowering his head, he turned away. He'd been dying to get her undressed in a bedroom, but this wasn't how he had envisioned it. "Then why are you angry?"

"I'm not angry. I'm furious," she said, and he could hear her changing clothes. "I can't believe I shared all that personal stuff with you. My past. My pain. That I let you in and put everything on the line. I trusted you. While this entire time, you've been playing me."

"What are you talking about?"

Her high heels clacking against the floor, Charlie prowled around to stare him in the eyes. She'd changed into a low-cut dress that showed off the lace of her bra, exposed her trim, bare thighs and clung to her body like a second skin.

It was so short, was it even a dress?

"You're friends with Seth Olsen," she said through clenched teeth.

Brian swore under his breath. "I told you to stop following him."

"So I wouldn't see you two together, acting like bosom buddies. Go on, deny it. I dare you." She marched out of the room, with her backpack slung over her shoulder. "You're supposed to be investigating him. Not hanging out with him. How could you lie to me?"

The sharp staccato of her heels striking the hardwood rang in his head.

"It was an omission. I never lied to you."

"I'm thirty years old. I've only been close to four people my entire life. My mother. Who was killed in front of me. Rocco and his parents. Even with them, it's easier, safer to hold back."

"Hold what back?"

"Letting it matter. If the disappointment, a lie, some offense mattered too much, it would grind me down until I was nothing. Been there. Disappearing in my grief and my guilt. I can't be nothing ever again."

She took his breath away.

Brian fought to think. To respond.

"I was a victim for most of my life. People pitying me. Making choices for me. Decisions. Pushing the buttons. Manipulating me. All for my own good," she said with such disdain and anger, he could only focus on the underlying pain.

"Is that what you think I'm doing?"

"Isn't that what's happening? How you twisted things," she said, "to make me feel bad about keeping secrets. Unreal."

He was right behind her. "I know how this looks. Give me five minutes to explain."

"Five minutes to reel me back in. I don't think so." She headed for the front door. "There's nothing you could possibly say to change this."

Desperate and at a loss, he said the one thing he could. "Rocco knew."

She stopped.

Glancing over her shoulder, she narrowed her eyes at him, giving him a look that could peel paint from the wall. "Knew what?"

"That I was friendly acquaintances with Seth. About us playing football together. Having drinks on occasion. Sometimes dinner with all the guys. When he called to ask me to help you, I told him. *Full disclosure*. He asked me to keep it from you. Didn't think you'd react well."

In hindsight, Brian should've told her. Not when he first

went to her house and was working on gaining her trust, but he should've found the right time. Rather than letting this blindside her.

Dropping her gaze, she pulled something from her pocket and threw it at him.

He caught it.

The key to his house.

"Thanks," she said. "Now I get to be angry at you and my cousin." She opened the door and stormed outside. "How dare the two of you decide what I should and shouldn't know? All in my best interest, right?"

"Where are you going?"

"None of your business!" She threw her backpack into the SUV and slammed the door.

Brian clenched his teeth until his jaw hurt. He tried not to explode. Or to go over and stop her, which would've required physical restraint. She would see it as hostile and then things would really spiral out of control.

"Do us both a favor and stay away from me!" She slid inside the vehicle and took off, tearing out of the driveway.

With Charlie's fixation on Haley, her destination most likely involved Seth and it was only going to lead to pain. For her. Never had he met a woman more prone to hazardous situations. Like danger was drawn to her. Or maybe she went looking for trouble.

Whichever the case, getting close to her meant an endless number of headaches—such as this, when he knew she was putting herself at risk—were in store for him. No amount of reason or persuasion was going to make her veer from a path once she'd started down it.

He ran back into the house and grabbed a shirt, his boots

and his gun. If he had any common sense, he should be the one running away from *her*.

But he couldn't do it. Because the problem was, he was into her. Helplessly in too deep to turn back now.

Like hell he was going to stand by and watch her get hurt. The devil himself couldn't stop him from going after her.

SECURITY AT THE DOOR—she remembered his name was Hammer—did a cursory check of Charlie's purse. She'd expected it and had left her SIG in the vehicle. Hammer looked her up and down, and then waved her inside.

"No cover charge for ladies," said the attendant at the register. "Have a good time."

Charlie eased inside the dimly lit gentlemen's club. The place was as she had imagined.

Well-stocked bar. Men seated at tables around the stage that had a couple of mostly naked girls dancing on the poles. Waitresses walked around in outfits that left little to the imagination, taking orders, carrying drinks and food. Other dancers circulating. Some were giving lap dances.

The place reeked of sleazy desperation.

Feeling like a fish out of water, Charlie didn't want it to show. She went to the bar, ordered a rum and Coke. Paid in cash with a generous tip. She didn't intend to drink much, only a sip here and there, in case anyone was watching her. Tonight, she needed all her senses firing at high speed, not dulled by alcohol.

She swept the place with her gaze. Little red lights from security cameras blinked in the corners of the club. Behind the bar was a long mirror. That would enable her to look around and see everyone, much like the bouncers, but subtly.

The night was young. The later it got, the more bodies would funnel inside. The harder it would be to find Seth and see what was going on.

For a minute or two, she watched the ladies onstage strut and dance and spin on the pole all while donning sky-high heels.

Charlie could barely walk in the pair she had on. It was beyond her how those women were able to manage acrobatics in stilts without face-planting.

Her cheeks burned again with renewed anger. The only reason she'd packed the heels and this dress was because she was staying with Brian. Their night together at the charity gala had been hard to forget. Part of her wanted to re-create it in some way. Maybe they'd have dinner. Light some candles. Instead of wearing her usual garb of a T-shirt, sports bra, workout leggings and sneakers—all of which did not scream come hither—she'd put on something feminine and skimpy.

Charlie huffed a breath. Who was she fooling? Her plan had been to seduce him. Little did she realize how hard that would be.

If only she could reconcile the things about him that didn't make sense. Why not sleep with her when he had the chance if he didn't care about her?

Maybe he was playing both sides. Appeasing her and protecting Seth.

Taking a sip of the drink, she banished Brian Bradshaw, his handsome face and hot bare chest from her thoughts. She looked around the bar in the mirror.

Where was Seth?

His truck was here.

Aubrey came out of a room off to the side, wearing dental floss and heels. She sashayed across the room, wending in between tables, over to a booth in the corner.

From this end of the bar, Charlie couldn't see much. She picked up her glass and moseyed down to the other side. On the way, she watched the girls dancing. She was hoping to blend in. Not act out of the ordinary for a woman in the club alone. Although she was the only one at the moment. After a stripper did an impressive full side split, Charlie raised her drink up to her. The dancer waved in return.

She slid onto a stool and looked up at the mirror.

In the corner booth, Seth sat with two men. One she'd seen before. The guy with wire-rimmed glasses at the gym. The third man wasn't familiar. She would've remembered the long dark hair and the scar on his cheek that ran from his ear to his mouth. His demeanor was a stark contrast to the guy with glasses. Scarface had a certain deadness about the eyes, a readiness to his posture—all that told her to be wary of him. The men weren't really paying attention to any of the girls. Except for Aubrey.

The redhead tried to cozy up to Scarface, but Seth shooed her away.

Charlie slipped her cell phone from her purse. She brought up the camera app. Extending her arms and hoisting the phone high, she smiled, pretending to take a selfie while getting Seth's table into the pics.

With the poor lighting and lack of flash, she wasn't sure if she'd be able to make out their faces in the shots.

A bouncer approached. "Hey, miss, no photographs allowed. It's a misdemeanor to take a pic of a stripper in any state of undress."

She wanted to tell him that no dancers had been in the photo, but she didn't think that'd help her. "I'm sorry," she said, changing her voice, making it more high-pitched. "Silly me." She put the phone back in her purse and sipped the drink.

Aubrey sauntered up to the bar. "Juan, get me my usual. Put it on Seth's tab."

"Sure thing." Juan poured two shots of vodka in a glass with ice. Filled the rest with soda water and added a squeeze of lemon. "Here you go." The bartender handed her the drink and moved down the bar to take another order.

Aubrey gave Charlie the side-eye. "What brings you in tonight?"

"You do."

"Is that right?" Aubrey asked, glancing around. "You got a boyfriend or husband here with you?"

"Nope." Charlie shook her head. "All by my lonesome. Want to keep me company?"

Aubrey smiled and stepped closer. "We don't get many ladies in here alone. With their fella, sure. In a big gaggle wearing veils and plastic penises on their heads, sure. But alone?" The woman scrutinized her under a laser-eyed gaze. "Not so much."

Possible that was true around here. But Charlie was ready with a story. A toss-up between her being into girls herself. Or she was a stripper at a club in Cheyenne who was scoping out a new place to work.

Since she had the woman that she needed to speak with in front of her, there was no need to play games. "You lied to me about spying for Haley when we spoke in the alley by the dumpster. I want to know why."

Aubrey reeled back. Her eyes narrowed to slits. Then she leaned in. "Charlie?" Panic flashed across her face. "You can't be in here."

"Why did you lie to me? I know you were spying on Seth for Haley."

"You don't know what you're talking about." Aubrey glared at her and lowered her voice. "Get out of here."

"I'm not leaving just yet. Not until you tell me who is sitting at the table with Seth and what they're discussing."

"You were taking pictures of them, weren't you? First time I've seen a woman on her own in here snapping a selfie." Aubrey took a gulp of her drink. "Do you have a death wish, lady? Seth has the instincts of a cobra. He will strike first at any threat, and something has already got him paranoid."

"What's he up to at that table?" Charlie asked. "What's he doing in here every day?"

Aubrey laughed, but the sound was grating. "Business. As usual."

"What kind?"

"The illegal kind. Now you need to get gone," Aubrey said, pointing a finger in her face.

"Why did you lie to me?" Haley was her friend. The stripper didn't have to talk to Charlie, but she'd volunteered. Only to spew half-truths.

The redhead heaved a breath. "Because unlike you, I don't want to die. I hope nothing has happened to Haley, and if it has, then I want that bastard to pay for it. But I've also got to protect myself." She chugged her drink. Slammed the glass on the bar with a clink. "You've got get out of here." Aubrey moved to leave.

Charlie hopped up in front of her. "What kind of business?" she demanded. "Give me something."

"I can't."

"If you don't, I'll keep popping up. Pushing and poking. I'll become your worst nightmare. That's a promise until you tell me."

"Drugs," Aubrey snapped in a harsh whisper. "Prostitution. Money laundering. Take your pick. All right."

"Did Haley know?"

"Yeah. Of course." Aubrey looked over Charlie's shoulder. Her eyes grew wide. "Time for you to get the hell out of here. Use the exit at the rear. Don't come back again." The redhead scurried off, disappearing behind a door marked Employees Only.

Charlie glanced at the booth in the corner.

Empty.

She headed for the front of the club.

Wire-rimmed glasses guy hurried through the doors after someone else. Seth lingered near the entrance, talking to one of the bouncers. He pointed at Charlie. The bouncer nodded as they spoke.

She swore under her breath.

Spinning on her heel, she hustled for the exit at the rear. Her heart pounded, thrumming against her rib cage. She pushed the door open and stumbled into the alley. To the right and around the corner led to the parking lot at the entrance, where Dustin's SUV was parked.

She click-clacked down the alley. Too bad she hadn't been wearing sneakers. The hairs at the back of her neck twitched to life. She stopped. Listened.

Nothing. No movement. No sound.

She crept to the end of the building and turned the corner.

A dark figure loomed, standing between her and the parking lot. Lean and wiry. Long black hair. He stepped into the light. Jagged scar on his cheek.

Oh, hell.

Chapter Ten

Her gaze clashed with a cold, black stare. There was a second of something close to recognition, even though she had never seen this man before tonight. She knew a predator when she saw one.

Time slowed. Charlie edged backward, clutching her purse. Wishing she had her SIG.

Her brain screamed at her to run, run. *Run!*

Charlie's heart raced, but her feet felt mired in quicksand as she turned and fled. A scrape of leather on pavement behind her, the man closing in. She heard him as much as sensed him.

Adrenaline overcame the initial jolt of fear. She darted to the side. Barely missed the hand that clawed out to grab her.

But he was fast. Much faster than her in those clumsy, loud heels. Fear flooded her veins. Maybe if she made it back to the rear door, she could—

He snatched a hold of her hair—the long tresses secured by well-placed bobby pins—and yanked her backward. Pain pulsed over her scalp, wrenching a cry from her lips.

Not panicking was the most important thing. That's

what she taught her clients. She had to get him off. Had to free herself.

Dropping her purse, she pulled out the pins from the front. The force of his grasp ripped the wig from her head. She stumbled at the sudden release. Floundered to find her footing.

A kick sent her reeling into a wall. Her bare shoulder and leg scrubbed against brick, her skin burning from the scrapes.

He swooped in. Clamped a hand around her upper arm and whipped her around. "You're coming with me," he growled at her, but Charlie knew that leaving with an assailant never boded well.

Ninety-five percent of the time if the woman complied, she was dead.

He reached into his jacket pocket.

She didn't wait to see for what. But she imagined a gun in a shoulder holster. Instead, she slammed the sharp point of her heel down onto his foot. He grunted in pain. Driving her knee up into his groin, she shoved him away as he doubled over. His hand fell from his jacket, and she glimpsed the shoulder rig.

If he pulled the gun, running wouldn't save her. It would only get her a bullet in the back or worse, in her head.

She stood her ground but didn't wait to strike again. Size didn't matter in a fight. As a woman, she was never going to get attacked by someone smaller or weaker. It boiled down to thinking outside the box, focusing and moving quicker than her opponent.

Scarface recovered, standing upright when she planted one foot—as best she could in the teeter-totter heels—and pivoted, swinging her elbow up and around. She used the added rotation to drive it hard into the side of the guy's head. If she had attempted to throw a punch that hard, she'd have broken her hand. But her elbow barely felt it.

The guy staggered. But this wasn't his first rodeo being hit in the head. Still off-balance and blinking from the blow, he reached under his jacket again. Charlie grabbed his wrist, holding it inside the jacket so he couldn't pull the weapon from the holster. He was strong, had lots of lean muscle. She rammed her heel onto his foot once more and threw a punch. But he jerked sideways, and she just missed his solar plexus. Had the blow struck where she had aimed, it would have immobilized him, giving her enough time to get away.

He flung her off him and slammed his fist into her gut. A cry crawled up her throat, but she could barely breathe, much less scream. Scarface drew a gun with an attached sound suppressor.

Not something you saw every day.

"We're going to go for a drive," he said, and this time she picked up on his slight accent, "and have a little chat."

The rear door to the club flew open with a clang as it banged on the wall. A blond guy in jeans and a button-down lurched out. "Is this the bathroom?" he asked, tottering deeper into the alley.

A drunk.

"Go back inside," Scarface said, waving his gun at him. "This isn't the toilet."

Dread ricocheted through her. Her lungs squeezed. While there was a witness, she scooted to the side, trying to ease away, but Scarface blocked her path. All he had to do was redirect the aim of the muzzle at her.

If the drunk left, Scarface was going to drag her away somewhere, question her and then kill her. She sensed it in her bones.

"What? Really?" the drunk said. "Man, I can't hold it." The blond guy stumbled over to the opposite brick wall and unzipped his pants. "Give me a minute." He shoved his hand in his pants, jiggled around. Then he spun around, drawing a gun. Something small, microcompact. "Police! Drop your weapon!"

For a dazed second, she stared at the blond man in shock. His feet were spread wide, his gun raised.

Scarface squeezed the trigger. Bullets bit into the brick facade near the blond's head as the other guy bolted around the corner. Footsteps thundered around the side of the building toward the front of the club.

Charlie swayed, balancing on her heels.

The blond turned to her with the gun in his hand and said, "I'm DCI Logan Powell. Give me your car keys."

A wave of confusion gripped her. *Powell.* Same surname as the chief deputy. "What?"

"Charlie Sharp, I'm a cop, who just saved your life. Give me your keys. I need to get you to safety."

She searched the ground. Found her purse. Fumbled for the keys. Hurled them.

"Here." He tossed her a key fob. "Go that way." He pointed to the opposite side of the alley. "There's a roadhouse on the other end," he said, and she knew the place. "You'll find my vehicle there. Meet me in the parking lot of the big-box store on Grand. Back end of the lot adjacent to the avenue. I'll explain there." He turned and took off in the direction Scarface had gone.

Charlie raced down the lane, hating the raucous clatter of her heels, but there was no way she was going barefoot.

The alley opened to A.J.'s Roadhouse. A rough, rowdy place. Lots of bikers. Brawls often broke out. All to be expected in this seedy part of town.

The guy hadn't told her what he was driving. She scanned the lot and pressed on the key fob.

Lights flashed at her nine o'clock. She wobbled over to a crossover SUV. A Subaru Forester. Was it the same one that had been following her?

She got in and sped off.

By the time she drove into the back end of the parking lot of the big-box store off Grand Avenue, she was still shaking.

The area was well-lit and buzzing with activity. Other cars were parked nearby. Shoppers moving back and forth between the store and the lot.

She plucked the rest of the bobby pins out and removed the wig cap. Her thoughts whirled in her head. She replayed the incident in the alley and shuddered.

Dustin's SUV pulled up alongside the Subaru. The blond hopped out, came around the side and climbed into his vehicle.

"Before you utter a word," she said, "I need to see some ID."

He pointed to the glove compartment. Reached for it slowly and pulled out a leather folio. He flipped it open.

Charlie eyed the photograph, along with the badge, the name and title beneath it: Logan Powell. Wyoming State Attorney General's Office, Division of Criminal Investigation.

"Okay?" he asked.

"Powell. Are you related to the chief deputy. Holden. And the fire marshal." She couldn't remember his name.

Staring at this man up close, she already knew the answer. The resemblance to Holden was unmistakable. Same golden blond hair and bright blue, earnest eyes.

"Sawyer. Yeah. They're my brothers." For a moment, he just looked at her.

"You've been following me?" she asked.

"I was following the guy you've been tracking. Seth Olsen. I was sent here to investigate him. Then last night, I followed him following you."

She shook her head. "No. I made sure I lost him."

"He made sure you thought you lost him. Olsen is a seasoned detective who has been at this a long time. It's his job to follow people without them knowing."

Brian had warned her. She should've listened to him. He was only trying to keep her safe. Maybe shouldn't have at the very least let him explain.

A shadow swept up to the window on the passenger's side. Rapped on the glass with a gun. Bent down and peered in the car. "Can I join the party?" Brian asked.

SITTING IN THE back seat of the Subaru, Brian gritted his teeth as Charlie got him up to speed about the attack in the alley and this guy's intervention. He hated that he hadn't been the one to protect her, but the only thing that mattered was her safety.

Brian figured that if he had waltzed into the strip club, he would've upset Charlie further, blowing her disguise—moot point now—and only sabotaged her efforts with his presence.

The second he saw that slick guy with the scar racing

around to the back of the club, with Seth standing near the entrance, he knew something was up, but prayed he'd spot Charlie leaving any second.

What he hadn't expected was to see some strange man getting in the vehicle that Charlie had been driving.

"I need to see your badge," Brian said.

With a sigh, the guy handed him the folio. Brian scrutinized it. Definitely real.

Brian gave it back. "How many of you Powell boys are there?" He'd gone to high school with at least two of them. But they hadn't run in the same circles.

"Five."

That's a lot of Powells. "Who sent you to investigate?"

"LPD chief. Willa Nelson. She made a formal request with the state attorney general's office," Logan said.

"To look into the disappearance of Haley Olsen?" Charlie asked.

"No. I'm afraid not."

"Then why are you here?" Brian asked.

"To look into police corruption."

"Maybe you shouldn't answer any more of his questions." Charlie folded her arms. "It's one thing to play me, Brian, but if your conflict of interest by being buddies with Seth Olsen is going to compromise this—"

"Now, hold on a minute. I'm going to say this one last time, and I want you to hear me. I am *not* friends with Seth."

"I've got pictures that say otherwise," she told him.

"I was trying to use the football game to my advantage. Hoping he might let something slip. Sometimes it's the smallest detail that can make the biggest difference. For instance, the way he talks about Haley. Never past tense.

Like he doesn't think she's dead. Or he wasn't the one who killed her."

"So, you're back to sticking up for him?" she asked, meeting his gaze in the rearview mirror.

Brian leaned forward and rested his arm on the seat. "I'm not. I swear it. I'm talking to you like a detective investigating. I don't think he blew up his own house. But I do think he and Colvin are lying about the alibi. Among other things." His gaze dropped to her shoulder. "You're bleeding."

She glanced at the scrape. "It stings, but I'll live."

"Can I interject, or should I give you two a minute alone?" Logan asked.

Brian clenched his jaw that this guy was here while he needed to sort things with Charlie.

"We've been digging into Detective Olsen for some time," Logan said. "I can assure you that Detective Bradshaw has been nowhere near him or his associates. From what we've observed, they're not even buddies. And Bradshaw isn't one of the cops being investigated or even under suspicion. In fact, he's one of the few that we believe for certain are clean. I hope that resolves the disagreement so that we can focus on business."

Chewing on her bottom lip, she met Brian's gaze again. Her features softer, her posture less defensive.

Maybe Logan Powell wasn't so bad after all. "You said *we've been digging*. Who is *we*?" he asked the DCI agent.

"A special task force. That's all I'm at liberty to say."

This was big. So much bigger than Brian had suspected.

"Once Haley disappeared," Logan said, "I was planning to come speak with you, Charlie, but things have been moving fast. A lot of different pieces and players on the board. Then Detective Olsen followed you and this opportunity presented itself."

Brian went rigid. The dread over Charlie's safety that had been dogging him since someone shot at her now intensified. "Say that again? Seth has been following *her*? For how long?"

"Last night he caught her surveilling him," Logan said. "I followed him following her. I kept watch in case he tried something."

Brian shot her a withering look.

Charlie lowered her head. "Please don't say something as cliché as *I told you so*."

His blood burned to say a heck of a lot more than that.

"Do you two need a minute?" Logan asked.

Brian nodded. "Yes."

Charlie shook her head. "No. Why did you want to speak with me?"

"I was hoping you could help us find Haley Olsen."

"Ask her husband," Charlie said. "I can't help you. Maybe you should try dragging the lake behind the house that blew up."

"We did."

News to Brian.

Charlie blinked at Logan, then she shifted her gaze to Brian.

He shook his head. "I didn't know."

"No one at LPD does. That's the point. We've been investigating under Detective Olsen's radar." He looked at Brian. "Not a word of this to anyone else in the department, okay?"

"Yeah. Sure."

"If you think Haley is alive," Charlie said, "why are you trying to find her?"

The dots were finally connecting for Brian. "You approached her, didn't you? Asked her to work with you on nailing Seth."

"You wanted her to testify against him?" Alarm rang in Charlie's voice.

"Not with spousal privilege," Brian said. "She wouldn't have been able to testify against her husband."

Charlie shook her head. "Then I don't understand how you expected her to help nail him."

"Haley was aware of her husband's activities. We needed her to wear a wire. To get him talking about the operation."

Not hiding the outrage from her face, Charlie glowered at the agent. "And jeopardize her life in the process."

Logan frowned. "The harsh reality is that her life was already at risk."

"She would've understood the danger," Charlie said. "There's no way she would've simply agreed."

"She didn't. We had to apply some pressure."

"Maybe too much pressure," Brian said. "Maybe you scared her off. When did you first approach her?"

"Back in May."

Sighing, Charlie slumped in the seat like she was deflating. "That's when she first came to USD. You, your task force, is the reason she came to me to disappear."

Logan nodded. "Unfortunately, you're probably right."

"I believe Seth got wind of it somehow and killed her for it," Charlie said. "You should be investigating him for murder."

"We are." Logan glanced between them. "But not Haley's."

"Then whose?" Charlie asked in disbelief.

"Teddy Williams?" Brian ventured a guess, and Logan nodded again.

She gasped. "What? Teddy is dead?"

"I found out earlier today that he's been missing since Monday or Tuesday," Brian said. "Detective Kramer, my partner on this, made a connection between him and Haley through USD."

"We don't know for certain that he's dead. But he vanished before Haley, and we have reason to suspect foul play."

"Why would Seth kill him?" Charlie asked.

"Haley and Teddy were having an affair," Logan said. "Someone on the task force threatened to expose her if she didn't come through with assisting us in the case. I disagreed with the method. Coercion rarely works."

"Oh, my God." Charlie shrank back. "Did some reckless, overzealous cop on your team leak it to Olsen?"

"I don't think so."

Brian didn't like the lack of conviction in Logan's voice. If someone on Logan's task force had, he wouldn't admit it to Charlie. Not when his apparent mission was to recruit her.

"If you were going to help Haley disappear," Logan said, "maybe you know how to find her. Start looking at this like she's alive. Think it through." Logan handed her a business card along with keys. "If you come up with something, if you're able to find her, will you call me?"

Charlie didn't respond. She snatched both from him and hopped out. "If Haley is dead, then this is on you and your task force," she said, before slamming the door.

Chapter Eleven

Emotions tangled in a knot in the pit of her stomach.

"We need to talk," Brian said behind her as she walked around to the SUV.

Anger simmered over how the boys, Brian and Rocco, had decided to hide things from her. *Poor, fragile Charlie.* While a warmth she'd never known filled her at knowing that Brian hadn't given up on her. That he'd followed her. Because he cared.

She pressed the button on the fob, unlocking the door, and reached for the handle.

But he put a palm to the door, stopping her from opening it. "Are you going to ignore me?"

"What is there to say?"

"Unbelievable. How about giving me an apology for hurling accusations and not giving me *five minutes* to explain?"

Brian had no idea the power he wielded—the things he stirred inside her. He'd slipped beneath the surface, had her revealing secrets, talking about her past. Stuff she never discussed. Not with Rocco. Not with Orson. Not anyone. Brian managed to break past the defenses she'd taken so long to build and made her feel raw. Exposed. Stripped utterly bare around him.

It was liberating and terrifying and beautiful.

She couldn't imagine what he would've accomplished in five minutes, especially if he'd touched her. "I needed distance. Time to think about it." She hated that she'd doubted Brian, and that he'd given her reason to. Because to her amazement she liked trusting him. "I'm not going to apologize for wanting space. Or for being relieved that I was wrong about you."

"Wow. I'll unpack that dodgy double-talk to evade an actual apology later. For now, you're clearly still upset with me. Why?"

"Your omission feels like a lie. A double standard. You hid it from me." She glared up at him. "Decided with Rocco that I was incapable of handling it."

"You're right. I'm sorry. I should have told you." He eased closer, close enough for her to feel his body heat, his breath across her skin. "But don't lecture me on double standards and hiding things. Not after I had to hear from another man what you've been up to." And then his hand was in her hair.

Her breath caught. Every muscle tensed as he crushed his mouth to hers. Hot and deep, full of wanting and need, he kissed her. She pressed against his hard body, sinking into it, savoring his touch. His mouth was warm and firm. The scrape of his stubble on her skin lit up her nerve endings. He tasted good. Felt even better.

His hands traveled over her body, lingering on her curves. The fluttering inside her went wild. Warmth simmered until she wanted to drag him into the car and strip off his clothes. Chuck hers as well.

"Come home with me," he whispered against her mouth.

His voice urgent, almost desperate. The suggestion delivered with a meaningful look.

Her heart threatened to beat out of her chest, reflexes struggling with her fight or flight response.

Then she remembered that there were more pleasurable options. She kissed him again, a soft brush of her lips, not wanting to stop. Not wanting to think. Or speak.

She nodded okay.

He pulled the key from the door, took her hand and popped the trunk. "Let's ride together. We can pick up the SUV in the morning." He grabbed her backpack and put it on his shoulder.

They got into his truck and headed to his house.

In the dark quiet of the truck cabin, he asked, "Is there anything else that you're hiding?" His tone gentle, teasing.

"I've been taking pictures of Seth and everyone I've seen with him. Including in the club." She opened her purse. Looked at the pictures on her phone. "It was so dark in there. You can't see the guy with the scar. The one who attacked me in the alley. But I have better photos of the man with glasses on my camera."

He shot her a heated look. "What am I missing? What possessed you to go to the Bare Back? Why would that guy attack you?"

"It's a long story, but a stripper who works there, Aubrey, she led me to Rafe. But she lied about not helping Haley spy on Seth. I went back to pin her down and get the truth. Find out what Seth is up to. Turns out it's drugs, money laundering and prostitution."

"Hold on. This Aubrey was working with Haley to do what? Collect evidence?"

She shrugged. "I'm not sure. Aubrey wasn't completely

honest. Considering everything I've learned over the past few days, it's obvious that neither was Haley. I think she manipulated me into her helping get the fake credentials. But if she's alive and fled, why wouldn't she wait for the new ID?"

"Maybe it's got to do with Teddy. If Seth did kill him, that might have been enough to push her over the edge. Drive her to do something rash."

"But she can't run far or for long without credentials. Or money. Or the place I was going to set up for her in Idaho." She'd worked out a lease with someone who would accept cash and not run a background check.

"Why there and not halfway across the country? Say Georgia? Alabama?"

"Her mom is sick, and she didn't want to go too far. Even though I warned that she wouldn't be able come back and check on her."

"You've learned a lot," Brian said, pulling into his driveway. "Any reason you didn't share all this with Powell?"

"You mean about Aubrey and possible evidence?"

"Yeah."

They got out and he carried her backpack and duffel bag inside.

"Haley was either killed or put under so much pressure that she bolted prematurely. I wanted to think before offering up another sacrificial lamb. It's a big decision." Meddling with someone's life.

He locked the door. "If she's on the run, any idea where she'd go?"

"No, but…" An idea came to her.

"What is it?"

"I don't know where she'd go, but I might know how to

find her." She dug inside her backpack and whipped out her flip phone.

Brian eyed it. "Is that your burner?"

"Same kind I gave to Haley." Not that it did her any good. She flipped it open.

"Who are you calling?"

She swallowed hard. "Orson."

He looked surprised. Then cautious. "Why?"

"He's the best at what he does. Genius level IQ. Hacked into some government agency when he was only fourteen." She stopped herself from saying more when Brian frowned, twisting his mouth like he tasted something sour.

"A real wunderkind," he grumbled.

On the phone, she pressed and held down the number one, putting the call through.

"You've got him on speed dial? As your first option?" He mumbled something and raked a hand through his hair.

She pressed the phone to her ear. The line rang. And rang. It wasn't like Orson carried the burner around with him. It was probably tucked in a drawer.

"Put it on speaker," Brian said.

She tensed. "Why?"

"Because I'm asking."

She'd asked him to prove that she could trust him. Over and over. And he had. Until the football hiccup, which turned out to be a misunderstanding that he'd wanted to explain. She stared in his eyes and realized she needed to show him that he could trust her, too.

With a nod, she hit the speaker button right as Orson answered.

"Hey, sweet lips." His voice was deep and sultry, warm as a summer night.

Her cheeks flushed and Brian scowled.

"I told you not to call me that," she snapped.

Orson chuckled, the sound reverberating in her belly. "Sorry. It's fun getting a rise out of you. Hey, at least I didn't call you sweet p—"

"I need a favor," she said, cutting him off.

"Of course, you do. It's the only reason you ever call. What is it this time?" Orson asked.

"My latest client, Haley Olsen. She really has disappeared. Possibly. I need you to help me find her if she's still alive."

"I'm listening."

She briefly recounted what happened the night Haley vanished.

"Sounds gnarly. That was Wednesday night?" Orson asked.

"Yes. So, look for someone who has been paying for a hotel in cash since then. Say a sixty-mile radius from here." Haley was worried sick about her mom. She wouldn't want to go far. Especially if she was trying to keep tabs on what was happening back here in Laramie.

Brian shook his head and extended his hands, like he was widening a circle.

"On second thought," she said, "double it. Make it a hundred and twenty miles."

Brian nodded.

"I can use my facial recognition program if you want," Orson said.

Her heart leaped. "Yes. That would be perfect."

"For a price."

He'd never charged her before.

"How much?" she asked. What she was asking for would come with a hefty price tag.

"I don't want your money," he said, sounding insulted. "Come to Denver. Spend a week with me. I miss you."

Sucking in a breath, Charlie turned her back to Brian. For too long, she had allowed this flirtatious banter that skirted a thin line. "You don't miss me. You miss the idea of me. You miss having dinner with someone and a person in your bed who actually knows you." A woman who recognized how special he was, what he was capable of. His brilliance. His drive. His staggering loyalty. He might not have been faithful as a boyfriend, but he was a diehard friend that she could count on in a pinch. "But mostly, you miss the pretense of a relationship. Not me."

They never talked when they were together. Not the way she did with Brian about things that mattered. Orson had never asked her questions, forcing her out of her comfort zone. He preferred to learn about people on the computer. And he certainly never admitted that he cared about her.

Silence stretched, seconds bleeding into a full minute, until it unnerved her. "Orson?"

He sighed. "I hate it when you're right. I guess I just regret the way it ended. You didn't deserve that."

Finding another woman in the bed that they had shared? No. She didn't.

"No regrets. Water under the bridge." Everything worked out the way it was supposed to. She never loved him. Nor him her. Two lost souls who had passed time together. She'd forgiven him ages ago for being disrespectful. It was ancient history now. "Hey, being right doesn't mean I'm smarter."

"I take a strange comfort in that," he said, and she could

hear the smile in his voice. "I'll call you when I have something. Keep the phone handy."

The line disconnected.

She exhaled a slow breath of relief, shoved the phone in her duffel and faced Brian.

He took her hands in his, and she realized they were shaking.

"Thank you, for trusting me," he said.

"Two-way street. Right?"

A smile tugged at his delicious mouth. God, he was gorgeous.

"Let's get those scrapes cleaned up."

"I think you were a medic in a previous life."

He laughed and led her through the house to his bedroom. She hadn't gotten a good look at it before.

The room was simple, understated, yet tasteful. A deep navy color on the walls. King size bed that took up most of the room. Chic curtains. The duvet looked like it belonged in a swanky hotel. A couple of nightstands with stylish lamps. A photograph of what she presumed was his parents on the dresser.

He sat her down on the bed. "Give me a second." He ducked into the en suite. Came back carrying a large red case that had a white cross on it.

"You brought me in here to flaunt all your medical supplies, didn't you?"

His smile deepened. He unzipped the kit and then she was really impressed. It was the best first-aid kit on the planet. He even the supplies to do sutures. *Show-off.*

He started with cleaning the bruise on her knee.

"Lucky me to have a once-upon-a-time Boy Scout tending to me again," she said, appreciative of his gentle touch.

"Nice to hear that said with affection." He blew on the scrape. Moved to her shoulder and did the same. His gaze raked over her. Not only like he wanted her, but as though she was precious. Valued. Appreciated in return.

Her fear. Her walls…her fences. All the time she'd spent protecting herself from getting too attached. From being hurt. None of it mattered.

Not in this sweet, safe space that she'd found here with him. She slid her hand into his hair and brought his mouth to hers. The kiss was soft and warm.

"I want to show you something," he said, but hesitated.

"Go on." She nudged him.

He opened a tiny little chest on the nightstand, designed to hold small knickknacks. He pulled something out and opened his palm.

Curious, Charlie stared down at the simple pearl in his hand. "What is that?"

"The night of charity gala for the women's shelter in Cheyenne, you lost an earring."

She'd never had her ears pierced and had worn clip-ons. "The clasp broke." Her gaze dipped back down. "That's the earring? You found it?"

"After you had abandoned me on the dance floor, I came across it. I'd intended to give it back to you. So you could have it fixed."

She reached for it, but he closed his fingers around the pearl.

"My first lie to you." He chuckled to himself. "And my last. I never intended to give it back."

"Got a thing for pearls?" she teased.

"More like for diamonds in the rough. Forged under pressure," he said, and something in her swooned. "This was the closest I could get. I take it out every night. Look at it. Feel it between my fingers. Think of you."

Her gaze went back to his. A sweet warmth coursed through her. Sweeter yet was that she saw he was embarrassed. "That's borderline weird," she said.

"You're being nice. I'm sure it sounds completely weird."

Who was she to judge?

He put the pearl back in the chest, shut it and rose, holding the first-aid kit.

She stood, stopping him with a hand on his chest. "It's also really romantic." In a weird way that she adored.

The night of the gala had been magical for her. Because of him. Running into him when she'd been alone and feeling a bit lost, uncomfortable. Talking to him. Dinner and dancing. Those smooth moves of his. That kiss.

All with him.

It was like Cupid had aimed, released his arrow. And she'd mistaken it for an assassination attempt by the gods.

"I meant what I said last night," he said, his gaze caressing her face the way she longed for his hand to.

"I know." She lifted onto the balls of her feet, still wearing those treacherous heels. And captured his mouth with hers.

Her arms went around his neck, fingers diving into his lush hair. Their bodies slammed together, hers vibrating as the kiss grew rough, nearly brutal with a wild recklessness. His mouth was hot, this time possessive, and she welcomed it. The shock of it sent flares rippling straight to her center.

And the warrior, the survivor in her who had been fighting for so long, so hard, shattered into a thousand pieces. The pain, the loss, the guilt, the anger she'd lived with every single day melted away. Like ashes in rain.

She loved his hair, thick and silky. His mouth. The way he kissed her. She loved his rough hands on her skin, his warm palms pulling her closer.

Desire pooled inside her as his lips moved over hers, kissing down her neck. She rocked her hips against him, aching to get as close as possible.

Pushing him down onto the bed, she straddled him. Kissed him harder, desperation sliding into every stroke of her tongue. His hand slid up, cupping her breast. The other was on her hip. He adjusted their bodies until she was nestled right on top of the rock-hard bulge in his jeans. For too long, she'd been avoiding and wanting this man. Every nerve in her body was alive with the anticipation of spending the next few hours naked with him.

She needed him.

"I want you," she said, the breath shuddering in her lungs as she rocked her hips on him.

"But I need more than the just physical."

Sex, when she chose to have it, was on her terms, always quick and satisfying a basic need. Even with Orson.

Maybe that's why he needed variety. Because she hadn't been willing to do tricks. Perform like a circus act.

But with Brian, there was a tangling of emotions. A war on her instincts. A battering of expectations. He wasn't looking for entertainment, some carnal thrill.

He wanted to go deeper. To connect by making love.

Another first for her.

"I know," she whispered, nibbling at his mouth, craving all of him. She had no idea that being vulnerable could make her happy. But it did. "I understand."

Making love to him would be taking a giant leap of faith...that he wouldn't break her heart.

But she wasn't blindly jumping in. Her eyes were wide open. And she saw Brian for who he was. A good, strong man. With a kind heart. Not perfect Captain America, but fallible. A guy who could take a licking and keep on ticking.

"What are you saying?" he asked, with a baffled look, cradling her face in his hands.

"I'm saying yes." She was giving him a chance. "Don't blow it."

Chapter Twelve

Driving into town, Brian checked the rearview mirror again. No one had parked near his house, and with the few cars on this stretch of the road, he was certain they weren't being followed.

He reached out and took Charlie's hand. She beamed at him.

"You're beautiful," he said. "Even prettier without the makeup."

She moved her hand from his palm to his thigh and stroked his leg. "Flattery will get you everywhere."

"I'm serious." He glanced over at her. "Did you do something different to your eyebrows?"

"Oh, Carey, *my stylist*, did. Altered the shape to give my face a different look. Subtle, but effective. Do you like it?"

He nodded his approval.

Smiling, she put her head back against the seat and gazed out the window.

After a while, he said, "Penny for your thoughts."

She shrugged. "I'm just happy. Feel like a weight has been lifted." Her smile spread wider. "And I can't stop thinking about last night. Or this morning. I was right about you."

She stroked his leg again. "You do know your way around a woman's body. I'm glad your brand isn't Captain America. I don't think he would've been capable of all the dirty, delicious things you did to me."

He chuckled. The night had been incredible. The intensity. The passion. Her guard had lowered and hadn't returned.

This morning had been different when they'd made love again. Sweet. Tender. But no less intense. He'd held her in his arms. Snuggled close, he'd loved the feel of her thigh nestled between his. Her breasts pressed against his chest. The way she kissed up his neck to his jaw. And made them run too late for him to cook breakfast. They'd barely had enough time to shower and grab coffee.

But it was worth it.

He stopped alongside Dustin's Jeep in the big-box store parking lot. "Are you going to get your Hellcat back?"

"If Dustin is willing to give her back that is."

He leaned over and kissed her. "Still want full disclosure?" he asked.

"Always."

"I think I'm in love with you," he said.

She stilled. The color and smile drained from her face. He wasn't even sure if she was breathing.

His heart shot like a missile to his throat. Why had he blurted it out like that?

"You don't have to say anything," he said. It was too fast for her. She needed baby steps. But also, the truth. "I get what I said might be scary for you. You're gun-shy about relationships, even though you're not timid about anything else in your life. This is new for me, too." He hadn't gotten serious about anyone. Until now. "My heart is every bit as much in your hands as yours is in mine. Okay?"

"How can you be sure it's love? It's only been a few days."

When you know, you know.

"It's actually been almost a year. I fell for you the first time I saw you sparring in USD. Then at the gala, well, I fell much, much harder." A complete goner. "I've never felt like this. I wanted you to know." He just hoped she didn't run.

She moistened her lips. "No heavy discussions allowed before breakfast. New rule."

Rules were a good sign. He could live with that.

"How about you pick up some food from Delgado's?" she suggested. "We could eat together at USD."

Even better, she wasn't running. He smiled. "I like your idea." He kissed her again.

She snatched the cowboy hat from his head and put it on. "I'll hang on to this for you."

"My hat looks good on you."

Her mouth curved into a slight smile.

Brian watched her get in the Jeep and drive off. He followed her. They were going in the same direction. Delgado's was just down the block from USD.

Since she hadn't told him what she wanted to eat, he got two different things. A breakfast burrito and prairie rose special: two eggs any style, hash browns and bacon. He'd eat whichever one she didn't want.

At USD, she took the burrito, but he suspected it was because it left one of her hands free to log into her computer.

"I noticed the note on the door about closing early the next few nights."

Taking another bite, she nodded. "Until I find out what happened to Haley. Or Seth's arrested."

"Both could take a while."

"That's not what I want to hear."

"I know." He finished eating and wiped his mouth with a napkin. "Have you ever considered taking a full day off, on a regular basis?"

"Why? Did you have plans for me?"

"A few dirty thoughts spring to mind," he said, and she grinned. "But I'm talking about time to recharge. Unwind. I'd love to spend a full day with you."

"Sounds nice. Let me think on it."

The front door opened. One of her trainers walked in, and she waved to him.

"I need to tell Dustin about Teddy." She stood and came around the desk. "I can't believe I was this close to firing Teddy in a voice mail for not showing up." Taking the hat off, she set it on his head.

Brian watched her approach Dustin and put a hand on his shoulder as she spoke to him.

A phone buzzed.

He checked his pocket, but it wasn't his. Looking around, he spotted Charlie's on the desk, but it wasn't that one either.

The buzzing came from inside her duffel bag on the desk. He unzipped it and took out the burner.

"Charlie!" He held up the phone, and she nodded.

She said something else to Dustin, who had lowered his head, his face in shock. She hurried into the office and grabbed the phone.

"Hey, Orson. Did you find something?" She listened. Then her gaze flashed up to Brian's. She nodded, grabbed a pen and wrote on a notepad. "You're the best." She smirked like Orson had responded with something saucy. "Knock it off. I've got to go. Thank you." She clicked off, flipped the phone closed and shoved it back in her bag. "Haley is alive. And Orson found her."

A wunderkind indeed.

"PULL OVER THERE and park," Charlie said to Brian, gesturing to the diner situated next to a gas station.

"Why?" he asked. "The motel is across the street."

"Please, just do it."

His jaw hardened, but he did as she asked. "Are you going to tell me why we're parked at this diner?"

"If Haley sees a cop before I've had a chance to talk to her and convince her that she can trust you, it's possible she might not tell me anything. But it's certain that she'll freak out." Charlie had plenty of questions, and she intended to get answers. "Give me twenty minutes with her. Then we'll either come to you or I'll call you and have you pull the car around. Okay?"

By the look on his face, she could tell that he didn't like it. "No. Not okay. I'm parking at the motel." He put the vehicle in reverse and backed away from the diner. "I'll position the truck where she won't be able to see me from the room. *Okay?*"

Not that he was truly asking because he was already pulling into the lot.

"What's the room number?" he asked.

She glanced down at the piece of paper in her hand that had the address of the motel in Kimball, Nebraska, less than two hours from Laramie. Brian had been right to expand the search radius, and she was grateful that Orson had come through, finding her.

The motel was right off the highway, not far after entering Nebraska from Wyoming.

"One twenty-five."

He parked in front of room 103 near the front office. "Haley's room should be all the way at the other end."

"Why couldn't you park across the street like I wanted?" she asked.

Unclicking his seat belt, he shifted to look at her and propped his forearm on the back of the seat. "Because I've got an uneasy feeling in my gut. Combine that with your penchant for finding trouble, and being across the street felt too far. Call it being caution, protective, whatever you want. But if you insist on going in there alone, this is how it's going to be." He tipped his hat at her.

She groaned, torn between arguing with him and kissing him. "Twenty minutes."

"You've got ten. Then we're bringing her in to DCI Powell."

Sighing, she slid out of the truck.

"Hey, be careful," he said. "When you first knock, don't stand directly in front of the door."

"Why not?"

"You don't know what's on the other side. She could be armed and jumpy. Not a good combination."

Charlie nodded, closed the door and hurried down the walkway. The High Point motel looked as if it had seen better days. Old and run-down it had plenty of vacancies, judging by the nearly empty lot.

Drawing closer to the end of the building, she eyed the

truck in front of the last door. A Ford F-150. Dark green. Older model. She knew the plate number.

Teddy's truck. Was he alive, too, and hiding out with Haley?

Rushing up to room 125, she noticed that the sheer curtains were drawn across the window, but not the heavy blackout drapes. A television was on inside.

She knocked, standing off to the side near the window while she did it. "Haley!"

No answer.

"Haley!" She knocked again. "It's me, Charlie. Open up."

She strained to listen. No movement on the other side of the door. The only sound she picked up was the whoosh of the traffic on Old Highway 71. Charlie turned and stared at the Ford behind her.

"Haley, it's just me, Charlie." She pounded her fist. "Are you in there?"

The sound of the television died. Rustling inside the room. Maybe one person.

"Open this door!"

A chain slid back and rattled. The door swung open, and there stood Haley, pointing a Smith & Wesson .357 level at her chest. "What are you doing here?"

"I could ask you the same question. Unless you're going to shoot me, lower that thing."

"Are you here alone?"

Charlie swallowed. She didn't want to lie, but she also didn't want to spook Haley by telling her that her companion was a detective who worked with her husband. "Do you see me with anyone?"

Wide-eyed and hair mussed, Haley stuck her head out the door and took a furtive glance around.

"Satisfied?" Charlie strode past her into the room.

Haley slammed the door, locked it and slipped the chain on with a shaky hand. "How did you find me?"

"That doesn't matter right now. What matters is that I did."

Trembling, Haley plopped down on the bed, clutching the revolver. She didn't look well. Pale skin. Bags under her eyes. She was bare foot and wore a T-shirt and jeans.

Charlie looked around.

The dim motel room smelled of mildew and traces of a hundred seedy encounters. Empty bags of junk food and cans of diet cola were on the nightstand.

"Tell me what you did." Charlie crossed her arms. "And why you did it."

Haley bent over, propped her elbow on her thigh and dropped her head into her palm.

"You better start talking," Charlie demanded. "What happened after you called Wednesday night?"

"I staged the scene at the house."

"You baited me and set me up."

Raising her head, a stranger with a steely glint in her eyes stared back. "Yeah, I baited you. But I was setting up Seth. Not you."

"Why?"

"Because he deserves it!" Haley jumped to her feet. "He's a soulless beast. He killed Teddy!"

It was true? "How do you know for sure?" Charlie didn't want it to be real. She wanted to cling to hope that he was still alive.

"Seth bragged about it. Taunted me with the fact that he killed him. After that I realized it didn't matter if my name changed, if I looked different, if I lived somewhere else. He would always find me."

"But we had a plan. It would've kept you safe."

"To hell with your plan."

All the effort and time and money that had gone into the process—wasted. The months of manipulation that Haley had invested in getting Charlie to even help her in the first place. For what? "Why come to me to begin with?" Then a sneaking suspicion settled in her gut like a rock. "How did you even know to come to me, that I could help you disappear?"

"My friend Rafe. You helped his cousin. Eva Johnson."

Eva's maiden name had been Martinez. But it was a common surname. Charlie hadn't made the connection. "Well then, you know how my system works. Why didn't you believe in it?"

"I did. I thought it could work, too. Then Seth took Teddy away from me." Haley seemed to collapse in on herself. "Seth can take anything away. Even my life." Tears glistened in her eyes and rolled down her cheeks. "I needed him to pay. Finally. For something. I don't know what he did with Teddy's body. Whether there's evidence of his murder somewhere.

"Speaking of evidence, do you have any on Seth that could put him away?"

Haley lowered her head. "Yeah, but…" She chewed her bottom lip. "Other people I know working for him will be hurt by it. They'll go to jail, too."

"People like Aubrey?"

Haley's shocked gaze flashed up to her. She nodded. "That's why I needed him to be convicted and jailed for something else. Like my *murder*. He deserves to rot in prison for all his crimes."

Charlie paced in the room, fuming at the lies and deception. "There was so much blood at the house. How did you pull that off?"

Grabbing a tissue, Haley sniffled. "I volunteer at the hospital. I got to know people. There was a phlebotomist with a gambling debt. I paid him to draw as much blood as possible from me. Two pints. But it wasn't enough. I bought two more pints of someone else's blood. That's why I needed the house to explode. To make sure the police couldn't analyze all of it. Only mine, which I mostly used on the porch and in the grass. A bit in the kitchen."

Every word out of Haley's conniving mouth infuriated Charlie. "Why rope me into this? Was the abuse even real?"

"Yes," Haley said, shaking the gun. "Seth not only beat me, but he got into my head. Never let me forget how small and insignificant I am. That the only value I have is what he gives me." More tears.

"Why me?" Charlie scrubbed the heel of her palm across her forehead. "You have family that you could've dragged into this. Called them to come running out to your house that night."

Haley shook her head. "Seth doesn't let them visit. They never would've come. But I knew you would. Knew that you wouldn't call the cops."

A sickening thought occurred to Charlie as the pieces came together. "Did you shoot at me, too, at my house?"

Haley sobbed now. "I'm sorry. I'm so ashamed."

"But why?" A misdirected bullet could've killed her. Or Brian. How could Haley have taken such a crazy chance?

"It made you angry, didn't it?" Haley dabbed at the tears and wiped her nose. "Fired you up with the determination to get Seth?"

And it had.

This woman was a master manipulator.

What was the point of asking her any questions? It would only be more manipulation. Spinning half-truths just like Aubrey.

"You're a real piece of work, lady." Charlie was disgusted with herself for being so stupid. So easy. "There's a DCI agent, Logan Powell, looking for you."

"What?" Haley asked, a horrified look coming over her face.

"He doesn't think you're dead. Convinced me to look for you."

"Wait a minute," Haley said, her tears drying up quicker than a mirage in the desert. "If DCI Powell thought you could find me, who else might think the same? Did you lead someone here? Seth? One of his people? Oh God, the cartel?" Haley spun around. "The money."

"What money?"

BRIAN KEPT CHECKING his mirrors. But the itchy sensation slithering up and down his spine didn't stop.

He climbed out of his truck and stretched his legs. Glancing over at the front office, he spotted the coffee machine. He checked his watch. Charlie had two more minutes with Haley, and then he was knocking on the door.

Time enough for a cup of Joe. He stepped inside and went

over to the small table set up for guests. As he poured coffee in a paper cup, he looked across the street.

Was that the same black SUV sitting at the gas station that had pulled in around the same time he parked at the diner?

He couldn't be sure. It was a Chevy. Dark tinted windows. They were a dime a dozen. He hadn't gotten the license plate. But it was in the exact same spot off to the side of the pumps.

They hadn't been followed from the house. That he was certain of. But it was entirely possible someone might have been waiting near USD. It was common knowledge that she went there every day. The best place to find her if someone was looking.

On the freeway he hadn't noticed a tail.

Sipping his coffee, he watched the SUV pull out of the parking spot and leave the gas station. Relief ebbed through him.

Until the vehicle crossed over Old Highway 71 and careened into the motel lot. The driver gunned the gas, tires screeching across the asphalt.

Brian sprinted to the door and bounded out into the lot.

A window in the back driver's side of the vehicle rolled down, and the barrel of an automatic weapon stuck out.

Terror clawed at Brian's chest as he dropped the cup.

A series of loud *RAT-A-TAT-TATS* exploded.

Bullets tore into room 125, riddling the door with holes and busting the window.

No! Charlie!

He drew his weapon and returned fire, shattering the rear windshield.

The vehicle took off, speeding out of the lot. As it turned, going around the corner, he caught a glimpse of a man. The one with a jagged scar on his face.

Brian bolted across the lot. He kicked in what was left of the door to room 125. His gaze flew around. Bullet holes everywhere. Shattered lamps. Busted TV. Feathers floated in the air.

"Charlie!" he screamed, racing around the bed. Charlie and Haley were on the floor.

Blood was splattered on both of them.

Chapter Thirteen

In the Kimball emergency waiting room, Brian threw his arms around Charlie, thankful that she wasn't hurt.

"I'm okay," she said, again, for like the twentieth time.

But he didn't believe it until an EMT had checked her.

The blood on her body had been Haley's. Other than a gash on her forehead from hitting her head on the nightstand as she fell, and a few stitches to close it, she was fine.

He stared at the stitches and caressed her cheek.

She looked composed, but he saw the nerves beneath the surface. "If not for Haley—" she paused, swallowed "—shoving me to the ground, I might be in surgery with her." She looked up at him, and the misery in her eyes made his chest squeeze. "I led them straight to her."

"We led them."

DCI Powell, who had arrived after Brian called him, spun on his heel. "This wouldn't have happened if you had notified me of her whereabouts as soon as you had located her. We would've brought her in quietly. Safely."

That was probably true. But Charlie had legitimate concerns about the way Haley had been handled by Logan

Powell's task force. Charlie felt better about bringing her in herself, and Brian had agreed to help her.

Haley had lost a lot of blood, for real this time, in the motel room and on the way to the hospital. Now she might not pull through the surgery.

He still couldn't swallow the story Charlie had repeated about all the things that Haley had done. The way she had taken advantage of Charlie's need to help victims of domestic abuse burned him to the bone.

The entrance doors to the ER whooshed open.

Kent strode inside. "I got here as fast as I could."

"You called Detective Kramer?" Powell asked.

"I did. He's my partner on the Haley Olsen case. You don't suspect that he's dirty, do you?"

The DCI agent clenched his jaw. "He's not under investigation or suspicion."

"Then I trust there isn't a problem here."

"Make no mistake, there is a problem. With the way you violated protocol, by taking your girlfriend on a road trip to see my informant, when you should have contacted me."

"This is my fault," Charlie said to Powell. "Not Brian's. I didn't trust you to have Haley's best interest at heart."

Brian wasn't going to allow her to blame herself for this.

He stared at Powell, forcing himself to keep his cool. "She's the one who found her. Something you couldn't do. Your mistake, or someone on your task force, is the reason Haley bolted. I'm certain that leaking to her husband that she was having an affair is violation of protocol. It's also what got Teddy Williams killed. So, if we're making a tally of mistakes here, I'd say that you and your task force have a longer column."

"For the record, the agent who leaked the information has been suspended pending an investigation."

As Brian had suspected. "You lied."

"I did what I had to get your girlfriend to cooperate." He stepped away.

"Is Charlie all right?" Kent asked, easing forward.

Brian nodded. He looked at her again, hating how close she had come to dying. How helpless he had felt. The desperation that had flooded him at the prospect of losing her. He brushed his knuckles across her bloodstained cheek before going over to the other detective.

"I can't believe you two found Haley Olsen and left me out of the road trip."

Maybe he should've brought Kent along. Another set of eyes keeping watch might have prevented this.

A doctor wearing scrubs pushed through doors and approached them. "You're waiting for information on Haley Olsen?"

They all nodded. Charlie rose and came to Brian's side.

"A bullet ruptured her subclavian artery," the doctor said. "She lost a tremendous amount of blood. Almost didn't make it. But the surgery went well. We were able to repair the damage and stop the bleeding. Then we gave her a transfusion of two units. She should fully recover."

Charlie leaned against Brian as if a burden had been lifted off her shoulders.

"When can I speak with her?" DCI Powell said. "I have some urgent questions."

"She's in the recovery room now. She'll be a bit groggy for a while."

"That's fine. I might get more truthful responses if she's

kind of out of it," Powell said. "Also, when will she be able to leave the hospital?"

"Not for a couple of days."

"We'd prefer to have her in a safe house, but we'll need to make arrangements to have her airlifted out of here as soon as possible to another hospital for her safety."

"Oh," the doctor said. "I didn't realize. It is possible to have her recover at a safe house, provided you have a nurse available for a couple of days who could change her IV and the dressing for her wound."

Powell nodded. "I can make that happen."

"Come with me. I'll take you to see her."

"Wait," Charlie said, going up to Powell. "She mentioned that she had evidence on Seth, but that she was worried about implicating people she cared about."

"My people are going through the motel room with a fine-tooth comb. The one thing your boyfriend did right was ensuring the police kept officers posted at the room. If she had any evidence in there, we'll find it. And if it's somewhere else, I will persuade her that it's in her best interest to cooperate and hand it over."

"Also, one of the last things she said to me was something about the cartel and money."

"Do you know what she meant?" Powell asked.

"She didn't get a chance to explain because gunfire turned the room into Swiss cheese and nearly us along with it."

"I'm glad you two are okay." Powell clutched her arm. "Thank you for finding her." He left with the doctor.

Brian put an arm around Charlie, bringing her close.

"Please tell me that you intend to take the rest of the day off. We'll go back to my place. Decompress."

She shook her head. "We've got booked classes this afternoon through the early evening, and Dustin has to leave by four. Decompressing will have to wait."

"At least let me take you to get cleaned up first." He looked over her bloodstained clothes. "Shower and change."

"Yeah, that's what I had in mind."

"To reiterate what the DCI agent said, I'm glad you two are all right also." Kent glanced between them. "Didn't know you were dating anyone," he said to Brian. "But good to see that you're putting yourself out there."

Not sure what to say, Brian simply nodded.

"I never showed you all the pictures I took of Seth," Charlie said. "And the people he's been associating with. Especially at those suspicious addresses."

"We'll take a look at when we get to the house," Brian said. He turned to Kent. "If there's anything worthwhile, I'll share it with you."

"Sounds good. In the meantime, we've got reports to fill out," Kent said. "I'll get started since you'll be *delayed*."

"Sure. The only thing is we need to keep all this from spreading around in the department. Especially the part about the DCI investigating Seth Olsen."

"I won't submit it through regular channels. Only the lieutenant and chief of police will see it."

"Works for me," Brian said.

AFTER COMING SO close to death, Charlie was astounded by the numbness that kept threatening to engulf her. Every time she felt the cold sinking in, right down to her core, she thought about Brian. His warmth. His light.

And it helped to plug her back in.

Is that what she had been doing since her mother's murder? Disconnecting?

Such a sad way to live.

She glanced at the USD schedule on her computer.

No one was on the books for the last two classes this evening. This was the one night a week where Rocco would usually take over as the instructor and close up for her if he was available. She hadn't realized how much she missed those evening hours off until now.

Changes needed to be made in her schedule so she could actually have time for a life. The school didn't need to be open seven days a week. Maybe she'd shut down on Mondays. Hire a dedicated trainer to teach three to four evenings as well as handle locking up the school.

She wanted time. To slow down and unwind. To spend with Brian, hanging out on his back porch, curled up in his arms.

Who would have ever thought she'd feel that way about anyone, much less a cop?

Charlie thought about the pictures she'd shown Brian. He'd been able to identify two other detectives, who were also possibly dirty. When he'd pointed to the one with close-cropped dark blond hair, Colvin, she'd caught a flash of anger in his eyes. She hadn't understood until he explained that Colvin was Seth's alibi. The balding guy with a paunch was a detective, too. Eklund.

But Brian hadn't recognized the man with glasses.

Haley needed to come through and nail all these guys.

Charlie went to the first of two private training rooms for

one-on-one sessions and started putting away equipment: pads, mats, sparring helmets.

"Hello," a female voice called out.

Charlie shut off the light in the room and stepped out into the main area where they held group classes.

"Hi." It was Aubrey. "Do you have a minute?" she asked.

This was the first time Charlie had seen her in regular clothes, a formfitting dress and heels. But it was even more surprising to see her standing in USD.

"Sure," Charlie said.

"I'm sorry I lied to you about Haley and about spying on Seth. It's just that my position is delicate. You came around asking dangerous questions, where I work. The last person I gave information to disappeared."

In hindsight, Charlie would've handled things differently. "I understand. I shouldn't have popped back up at the club the way that I did."

"No, you shouldn't have," Aubrey said, with a frown. "But I get why you did. We're both worried about Haley. She's lucky to have someone like you on her side. Have you found out anything more? Do you know if Haley is dead or alive?"

A chill moved through Charlie like someone had walked over her grave. She tensed. Hesitated. "She's alive. But I can't say anything more than that. To protect her."

Aubrey exhaled a big breath, relief washing over her face. "Thank goodness she's all right. If anything had happened to her, I don't know what I would do."

"You don't need to worry about her. She's going to be okay." Charlie waited to see if this supposed friend kept pushing for information or let it be.

"Do you think I could start taking some classes here? It'd be nice to learn how to defend myself."

"Of course," Charlie said, feeling more relaxed at the change in conversation. "Everyone is welcome. Your first two will be free."

"That's real nice of you." Aubrey smiled. "Mind if I use the bathroom before I leave?"

"Go right ahead. The restroom is around the corner and down the hall."

Aubrey's heels clacked away against the linoleum, and Charlie went to the second training room. Once she was done packing up the equipment, she grabbed the laundry bag.

"Good night," Aubrey called out.

"Night!"

As Charlie stuffed dirty towels in the bag that she'd drop off at the cleaners in the morning, she thought she heard the door again.

"Aubrey?" Charlie switched off the light in the room and headed back into the main area.

No sign of her. There was no one outside on the sidewalk. The space inside was still. Yet, something tickled at her senses.

Her cell phone rang. She hurried to her office and dumped the laundry bag in front of her desk. Seeing Brian's name on the caller ID made her smile. "Hey. I'm locking up now."

"How does homemade wood-fired pizza sound for dinner?" Brian asked.

"Delicious." Right on cue, her stomach grumbled. "I'm starving."

"Excellent," he said. "I just finished making the dough. What's your preference for toppings?"

"I'm easy. Anything except pineapple."

"My kind of woman." His whiskey and velvet voice sent a tingle through her.

Her smile deepened.

"Just to give you a heads-up," he said, "I think we should talk after dinner." His tone was easy-breezy.

She loved the way he kept things light. "Is that a euphemism or is this going to be an actual conversation?" she asked.

"A conversation. About things. About us. But we could make it pillow talk."

That was the best kind. "The forewarning is appreciated." But unnecessary. When it came to Brian, she wanted to run to him. Not away from him. Not anymore. "See you soon." She disconnected.

She grabbed her duffel bag, left the office and locked the front door.

Switching off the interior lights, she peered into the darkness out front, listening, looking. Nothing appeared amiss.

Curiosity poked at her. She opened the GPS app on her phone and stared at the map. Seth's truck was out at the ranch. Actually, his brother's piece of land. The first time she'd seen it there since she'd been surveilling him.

Still, something wasn't right. She unzipped her duffel bag, dropping her cell phone inside and pulling out her .45.

Heading for the back door, she passed the bathroom. She reached for the dead bolt on the back door and froze.

It was already unlocked. Her gaze flew to the alarm keypad on the wall. The screen was blank. No green light. The security system had been disabled.

The hair on the nape of her neck rose.

Clutching the SIG in both hands now, she crept backward from the door. Not knowing what, or rather who, was waiting to ambush her on the other side in the dark parking lot.

The door swung open. She sucked in a breath.

Two men wearing black ski masks stood across the threshold.

She took aim. A creak came from behind her. Dread spilled down her spine. She turned.

A third man lunged from the bathroom, tackling her.

The gun went off. They crashed to the floor. Air whooshed from her lungs as he landed on her with sickening force. Pain sliced through her.

They wrestled over the gun. She threw an elbow to her attacker's face, but he slammed her forearm against the floor. Her .45 went skittering.

A different man grabbed her ankles, trying to pin her down. She lashed out with a foot. Her heel hit flesh. The man groaned. Another knelt beside her. The dark figure loomed over Charlie, holding something in his hands.

She kicked and punched, battling to twist free. Desperate to escape their grasp, but it was three against one. *Cowards.*

Duct tape was pressed to her mouth and a black hood was shoved over her head. Three sets of hands tossed her onto her stomach. A knee was thrust into her spine. The man's weight bore down on her, flattening her against the floor, until there was no more air. She couldn't breathe. Couldn't scream.

Zip ties tightened around her wrists, pinching down to the bone. They restrained her ankles next and hoisted her up.

She struggled to move her arms, her legs. To keep fighting. It was futile, but she refused to stop.

Something hit the side of her head. The darkness lurched. She tried to hang on to the threads of consciousness unraveling, but failed.

WHERE WAS SHE?

His tenth time calling Charlie, and she still didn't answer the phone. Brian hung up again. After the pizza had grown cold and he hadn't been able to reach her, he'd gotten into his truck.

He zipped down Third Street and turned into the parking lot behind USD, tires screeching. Slamming on the brake, he stopped next to Dustin's SUV.

The back door was wide open.

Drawing his firearm, Brian hopped out of his truck.

"Charlie!" he shouted as he ran inside the building. "Are you here?"

Nothing.

"Charlie!" He swept the corridor with his gaze. Fumbled for a light switch. Found it.

Brian's blood ran cold as he took in the scene.

Everything stood out in jarring relief. Her duffel bag was on the floor. Unzipped. The .45 SIG Sauer she carried was against a baseboard. Black scuff marks on the linoleum. A bullet hole in the drywall.

Fear tightened in his gut as he peered in the bag. Inside were clothes, her wallet and cell phone.

She wouldn't go anywhere without it. She certainly wouldn't leave a loaded weapon on the floor.

Oh, God. Charlie.

Seth must've taken her.

A hard lump rose in his throat. His mind whirled, the detective part of his brain strategizing how to possibly find her.

She didn't have her phone. Wherever he took her would be out of town, beyond traffic cameras. Limiting Brian's ability to track her.

He growled his frustration. *Think, think.* Drawing in a deep breath, he clenched his fist tighter.

An idea came to him. A long shot. But possible.

He knelt by her bag, rummaged through it until he found her burner phone and dialed the one person who might be able to help him save the woman he loved.

"Hey, beautiful," Orson said. "Did everything work out with your girl?"

"My name is Brian Bradshaw. You don't know me, but—"

"Then we shouldn't be talking," the man said. "Especially not from this number."

"Orson, don't hang up. Charlie is in danger. She needs your help. It's life or death."

Silence.

It was better than a dial tone.

Brian pulled out his cell and fired off a text message to Kent.

"What do you need from me?" Orson finally asked.

"For you to do what you do best. Hack her cell phone. Her laptop. Something."

"What you're asking is illegal. Are you a cop?"

Brian cursed as something in his chest wilted. "This isn't entrapment."

"I take that as a *yes* and it would make this a classic example of entrapment."

Damn it. "You're right. Entrapment is illegal. Therefore,

you've got a solid defense for any potential criminal charges. But if you don't help me, Charlie is going to die. And I'm willing to risk prison to keep that from happening."

More silence. But Orson didn't hang up.

"Please," Brian said. "I'm begging you."

"What are you looking for on her phone and laptop?" Orson asked.

"Someone's kidnapped her. He's going to hurt her. Then kill her. I need to find her before that happens. But the only thing on her person that I can think of to locate her is her smartwatch. The app linked to it will be on her phone and laptop. I need you to access the app. It'll show her GPS location. Can you?"

"Yeah, I think so."

Think wasn't good enough. "This needs to happen. Now," Brian snapped. "The sooner the better. Understand?"

"The thing is, you need to find her ASAP and that'll take too long."

If Seth had Charlie, this might be their only chance of getting her back. It might already be too late, but Brian wasn't going to give up. He wanted to yell, to punch the wall, to find Seth and put an end to this, but he took a deep breath. Strained for self-control. "I need you to find her. There has to be some way. Charlie said you're a prodigy. Some kind of genius." Even after their breakup, Charlie still worked with him, believed in his skills.

"There is a way," Orson said. "Faster, too. We don't need to go through her cell or the laptop. What kind of smartwatch is she wearing?"

Brian told him the brand.

Rapid-fire clicking on a keyboard sounded over the

phone. "She hasn't changed," Orson said. "I'm pulling up the website now. She uses the same email as her log-in for stuff like this. All I have to do is crack her password for this site. And bingo. Pull up her location."

"Then do it. Hurry. *Please.*"

"I have to ask, who is Charlie to you?"

Everything. His heart squeezed at the realization. "She's my future."

"Well, that explains the stern talk she had with me. Put me in my place. It was overdue. Are you going to make an honest woman out of her?"

He caught the double entendre. One day, he'd love to make Charlie his wife and have her operate aboveboard. No more gray boxes. "Yes."

But first they had to reach her in time.

Chapter Fourteen

Charlie's head throbbed. She swallowed. Her tongue felt heavy, her throat dry as cotton as she came to in confusion. *In darkness.*

What was happening?

Men in ski masks.

At USD.

It came back to her in a rush.

She tried to sit up, but she was on her belly, with legs bound and arms restrained behind her back. Duct tape over her mouth. In a vehicle.

She could tell from the sounds, the movement. The change in inertia pitched her to the side, jostling her body.

"I don't understand why you need me." A woman's voice. *Aubrey.* "I did my part like you told me. Just let me go. Please."

Aubrey had helped them get in. The conversation, talking about wanting to take classes, asking to the use the bathroom, had all been a ruse. To give her a chance to unlock the back door for those men.

And Charlie had fallen for it. How stupid could she be.

"There's something else I need you to do first," a man said.

At the sound of that voice, Charlie's heart dropped. *Seth Olsen.*

His truck was at his brother's ranch, but he hadn't been there. Instead, he'd been lurking behind USD, waiting to ambush her. Had he found the GPS tracker?

"What else?" Aubrey asked, her voice panicked. "Tell me and I'll do it, so I can get out of here."

"You'll find out soon enough," Seth said. "We're almost there. In the meantime, be a good girl and keep your mouth shut."

Momentum rolled Charlie to the side. They were turning. From the change in the sound of the tires, they had left a paved road for a dirt one. A little bumpy, too, as they continued along it for a while.

Finally, the vehicle came to a stop.

"Get her up and out," Seth ordered.

There was a tug at her ankles, and the restraint fell away. Someone had cut the zip tie, but her wrists were still bound together.

The hood was snatched from her head. She blinked, getting her bearings. Her gaze flew around wildly. She was on the floor of a cargo van.

A man wrenched open the side door and grabbed her arm. "Come on." He hauled her out of the van.

Cool night air brushed her face. A stark relief from the hot hood that had been suffocating. In the bright moonlight, her vision cleared. They were in the woods.

None of the men wore their masks. She was able to make them out clearly.

Seth led the way down a path. Detective Colvin shoved Aubrey forward, causing her to stumble in her heels while

Detective Eklund kept a tight grip on Charlie as he hurried her along.

The fact that they were no longer hiding their identities meant they didn't intend for her to survive this encounter. Charlie swallowed the bile in her throat.

She wasn't ready to die. Not like this.

Brian. The thought of never seeing him again was too much to bear.

The meaty hand on her arm jerked her forward. They passed Seth's truck along with two other vehicles.

The air held an unpleasant stench that only became fouler the closer they got to a barn. A cacophony of squeals and grunts rose, filling the air. As they came around the side of the barn, about two dozen pink hogs came into view.

The pigpen was dimly lit by the flames crackling in a stone firepit.

Charlie tugged her arms, trying to weaken the zip tie. Maybe she could pop it if she got her wrists at the right angle and put enough force behind it, or wriggle one hand out. She dug her heels in the dirt and tilted back to slow down their approach.

Eklund yanked her to his side, nearly taking her off her feet.

"Do we need to worry about your brother coming out here?" Colvin asked.

"No," Seth said. "I keep Abel out of this. He doesn't know anything. Only to stay inside the house when I'm out here working."

Colvin released Aubrey, and she stopped near the firepit.

"Now what?" Aubrey asked.

"We wait for the rest of our party to join us," Seth said,

glancing at his watch. "Should be here any minute. He's always punctual."

Charlie glanced around. Forced herself to concentrate. Sharpen her senses. She needed to think of a way out of this. Find an advantage.

The farmhouse was about two hundred feet upwind from the pigpen. Seth's brother lived there. If she got free somehow and made it to the house, she could call for help if there was a landline. But would she be able to make it with three armed men in pursuit?

A vehicle approached. Headlights cut through the darkness, drawing closer. The SUV stopped. The engine cut off. A car door slammed shut.

Someone heavy-footed came up the path. A man wearing a white button-down and slacks came into the light of the fire. Blond and balding. Average height. Lanky.

Charlie recognized him from the photos. He was the unidentified man.

"What in the hell is going on?" he asked, his gaze bouncing between Aubrey and Charlie. "What are they doing here?"

"We've got some business to take care of," Seth said.

"I don't get involved with this side of things." The guy backed up, raising his palms. "Just give me my cut. That's why I'm here. Then I'm gone."

"This does involve you. She's been taking pictures!" Seth pointed to Charlie. "Of us together. Including you."

His gaze swept to Charlie, his eyes growing wide with panic. "What?" He turned to Seth. "I can't be implicated in any of this. I'll be disbarred. I could go to jail. You have to handle it."

This was their lawyer. The one who was helping them make all this possible. There must have been layers of legal red tape used to hide their identities with the offshore shell companies.

"That's what I'm doing. Fixing it." Seth put a hand on the wood rail of the pigpen and leaned against it. "Come here," he said to Aubrey, beckoning to her with a gloved hand.

"Please. Let me go," she said. "I told you a million times that I'm sorry."

"Don't make me tell you twice."

Trembling, Aubrey treaded carefully over to him, holding out one arm to maintain her balance on the uneven ground and clutching her purse with the other.

"Good girl," Seth said, like she was dog, and Charlie gritted her teeth. "Give me that switchblade you carry around all the time."

Tears leaked from Aubrey's eyes. "Remember I was the one who told you to watch out for her. That she was following you. Taking pictures of you. Of all of you," she said, pointing a finger at Colvin and Eklund.

"Only after she made that little scene inside the club," Seth said. "When you had no other choice but to tell me."

"I never should have talked to her." Aubrey glared at Charlie, and then looked back at Seth. "Lesson learned," she sobbed. "Okay."

Seth held out his palm. "I'm waiting."

With shaking hands, Aubrey unzipped her purse and gave him the knife. "You've got to believe me," she pleaded. "It'll never happen again."

"I know it won't." Seth smiled as he caressed her cheek. In the firelight, his eyes were dark and empty like those of a snake. "Because I'm going to make sure of it." He pressed the button on the handle. The blade slashed out with a *flick*.

"What are you doing?" the lawyer asked, a terrified look stretching across his face.

Aubrey cringed. "But why?" she cried. "I didn't tell her anything useful."

"No loose ends." Seth slit her jugular in one smooth motion.

Gurgling blood, Aubrey clutched her throat.

Charlie reeled back in horror, but Eklund's tight hold on her didn't let her take more than two steps.

"What the…" The lawyer stumbled away from the firepit.

Seth shoved Aubrey backward, over the top rail into the pen.

The pigs surged, swarming all over the body, in a snarling, squealing frenzy.

Disgust and rage rolled through Charlie.

"Have you lost your mind?" the lawyer screamed. "You murdered her. This is crazy!"

"Shut up, Alcock." Seth pointed the switchblade at him. "I'm working. Trying to clean up this mess."

"I didn't sign on for this!" Alcock started hyperventilating. "You've made me an accessory!"

"Now your hands are just as dirty as ours," Eklund said, sneering. "Covered in blood."

Alcock swore. "You dragged me here to set me up?"

"Be quiet," Seth ordered.

The men stopped arguing. The sound of jostling, grunting and squeals drew everyone's attention to the swine in the pen.

"Did you know pigs are opportunistic omnivores?" Seth

asked, now stalking toward her. "They'll eat almost anything they can chew. Even bone."

Charlie's stomach heaved. She thought she might puke.

Stepping in front of her, he obscured the light of the fire. He was a big guy. Broad-shouldered and muscular. A dark nightmare. "I have my brother keep them a little hungry. For times such as these, when I need them for disposal. Even with twenty-six of them, it'll take hours for them to finish. They haven't eaten this good since I fed them Teddy."

Oh, God. Teddy really was dead. Not missing. Haley had been telling the truth.

Alcock put a hand over his mouth like he was going to be sick.

Still holding the bloody knife, Seth gripped her chin, and she flinched. "There's no way out of this for you Charlotte."

Hearing her full name that no one ever used sent a fresh jolt of fear through her.

"You're as good as dead," Seth said, and a knot swelled in her chest, tightening through her rib cage. "But *how* you go is up to you. I can strip you naked. Cut your Achilles tendons and toss you in the pen with your hands bound. That'll be agonizingly slow. Excruciating. But fun to watch."

Her skin turned to ice.

"I wouldn't wish that on anybody. Or…" He paused as a smile stretched across his ugly mouth. "It can be quick and painless." Releasing her chin, he put the knife away. He pulled a pack of cigarettes from his cargo pants. Tapped one out. Lit the cigarette from the fire in the stone pit. All while the pigs did their ghoulish work, the sound of crunching bone piercing the night. "Your choice," he said, his tone taunting as he prowled back over.

Pulse pounding at her temples, her head aching, she wished her hands were free and this was a one-on-one fight.

Seth sucked in a deep drag on his cigarette. Held her gaze. Exhaled through his mouth, blowing a cloud of smoke in her face.

She'd held her breath but coughed, nonetheless.

"All you have to do is tell me where I can find Haley," he said, like a used-car salesman trying to make a deal that only benefited himself.

Seth reached for her and ripped the duct tape from her lips.

Fire bloomed across her mouth. She sucked in a breath. Gasped from the lingering smoke in the air.

He bent closer, reeking of gin and sweat that almost made her gag as her stomach clenched. "So, what do you say?"

Nerves shooting into overdrive, Charlie said, "Drop dead."

No matter what she told him, he was going to kill her anyway.

"Bad choice." Seth punched her in the stomach.

Pain tore through her abdomen, stealing her breath, blurring her vision as she dropped to her knees. He snatched her by her hair and yanked her back up to her feet.

"I never did care for a woman with too much fire in her blood. Let's try again. Every time you refuse to tell me what I need to know, we'll strip an item of clothing from you. Maybe that will persuade you to talk."

DREAD BURNED IN Brian's gut as they sped down Highway 230 in his truck. What he wouldn't have given to be behind the wheel of Charlie's Hellcat instead of his vehicle. The clock ticking in his head rapped louder and louder, a bad feeling swelling in his gut.

"We'll reach her in time," Kent said from the passenger seat as though reading his mind.

They had better. For Seth's sake.

Brian believed in the law and justice. But if Seth killed Charlie, there was no power on earth that would stop Brian from getting vengeance.

He had been drawn to Charlie since he'd first seen her. Had a feeling about her. Once she had opened her mouth and snapped at him with that icy indifference, he was hooked. He hadn't been able to get her out of his head. The woman was a warrior, with steel running in her veins. But when she let her guard down, showed him how big and warm and vulnerable her heart was, he'd known...she was the one for him.

Now that she finally trusted him, finally accepted the love he had to give, he couldn't lose her. They'd barely been given a chance.

Kent had done good getting to USD within minutes of receiving Brian's text about what was happening. He looked at the smartwatch app that they'd pulled up on one of the phones. "We're only ten miles away," Kent said.

Brian didn't need the app to navigate, but they were monitoring it anyway just in case Seth moved her.

Flooring the accelerator, Brian tightened his grip on the steering wheel, his knuckles whitening. He flicked a glance in the rearview mirror. Not sure what he was expecting to see. He'd reached out to DCI Powell, who'd assured him that reinforcements would be en route to assist.

Seth Olsen wasn't operating alone. They had no idea who was with him, or how many, but it could've been half the badges in the LPD. Brian wasn't sure how far the corruption had spread. Whether it had tainted the sheriff's department. There had already been a scandal involving the previous sheriff. Brian was only willing to trust the DCI's office, but he and Kent hadn't waited for backup. There wasn't a second to spare.

"Look on the bright side. If he'd wanted to simply kill her, he could've done that at USD. Staged it like a robbery gone wrong. That would've been the cleanest way to eliminate her." Kent was continuing the pep talk he'd started after they'd raced out of the USD parking lot. "It's a good thing that he dragged her out here. Shows he's desperate. And desperation can drive a person to do dumb things. Like bringing her to his brother's ranch."

"Plenty of reasons for him to bring her out here," Brian said. "Interrogate her. Torture her. Dispose of evidence. Get rid of a body." Cold sweat slid down his spine.

"Hey, doesn't his brother have a pig farm on that ranch? I read that's how the Mob used to get rid of people in Sicily."

Brian shot him a glare. "Yeah, yeah, he does."

The car fell silent as Kent checked the app again.

Hoping that Seth wanted information out of her, Brian pressed harder on the gas pedal, driving faster than ever before in his life. The speedometer had reached triple digits. He swerved around a sedan that was going the speed limit. At least traffic was light. One more thing, besides Orson's assistance, that was working in their favor.

"I emailed the Internal Affairs point of contact Charlie's pictures, along with the locations of the houses and businesses owned by the offshore LLC," Kent said.

It had been time that he had shared everything he'd learned with his partner.

Those pictures were the product of Charlie's snooping. Even though it had been dangerous, and he'd warned her against it, she hadn't backed down.

But that was her. Headstrong to a fault. All fire and ice. And he loved her for it.

"Good." No matter what happened tonight, the truth would come out. Every dirty cop involved was going to be exposed. "I made sure DCI Powell also got the information, too." Although he probably already had his own surveillance photos.

If not for Charlie and Haley, Seth and his crew might have gotten away with their crimes. Everything from prostitution and drugs to murder.

It sickened him that there were so many dirty cops on the force. As well as shamed him for not being more open to the idea when Charlie had suggested it. He never should've dismissed her suspicion as paranoia.

Rage replaced his gut-wrenching fear. He funneled his white-hot anger into driving.

"Any idea who the one guy in the picture is that we didn't recognize?" Kent asked.

"No, not for certain."

"We're almost there," Kent said.

Brian turned off the highway and took the road that led to the ranch. Gritting his teeth, he raced down the street. One more turn and they reached the fork where the road split for the two ranches. Killing his lights, he made a left.

He spotted an opening in the thicket on the side of the road. Pulled off into a spot in between the trees. "We should go on foot from here. Use the app to pinpoint exactly where she is on the property."

"Are you sure you don't want to wait for backup?" Kent asked.

Brian clenched his jaw. "Charlie can't afford for me to wait. But if you want to hang back until the sheriff's department arrives, I'll understand."

"We're partners on this, right." Kent his drew gun and handed him the phone with the app.

"Thanks." Brian reached into the back, snatched the one bulletproof vest that he had and offered it to his partner.

"Keep it." Kent shoved it back at him.

"We're probably outmanned and outgunned. I don't need you adding to the list of problems by taking a bullet."

"Wanna know why I drink every night?"

Brian nodded.

"To forget I have to go home to an empty house. We never had kids. Some nights I wish like hell that we had. Or at least had gotten a cat."

His grief was too fresh for Brian to point out that it wasn't too late for him to find love again. Although no one would ever replace his wife, who he'd cherished, he could still share his life with someone.

Kent gave a dry chuckle. "Put the vest on, Bradshaw. I've seen the way you look at Charlie. I remember that feeling. To have a great love is a miracle. To have it for twenty-five years was luckier than I deserved. I've got nothing to lose. You can't say the same."

Brian strapped on the vest, grabbed the extra loaded magazines, divvying them up between the two of them, and stuffed his compact backup weapon, a Beretta Nano, into his ankle holster. "When this is over, I'm buying you a cat."

Clasping his shoulder, Kent flashed a sad grin.

They both got out, closing their doors without making any noise. Brian crept through the woods, with Kent alongside him, headed toward the blinking red dot on the app.

To Charlie.

Be alive.

Please. Be alive.

No SHOES, stripped down to her sports bra and underwear, Charlie shivered under Seth's hateful gaze. Rather than untie her, he'd cut her T-shirt from her with the same bloody knife that he had used to slit Aubrey's throat.

"Changed your mind? The end doesn't have to be unpleasant. But I need you tell me where my wife is hiding. She took something. I need it back."

Charlie had no idea of the location of the safe house. Even if she knew, she'd take it to the grave. Haley had made mistakes—awful, manipulative choices—but Charlie would not give her up to spare herself a nightmarish death.

"It's not as if anyone gave me the address so I could keep in touch," she said.

"Who has Haley? FBI? Marshals? Tell me the agency and name of the agent. I'll manage the rest."

She didn't want to imagine how. Bribes? Torturing others? A vicious, never-ending cycle. The buck stopped here. "You want her bad. What did she take from you? Your pride? Peace of mind?" Soon, it would be his freedom.

Seth chuckled. "She stole money. A lot of it. The cartel's cash. When they come looking for it, I need to have it."

A string of filthy curses flew from Alcock. "You didn't tell me Haley stole from the cartel. We're all as good as dead."

"Sounds like your list of problems is getting longer and longer," Charlie said to Seth. "I'll tell you what you want to know. But you've got to fight me for it. One-on-one. No restraints."

"What?" He laughed again. "You fellas believe she's actually asking me to spank her pretty butt?"

"I would've thought it would be a dream come true for you," she said. "But from the look on your face, I'd say you're scared." When he narrowed his eyes at her, jaw tightening, she knew she had him. The emotional attack worked. Such a fragile ego. Easy to bait. The hubris would do Seth in. He was so used to getting whatever he wanted, threatening, using violence, any means necessary. It's what allowed him to believe that he was above the law. That he could avoid retribution. He'd grown to see himself as invincible. "Afraid a woman will give you the beating you deserve? Should be. You pathetic excuse for a man."

Even in the dim light, she saw Seth's face redden.

"She's not going to tell you," Eklund said. "Stop toying with her. Just throw her in the pigpen and be done with it. We've wasted enough time on her."

"We need that money!" Colvin stepped toward Seth. "Or we'll be the ones in the pigpen."

"Get the lieutenant to help us," Eklund said. "He can find out who has Haley. Maybe even where they're keeping her."

Seth shook his head. "Jameson washed his hands of us the minute he learned IA was going to get involved."

"IA?" Alcock's gaze flew around, his visible panic rising.

"The lieutenant wants as much distance as possible," Seth continued. "Telling us about Haley being taken to a safe house was the last help he was willing to give." He glared at Charlie. "The agency that has her wasn't mentioned in the report. But you know, and I'm going to make you tell me."

"Make him a sweet offer he can't refuse," Eklund said, his voice desperate. "Double what he usually gets. If that doesn't work, threaten to name him as an accomplice if we all go down."

Colvin raked a hand over his close-cropped hair and paced in a circle. "Is that a joke? The lieutenant will sooner put a bullet between our eyes and bury us himself than give in to a threat. He might even be the first in line to take a plea deal or to get immunity to testify against us. Just out of spite. We need Haley. And the money."

Charlie met Seth's evil gaze. "Only one way I'll talk, if you're man enough for it."

No way she was going to make this easy for him. The fear was there, like a shadow in her soul, eclipsed now by the anger running through her like a cold iron bar. These might be the last minutes of her life. She wanted to spend them fighting.

"Cut her loose," Seth said, fury rife in his voice.

"Are you kidding?" Eklund asked. "You're going to fight her?"

"Why not?" Seth shrugged, slipping the switchblade in his pocket. "I've got no qualms about hitting a woman. Especially if means getting what we need. I'm happy to beat the answers out of her."

"This is beyond sadistic," Alcock said.

"Shut up." Seth stepped toward him. "Ortega is on the

way here. We need to be the ones getting the answers. The ones showing that we're still in control. Not him."

"The cartel's rep is coming? I'm out of here." Alcock took off down the path toward his vehicle.

"Do you want me to go after him?" Colvin asked.

Seth shook his head. "Let the bottom-feeder go. He won't talk. Too much to lose. His license to practice law. His reputation. His picture-perfect family. All those luxuries he enjoys."

Eklund drew a bowie knife from a holster on his hip, sliced the zip tie around her wrists and shoved her forward.

The ground was cold and damp beneath her bare feet. The feel of the mud and grass grounded her. To get the circulation going, she shook out her arms, and then hopped up and down to warm up. Sparring with Rocco kept her nimble, her reflexes sharp.

Getting out of this alive wasn't her aim since the odds were slim. All she wanted was to give Seth hope. Hope that she'd cave under the pressure of violence. But she knew the truth. Nothing he did would work.

You couldn't break what was already broken. Her father had done the job a long time ago.

Her one goal was to use every punch and kick she threw to crush Seth's hope. And her only regret was that she hadn't told Brian that she loved him. She did. She'd thought it rash to say it. That it was too soon. She'd also been scared.

But now her greatest fear was that he'd never know how deeply she felt for him.

The car engine fired up. Tires sped down the road as Alcock fled from the farm.

"Did Haley ever tell you that I like it when my women

fight back?" Seth asked. "Makes it more enjoyable. And my wife brought me a lot of pleasure. She was a scrapper, too."

Steeling herself, Charlie lifted her fists as she and Seth circled each other in the space between the barn and firepit. Eklund and Colvin drew their firearms but kept them low at their sides. Even if she won, they were going to make sure she didn't leave this farm alive.

With a feral smile, Seth lunged.

She deflected his fist and whipped her forearm upward as though she was smoothing back her hair. The tip of her bent elbow hit his chin, splitting the flesh to the bone.

Seth's head lashed back, blood ribboning from the wound, as he sucked in a breath.

Yes.

She needed this bastard to feel pain now. Not tomorrow.

Seth jabbed with one hand and swung a right hook.

Charlie feinted left, then threw a thunderclap to his ear with the heel of her palm. His eyes rolled into the back of his head, but he recovered quickly. She waited for him to retaliate defensively. When the blow came, she sidestepped.

But her attacker swung again and again. Each time he missed. Barely.

Once there was a break in Seth's momentum for her to capitalize on, she seized it. She threw a kick to his knee with her heel. He dropped to the ground with a grunt. Then she launched a punch, making contact with his eustachian tube at the hinge of his jaw, her knuckles sinking into the soft skin at the delicate spot. But she'd slipped too far inside Seth's reach.

Instantly, she realized the mistake would cost her dearly.

He caught her wrist. A switchblade flashed open, slashed

up her arm, then down across her midsection. The fiery sting drew a ragged gasp from between her teeth.

"Never said it would be a fair fight, bitch."

Chapter Fifteen

A car raced down the road, leaving the ranch like a bat out of hell.

Brian and Kent ducked behind a stand of trees, ensuring they weren't spotted. Once the car tore out on the main road, another one approached the farm. A black SUV. Chevy. Moderate pace like the driver had all the time in the world.

His gut tightened. Brian double-checked the GPS app.

The blinking red dot was up ahead and not in the vehicle that had just left. "She's still here."

Kent gave him a thumbs-up.

"Come on," Brian said. They needed to hurry.

He and Kent pressed forward.

As they passed a black van, three pickups and the now parked SUV, a foul odor in the air grew stronger. Brian signaled Kent to go through the back door of the barn. If it was locked, then he'd have to ease around the left side. Either way, it'd not only give them two angles of coverage, but it would maximize the element of surprise.

Kent nodded and moved into position as silently as he could. Brian watched him tug at the back door to the barn.

In a back-and-forth slashing motion, Kent waved across

his neck. *Locked.* He gestured to the left of the barn. Then keeping low and moving fast, he crept into the darkness, disappearing around a tree.

Going around the right side, Brian took stealthy, measured steps.

Seth was a seasoned police officer, which made him even more dangerous. If he or the other dirty cops with him heard or spotted Brian and Kent coming, there was nothing stopping them from killing Charlie.

The timing had to be just right. He hoped and prayed that nothing went wrong. The need to have Charlie safe and back in his arms was overwhelming.

His heart thundered so hard the frantic beats filled his ears until other sounds rose in the air.

Squeals. Grunts. The slap of flesh against flesh.

Pressure gathered in Brian's chest as a rush of adrenaline flooded his veins. With his back to the wall, he eased up to the corner of the barn, Glock drawn. He peered around the side, every muscle, every cell in his body coiled tight and ready.

Charlie.

She was alive. Standing in her underwear, blood streaked across her abdomen, her arm, she was in a defensive position, fists up. Horror screamed through him.

Seth was holding something that gleamed in the firelight. A knife. Brian ached to blow a hole through him, but Charlie was in the way.

Colvin and Eklund both had guns drawn.

Brian wanted to leap into action that very second, but he needed to give Kent a chance to get into position on the other side of the barn. Otherwise, one of them might shoot her.

"If you don't get her to talk, I will," said the man with the ugly scar. "I'm rather good at it. Taking fingers. Toes. I guarantee once she smells her own flesh burning, she'll tell me all her secrets."

Tension knotted in Brian's chest, his heart throbbing like an open wound. He had to prevent that man from ever touching her and get her out of there.

Charlie threw a punch, her fist hitting Seth's jaw.

The big guy staggered back. "You're going to talk, so help me, even if I have to break every bone in your body." He kicked her in the gut, slamming her backward down onto the ground.

Waiting any longer wasn't an option. Brian took aim on the guy with the scar. He was the closest armed man to him and the scariest. His police training had taught him to go for center mass. But Special Forces had taught him sometimes you only had one shot to eliminate a threat. On an exhale, he squeezed the trigger.

A shot to the head. The man dropped.

But everyone else spun around, now on alert.

Quickly, he shot at Colvin, who was moving. Two bullets hit him. One in the arm. The other in the shoulder.

As Colvin aimed to return fire, Brian caught a glimpse of Charlie. She rammed the heel of her foot into Seth's groin and kicked the knife from his hand right before Brian took cover.

Bullets bit into the barn not far from his head.

On the other side of the building, gunfire erupted. *Kent.*

Ducking low, Brian darted out. Locked Colvin in his sights. Fired. The detective took one to the chest, lurched back and fell to the ground.

Seth pulled a gun and snatched Charlie by her hair, yanking her up in front of him. He hauled her back to the barn door. Flung it open. Dragged her inside at gunpoint.

Busy firing at Kent, Eklund hunkered down behind the stone firepit. He was too big to fully conceal himself, but a tree blocked Brian's line of sight for a clear shot.

Kent maneuvered off to the side behind a tractor.

"Cover me!" Brian called out, grateful for the extra ammo he'd given to him.

His partner squeezed off rounds, keeping Eklund pinned down and unable to shoot back.

Taking the small opening, Brian ran to the barn door and slipped inside. He stopped cold.

Seth had an arm curled around Charlie's throat, his gun pressed to back of her skull, her body shielding his. "Drop it. Or she's dead."

"Don't do it," Charlie said.

"I've had enough of you!" Seth growled, tightening his hold until she gasped.

Outside more gunfire was exchanged. Brian hoped that Kent could wear down Eklund, getting him to run out of ammo and then neutralize him.

Seth shifted the muzzle of his gun from the back of Charlie's head, jamming it against her temple. "Unless you want to see her brains splattered across the wall, you'll drop it."

Fury like Brian had never experienced surged inside him. Instead of suppressing it, he let it fill him, fuel him. If there was going to be a hostage, it would be him. He'd trade places with Charlie. His life for hers. He was willing to make any sacrifice. But first he made a solemn vow. "Hurt her again, and I will kill you."

"No, you won't," Seth said. "Not while I have her."

The gunfire outside stopped. Either Eklund or Kent was dead.

If it was the former, Kent would reposition around to the back of the barn, cutting off any escape for Seth. But if it was the latter, and his partner, his friend, was dead, Eklund would put a gun to the back of Brian's head, and this would be over.

He didn't glance over his shoulder. Instead, he focused on Charlie. Her face was bruised. She was covered in mud. Blood ran down her bare arm and stomach where she'd been cut. But there was something so hard and cold in her expression that it was startling.

"Me for her." Brian raised his hands. His finger off the trigger, but his grip still on the gun. "Let her go and take me instead."

"Brian." The intensity of Charlie's stare burned through him. Those green eyes were laser sharp. "Aim and pull the trigger." She tried to nod, but Seth's grip was too tight around her neck.

"Don't test me," Seth warned. "I will put a bullet in her."

The urge to beat this guy to a bloody pulp flared hot through Brian, but he stayed put. For Charlie's sake.

She clutched the arm at her throat, struggling to push it down. "I should've said this sooner. I love you." Her whispered admission cut through the barn, gutting him. "It's okay."

She was making the tough call, giving him permission to take the shot. To do his job.

But how could she think that he would risk her life? "No, Charlie. I can't." Not now. Not ever.

"You have to do it," she said, her voice like steel.

"Here's what's going to happen," Seth said. "I'm going to walk out of here with her. And you're not going to follow me.

"If he takes me," Charlie said, "I die anyway."

The ways this could play out right along with the odds had already gone through his head. Seth wasn't taking her anywhere. But he needed Charlie to trust that he had a plan.

"Toss your weapon!" Seth ordered.

Brian dropped it. His Glock landed on the barn floor with a thud.

"Kick it away!" Seth scurried toward the back of the barn with Charlie in tow. "Right now."

Brian swept the gun aside with his foot, sending it skidding into a dark corner.

Seth reached the back door and shoved on it, realizing it was locked. Moving the gun away from Charlie's temple, he popped the padlock with two bullets.

The door swung open. Kent, DCI Logan Powell, Chief Deputy Holden Powell and another deputy appeared on the other side.

Charlie thrusted backward, forcefully, giving Seth a sharp headbutt.

The violent blow over her skull to his face stunned him.

Brian bent down. Snatched the Beretta from his ankle holster.

Seth scurried backward into a corner, into the protection of two walls with Charlie as his shield. Before he could reposition the gun to her head, she sank her teeth into the arm around her throat. Seth howled in pain and slammed the butt of the gun down against her head.

Brian's stomach went into freefall as she went limp like a rag doll. Her deadweight tugged on him, forcing him to let her go. As she hit the ground, Seth turned the gun on her.

But Brian aimed and fired. He shot him twice in the throat, putting an end to him.

He hurried to Charlie, hauling her into his lap, cradling her head. "Open your eyes, honey."

She didn't move. Her skin cold and clammy, her face pale.

The other men charged inside. One checked Seth for a pulse.

Kent dropped to a knee beside him. "Is she—"

"No," Brian said. "But we need an ambulance."

But then her eyes fluttered open.

His heart squeezed with relief, and it was like he could breathe again.

Three days later

CHARLIE SAT ON Brian's lap in the living room, scrolling through the news article he'd wanted her to read.

She skimmed through the story.

According to the *Laramie Gazette*, Chief of Police Willa Nelson had finally issued a statement. A task force operating out of the DCI's office had been formed six months ago to look into the alleged ties between the Rios drug cartel, out of Mexico, and several police officers in key positions throughout the Laramie PD, as high ranking as Lieutenant Malcolm Jameson. The probe had started with a few narcotics detectives but had been expanded to include a huge array of civilians working in the organization. Real estate attorney Timothy Alcock had played a key role in using his legal expertise to help the cartel and officers create shell companies to hide behind in purchasing foreclosed homes to use as meth labs, and sites of storage and distribution. Charges included trafficking and selling drugs, prostitution, money laundering and racketeering. Based on DNA recovered from Olsen Ranch A, Detective Seth Olsen was also found to be responsible for several murders, including those of Theodore Williams and Jane Aubrey Dunn. The owner of the ranch, Abel Olsen, was not found to be complicit. An unidentified informant was key to breaking the case and turned over half a million dollars in cartel money. Chief Nelson has pledged to clean up the LPD.

"Wow," she said in a whisper. The informant was clearly Haley, who was still in an unidentified location. "I had no idea it was so big and deep. Are you all right?"

"Yeah."

But Brian was an idealist. He couldn't possibly be fine. "You can tell me."

He shook his head. "Those cops abused people and their positions. They violated the public trust in every way that counts. They've put a stain on the department that won't go away anytime soon."

Such a good man.

She kissed his head, pressed her palm to his cheek and ran her thumb over the evening stubble on his face. "Justice will be served. Take comfort in that. I'm just glad this nightmare is over."

"Me, too. But Chief Nelson still has a lot of work to do with the LPD."

She slid her fingers through his hair. "You know, I'm still surprised that you called Orson for help."

A smile pulled at his gorgeous mouth. "I'd do anything for you."

She believed him and was grateful to have Brian in her corner.

"I need you to do a favor for me tomorrow," he said.

"Anything. What is it?"

"Help me pick out a kitten. For Kent. I promised to buy him a cat."

Smiling, she kissed him again. This time on the lips. "It would be my pleasure."

Putting her down on her feet, he stood. "Go shower and meet me outside. I've got a surprise for you."

"What is it?"

He gently bopped her nose with the tip of his finger. "If I told you, then it wouldn't be a surprise."

"I thought we were having dinner."

"Food is a part of it."

"How long do I have?" she asked.

"As long as you need."

She frowned.

"Can you meet me out back in ten?"

"Sure," she said, but she'd do it in five.

She hurried through a shower, gritting her teeth every time the warm spray of water hit a scrape or bruise, and there were many. Exfoliating and shaving were musts since she was with Brian every night.

In a relationship.

The words still sounded weird in her head. Even weirder rolling off her tongue.

Wait until she told Rocco. He was going to lose his mind. In a good way.

She threw on Brian's T-shirt and padded down the hall.

The back door was open. The light on the porch was off. But a trail of candles lit a path.

Nerves fluttered in her stomach.

Smiling, she followed the candlelight out onto the lawn. Wearing his cowboy hat, Brian sat on a blanket that was surrounded by dozens of blazing candles. There was picnic basket, champagne flutes and bubbly.

She stepped on the blanket and sauntered over to him. "What are we celebrating?"

"Besides, being alive and being in love?"

She gave a little nod, her smile spreading wider.

Brian rose to his feet, then got down on one knee. "A proposal."

Her heart started pounding so loudly she could hear it.

He reached into his back pocket and pulled something out. But it wasn't a ring box. It was an envelope. "Open it."

She peeled back the flap that was sealed and took out two tickets. For the upcoming charity gala to support the women's shelter in Cheyenne. The same one they had gone to and found magic in each other. "I didn't realize this was in less than a week."

"Good thing I did. Charlie Sharp, will you be my date?"

She wanted to be his everything.

Funny how coming inches away from death, especially twice in one day, made her clearly see all the things lacking in her life.

Emotion ballooned inside her, but she refused to cry, even if they were tears of joy.

"Of course, I will."

He stood, put his hat on her head and wrapped his arms around her, tugging her flush against him. "I love you."

Every time he said those three little words, her heart rolled over slow and dreamy in her chest.

She'd already shown Brian her soft underbelly more times than she liked, and quite honestly nothing in her life had ever felt as good as having that level of trust. So, she gave herself permission to say it and revel in how deeply she meant the words, without having a gun to her head. "I love you, too."

* * * * *

COMING SOON!

We really hope you enjoyed reading this book. If you're looking for more romance be sure to head to the shops when new books are available on

Thursday 8th June

LET'S TALK
Romance

For exclusive extracts, competitions and special offers, find us online:

f MillsandBoon

𝕏 @MillsandBoon

◎ @MillsandBoonUK

♪ @MillsandBoonUK

Get in touch on 01413 063 232

MILLS & BOON

THE HEART OF ROMANCE

A ROMANCE FOR EVERY READER

MODERN Prepare to be swept off your feet by sophisticated, sexy and seductive heroes, in some of the world's most glamourous and romantic locations, where power and passion collide.

HISTORICAL Escape with historical heroes from time gone by. Whether your passion is for wicked Regency Rakes, muscled Vikings or rugged Highlanders, awaken the romance of the past.

MEDICAL Set your pulse racing with dedicated, delectable doctors in the high-pressure world of medicine, where emotions run high and passion, comfort and love are the best medicine.

True Love Celebrate true love with tender stories of heartfelt romance, from the rush of falling in love to the joy a new baby can bring, and a focus on the emotional heart of a relationship.

Desire Indulge in secrets and scandal, intense drama and sizzling hot action with heroes who have it all: wealth, status, good looks…everything but the right woman.

HEROES The excitement of a gripping thriller, with intense romance at its heart. Resourceful, true-to-life women and strong, fearless men face danger and desire - a killer combination!

To see which titles are coming soon, please visit

millsandboon.co.uk/nextmonth

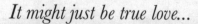